I0715169

Heart & Hope

ROSEWOOD RANCH SERIES

ALEXANDRA BANKS

WILLOW HOUSE Publishing

For more information, or to book an event, contact:

alexandrabanksauthor@gmail.com

Book design by Alexandra Banks

Cover design by Alexandra Banks

ISBN (ebook): 978-1-7635496-8-5

ISBN (paperback): 978-1-7635946-9-2

First Edition: October 2024

Also by Alexandra Banks

Rosewood Ranch Series

Tough Love

Heart & Hope

Saving Grace

True North

*For the women who get shit done
with their whole heart.*

Author's Note

TW –

Vehicle accident.

Mature, explicit intimate scenes.

Coarse language.

The location and topographies of the places in this story have been fictionalized. They may not accurately represent actual location and terrain.

P.S The playlist is in the back!!

HEART

&

HOPE

Chapter One

RUBY

The guest list is far too small. Big corporate gatherings, especially openings, are the reason the saying *the more the merrier* was coined. I would bet my inheritance on it.

All twenty-eight million, at last count.

The consolation prize for emotionally unavailable parents, who provided a less than loving childhood for me and my two sisters. I shake my head, dislodging the thoughts that slip in whenever business overwhelms me.

But I wouldn't have it any other way. Idle hands are the devil's work, if you believe the sentiments my father instilled into us girls growing up. It was his excuse for never being around. Don't understand how that explains his absence in other areas . . .

My cell vibrates, dancing across the glass desk. I ignore it for a moment, staring out into the now bright morning sunlit buildings of Lower Manhattan. The phone continues its solo dance.

Marina.

I tap the answer button and then put it on speaker. "Talk to me, Mari."

"Your eight o'clock postponed until the end of the week, and I have an influx of replies for the gala from the food and beverage vendors. Do you want me to email them through?"

"Sure, I'll check them out and send the short list for you to vet. Thanks."

"What time did you get here, Rubes? Or did you sleep under your desk again?"

I chuckle, leaning back on my white leather business chair. It reclines as I sink into the soft as butter padding. Nobody is this put together from sleeping at work. My hair would never be this straight. And over my dead body are these designer clothes touching the filthy floor . . . It's bad enough my favorite red Dolce & Gabbana stilettos take minor scuffs from the poor quality carpe—

"Ruby?"

"Only a little earlier than you. You worry too much."

"And you, my girl, work too much." The tone of her voice is laced with concern. She's right. But I have no intentions of slowing down. The last thing Ruby Robbins will ever be is lazy, or worse . . . redundant.

In fact, it's one of my rules.

Number three, actually.

Rule number three—Give it all you've got, or don't bother at all. No hoping or praying—hard work, all the way.

Addy says my rules are too rigid. But as my best friend and honorary sister, she gets away with it. What she doesn't get a say on is how hard I am willing to work for my dreams. I will own my own event planning company one day and only doing the bare minimum is no way to achieve anything.

I devote my life to my career. No husband, no dates. Rule number one, I don't date or do relationships. Period. It's easier that way, and no distractions means ultimate productivity. And that makes this girl very, very happy.

My phone rings.

Addy.

I swear that girl reads my mind. I shut the laptop and swipe the screen open. "Adds, so how's it going?"

"A few equine visits for today, then clinic. How's your day so far?"

"Busy. I have that gala in the works, and Olive wants to meet later; hopefully, she has something more upmarket for me to sink my teeth into."

"More upmarket than a Manhattan Christmas gala ball for the elite?"

"You know what I mean. I want to work on something huge. Like inter-corporation merger, and all the HR and PR events that go with that. That's where the opportunity is."

"And the fancy wine . . ." She chuckles.

"You know I do love my wine. Wish you could come over to my place tonight. Le Du's is having a tasting night and then we could have gone out for tapas or whatever."

"Montana might be a bit far for that. Sorry, babe." She pauses. I guess, she's checking her phone of the time. "But only five months 'til I can come back and hit that joint with you."

"Don't sound so excited you've left me, Adds."

"It's only a short stint, and you know I couldn't stay there with everything that happened with Adam."

"I know, but I miss you. Promise you will come home when you're done. No running off into the sunset with some muscle-bound cowboy."

"Ride off," she says with a laugh.

"Huh?"

"I think they ride off into the sunset, Rubes."

I scoff and close my eyes. Of course they do. My cell vibrates and emails flood in. Mari. "Hey, I have to get back to it. Please stay safe, Adds. And text me if you need me, promise."

"Yes, Mom. Love you, Rubes."

"Love you too, Addy."

I tap the red circle as emotion clogs my throat and my office door swings open. Addy and I have always been close. People mistake us for sisters, our eyes both dark brown, similar complexion. Figures, since the only difference really is our hair. Hers is curly and brown, mine is wavy and natural blonde. A voice clears to my left. Olive stands, arms crossed, in my doorway as I swivel the chair to face her.

"Ruby, do you have a sec?"

"Ah, I thought I was coming to you, at eleven?"

"We can do this now."

As if I didn't have my day scheduled to the minute, but hey, it's not like I'm the boss . . . yet. "Sure, Olive, take a seat."

She waits by the door and when she doesn't move, my gut sinks. I push out from my desk as she nods toward the door. Following her down the hall, we reach the elevator, and she punches the button for the ground level. When the door pings, we step inside and turn to face the sliding doors automatically. My heart pounds in my chest as the elevator drops. I don't like things out of routine. And taking a walk with Olive, trying to make it casual, is making my nerves sing.

"Ruby, you know I love the work you do. Your events are top-tier. Always."

Oh wow, here goes.

Here comes the *but*.

"But?" I ask, deciding to rip the Band-Aid off.

"Some of the clients have given us some feedback about your relations and the way you have been handling staff lately."

"Efficiently?"

"Bluntly. And very inflexible."

"Olive. You know how I operate. Events of that caliber aren't accidents. And someone has to hold the ship together or it fucking sinks."

She cringes, her fifty-something wrinkles pulling at her blue eyes as she sighs. "Ruby, you need to relax a little, or we are going to start losing the larger accounts to those hacks across town."

She is referring to Premium Events. Original. Honestly, who chooses a company name so basic? Surprised they bring in any business at all.

"Fine, I'll tone it down a little. Let a few things slip. And when complaints come pouring in, I'll direct them straight to management."

She tilts her head, muttering my name exasperatedly.

The elevator bings and the doors swing open.

"You can tone it down right now, Ruby. I understand you have standards and not everyone lives up to them. But this controlling side of you isn't healthy. So . . ."

She steps out into the central garden that sits between our high-rise and the next.

"You can tone it down in Montana. I'm assigning you to an inn opening. It's been taken over by new ownership. And the owners want a stellar event to bring in commercial backers and then a grand opening for the public to fill the books for the following six to twelve months."

I know I'm staring now. And the elevator door slams into my side where I jerked to a halt at the word Montana. It hits my shoe. Fuck. I jump from the doorway and vent a string of curses as I bend down to brush the scuffed side of my heel. When the mark doesn't budge, I suck in a breath.

Okay, stay calm.

Maybe Olive is right?

Fuck that elevator door right into hell.

"Ruby?"

"If you want me to resign, just say so, Olive."

She rubs the bridge of her nose and closes her eyes briefly. "No, that's not what I want. I want you to succeed; you are a diamond in the event space. But at this level, you will end up crushed under the pressure of everything. You need perspective, hon. I'm handing it to you in the form of a small-town country inn. It's a challenge. Not a punishment. I want you to find something else you love, workaholism aside."

I count each breath that comes in. Not in the habit of burning essential bridges, I nod before the *fuck you* that is sitting right there on my tongue flies out of my mouth.

Olive steps toward me in her gaudy, generic beige pumps that trim out her black pencil skirt and sheer pale pink top. "I will see you in three months. And the next time I look at this pretty face, it will be wrapped in that megawatt smile I know is in there somewhere."

I try to find it. To prove to her that all this is a wild goose chase. A waste of my time, and her best planner to Hicksville.

But I can't.

And it kills me to know she's right.

I don't remember the last time I smiled at work. Or on a weekday, actually.

Structure. Rigid, unbending structure has been hammered into me since I was a little girl. I wasn't aware there was another way of working. If Olive thinks I can hunt it down in the mountainous west, who am I to argue? I mean, Adds will be there. How big is Montana, anyway?

"Fine, one stint in redneck world and one megawatt smile, and then I'm hightailing it back to the city," I say to her.

She smiles at me as if there's something she knows that I have to go figure out.

Fuck you, Olive.

I will find out what it is.

Montana, here I come.

At my desk, I take a moment to wonder at the glittering city outside before plucking my phone. I tap out a text to Adds before letting my phone fall onto the glass.

Guess who's coming to Hicksville, babes.
Ugh. See you soon.

The rental Mercedes rolls into the driveway of the Heritage Inn in the heart of Great Falls, Montana. And I jerk, snapping a foot onto the break when I remember I'm driving, not a passenger. It is not what I expected.

At all.

The impressive building is elegant and upper class. I slide the car into park and kill the engine, pushing open the door. Stilettos clicking on the stone-paved driveway, I head into the reception area.

I gasp, taking in the grand entrance. It's all rustic yet gorgeous, oversized brass chandeliers and shining marble floor. Again, I was not expecting this. In the middle of some redneck town. But here we are.

When I reach the back of the enormous room and step up to the long, polished wood counter, I meet a bright-eyed young girl, maybe five years younger than me. I'm sure she couldn't be any older than twenty-two. Brunette curls frame her face, her dark eyes studying my clothes. She reminds me of Addy a little.

"Checking in, ma'am?"

Ugh. I'm not that old. "Yes, and it's Miss Robbins."

She scans the computer screen with a half-baked smile.

Too harsh?

"I only have a reservation for a Mrs. Robbins, and it says here you're our new events manager?" Her eyes light up. Guess she likes a good party. A door to the side pushes open, and an older lady wearing some god-awful vest over her crisp white blouse steps up beside the young attendant.

"Ah, I am she, but—"

"Mrs. Robbins! So glad y'all arrived safe. I'm Mary-Sue, new co-owner." She beams. "We have you in one of our best suites, and I can show you this wonderful old building. Oh, wait, what am I sayin'! You must be exhausted. I'll let you settle in, and we will see y'all at breakfast. Bill—my husband—and I have you slotted to meet about the gala first up tomorrow."

I stare at her. Neurons are firing in my brain right now, I'm sure. They're just not connecting in any meaningful way. Mrs. Robbins? Opening? The place appears up and running to me. "I—"

"Is Mr. Robbins with you? A super successful gal like yourself; I bet he follows you around all over the country-side. It's no bother if he arrives later, we have an after-hours attendant and a twenty-four-hour call button right out front. Miley, show Mrs. Robbins to her suite, I'll get her checked in. No need for charges, your boss phoned ahead."

"Oh, wonderful, thanks."

Miley is by my side a second later, scanning the foyer for the bags that she must have assumed I would haul in myself.

"They're in the trunk of the rental outside," I offer.

"Sure. I'll meet you at the elevator, Mrs. Robbins."

Before I can get a word out to correct their mistake,

the young girl is out the front door and popping the trunk. Deciding to let it go, I wander to the elevator foyer with a smile and a wave to Mary-Sue.

Grunts come from behind me as I tap out a message to Adds. I turn back to see Miley dragging my bags behind her. All four of them. I drop my phone into my tote and relieve her of two of them. Louis Vuitton should not be dragged. Ever.

"Wow, y'all's luggage is—"

"Expensive, please be careful."

"I was goin' to say heavy." Miley's gaze swings to the elevator as it bings.

I step inside and turn back, settling the two bags on either side of me. The young woman's focus is fixed on the floor.

"Your boss is lovely," I say, trying to crack the frozen tundra between us after my lack of tact with the bag.

"She's the best," she says, a little too deadpan, the smile on her face forced. "Her and Bill, they're kind of traditional."

"Oh, in what way?"

"The traditional way? I don't know. It's a good thing your husband is coming soon. Bill ain't real big on unmarried women traipsing across the country. Even less fussed on us having a career, so to speak."

I press my lips into a thin line, my now dropped brows a good half an inch closer to my nose. "It's 2024."

"Yeah, they know. But reckon some things are best left

to the old ways. And women working *inside* the home is one of them."

"But you work here, and Mary-Sue?"

"Yeah, that's just until I'm married, I guess."

My face twists.

"What about Mary-Sue?"

"Well, Bill is here and he's my uncle's cousin, so . . ."

"You can't be serious. Just how far back in time have I traveled in four days?"

She chuckles, running a hand over the now finger-print-spotted brass of my luggage. "I mean, I'm all for it, you know. Going off to college and seein' the world. Maybe one day."

"Uh-huh" is all I can say.

Good Lord, what the hell is this place?

And how on earth am I going to convince Mary-Sue I have a husband when he doesn't exist? Surely, Olive can sort this out?

The elevator pings, doors sliding open.

Top level.

Miley shows me to my suite. With the swish of a card, the door clicks, and she pushes it open. The inside is huge, almost bigger than my apartment. The marble floor, the same as in the foyer, shines; the linens give off a crispness that floods the room. And at the far end are two wide double doors with a sprawling balcony. It's brilliant.

And if I can make it through this job without being

burned at the stake for my sordid unwed existence, maybe I can relax.

A little?

My phone vibrates in my tote.

"I'll show myself out," Miley says, lingering in the doorway.

I smile and wave her off as I answer.

"Olive! We have a problem."

Chapter Two

REED

"RAW-LINS!"

"RAW-LINS!"

"RAW-LINS!"

Fists pound the table on either side of me. The huge guy about to shatter my wrist with his enormous mitt scowls inches from my face. Must be the direct descendant of Popeye, 'cause he's set to snap me in half.

Bare-chested and sweating up a storm, I buckle down for pain, re-affirming my grasp on his hand. I strain against his twitching forearm, holding my own for a moment.

Arm-wrestling isn't one of my finer moments. But tonight, it garners the attention of two women at the bar. And I have every intention of milking those sympathy looks until at least one of them is in the bed of my truck.

If Hudson were here, he would have slapped the back

of my head by now. But he's not, and my chances of losing spectacularly are high. The way I want them. It's easy to be the loser when your entire family expects it.

A role I have long known how to fulfill.

But it has its perks.

It absolutely does. I snap my gaze from the brunette at the bar who's about to have kittens over watching me die a slow and painful arm-wrestling death. I would smile, if I wasn't about to be in a world of pain.

At least the ER in Great Falls is well-stocked and staffed. This isn't my first rodeo.

"Reed, it's fine. You don't have to defend my honor!" With a whirl of cheap perfume and cigarette breath, the brunette closes in. A second later, she is hanging off Popeye's flexing forearm. "Please, it's not a big deal. Let him go. I'll take the drink, please. Just don't hurt him."

The big guy's scowl slides to her. A blush floods her neck and face. If I didn't know better, I'd say she only did it to egg him on in the first place. When his eyes dip to her breasts, almost spilling from the neckline of her tank top, his hand on mine loosens.

"You're not goin' to let her distract you that easily, are you, buddy?" I growl.

"Huh?" he rasps, grip turning painful.

A second later, my arm is wrenched in its socket and the back of my hand smashes into the wood.

Fuck.

Sweet Jesus, that's goin' to hurt tomorrow. Cheers go

up around him as his friends celebrate his win. My loss is commiserated by the remaining two women at the bar, who fawn over my quickly reddening hand.

"Oh my god, do you need some ice?" one asks, the redhead, I think.

"Can we take you to the ER?" the other swoons.

"Nah, all good, ladies. A beer and a little love and I'll be right as rain."

"Oh god, yes, let me get you a drink." The redhead scoots off to the bar as I drop into the couch on the back wall. The establishment is small, but central to town and filling up as the hour gets on. The redhead walks back with two drinks. The brunette drops into my lap, resting my hand in her palm, inspecting the bones, moving each finger as if she has a clue what she's doing.

"I don't think anything is broken," she says softly.

"Only my pride then, hey?"

She dots a kiss to my cheek, and I take her chin with my free hand. She covers my mouth with hers a second later. My cock stretches in my pants, digging into her ass.

"Don't forget about me, Reed." The couch dips beside me as the redhead settles in close, placing the drinks on the coffee table in front of us.

"We should call it a night," I say, knowing full well they will protest.

"Can we come with you?" the woman on my lap says, tilting her head to one side, biting her bottom lip. The redhead leans over and nips my ear. "Both of us?"

Plan prepped, executed, and successful. All blood has migrated south, and my rational brain has closed up shop for the night.

"Are you sure?" I put on my most innocent face, nursing my injured hand, but my grin pokes through.

The redhead slaps my shoulder and giggles. "Don't play dumb with us, we know all about your reputation. That's why we're here—to fuck the Great Reed Rawlins."

And just like that, my boner is as limp as a dead fish.

They are chasing *me*.

Resisting the groan that wants out of my throat, I say, "Right, I gotta be up early in the morning, ladies. If you don't mind." I widen my arms and raise them, palms up.

The woman on my lap stands, confusion twisting her face. "Ladies?"

It's one thing to have a reputation. But something else entirely to be hunted down because of it. Who volunteers to sleep with a ladies' man? Pretty sure that's what Huddo calls me. If anyone needs these two cock jockeys, it's my oldest brother.

Me? I'll see myself out.

I push through the doors of the bar and onto the quiet paved sidewalk of Great Falls. The street is lined with glowing heritage lamps. A few people mill about, nothing much for a Friday night. Shop fronts are lit up and one restaurant is still open. My truck is parked a block away. With only two beers under my belt, I may as well drive back to the ranch on the other side of Lewistown.

I hear clacking heels before I see a blonde with her head down, gorgeous brown eyes lit up by her phone. Her shoulder bumps mine. She throws a manicured hand up with a breathy apology, not taking her eyes off the screen.

She didn't even see me.

But I stand and watch her walk away. Blonde waves bouncing over her shoulders. Hips swaying with every long stride she takes in the most ridiculous red high heels. The fancy suit she wears fits her shape, cinched in at the waist. Now *she* doesn't belong in this backward backwater town.

Her fragrant perfume hits me a second later. And something heavy tugs in my gut.

Strawberries.

Something is moving in my back pocket. The hum of my phone vibrating fades in.

Shit.

I pull it out.

Hudson.

> Don't get fucked up tonight, Reed.
> There's a fence line with your name on it,
> little brother. Bright and early!!!!!

Ugh, the only thing worse than early starts? Early starts for ranching chores I fucking hate. And fencing is top of the shit list. In fact, apart from being in the saddle, there isn't much I like about ranchin'. Mountains and fields only entertain you for so long. I'm more of a people person. Maybe one day I can go someplace else and explore some of the world.

The clack of heels comes back my way. Still glued to her phone, the woman walks past me. My usual Reed Rawlins swagger is nowhere to be found as I open my mouth to ask if she's lost. But nothin'.

Not a word falls out.

Fuck me.

Head down, I cross the street and head for the truck, shoving my hands in the back pockets of my Wranglers. I glance back as she turns onto the avenue the Heritage Inn sits on, disappearing inside the giant old building a moment later.

I run a hand through my messy hair before rubbing it over my three-day scruff that I wasn't self-conscious about 'til five minutes ago. Sliding into my black F-250, the sweet Napa leather seat hugs my ass as I slam the door shut and drop my forehead to the steering wheel.

Mind stuck on loop, blonde waves and dark eyes flying past, I breathe deep and close my eyes. That damn scent. Would be enough to drive a preacher crazy. I stare at the Heritage Inn as I fire up the engine. The rumble of eight cylinders brings me back to reality. The only thing I love more than my family, and a quick fling in the back of my truck, is my actual truck.

F-250, 6.7-liter Power Stroke V8 diesel. Blacked-out mag wheels and twin sports exhausts, black Napa leather interior. Rumbles at an idle. Pulls like a sixteen-year-old.

Roars like nothing else when I open her up on the highway.

I let her roll to the first set of lights and glance back down the street. No gorgeous blonde. Probably for the best. A girl like that wouldn't last two minutes with the red-blooded hicks in this town.

The light turns green, and my foot flattens to the floor. The rumble rattles the street, and rubber burns in our wake. A smile grows across my face. This, right here, is almost as good as what I was chasing in the first place.

The hour and a half it takes to drive back to Rosewood Ranch, the woman in the red heels fills my fantasies. I imagine her looking up at me. Me not losing the ability to speak at the most inconvenient time. I say hi, and she says hi back.

Nope.

This is getting way too Dear Diary.

Maybe, the blonde wearing only the red heels.

How about those heels over her head . . .

Oh fuck.

I'm goin' to have to pull over if I don't shut that down real fast.

When the familiar lights of home come into view down the long dirt road I have been driving for the last twenty-eight years of my life, I yawn. Bed sounds like a fantastic place right now. At a quarter past midnight, I roll into the barn and turn off the engine. With a little luck, Ma will be sound asleep.

Hudson, too.

I can count on Pa being out like a light; that man sleeps like the dead, luckily for me. Mack is away on tour again. And it's hard without him here. The two of us have been peas in a pod since we were little boys. Huddo was always busy trying to be just like the old man. And Lawson left for the city for college the second he graduated.

Smart.

I push through the white gate to the yard of the homestead. Charlie, Hudson's little mutt, growls at me from the far end of the porch. "Shut it, gremlin boy."

He pops his head up and yaps.

Fuck.

I slip inside, and the smell of Ma's cookin' greets me. A covered plate is in the still lit up oven. God, all of a sudden, I am fucking starving. I open the door and go for the plate. It burns my hand, and I hiss a curse, grabbing a tea towel.

"You're home early, my boy," Ma says from the end of the hall, leaning on the corner in her robe pulled closed, the tie knotted. Her dark blonde hair is plaited to one side. Her green eyes, identical to my own, hold nothing but love and kindness. At twenty-eight, I'm still her boy. It's sweet, I guess, but being the youngest, it only reminds me how far I have to go.

"Town was quiet. Huddo should have come; that's his style."

"I wish he would. Your brother needs to get out more. Maybe Addy could get him to town; he could use some more time with her. I like her, she's good for him."

If Ma knew what I did when I am "getting out," I doubt she would approve. Huddo is too caught up in his head and his horses to make time for women. Well, usually, that is . . . Addy, the new vet, certainly has his attention. And to everyone's surprise, even Charlie the evil hound-dog likes her. From what we can tell, he's keeping their relationship strictly professional.

Sucks for Huddo.

"I'll see you in the morning," Ma says, pushing off the corner and walking back down the hall.

"Yeah, night, Ma."

I pull the drawer open and dig into the pot roast with maple veggies. My favorite. Guilt pangs at my gut for missing dinner. But it was worth it for a glimpse of the prettiest girl god ever made. I chew and savor the flavor, running her face and the swaying of her hips through my mind one more time.

Yep, that's goin' to keep me entertained for months.

Sweet Jesus, now I'm fucking hard.

Urgh, thank god Ma's not still here.

I shove my dirty plate and cutlery in the sink and run the water over it. Pulling my shirt over my head, I head down the hall to my room. Still living with my parents. World's biggest loser, right here. Don't let the shiny, fancy truck fool you, folks—this man does *not* have his shit together.

Not even close.

If I could be half the person my mother is in this life, I'd die happy.

Plans for the future?

Nope.

Marriage and kids?

Nada.

Career and savings . . .

Say what?

Floundering in my own cesspool, that's me. Reed James Rawlins, six feet of muscled, cheeky, live-wire, good-hearted (so I have been told), dark blond, and unintentional facial hair—a hunk of useless burden. All because I can't pick a trade or find a path that excites me. And I'm definitely not a rancher.

Not a willing one, at least.

I lay on my unmade bed and push my boots off with my toes. The duvet doesn't even bother putting up a fight when I toss it aside to get inside the warmth that calls my name. As my eyelids droop, her beautiful face fills my drowsy mind over and over.

The woman that is the makings of a man. His captain. Pa's words. Always tossing them around when one of us relents to listen. A man could do anything with a captain like her. I could man up for someone like her.

Or live the rest of my days in a fantasy that will eventually break my heart.

Fuckin' hell.

A girl like her ain't never goin' to want a wanderer like me.

I roll over and shove my face in my hands.

Fuck this bullshit.

S itting on Addy's front step of her townhouse in Lewistown, I tap out yet another text to Olive about the presumed marriage situation. And I still can't believe I am typing this drivel. But so far, the only response I have gotten back is from her secretary.

After driving through so many small towns and middle of nowheres, my directional skills are still zero. The GPS is the only thing that has saved me this past week. But when I pulled up at Addy's new address, I could almost imagine what it would be like to live here, amongst the slow-paced life and laid-back folks.

Almost.

It's kind of beautiful out here. Something I didn't expect at all.

My phone vibrates as another bar of service appears

and my emails flood in. I skim through them, hunting for Olive.

Nothing. Nada.

I swear, if she is ghosting me to teach me some sort of left-field old wives' wisdom. Ugh! Alright already, I get it.

You think I'm a lone wolf.

But I'm happy, honestly.

Boots appear at my feet. Scrubs.

Addy.

I fly up from the step, wrapping her in a hug. "Damn, have I missed you, girl."

She chuckles. "You have no idea. Please tell me you're staying the weekend?"

"Of course; as long as you need me. My office is right here." I wave my phone at her, and she steps around me, opening the door. I file inside.

Oh, this is just . . .

The elegant, spacious townhouse is farmhouse style, and so gorgeous. "Wow, Adds, all this for one girl. Geez, I should have been a vet."

"Ha! You would be fine until there was blood or poop, Rubes."

"Ugh, you can keep it. I'll visit lots and soak up the country living and wide-open spaces."

"Speaking of wide-open spaces, I have visits tomorrow for some of my equine clients, and then I'm off to Rosewood Ranch for another riding lesson."

"Oh, yes, how is that going? Come here and tell me." I

flop on the couch and pat the seat beside me. Addy rolls her eyes at me, but it's playful. I want to know it all. Every detail I missed while we have been apart. It has been like having half of my heart missing. She is closer to me than any of my actual sisters. And I have missed her so much.

We talk about her riding, her asshat of a boss, and everything concerning Hudson. He sounds amazing. Any man who can give back that huge part of her life that she lost is a literal god in my opinion. I can't wait to meet him and his family. They sound incredible.

When the conversation lulls a little, I lean on the sofa and sigh.

"What is it, Rubes?"

"Am I self-absorbed, Adds?"

"Not at all! Who said that?"

"No one, really. I kind of got the impression that's what they meant."

"Olive?"

"Amongst others."

"Well, this is how I see it. You are driven and focused. You have rules and you follow them. Especially number three."

"Hard work, all the way. No hoping or praying."

"Yeah, that one."

She shifts forward and wraps both hands around her almost empty wine glass. "But Rubes, what do you do for yourself?"

I stare at her. I was accused of being too selfish. Apparently, I do everything for myself. "I don't understand."

"You have all these rules to follow to make sure you're successful. But are you happy?"

Oh.

Happiness is for people with no direction.

My father's favorite words whenever one of his daughters would complain we were miserable with the overloaded schedules the three of us had during our high school years.

"I'm happy, I think?" But the air leaves my lungs, and my grip on the glass stem tightens.

Addy puts her wine down and pulls me into a hug. I swallow past my fast-closing throat and slam my stinging eyes shut.

"You should come with me tomorrow. Stay as long as you can. See what else there is to the world, babe. And maybe you use this as a working holiday or something. Just breathe, Ruby Jane." Addy's words are soft, and I know she will always have my best interests at heart. Maybe I will stay longer? For a little while, anyway.

A little bit of time to breathe never killed anyone, right?

Head out the rolled down window like one of Addy's canine patients, I close my eyes against the bright Montana sun and hold my hand up into the wind as we drive down the longest dirt road known to man. The breeze whips through my straightened hair, tossing it around. It feels like fingers running through it.

It's been a long time since anyone has done that.

Like, a *really* long time.

And if I'm honest, it was quick and shallow. No foreplay, no talking, no loving touch. Purely sex. All business. Need, not want.

"What you thinking about, hanging out the window there like Charlie?"

Huh?

Oh shit!

I pull my arm inside and straighten my hair, huffing a laugh. "Charlie, hey? At least I know I did it right."

Addy laughs as she turns the Cherokee into a driveway. A tall sign arches across the entrance.

Rosewood Ranch
H J & L M Rawlins

The ranch is enormous. A magnificent sprawling homestead and twin red barns sit on the other side of two front white-fenced paddocks, a horse in each. This place is something else. A man rides away from us on a horse, heading toward the mountains that rise behind the barns.

Wow, this really is the west.

"You're going to kink your neck, Rubes."

"I can't believe how amazing this place is."

"You have no idea. Wait 'til you see the ranch, some of the places Hudson has taken me."

"How have you been living here and not sent me pics? Rude, Adds. Just rude."

Those mountains are something else. Stunning. The life they must lead living here . . .

Addy pulls in by the homestead at a small white gate and shuts off the engine. "I'll introduce you to the Rawlinses. Did you want to tag along or stay at the house with Louisa?"

"I'll tag along, if I can."

Addy grins and pushes out the door in her jeans and long-sleeved, button-down shirt. I follow in capri-length jeans and boat-necked, ribbed white-and-navy striped top. The smile on my face is so wide it hurts. A small white dog with tan ears speeds toward her. She is crouched a heartbeat later, loving him up. He ignores me, licking her up.

I huff a laugh, not sure if I'm disgusted or amused. Addy stands as trotting hooves head toward us.

I grab her arm with a gasp when a guy trots over to the car on a horse, bringing with him another saddled-up mount. His brilliant blue eyes fall automatically to Addy.

"Oh wow, you must be Hudson!" I grin, waving a hand.

He tips his hat, giving me a happy but somewhat confused glance.

"Hudson Rawlins, this is Ruby Robbins, my best friend," Addy says.

"Hey Ruby, it's a pleasure to meet you. This is Rocket, and this here is Addy's current loaner, Sergeant."

"Hello, boys," I gush.

"Why is he all saddled up and looking like he is about to head some place big and open?" Addy says.

"'Cause he is, Howard. Sorry, Ruby, I didn't realize you were coming, otherwise I would ha—"

He calls her Howard?

Must be a country guy thing.

"Addy! How's it going?" A younger guy swings an arm over Addy's shoulders and tips his hat to me. When his brows shoot up and his mouth gapes, he extricates himself from my friend and shoves his hands into his back pockets. Okay . . .

His face slackens before he raises an eyebrow. Clearing his throat, he holds out a hand to me.

"Ah, Reed Rawlins. You must be Addy's friend from the Big Apple?"

"Ruby. It's nice to meet you." I press my hand into his.

He takes me in, releasing a breathy huff and then my hand. "If these two are riding off into the sunset, I can give you a tour of the Montana mountains. If you'd like."

"Um, is that okay with you guys?" I ask Addy.

A cheeky smile pops up on her lips. "Sure. Looks like I have plans."

Addy takes the stirrup iron in her hand and mounts like an absolute pro. I cover a hand over my mouth for a moment. She really did it.

She flashes me her happiest smile and waves as she turns the horse to follow Hudson and Rocket.

Reed shuffles a little closer, and I turn, offering a smile. His face is lit up by his green eyes as he returns the gesture. Shaggy dark blond hair flips in his face and he sweeps it away. His biceps flexes as it moves. I purse my lips and shove my hands in my back pockets.

"So, first time in Montana?" he says cautiously.

"First time out of the city, actually."

His eyebrows shoot up. "Oh, wow. Well, in that case, let me take you on the *deluxe* tour." He crooks his arm as his happiness grows into a grin that splits his face.

He's gorgeous.

I huff a small laugh and watch as Addy and Hudson disappear behind the barn and into the field. "Sure, show me what you've got out here."

"It would be my pleasure." He nods to his arm.

I roll my eyes and weave my arm through his.

"This way, mademoiselle."

When he takes off at a high stepping walk, I laugh. He's funny and so friendly. I like him already.

"We'll take Huddo's truck. It knows these hills backwards."

When we reach the old Chevy, he opens the door for me, and I climb in. The door closes, and he walks around the front of the vehicle and hops in. With a flip of his hair, he starts the engine and backs away from the barn.

"So, lived here your whole life, Reed?"

"Born and raised. But don't hold that against me, will ya?" He winks, and I roll my eyes at him.

"I wouldn't dare," I finally say, looking out the window.

"Wouldn't you?"

Are we still talking about the same thing?

"How far are Addy and Hudson going?"

"Not sure, maybe to the river. But we have to take the long way, no loping across pastures today, Miss Ruby."

"Do you ride, too?"

"Yup, kind of a mandatory skill round here."

"Oh, yeah, I guess it is. I've ridden a couple of times with Addy, when we were younger. Before . . ."

Do I tell him about the accident? Do the Rawlinses know the details of that day? It has affected Addy for so long. If she doesn't want them to know everything, I won't be telling them.

"Yeah, I bet," Reed simply says. "Addy said you two were like sisters."

"She did?"

I can't flatten the smile that lights up my face. Of course she did. But it still fills me with happiness every time someone brings up the fact that Addy loves me like a sister. And I guess it also stings a little. I have actual sisters. None of them treat me the way Addy always has.

"Addy's somethin' else. I know Hudson likes having her around," Reed says, but his eyes don't leave the road. I take a moment to study him. Big hands grip the wheel, forearms flexing as the road tosses the wheel side to side. His pale blue Wranglers are fitted, the checkered shirt he's wearing has the sleeves rolled up, white t-shirt underneath. The top three buttons are undone. He's sexy, and he's not even trying.

As if he read my stupid, wandering mind, his green eyes flick to meet my gaze. "You okay?"

I shoot my focus back to the road ahead and grip the door handle, the other hand holding the front of the seat as the truck lurches a little to the left. "Sure, all good."

He chuckles softly. And I fight the urge to turn back and see the smile I can hear in his voice.

Shit.

Rule numero uno, Ruby Robbins.

No distractions.

Tell that to the hammer in my chest right now.

When we finally turn with the road and head toward a line of trees that flanks the river, I sit up straighter. Addy is still sitting on her horse as we roll to a stop. Hudson stands at her side, looking up at her. *Addy, girl, if you can't see the way he looks at you, you're blind.*

It's like he's going to fall apart if she so much as breaks a nail.

"Shit," Reed mutters, his face twisted with worry, eyes locked on Addy. These two guys . . . they're all heart. He shoves the truck into park, rushing from the vehicle, and rounds the front to open my door. With another cheeky grin, he crooks an arm, and I slide mine through. We walk to where Addy is still sitting on the horse.

"You okay, Adds?" Reed says, the grin slipping from his face.

"Yeah, a little achy."

Hudson glances up, brows dropping, head tilting.

"Get her down, Huddo. She should stretch or something." Reed stops at Sergeant's head, and I rub the gelding's face.

"You ready?" Hudson asks.

Addy nods, and Hudson lifts her from the saddle. She slides down until her feet hit the ground.

"Better?" Hudson whispers.

Addy dips her head. "Thank you."

He hovers like he wants to fold her into his arms, but he hesitates and lets her go.

"Nothing a good skinny dip won't fix, Addy," Reed quips.

I track my gaze between Hudson and Addy. "We should leave them be. Come on, show me your mountains. I'm dying to see them, since Adds hasn't shut up about them the whole time I've been here."

"Really?" Reed's eyes widen.

"Really. Take me away from these two."

But Addy doesn't hear me—she's staring at Hudson like he's the last drop of water on the planet. *God, girl. You are so gone.*

I spin back to the truck and tug Reed along with me. He catches up, closing in. "You sure you don't want to go skinny dipping, Ruby Robbins?"

His voice is deep and soft and close to my ear. My stomach flips, wild and messy. I suck in a breath before looking up at him.

"Mountains, Rawlins. I want my tour. Or I am going to have to talk to management," I say as seriously as I can muster.

He runs a hand through his hair and groans. "God, don't talk to Harry, please, whatever you do. Not management."

I laugh but the pained expression on his face almost looks real. When he holds the door open for me, I slip my arm from his. I still, hand gripping the side of the truck. That gorgeous face, those green eyes that could bring a girl to her knees, and his cheeky, playful way could have this girl in a whole lot of trouble if she let it.

But Ruby Robbins has rules.

Rule number one, no distractions. And Reed Rawlins could quickly become a very big distraction if I let him. We will be keeping whatever this is strictly in the friend zone.

You're out of luck, Rawlins.

When I climb into the truck, he watches me for a

moment before closing the door and disappearing around the back. When the driver's door opens, he climbs in without a word.

I want to crawl over the bench seat between us and let his gaze wander wherever it wants.

Good Lord, Ruby. Get a hold of yourself, woman.

Instead, the truck roars to life, and he shoves it into drive.

"First stop, the northern hills and Rosewood Ranch vista. Buckle up, keep your tray tables stowed away at all times, and remain seated until the captain turns off the seat belt sign. Enjoy your flight, and thank you for flying Air Rawlins."

I force a small smile. Because his voice is strained, his face expressionless, and the rise and fall of his chest is almost faster than mine.

Ruby Robbins. Hell's hounds on heat, that's a pretty fuckin' name.

Fuck, she's like nothin' else.

Gives a completely new meaning to the phrase R & R. But . . .

The silence in the truck is too loud. My breathing matches my thoughts—rushed and stunted. And I still can't get over the fact that the girl I saw Friday night on the street at Great Falls, in those red heels, is sitting right next to me. Goddamn, she is even more beautiful in the daylight.

In the space of an hour, we have gone from newly introduced to me being hard as fuck every time she glances my way. Hair blowing in the breeze with the window rolled down, she smells just like a flower.

When we make it back to the barn, I park the old

Chevy. Addy and Huddo are still out on their ride. Or lesson, or whatever it is they do while Harry's not around.

"Thanks for the tour," Ruby says. Her words jerk me back from my daydream.

"Sure, no worries."

"Your mountains are lovely. You're incredibly lucky to live here, Reed."

"Beats the city." I shake my head. "I mean, if that's not your thing, I guess . . . It's not mine, yours, though—"

I run a hand down my face as it heats up. *Geez, not much better.* Embarrassment right here, folks. Come get your fill. Going so cheap, it's free. Sweet Jesus. Since when am I flustered around girls?

Fucking hell, Rawlins.

But a megawatt grin lights up her face, and I almost lose my load there and then.

"It is mine. I haven't ever known anything else, so . . ." She taps her phone on her pants and says, "Can I hop out?"

"Oh shit! Sorry." I jump from the truck, properly mortified, and grab her door. She slips out, her feet landing on the ground. Those big brown eyes find me, and my gut bottoms out like it has fuckin' permission.

"Thanks, Reed. I'll wait here for Adds."

I shut the door as she wanders around aimlessly, looking at her surroundings. *Take your time, Huddo.*

"Ruby, come say hello to Ma. She'd love to meet you."

She spins back from looking into the barn. "Oh, sure."

I walk her to the small white gate, no crooked arm this time. And it feels more awkward without it. When I hold the gate open, she walks into the yard, gazing up at the old oaks and weeping willows that Ma treasures.

"Your place is stunning," she breathes, bumping into my shoulder before looking back from the canopy around us.

"Sure is. Come on, she'll be in the kitchen."

Ruby smiles and walks beside me. When we cross the threshold, Ma looks up from her chopping. As always, she is busy whipping up something delectable in her favorite space.

"Reed! Where did you two come from? You must be Addy's friend! I'm Louisa." She wipes her hands on the tea towel slung over her shoulder and wraps Ruby in a warm hug.

A small squeak falls from Ruby's pink lips as she shoots me a wide-eyed stare. I beam, shoving my hands in my back pockets. When Ma releases her, she holds her at arm's length and takes in her clothes. "Well, you are a stylish girl. Oh, I love this top."

"Thanks, it's Gucci."

"Oh my. The only brands you'll find in this homestead are Wranglers, Stetson, and Winchester." Ma laughs.

"What's a Winchester?" Ruby asks.

Ma waves a hand at her. Ruby's confusion turns to a smile as she admires the sprawling kitchen. "You have an amazing spot here, and your home is . . ." Her gaze snags on the plethora of family photographs on the fireplace mantle and she inhales a long and slow.

Ma tilts her head with brows lowered as Ruby's words fade out after the mention of home.

"Well! Introductions done, we should head back and see if Adds and Huddo are back," I offer up, this time crooking my arm, as if it's her safe place.

"It's lovely to meet you, sweetheart," Ma says, resting her hand on Ruby's cheek as if they are old friends.

Ruby opens her mouth to answer, but her face is vacant, those brown eyes stuck on Ma's face.

"Ruby?" I say.

She shakes her head. "Yeah, sorry, coming. It was wonderful meeting you, Louisa."

"You too, darlin'," Ma says, but soft concern still lines her face.

Outside, Huddo is stalking toward the house. I stop Ruby in the middle of the yard. She waves me off and tries to step around, but I don't let her pass. "What was that?"

"Nothing, I . . . I—Your family, your home is amazing, Reed. You're lucky, is all."

"I take it yours isn't?"

"Huh, well Addy, she's—"

"Adds is your friend, not your family."

"I—" She closes her eyes.

I wrap an arm around her shoulders. Don't care if she

thinks it's appropriate or not. She's upset. Utterly unacceptable. I walk her to the gate. Mackinlay is standing by the barn, Addy crouched on the ground. I had almost forgot he was home. Been back a week, and still it feels like my big brother's time home from tour goes way too fast.

I guess that's my cue to deliver her back to her friend. And apparently the only person she has. That fucking makes me livid. When Ruby hesitates at the gate, I stop and remove my arm. "What is it?"

"Don't— Don't bring this up with Addy, please. She has enough on her plate. And I don't need to burden her with my shitty family. Or lack of. I mean, she knows what my family's like. This is not a normal reaction for me."

I study her face but nod. Huddo walks out of the house toward Addy who is now sitting against the barn, Charlie on her lap. I make my way over to my brothers and Ruby falls in beside me.

"Hey, I'm Mackinlay." He offers Ruby his hand with a glance at me. She takes it and says hello.

Addy looks up to Hudson. "Everything okay?"

"Yup." Hudson eyes Charlie. "Happy, buddy?"

"Pretty sure at this point he thinks he's Addy's dog. Sorry, Huddo," Mack says.

"I see that." He bends down and tugs his little ear playfully. "Ma wants you two to stay for dinner, if you can. She wants help planning her birthday party."

Ruby claps her hands, jumping on her feet. "Yes! We are so doing that."

"Sure, we can stay a while," Addy says, smiling.

Mack glances between us, raising a brow. I clear my throat and crook an arm for Ruby. "Milady."

She giggles and hooks hers through mine. And I would make a fool of myself every day of the week to make sure sorrow never crosses her face again. She bumps my shoulder with hers and mouths *thank you.*

I lean down until my mouth is an inch from her ear. "Anytime, Ruby Robbins. That's what friends are for."

"Friends already? That was quick."

"What can I say? I'm a friendly guy."

When her beautiful brown eyes flicker up at me, her smile blooms and wobbles.

Sweet Jesus, what the fuck, gorgeous girl?

It's a Wednesday, but I stand at the gate waiting for a girl like it's fucking prom night and I'm seventeen all over again. And I feel it. The same feeling that's reared its ugly head on occasion over the last decade, the tight ball consuming my gut, rising behind my ribs.

Ruby is coming out today to work on the details for Ma's party. When Harry found out this is what she does for a living, he insisted on paying her, but she refused to take his money. She stood Harry down. That made Ma laugh. I think the old man has met his match in this small blonde with more spark than a wildfire in summer after the driest winter.

When her not-so-white Mercedes rolls into the driveway, Charlie takes off after the wheels. I shoo him away before he gets any ideas about barkin' at her and open her door.

"Hey," she says, holding a hand up. "Olive, that is the most ridiculous thing I have ever heard. Can't you sort this bullshit out? Honestly, it's 2024, not the 1970s."

The woman on the line, who I'm assuming is Olive, talks fast. Her East Coast city jabber assaults the phone. How it doesn't make Ruby flinch, I have no idea. "Fix it, or I'm out, Olive."

Olive snaps out a few short words.

"Fine, whatever." Ruby glances at me, lost in thought. "Never mind, I'll figure it out. Thanks for your help."

The sarcasm is dripping from her pretty tongue, and I hope to hell those fighting words don't land her in trouble with whoever Olive is. Ruby hangs up and tosses her phone into her tote bag, groaning as her head hits the steering wheel.

"Baby, you work too much. You know that, right?" I drawl.

The second I realize the words I used, I curse under

my breath. But to my surprise, she doesn't miss a beat. Nor does she object to me calling her baby.

"Reedsy, you have no idea."

Reedsy. I'll take it.

I grin back at her and extend my hand. She grabs her tote and pushes out of the driver's seat. When I close the door behind her, she turns back. "Your mom, how old is she going to be? Is this a milestone birthday? I don't want to organize a party and miss any of the details."

"Not a milestone, and she will never tell."

Ruby laughs at that and follows me as I lead her through the gate and into the house. Ma's at the kitchen table and stands when we walk in. She leaves her seat and is wrapped around Ruby the second she reaches the table. Something warm grows in my chest.

"Hey, Louisa." Ruby chuckles.

"I have been thinking about the things you asked me to. I have a list; I hope that's okay?"

Ruby sits in the spot by Ma's and dumps her tote on the floor. "Of course! This is an amazing start. You're very organized." She smiles at Ma as she sits and waves me off. I stand, my frozen gaze swinging between them, before I clear my throat, wipe a hand through my hair, and head to the kitchen. There's gotta be some iced tea in here somewhere. I pull the refrigerator open and listen as they chatter away.

Two peas in a pod.

I pour three glasses of iced tea and deliver two over to

the table. Ma glances up with a smile and Ruby takes one from my hand without looking up. Her fingers brush mine as the glass leaves my hand. She continues to talk to Ma about whatever they are planning. Flowers or something.

I glance at the clock in the kitchen. Ugh, almost ten. Hudson will be hunting me shortly. Or worse, sending that hellhound of his after me.

"Alright, I have chores to get to ladies, have fun." I wave as I wander out the back door, grabbing my hat from the hook as I go.

Ten minutes later, I have Magnet saddled and mounted up, before pushing him into a trot down the lane toward the southern paddocks. Harry wants the herd of weaners shifted further downfield to let the pasture rest. Shouldn't take more than an hour or so.

Hudson's truck is at the paddock gate of his brood mares. He walks around between them, checking them over. Always fussing over them, my big brother. And Ruby is back at the homestead, completely immersed in planning Ma's party. You can tell she loves it, the way she lights up talking about her work. I wish I had that. Something I loved to sink my teeth into.

I push Magnet into a lope.

The grey gelding picks up a steady rhythm. I sit back in the saddle. This is one of the few parts of ranching I actually enjoy. Me and Magnet, the wind whipping past. A thousand pounds of pure power.

When I reach the paddock with grazing cattle, I slow Magnet to a walk and lean down and slide the gate latch open. Maneuvering the gelding around, I pull the gate shut and trot around the herd. The gate for the next pasture runs along the back fence. I head for that, running an eye over the animals as I pass.

No obvious signs of anything amiss.

Harry always wants an update. I open the gate and lope back before pushing the herd onto greener pastures, literally. When all are squared away in their fresh field, I head home. Hopefully, I can catch Rubes before she goes.

Rubes.

Reedsy and Rubes.

R & R.

Now *that* could be a very dangerous thought . . .

I chuckle at my lame joke and urge Magnet into a flat-out gallop. Something about the chance of not seeing her before she heads back to town has my gut in knots. The gelding obliges, ears flat back as we sail over the dirt road that winds through the laneway.

When we reach the paddock before the barn, I slow him to a trot. Something Huddo taught me a long time ago—the last leg home should always be controlled. Bolting horses is not something you want to build into your riding repertoire.

The dirt-covered Mercedes is still there. I all but fly out of the saddle and lead the gelding to the wash down bay, before making quick work of his rinse off and returning the tack to the barn. As I let Magnet loose in his paddock, Ruby walks from the front door with Ma.

I jog over, halter still in hand. "All done?"

Ruby takes me in from head to toe and smiles. "For the minute. There's some more prep work, and we need to confirm some things before anyone gets to relax. Oh, and I need you to help me with something."

"Thank you for coming all the way out again, Ruby," Ma says, giving her a tight hug before walking back to the house.

Ruby's gaze snags on my hat. "Stellar hat, Reedsy."

I dip it before tugging it off and plopping it on her head. It falls forward as she lifts her chin, trying to peer out from underneath, her hands still tight around the handles of her tote. I lift it up for her as she huffs a soft laugh. "Think it's a little big."

"It looks good on you. You should come for a ride with me one day before you head back to the city. If you want, that is . . ." I run my hand across the back of my neck. I have no idea what her plans are, really. Or how long she is staying here for. "What did you need?"

"Oh. Was there anything you think your mom would like for her party that she wouldn't have told me about?" she asks, handing the hat back.

I let it hang between my fingers.

"Fireworks." I nod and pull the best serious face I can muster.

"Really, fireworks? She doesn't seem like an explosive sky kind of gal." Ruby is grinning at me now.

I laugh and shove the hat on my head. "Yeah, that one may have been my childhood dream ever since these birthday parties of Ma's have been a thing. Which is my whole life, come to think of it."

"Okay, well, if you think of anything, text me, okay?"

"Will do."

She starts for her car. "Oh, and Reedsy. I'll be back next week, maybe we could go for a ride then?"

The grin that stretches my face won't quit. I will be counting down the seconds to that little bit of Ruby and Reed R & R.

"Yes, ma'am."

Chapter Five

RUBY

Louisa is like the mother I never had. Except I have a mother—a shitty one. A thousand percent sure I'm going to hell for that thought. But I swear, this is the first time in my life that I have ever had companionship with an older woman that I enjoy. The first time I have wanted to share my thoughts and life with a family member. Period.

Not counting Addy, that is.

Reed appears at my side. He smells divine. Not that I am letting myself take notice. He's a first-class goof. And despite his constant presence when I'm here at the ranch, I like having him around, which has surprised me more than anything else.

It has been a long, long time since a guy has been able to claim that title: Non-Annoying Male Presence. It's a start, I guess, to my new, more relaxed semi-vacation.

"Done already?" I glance at him.

He leans on the counter and glimpses the wine in my hands. His eyes wander from the bottles to my face and back. And I wonder what is going through that gorgeous head of his.

"Yup. What's next, Captain?"

I chuckle and point to the stack of boxes bulging with strings of warm white fairy lights. "I want those gorgeous old trees all lit up, Reedsy."

Surveying the trees outside as he leans on the counter, he groans and drops his head on my shoulder. "Fine, you want Tarzan, little lady? I'll be your monkey."

When his head pops back up and his green eyes find mine, I cant my head, giving him the *go on* look.

"Lucky you're cute, little miss."

I pull a face at him, and he chuckles and wanders to the boxes, hauling two onto his shoulders. His biceps bulge under his shirt and his forearms flex, and I snap my attention back to the boxes in front of me. Wine, beer, and whiskey.

I stack the alcohol into the oversized wine fridge Harry bought for Louisa three years ago, making sure each bottle is stacked with its own category of wine. I close the door after one last count. The catering arrives in an hour, so I reshuffle the double refrigerator to make room for the platter and trays of food for the menu Louisa painstakingly created.

She's a stickler for her food. The size of this kitchen

should have given that away, but she is a foodie and cook of decades, and this woman knows her way around a menu. Addy's mom and Louisa would get on like a house on fire. Right now, she is chopping away in a frenzy of speed that would put Martha Stewart to shame.

The entire house smells divine with the entrées Louisa insisted on making herself.

"Ruby, sweetheart, can you taste this for me?" She holds out a wooden spoon with something steaming in it. I wander over, and she nods to the sauce she has ladled up. I dip a finger into it and pop it into my mouth.

Oh. My. God.

I swallow the hot, delicious liquid. "Lou, this is incredible."

Shit, that just slipped out. But, in my defense, I'm so comfortable with Reed's mom. And the smile that beams on her face warms my heart. It's a somewhat foreign feeling, being with family that talks, interacts, and includes you, but it's growing on me. Real fast.

"Try some more," she says. Her gaze shifts behind me for a second. I don't hesitate, plunging another finger into the liquid. More this time. And when the flavor hits my tongue, I moan and close my eyes, sucking my finger clean.

A throat clears behind me. Snapping my eyes open, I spin back to find a flustered Reed looking anywhere but my face as he starts to say something but shoots a hand up and hightails it out the door.

When I turn back to Louisa, the shit-eating grin plastered on her face is too much. I burst out laughing. She totally set me up. Now I know where her son gets his sense of humor.

I slap her arm. "Lou!"

She doubles over in a fit of laughter, and I try and fail to tamper my own chuckle.

I'm certain Reed Rawlins has never been flustered around a woman in his life. And the revelation on his gorgeous face was priceless. But when Louisa stills and her mouth gapes, I turn back to see what or who she is gaping at.

A guy with similar features to Hudson stands in the doorway. But he's different from the cowboys, dressed in Levi's and a Tommy Hilfiger polo and loafers. A leather overnight bag swings in his hand.

"Oh, my lord!" Louisa springs around the counter as he drops the bag and opens his arms.

"Hey, Mama."

She lets him fold her in tight as he drops his head into her wavy dark blonde hair. All I can do is stand and watch, gawking at the love that is shared between them. The way he holds her, as if she is the most precious person on the planet.

This scenario isn't something I've ever had with either of my parents. Or sisters, for that matter. The air leaves my lungs, stolen by emotion. I spin back, refusing to stare or be seen choking on my own inner childhood grief.

"Ruby, this is my second eldest. Lawson."

I plaster a smile on my strained face as I turn around and move closer. He steps forward, hand held out. I take it, and he shakes it, his firm grip all warmth.

"Hi, good to meet you. Reed has told me a little about you," I say, a little breathless.

"Where is that little brother of mine? Or any of them, come to think of it . . ."

"Ruby has them all off working on the party." Lou opens her arms, as if to say *check out what we've done*.

"Wow, anyone who can get Reed to toe the line has my instant respect." Lawson chuckles. "Do I have a job, too, ma'am?"

"Go hunt down Tarzan." I nod to the yard outside. "He's going to need backup and the rest of those boxes." I wave at the boxes of fairy lights still sitting in the center of the living room floor.

"Sure thing, let me change into my old clothes before I start scaling trees."

Louisa watches the two of us. A string of curses comes from somewhere high outside.

"Excuse me. Sounds like Tarzan could use Jane's help."

I jog outside to find Reed hanging upside down, cable between his teeth as he ties the lights to the branch below. God, how fit is this man?

"Reed Rawlins, don't you dare fall from there!" I call up the tree.

His head jerks in my direction and he smiles, the cable still between his teeth. I shake my head at him, huffing a laugh.

"Lawson will be out to help you in a minute, please don't kill yourself over the lights." Concern lines my every word.

"Laws is here?"

"Yeah, just got here. Getting changed. He's nice."

Reed's face slackens for a second before he glances back up the tree and curls up, grabbing the branch with his hands and sliding his legs from the one they were hooked around. When he comes to rest sitting on the lower branch, he stares down at me.

"Need some cold iced tea, Rubes?" He studies my face, and it takes me a moment to understand his meaning. *Oh, he thinks I'm into Lawson.*

"I don't need cooling down from meeting your brother, thank you. But you in that tree? Now, that could have me hankering for something . . ."

When his mouth gapes, I stifle a giggle and walk back across the yard, leaving him hanging. Literally. That was too easy. I chuckle to myself. Leaves rustle behind me before something heavy hits the ground. Footsteps lope, catching up to me, and I stop, staring inside the house. Louisa putters around the house as I force air in and out of my lungs.

Nope.

Not going there. I close my eyes. But all I see is Reed

hanging in that tree, muscle-bound and happy. Internalizing a groan, I open my eyes and start for the house.

When a warm hand wraps around my wrist and spins me back, the last of the breath falls from my lips as Reed's green eyes drop to them.

He's too close.

I'm too close.

His hair is all ruffled up from climbing trees like an utter child.

But the place it cracks deep inside me feels like nothing else. This wild and free man—the opposite of everything I have ever been, ever wanted—has me coming apart at the seams with one sweep of his hand through his unruly hair.

He opens his mouth to say something but closes it again. And when he doesn't say anything, standing impossibly still, I rest a palm on his old shirt, sleeves rolled up, scattered tree debris on the worn fabric. "Those lights ain't gonna hang themselves, cowboy."

"Sweet drawl, baby."

He messes up my hair with a languid look before turning back to the tree.

Rooted to the spot, I can't take my eyes off him as he springs back up into the tree, arm and back muscles working. My gaze drifts to his ass, and I clear my mind with a shake of my head. I have details to attend to. *Party ain't gonna make itself, Ruby Jane Robbins.*

I roll my eyes at my own stupid southern talk. My parents would be appalled.

When Louisa meets me at the door, she glances over my shoulder as Lawson walks past and toward the tree Reed is hanging in again. Louisa laughs as he screeches like a monkey and scales the tree like his younger brother did.

God, these people have no idea how lucky they are.

"How's the entrée coming along?" I ask.

Louisa's eyes snap back to me. The love and adoration on her face for her sons transfers to me as she wraps an arm around my shoulders. "All done. You want to climb a tree, too, hon?"

I huff an indignant laugh. "Not likely, Lou."

"You can, you know. Out here, you're free. And we love having you around, Ruby Robbins."

I can't look at her. The burning behind my eyes is too much. She squeezes my shoulders and rests her head on mine for a moment.

When Harry pushes through the white gate followed by Mackinlay, Louisa releases me and wanders back inside.

"Ruby, how's things comin' along?" Harry says.

His rugged features are an older version of his eldest son. And the man has intuition like I have never seen before, even in the events and planning business, where it is our job to anticipate what other people need without saying. He makes us come across like a bunch of hacks.

"Good, Harry. You get that little task sorted?"

He winks at me. "All set, darlin'." He glances at his wife inside and then to his youngest son hanging in the tree. "Mum's the word."

Mackinlay, quiet as always, dips his hat and follows his father. He's an enigma, that one. I know Reed loves him dearly. Every story he has told me so far has had his closest brother in it. I know Addy thinks highly of Mack.

When monkey sounds let loose in the trees again, I turn back to find the lights all done. Every ancient oak and willow is adorned with strings that will illuminate them into something like pure wonder in a few hours. Lawson jumps down from an old oak, brushing off his jeans and shirt as he goes.

He shoots me a smile as he heads inside. I wait for Reed. When he doesn't appear like his brother did, I wander over to the last weeping willow and push my way through the curtain of swaying green. I don't see him at first. Legs stretched along a branch, he's sitting, leaning on the old trunk.

"Hey?" I call up.

A sad smile brushes his lips as he dips his head. "Hey, baby."

It should be weird that he calls me that. But for whatever reason, it doesn't bother me; it simply feels like something we have. This friendly banter that is sweet and casual.

"You coming down? We have a few other things to finalize."

"Nope."

"Reed, I need your help."

He doesn't respond, resting his head back on the trunk and closing his eyes.

Oh boy.

"Fine, I'm coming up."

With that, his eyes snap open, and by the time his mouth opens to object, I'm on the second branch. I kick off my shoes and slide my sleeves up to my elbows as I find the next branch with one hand and push up with a manicured foot wedged in the fork below me.

As I reach the branch he sits on, his hand drops down and I slide mine into it. It's warm and covers my own completely. Butterflies take flight deep in my belly, and I will the heat that has flooded my face to take a fucking hike.

Gentle hands guide me to the branch beside his and I plant my ass on it, not letting his hand go.

"You good?" he asks.

"Yes, thank you." I let my gaze wander around the inside of this magnificent nature palace. It's beautiful. The breeze that sways the soft tendrils of green adorning every single thin branch hisses. It's magical. "This is epic, Reedsy. I love it."

He chuckles. "Yup, one of my favorite spots."

"I can see why."

The silence that hangs between us is comfortable. I lay my head back and close my eyes. The overwhelming feeling of the world turning without me crashes in, and I snap my eyes open a heartbeat later.

"Thanks for doing this for Ma. She deserves it."

His face is soft, eyes studying my face.

"You're most welcome," I breathe.

"Every year we always have big plans to make it special, but the five of us ain't exactly party planners. Or that organized, come to think of it."

"I'm sure she loves whatever you guys create."

"Yeah, she always does." He sounds wistful.

"Reed? You have no idea how lucky you are to have a mom like Lou."

"Lou, is it? You two are gettin' on like fire, then?" He chuckles.

"Huh, yeah, I guess."

Happiness fills me up. And when his hand reaches across, I don't flinch or pull away. Only meet his gaze. His chest hollows out in a second. His thumb rubs the back of my hand before he flips my hand over and traces a finger over my palm and down my wrist.

"Rubes."

I swallow hard.

Rule number one.

Rule number one.

Rule nu—

"How can I ever repay you for all this?"

And for whatever reason, my brain flicks back to the inn. Mary-Sue's ridiculous rules about working women being married. Olive's insistence that I figure this out on my own. So, I need a fake husband.

No. That's a fucking stupid idea. I refuse to play a role in their outdated, insane, old-fashioned mindset. But then I say . . .

"Be my husband." The words blurt from my mouth like vomit.

Reed stares at me, stunned.

I pull back my hand like a hot coal.

Fuck.

"No, I mean—I need a *fake* husband, for work at the inn. My client has these stupid old-fashioned ideas about working women having to b—"

"Sure, I can be your husband, Ruby Robbins. Or should I call you Ruby Rawlins?"

I gape at his cheeky face, the way he so confidently slung those words out. Uncertainty flashes through his eyes, so fast anyone not paying attention would have missed it.

"Are you sure? We don't have to make out or anything. Only need you to be my marital plus one for a week or so when I'm at the inn. The first event is when I come back."

"Come back?" His voice is raw.

"Yeah, after your ma's party, I have to go home for a few months. But I'll be back for the gala and grand opening. Then again for the Christmas bash they want now.

That is an add-on that needs to be ironed out back home."

"Not an email kind of meeting, hey?"

He sounds disappointed, and I can't tell if it's because I'm leaving or the fact that I'm staying longer than planned.

"Not an email. But hey, we might find time for that ride in your spectacular hills?"

"Anything you want, Ruby Rawlins."

He grins at me like a Cheshire cat. My seat aches against the hard wood of the branch and I shift uncomfortably.

"Actually, it's Reed Robbins. Mary-Sue thinks my married name is Robbins."

He screws his face up for a second before canting his head. "I'm surprisingly okay with that. Either way, I'm all yours. Let me know when you need me, baby."

"First, please get me out of this tree."

He chuckles and swings off his branch, clinging to the trunk with both hands as he nods behind him. "Hop on, wifey."

I shake my head. "Uh-uh."

"Come on. If you're gonna be my wife, Ruby, you're gonna have to trust me."

I groan and hang my head. "Fine."

The moment I'm pressed against his back, the air leaves my lungs. I close my eyes as he descends the tree. I'm sure my grip is way too tight. But he doesn't say anything, and when we hit the ground, his head turns. "You can let go now."

His words are breathy and soft, making me never want to let go.

But my rules and my head override that sappy thought, and I drop to the ground.

"Time to wash up, Reedsy. Oh and, can we keep this fake marriage thing between us? I don't want to annoy your ma. She's so sweet."

"You got it. Happy wife, happy life." He winks at me and walks inside.

Oh god.

I've created a monster.

How the hell am I going to keep this professional?

I straighten my shoulders and suck in a breath.

You got this, Ruby. Keep your play inside the rules. Rule number one. And rule number three.

That won't be hard; I've done it all my life.

But my life was never out here, in this place, with these people.

My heart flings against my ribs as Reed disappears down the hallway, pulling his shirt over his head. His back muscles move, and his arms are all ropey veins and bulging tone from climbing trees.

Fuck.

Chapter Six

REED

I'd sell my soul for her name to be Ruby Jane Rawlins. But fake husband . . . I'll take it. Figures— no one has ever taken me seriously, why should she? Never before have I been so helpless when it comes to a girl.

A woman.

But fuck me if she doesn't have me dancing on the strings she pulls. And worst of all, I fuckin' love it. Without her around, I would come undone like a puppet with his strings cut.

And if she needs my help, I'll be damned if I'm not there. In any capacity she wants me to be.

Right now, I can't think of Ruby. I have to greet guests and entertain Ma so the boys can sort out the finishing touches. Mack's orders.

Mack, who I have rarely seen since he got back from

tour. And I'm not okay with that. I know you're not supposed to have favorites. But he's my favorite brother. There isn't a childhood memory I have without him in it.

Dressed up and ready to go. Best Wranglers, check. Best dress shirt with my sleeves rolled up, check. Shiny goin' out boots, check. The belt and buckle Ma gave me when I turned twenty-five, check. Hair washed, face shaved, and aftershave donned, check, check, check!

I give the complete look a once-over in the mirror before heading to the living room to intercept Ma. She is fawning over a small gift the ladies from her book club have given her. Well occupied, I leave her alone and pad outside to find Ruby at the gate with Addy.

A large box sits in Addy's grasp. The cake.

I jog over and drape myself over Ruby like a rag doll from behind, letting my chin rest on her head, arms hanging over hers. She smells like strawberries. Her soft, silky blonde hair is curled and down, her slim figure wrapped up in some designer dress that makes her look like a million dollars.

So when Addy gives me a curious glance, I drop my mouth to Ruby's ear.

"Do we tell her now or later that we're fake married?" I whisper.

She slaps the side of my head like you would a sibling. I wince, chuckling, and rub my head, glancing sideways at her with narrowed eyes before extricating myself from her soft body to open the gate for Addy.

"Keep your comments to yourself, Reedsy." Ruby scoffs.

Addy chuckles at us, and I take the cake as we head inside.

"Reed!" Hudson calls me over, standing by the stereo and speakers. Right, that's my job tonight. DJ. Oh, yay.

I deliver the cake inside, securing it in the space Rubes made in the fridge earlier. Hudson is at my back a heartbeat later. After a minute or so of him relaying the instructions he and Pa have been reiterating all day, I sigh. "Yep, got it. Music, then dinner."

"Right. Make sure you're on top of this, Reed; it has to run perfect, okay?"

"Yup, got it. Drink your beer, man; loosen up. You're getting all weird."

He swigs his own beer as Lawson appears through the door and onto the patio.

"Where's Addy, Huddo? Haven't met her yet." Lawson glances around.

Like Hudson oughta talk. Has been hiding out here since Addy showed up. Wish those two would get a room already. Like a fucking matchmaking service, I hunt Addy down in the kitchen, only to find Ruby neck-deep in the wine fridge, her friend right behind her.

"You need another beer, Reedsy?" Ruby says without looking back.

"Nope. Addy, Lawson wants to meet you."

"Oh, sure. I was getting there, I promise, but I wanted

to talk to your ma first." Addy is as pent up over this as Hudson.

I glance to where a gathering has now blossomed around Ma. She is holding up a bracelet. I guess she likes it.

"I'll be out in a sec," Addy says.

She is all dolled up in a dress that's gonna break my big brother's heart. And I can't help but let my attention wander to Ruby. Bent over, I'm getting a perfect view of her ass and those long, slender legs. And then I see them. Those ridiculous red heels.

The ones that made me salivate over her the first time I saw her. I lean on the bench and force my focus to somewhere less volatile for my mind. *The woman is working, Reed. Jesus fucking Christ, mind out of the gutter, man.*

An hour later, and three more prompts from Pa and my brothers, I stand behind the table, working the music. With a break for dinner, I schedule a string of slow country songs to play. A small hand slips into my own as I make my way to the long tables. Ruby bumps my shoulder and leads me to my place setting, right next to hers.

Now, in the fading light, with the miles of fairy lights we hung earlier, I take in her vision. Each of the tables is adorned with Ma's favorite flowers, silverware, cream linens, and porcelain plates. Candles are dotted between the centerpieces. I hold her chair out for her and tuck her in before dropping into my own beside her.

It's magnificent.

Ruby has outdone herself.

The way Ma's face lights up when Pa brings her out for the meal and she sees every single guest seated and waiting sends a stone to my throat. I squeeze Ruby's hand.

When I dip my gaze down at her, tears line her eyes.

Damn, beautiful, don't go lookin' like that or I'm goin' to have to pull you onto my lap and make it all better.

"I think she likes it, Rubes," I whisper into her ear.

She nods, and her face crumples a little as she leans into me more. I can tell this makes her happy, the way the emotion takes over her beautiful face, filling those brown eyes. This work lights her up. Seeing her happy makes me want to kiss that beautiful mouth like nothing else.

But she's not mine. And I'm not hers. And the best it's going to get for us is a fake deal that only lasts a week or so.

I am a thousand percent not okay with that.

Right then and there, beside the most amazing, talented, sweet, beautiful girl in the world, I make a promise to myself. I will give this, whatever it is between us, every fucking thing I got. And more.

When the meal is done, people stay sitting to chat and drink their fill of the alcohol that Pa brought in. Hudson and Addy disappear as I'm stuck talking to one of the neighbors. Ruby whips around, checking on things, ushering people outside. And when I drain the last of the suds from my beer bottle, a loud whistle followed by a crack explodes over the sky.

Gasps and oohs come from the crowd gathered in the yard. A dazed smile cracks slow over my face. Warmth presses into my side. I tilt my head down to find her brown eyes staring up at me. Elated.

"This part is kind of for you," she whispers, pushing up onto her tiptoes.

Fireworks.

She took that and ran with it. The little boy in me right now is overwhelmed, in the best way possible. When she lifts her gaze back up to the sky, now popping with every color of the rainbow, I wrap an arm around her and pull her into my arms. "Thank you, baby."

"Anything for my fake husband, Reedsy."

She pats my chest and untangles herself from my hold. The second she's left arms, my gut plummets. All I can do is stare at her back as the girl of my dreams walks away from me.

Indifferent.

Mack is silent beside me. It's been two months since Ma's party. Addy and Hudson have kissed and made up after a whole debacle over him not wanting to tie her down. Her not wanting to break his heart. Good Lord, those two are hard work. But it turned out okay in the end.

Thanks to Ruby's help.

We have had constant contact via text since she left. Work is riding her ass about coming back for prep at the inn over in Great Falls. And if I'm honest, it has been a long fucking few months.

Right now, I stare at the dotted line on the bunch of papers in front of me. My own ranch. All I gotta do is sign my life away. And that is exactly what it feels like I'm doing. It's stupid not knowing what you want at my age. But I don't. At least I know what I don't want. And that is to end up like my old man. Tied to the land and the animals it supports. That's Huddo's dream, not mine.

"You need me to read it to you, little bro?" Mack quips.

"Shut up."

"This is only the beginning, my boy; it's not the only thing in life, but it's a start for you. A foundation to build from," Ma says. I glance at her. A kind smile lights her face. Pa sits, arms crossed, staring me down, as if that's going to make me sign faster.

Ruby's determination and focus when she's working slides into my mind. I want that, too. Something I can sink my teeth into. I pluck the pen from the table and scratch out my signature.

Done.

My stomach roils.

Mack takes the pen from my hand, signing his life away to a ranch similar to the one I have just landed, ten miles down the road from mine. At least he will be close by. When all the paperwork is finalized, we head over to the new ranch. I hop into my truck, and Mack piles in after I fire her up. Nickelback screams at me the second the music comes on.

For a moment, I think maybe I can do this.

I mean, I should be grateful. I'm being handed the best start a country man could ever ask for. I know Harry has a plan; he always does. But I'm not supposed to feel like a pawn, a piece of the puzzle that is my old man's larger vision. He's a fantastic businessman and reads people like nothin' else. Wish I wasn't part of it sometimes.

I turn the truck onto the dirt road and head north, hands gripping the steering wheel.

Mack turns the music down. "What's eatin' you, bro?"

"Nothin'," I say, a little too fast.

"Yeah, right. Spit it out, gunny."

I meet his gaze. His military-short hair is dark, his blue eyes like Huddo's are scanning me now. *Don't look too hard, Mack, you'll discover all the shit I never let anyone else find.* Like the fact that most days not knowing who I am and what I want gives me anxiety so bad, I have to force myself from my room. That I use alcohol and loose women to soothe my deep and utter self-loathing.

The infamous Great Reed Rawlins.

Cowboy hack.

Loser.

And my parents handed over millions of dollars' worth of real estate to this sham of a son.

"Reed!"

I slam on the brakes, shaking my head, trying to focus on what is flying up at us fast. Mack grips the dash. No, we are the ones going too fast. We slide to a stop, inches from Pa's tailgate. His silver truck idles at the gravel road crossroads.

Holy fuck.

"Man, get out and let me drive. You're not okay."

Mack doesn't wait. He slides over the seat, and I hop out and walk around the back of the truck, hands crawling through my hair, tugging as my nerves play havoc with my insides and my mind all at once.

"You wanna talk about it?" Mack says, shifting the truck back into drive as he looks both ways and follows Pa's truck.

"Nope."

"This about Ruby?"

I wish.

"Nope."

"Geez, Reed. Give me something to work with here."

"Drop it, Mack."

When I stare out the window, ignoring the eyeballing he's giving me, he returns his attention to the dirt road, and we make it to the ranch in short time. At least they are close together.

Ma hops out of the truck before Pa does. She is spinning around, arms out, delight on her face. The ranch is a smaller scale compared to ours, but it stills lays claim to two big barns, a homestead, and another small cottage-type building. A stream runs behind the house, about a hundred yards away. A set of cattle yards sit halfway up the nearest hill to the south, and stables are tucked in behind the closest barn to the house.

Yeah, this is definitely real now.

Bile rises in my throat. But before I can retch my insides onto the grass, Ma folds her arm around my shoulders. "What do you think?"

"Yup, it's epic, Ma."

My words are strained. I force a smile, and she rests her head on my shoulder for a moment.

"Your mother can show you inside while I help Hudson and Addy," Pa says.

Huddo's truck pulls into the driveway with the gooseneck towing behind. Addy sits in the front with him, beaming a smile my way as she waves. I wave back as Ma pulls me toward the house. The porch wraps around the front and one side of the house. A white swing seat hangs by the front door to the left.

"Right, so it's a bit of a fixer-upper at the moment. But despite the outdated kitchen, the rest is still good. Could use a woman's touch." Ma opens the door, and we wander inside. Mack jogs over and walks in behind me.

The front room is something like a mudroom-slash-short hallway before opening into a living room with a fireplace. Sweet. The kitchen is pale wood with a navy counter. The small dining table sits between the front window and the kitchen bench. It's homey.

"Where's the bedroom and stuff?" I ask.

Ma almost skips down the hallway, waving to steps that lead to the upstairs. The house didn't even appear big enough for an upstairs from the outside. We walk up the creaking stairs. When we reach the top step, three doors end the small landing.

"Your guest bedroom is here," Ma says, opening the first door. A white room with a wrought iron bed sitting on hardwood floors. When she opens the center door, a full bath, white also. Neat and clean, not bad. At the final door, she hesitates.

"What?"

"This is your master." She pushes the door open and steps aside, letting me go in first. I step through, and the giant rustic wooden bed sits on the wall to the left, a fireplace on the right. A huge bay window looks over the southern fields. I pad to the window, running a hand behind my neck. Below, Hudson is leading Magnet to the barn. Addy follows with Charlie in tow.

"Do you like it, hon?" Ma asks.

I turn back to find her hands clasped in front of her chest. Eyes filled with hope and love.

I close the distance and hug her tight. That's all the mettle I need.

"I love it, Ma. Thank you."

"Oh, your brother brought your horses over. And Pa has a surprise in the barn."

I chuckle and lead her down the stairs. Mack is stocking the fireplace full of wood, with extra in the iron cradle beside it. "Now you're all set, bro."

"Thanks, man."

"Sure, I'll take a beer as payment later."

"Boys, come outside." Ma is waving at us from the front porch.

We wander into the small front yard flanked by trees, and Addy stands by Hudson, Charlie between them.

"Hey, Adds."

She pecks a kiss to my cheek.

Hudson nods to the barn by the stables. "Magnet's in the barn with two other horses. Tack's put away. All that's left to do is find Pa, he wants to show you some of the pastures. Oh, and the thing in the barn."

We make our way over, and when everyone hangs back, I step inside with a knot in my gut. I find Pa standing by a tractor. A brand-new, shiny red tractor.

"Holy shit, Harry!"

"Language, son. But you're welcome. You're gonna need it. Lot of improvements to make around this old place."

A huge Case IH tractor, an 8.7L Power Drive Magnum. I run a hand over the red hood of the engine as he opens the door and climbs in. He starts her up, and she rumbles to life. Lower and with more heart than my truck. The sound reverberates through my entire body. Pretty sure it lights up my soul.

Pa jumps down from the tractor and claps a hand on my shoulder. "Take her for a spin."

"Geez, it's too much, Harry."

When his gaze levels mine, my old man simply nods and says, "It's just the right amount. Now hop in, I'll ride rumble, you can drive, we'll talk numbers and plans."

And like that, my elation fizzles to nothing.

Expectations are nothing new with my old man. We head to the western fields first, and Harry runs down the list of improvements he wants done in the first twelve months.

Should have known. Still a lackey in his eyes.

"We want the first round up to bring in enough to cover the first lot of installments before we start stacking it against the assets and turning a profit, so every day counts from here on in."

With every word that comes from his mouth, my gut sinks further and further. Not even the hum of the tractor that turns on a dime with the slightest motion of my hand drowns out the sinking feeling that is growing, suffocating, slowly asphyxiating me. The weight of needing to be something I'm not crushes the air from my lungs.

I can't do this.

Knuckles turned white on the wheel, I swing the

tractor round and head for the barn. When Harry talks away minutes later, his words are only just audible over the roaring in my ears. My head is fuzzy. My gut a sea ravaged by the darkest storm.

I cannot do this.

I cannot let everyone down.

Not Ma.

Chapter Seven

RUBY

The second I step out from the car in the driveway of the inn in Great Falls, I see him. Leaning against his black F250. And instantly, the past few months feels like a year. A long, greyscale, boring year.

He's looking straight at me. Cap on his head, shaggy dark blond hair poking out under it, his green eyes covered by aviator glasses. A pale blue polo shirt accentuates his arms. And is he wearing Levi's?

Talk about putting in some serious effort, Reedsy. I close the distance between us, and he slides the glasses from his face and drops them inside the truck. "Hey, darlin'."

"Hey Reedsy," I say. It sounds too soft. But the last of my breath disappeared when those green eyes found mine and a smile split his gorgeous face. It should be awkward; we haven't seen each other for months. But it isn't.

"Where do you want me, baby?" he says as he tugs me into a hug. Oh yeah, fake husband. How could I forget?

"Ah, you can park your truck by my car, and they will valet it for you."

He unfolds his arms and leans inside and fires up the engine. It's loud, really loud. I don't know much about cars, but that sounds like a V8 or something.

"You want to jump in and run away?" Reed whispers.

I huff an indignant laugh and lay a palm on his chest. "Nope, no can do. Mary-Sue will have my guts for garters. And I really need to have some things ironed out before tomorrow night."

He tugs the door open and climbs in. "Okay, but if you ever change your mind . . ."

His truck rolls forward, stopping behind my car. He kills the engine and grabs a bag as he shuts his door.

"I'll grab my bags," I say. The trunk swooshes open with the click of a button.

Reed leans in and plucks them up with one hand. "I got 'em, baby."

He's sweet. Nothing like the city jerks I've dated before. Chivalry is certainly not lost on this man. And when he manages to hold the door open while carrying all three bags, I slip past and give him a shy smile.

We check in, and when Miley hands us two key cards, Reed thanks her in his polite drawl and we head to the elevator. We stand waiting for the silver door to slide open, and Reed steps closer, running a hand through my hair as he dots a kiss to the crown of my head.

"I missed you, Rubes."

Butterflies fling around my insides like they were shot from a cannon.

Fake husband.

Fake husband.

It's only for show.

But I missed him, too, and when I open my mouth to tell him, his eyes are shining with mischief and adoration. Good Lord, it is going to be impossible to keep the lines straight between us. "Missed you, too," I finally say. The words are almost a whisper.

The elevator dings, and the doors slide open. I walk inside as Reed hauls our bags in and comes to stand by my side. When the doors clunk together, his woodsy scent, something expensive and fragrant, swallows me whole. I turn and put space between us. "You don't have to be affectionate when no one is looking."

"Break a man's heart, Ruby Robbins."

"If it makes you uncomfortable, you don't have to."

"Nothing about being around you makes me uncomfortable. I like being around you. But if you—"

"Oh no, please. You're the best company I've had since Addy up and left me."

"Oh, yeah right. I forget you two are a thing." He grins at me.

"Haha. I—"

"You don't do people. I get it. I've seen you with others. Tell me what you want, Ruby. You have held up your end of the deal. I'm more than happy to hold up mine."

My face slackens. "I didn't mean it like that. I was happy to work on your ma's party. It was my pleasure." My gaze hits the floor. That weekend will forever be engrained into my memory. Being part of the Rawlins family for a few days was extraordinary. The relationships they have are so real and deep. And I wish . . .

The heat that floods my face and neck is ridiculous. So, I decide to change the subject. "How's the new ranch? You've been quiet since you moved in."

His humor fades. "Yeah, it's been a lot. Harry has a thousand plans and even more jobs on his task board. Some mornings I lie in bed and wish I could go back six months, you know?"

"You don't like having your own place?"

"I do, but it's a lot and it's not—"

Ding.

The doors swish open. I step out, glancing back at Reed. He grabs the bags and follows behind me. I unlock the door and hold it open for him.

He dumps the bags down and looks around.

One bed.

Guess we are married.

"I'll take the sofa," Reed says, kicking off his shoes as he sinks into the too soft, lumpy cushion on one end of it.

"You don't have to. I can get another room." I'm sure I resemble a deer caught in headlights right now. I scramble in my tote for my phone.

"And have them think our marriage is on the rocks, baby? Never."

I chuckle, but it's strained, and he's right. It wouldn't look good. I sink onto the bed and drop my bag onto the floor and flop backward with a sigh. Something hits my stomach, and I sit up. His cap falls into my lap.

"You bought a Yankees cap? Just for this week?"

"Laws sent it to me; told him I needed one."

He leans forward, elbows on his knees, hand under his chin, green eyes studying me. I turn the hat in my hand, running a pink painted nail over the stitching. Reed shifts on the sofa. I bite my lip and hold it out for him to take.

When he slides the cap from my fingers, his brush over mine. The zing of electricity that floods my body with the smallest touch from him is insane. I clear my throat and decide it is as good a time as any to change into jeans and a shirt.

I don't need to be in these crushed suit pants any longer. I kick off my black pumps and slide the jacket from my shoulders and hang it over the chair at the small desk by the bar, fridge, and TV.

Reed watches as I putter around, unpacking.

"Oh, you want half the closet space?" I ask as I pull my hangers from my larger bag.

"Sure, whatever you want."

He's in a daze. And when his Adam's apple bobs with a rough swallow, I hide my face in the closet and hang each item as slowly as I can. If I glance back at him now, I'm likely to end up on his lap. He jokes about almost everything, but being in close proximity to him makes me feel undone.

And I have rules. Which I intend on following.

No dating.

No distractions. Not in the city, and certainly not here. Period.

"You want a shower or something after your drive? I can head down the street if you need," Reed offers.

His words are like a slap to the face. Guess that would be the responsible thing to do. When the sofa creaks and the door opens and closes, I slam my eyes shut.

I have to concentrate on my job.

My reason for being here.

Not Reed.

Or the way my entire body responds to him simply being in the same room as me.

But when I finish unpacking and head to the bathroom to shower the four days' worth of gas station grime from my skin and travel weariness from my bones, all I can think of as I stand bare under the falling, steaming water is Reed fucking Rawlins.

Rules, Ruby, remember your rules.

For the love of god.

Rules.

Wi-Fi at the inn is patchy at best. I hold my phone up to the air, hoping that will solve my internet problems. It doesn't. Outside in the café area of the inn's restaurant, I tap out another email, double-check the vendors for tomorrow night, and recalculate my orders, to make certain I haven't under-catered.

People mill about, cutlery clinks, and the smell of coffee, even this late in the afternoon, is a comfort. When a figure drops into the chair opposite me at the table, I peer up from my numbers and overflowing inbox to green eyes.

"Do you ever quit workin'?" Reed drawls.

"Some of us need to be on top of things, Rawlins." I drop my eyes back to the screen and hit reply to a query from a guest. And I tap out a message, fingers flying over the keyboard.

"Do you ever take a break, Rubes?"

I snap my focus up. Reed's face is scrunched under a frown and his arms are crossed over his chest. I sit back in the woven café chair and sigh. "I have to make sure everything's as planned. It's my job."

"Yeah, but you just drove four days to make it back here, and you haven't seen your husband for ages. Can't leave a man hanging like that, baby."

The waitress who also works the front desk at night walks by with a tray full of dirty cups and plates. She smiles at me and then glances at Reed before wandering inside.

Nice one, Rawlins.

"I guess I could have the rest of the day off. I mean, everything appears to be in order. At this point, I'm triple-checking."

"Good, now let's ditch this joint."

He pushes up from the chair and helps me pack up my stuff. As a good husband would. When he shoulders my tote and holds out his hand, I stare at it. We haven't talked about PDA and what we will and won't do for this facade.

"It's okay, we're just going for a walk."

I slide my hand into his. It's warm and snug, like it belongs there. And when he rubs a thumb over the back of my hand and tugs me closer, I force my gaze on anything else but his face. This closeness, the way he is with me, it's so foreign.

Like he actually enjoys spending time with me, not hanging out purely for whatever he can glean from me. Money. Sex.

Like the guys before him.

"You should ditch those shoes, walkin' around Great Falls in those is gonna have you in a hospital bunk with a broken ankle. So impractical, Rubes."

"I like them."

"I never said I didn't like them on you. But where we're goin', they won't be sufficient."

"Okay, let's go up and change. You always surprise me, Reedsy."

"That's *my* job, beautiful."

Huh.

Well, fuck.

A breathy huff chokes from my throat as we reach the elevator. Despite my rules and this being a temporary fake relationship, the butterflies in my belly are very real. The way my body responds to him being in the same room as me. Too goddamn real.

When the elevator dings, and he leads us back to our room, I fall back and admire that perfect ass in those Levi's. The door beeps and we are inside a moment later. I pull my sneakers from my bag and slip them on. Reed inspects one of the black heels I was wearing, running a hand over the four-inch narrow heel like some sort of connoisseur.

"Don't think they'll fit you," I quip.

His eyes meet mine, darkened and piercing. And the heat that washes through my body burns. *What the hell is he thinking about?*

Breaking eye contact, I slide my phone into my back pocket. "You ready?"

He drops the stiletto on the bed with one hand and runs the other through his hair, arm flexing. His hair falls into his face as he turns and swoops up his cap, fixing it on his head. "Yup."

We walk in silence all the way to the front desk, where Reed requests his truck. Mary-Sue makes polite conversation with him. He drawls back about his drive out here, making it sound as though he drove from another city, not a couple hours away from his new ranch.

He charms the older woman with a few lines about the beauty of Great Falls and her magnificent inn before his black truck rolls into the driveway.

"Thanks, darlin'." Reed waves to Mary-Sue, and we head outside.

"Darlin'?" I scoff, getting into the truck as he holds my door open.

"Jealous, Ruby?"

"Huh. You wish, Reedsy."

He shuts the door, but his face flattens as he walks around the front to get in. The rumble of his truck is deep and heady. And when Reed lets it roll onto the street and accelerates, it's nothing short of pure thunder. And the smile that blooms over his face tells me everything. He loves this truck.

I chuckle at him, and he turns to look at me. "What?"

I study him for a moment. "It's true, then, what they say about cowboys and their trucks?"

"I thought it was cowboys and their horses?"

"I don't know, you seem more of a truck man to me."

"You got it, baby."

I smile at him, and he shifts his focus back to the road. Ten minutes later, we are at a park of some sort. He pulls up and kills the engine. The second I open my door, I hear it. Gushing water.

"Where are we?" I call over the hum of the turbulence.

"Giant Springs State Park. Mary-Sue suggested it."

"So you haven't been here before?"

"Nope. You wanna wander around?"

"Sure."

He takes my hand, and we meander down the first pebbled path we come across. The springs are spectacular. Calming and wild all at once. When we reach the edge of the stream that is fed by the springs, Reed releases my hand.

"This is stunning, thank you," I say.

Reed sinks onto the ground, knees up, and pats the grass beside him. I drop down and pull my phone out, resting it next to me.

"You seemed stressed out."

"Focused. I don't stress, I get busy."

He chuckles.

"Tell me about your new place. The ranch must be something?"

"Yeah, it's something. Harry thinks so, at least."

"You're not happy with it?"

He huffs a strangled breath and plucks at the grass at his seat. I can barely see his face under the cap.

"Maybe. I just . . ."

"It's not what you wanted?"

He stares at me now, eyes narrowed, mouth a thin line. "I don't know what I want. That's the problem. Everyone is moving forward, or already knows. Look at you. Ruby Robbins, career woman. And I can't even make the first step. I can't even decide."

The expression on his face and the defeat in his voice make my heart crack. Like he feels like a failure at the ripe old age of twenty-eight, because what he has isn't what he wants.

"Well, what are your options?"

"Ranching. Ranching, or . . . ranching."

"Reed," I say breathily.

"I'm serious, Rubes. Harry doesn't take no for an answer. And he's handed me millions in land and equipment. I can't walk away now. It's not an option. I'm all out of those."

"But if it's not what you wanted, why didn't you say something?"

"The old man reads people. Probably figured that's what I wanted. I mean, I never gave him a reason to think otherwise."

"Well, his comprehension could use some work."

Reed laughs and lies on the ground, hands under his head. "You tell him that, baby."

"Maybe I will." I roll onto my side, hand propping my head up as I study his face. He closes his eyes, and the only sound is the rushing water and the heartbeat in my ears.

"You want a Polaroid?"

I smile, and when I don't respond, he opens his eyes and meets my gaze.

"We'll think of something, Reed. I promise."

He pulls a hand out from under his head and touches my cheek, thumb running along my jawline. All I want to do is melt into his touch. But I don't. I hold my breath, counting the seconds until his hand falls from my face.

"It's okay, Rubes. It's my lot. I'll have to deal with it and man up."

With that, I sit up, knees up, and fold my arms around myself. He sounds like my father now. And I don't like it. Not one bit. Something about being out here feels so far removed from that single-focused mindset my father has always had. Like out here they know there is more to life than working every waking hour. And I don't want that for Reed.

I'm used to it. It's all I know. But somehow for him, I figure that's a life sentence, not an actual life.

"Hungry?" Reed breaks my train of thought.

"Yeah," I say, but my voice is weak.

He stands and drops a hand to pull me up. I take it, and he tugs me to my feet. The sun has gone down, and the first stars have poked from the dark grey blanket to the east. The sky is stunning out here. The mountains around us create a border, showcasing everything Mother Nature has to give.

I shiver. The chill in the air is noticeable now.

"Cold?" Reed says, pulling me into a tight hug.

I should resist, but he is so warm, and I berate myself for not remembering a jacket. When my shivers subside, he unfolds himself and drops to the ground in a crouch.

"Ah, what are you doing?"

"Get on. It'll be warmer, and I can make it back to the truck faster."

"I, no—"

"Hop on, Robbins, you're gonna freeze."

Snatching up my phone from the grass, I sigh. "Fine."

I climb on, and he pushes up and takes off into the dark down the path. He's fast. And I laugh, letting the happiness that he brings rumble through my chest and fill my veins. His long strides see us back at the truck in half the time it took to get to the spring.

He lets me down, breathing heavy, and holds the door open. I turn back as I go to step inside and hesitate, hand suspended between us. His gaze drops to my lips. In the dim light, I could so easily kiss that gorgeous smile. Take his face in my hands and claim that mouth.

But we are friends. This thing between us is fake.

Totally pretend.

Made up.

Not real.

And I am fighting so hard to remember that.

Every single time he is this close.

Every time he opens his mouth with that goddamn cowboy drawl.

Every moment between us that's deeper than a simple friendship.

I turn back and hop into the truck. The door closes, and I fix my gaze to the windscreen. The driver's door opens closes as the truck dips a little with his weight. The engine rumbles to life. The headlights flick on. The only thing moving in this truck is our heavy breathing.

The burn of his eyes on me is scorching as I force each fiber in my body to still, resisting the urge to return the look. To touch. To tangle myself around him.

Because the line that wobbles between friendship and much more is blurring at a rapid rate in this head and heart of mine.

No, Ruby.

Rule number one.

Chapter Eight

REED

I lie on the shortest sofa known to man, washed up and in my t-shirt and boxers. Guessing I'll have a crick in my neck at the very least in the morning. The door to the bathroom is open an inch, and I stare at the ceiling as Ruby moves about in there, getting ready for her shower.

The springs were a good reprieve. And I'm glad I made her laugh, let her de-stress a little. She deserves a break. She deserves so much more from the people in her life. Period.

The rustle of clothes hitting the floor sees my gaze flick to the bathroom door.

Shit.

I force my eyes back, staring at the hideous popcorn ceiling and counting backward from one hundred. I shouldn't look.

Ruby should shut the door.

And when she slips past the door on her way to the shower without a stitch on, I stifle the groan that rattles up my throat. I slam my eyes shut and force air into my lungs as my cock stretches my boxers. With loose underwear, it makes an unwanted hard-on that's much more difficult to defuse.

When the water turns on and she sighs, I roll over and drag my hands down my face. I stare at the horrid baby-puke-colored upholstery and try to count the threads in each inch. Like that will save me. I fill my mind with anything that I hate.

Harry's tax papers.

Seeing Mack off on another tour.

Disappointing Ma.

Nothing douses the fire that is building in my core, not even that last one. Or dulls the thunder of the blood bounding through my ears. When the tap squeaks and Ruby curses, I roll back and shove my hands under my head, closing my eyes.

"Reed?"

Shit.

"Reed? Can you grab me a towel off the bed? I forgot it."

My heart hammers as I glance at the rolled-up white towels on the queen-size bed. Of the two that were there, one remains. I roll off the sofa and stride to the bed and swipe up the towel. When I reach the bathroom door, I knock on the wall beside it. "You decent?"

Sweet Jesus, you idiot, Reed.

"Um, no? But I'm freezing. Towel!"

I hold the towel around the doorjamb. I hear as she sweeps the curtain back and steps onto the tile. The towel is tugged from my hand, and I hear the rustle of her wrapping it over her body. I rest my forehead on the wall and suck in a breath. The door opens, and Ruby steps out, hands twisting her wet hair into a messy bun on her head. I push off the wall.

Water droplets sit on her elegant shoulders. Her brown eyes find mine, and she smiles. "Thanks, didn't want to have to streak across the room for it."

I drag my gaze from her neck and jaw to her eyes. "Huh?"

"The towel. Thanks."

"Sure."

"You want to order in? The kitchen isn't fully operational as yet, and I don't think I can take any more Mary-Sue today."

"Yeah, sounds good," I say, but my voice is raw.

Ruby studies me. She steps closer and then eliminates the space between us. "Thank you, for this."

I dip my chin, taking her in. So close, I can smell her skin. The fire in my core from earlier roars back to life. How the hell am I going to be in close quarters with Ruby Robbins and survive?

"You're welcome, baby." Now my voice is pure gravel.

And she notices.

"Reed . . ."

I put space between us. Dragging her down with my pitiful existence was not part of the Reed-and-Ruby fake marriage deal. She deserves so much better.

I drop onto the sofa and pluck the takeout menu from the small table beside it. I'm looking at the words, but none make sense. I wait for the pounding behind my ribs and the fire in my veins to peter out. And when I can finally breathe without feeling like I'm gasping for air, I run my eyes over the options.

"Steak and veg for me, well done, Diane sauce."

I hand her the menu. She takes it, and her fingers brush over my hand.

"Sure, what's good on here?"

After a minute, she chooses a chicken salad and a bottle of white and calls it in, still in her towel. I grab my phone from the side table and check my messages. One from Ma, wishing me and Ruby a fantastic weekend. Poor Ma, she's gonna get her hopes up about this. One from Huddo, says he needs a few things for the barn at my place.

I send back responses to both and lock the screen, returning the phone to the table when Ruby steps out of the bathroom, dressed in her PJs, her hair almost dry and loose around her shoulders. She's beautiful, even in her PJs.

Good Lord, I am a dead man walking.

When she flops on the bed, she pats the mattress and turns on the TV with the remote, flipping through channels. I hesitate but make my way to the bed and take the left side, sitting up near the pillows, leaning on the headboard like she is.

"What do you want to watch?" she asks.

"I'm not fussy. Don't really do TV."

She turns to me, her mouth open. "Really?"

"Yeah, not my thing."

She wriggles, settling down into the pillows before choosing a channel. Something about people renovating houses.

"This one, they have to buy a property and have a set budget to renovate before turning it over within a set time frame."

She points to the screen with the hand still holding the remote. I stare at her in awe. Little nerd.

A knock rattles the door, and I jump up and grab the food and wine we ordered. It comes in a carton, the chilled bottle swinging from the delivery guy's hand. I place the bottle on her bedside table and pour her a glass of wine before placing the cardboard container of food in front of her. It feels natural, like the two of us having dinner at home. Not that this is home, or we are a thing. Or could ever be.

Ruby wastes no time digging into her food, making short work of it. And as she pours her second glass of wine, she starts to clean up, popping the now finished plates back onto the tray, pushing it to the door with one hand and sipping on the wine with the other.

On her way back, she drains the glass and sets it on her bedside table before climbing under the covers, still sitting up. But she yawns. It's been a long day for her.

"Oh, I forgot something," she says, turning to the bedside and opening the top drawer.

As she twists back to face me, she grabs my hand and drops a ring into it.

"Thought we might need these for tomorrow night, at least."

I stare at the silver wedding band in my hand, her fingers still wrapped around mine as our hands hang between us. She holds up her left hand and waves her fingers, flashing a white gold wedding band at me. A small smile peeks across her pretty lips.

Heart pounding, I say, "Good idea. Can't have guys thinking my wife is available," I joke, but it comes out flat.

"Didn't want Mary-Sue sussing us out before the gala. Olive would have a fit if this didn't work out. She is oddly attached to me pulling this off."

"Sure, can't have that."

When she drops my hand and starts to fluff the duvet, I take that as my cue to head to the sofa. Ruby organizes the pillows before rolling over and turning the lamp off. I pull the sheet I found in the cupboard over my frame, now draped over the couch. This is goin' to hurt in the morning. My neck is pinching already.

I punch the pillow underneath my shoulders.

Then the only sound in the room is our breathing. The soft humming of the town outside fills the spaces between. Ruby tosses and turns before sitting up in the dark. And despite the dimness, her gaze is on me.

"Reed, come sleep on the bed."

"I'm fine, Rubes. Honest. Go to sleep."

She sighs and lies down. And when another ten minutes passes, I stifle a groan at the ache in my lower back. Well, almost.

"That's it," Ruby says.

She is beside me, looking down at me in the dark a heartbeat later. "In the bed, Reedsy. I promise not to steal your virtue."

I chuckle as she grabs my hands. "Come on. Can't have a broken husband."

Who am I to argue with the woman? I pry myself from hell's sofa and follow her to the bed. She leads me to the left side, pushing on my shoulders until I sit on the edge of the bed. What I wouldn't give to wrap my arms around her waist and drop my head to her stomach. To breathe her in.

"You want a pillow wall between us?" she quips. I can feel her smile in the dark. Hear it in her voice. Can imagine her eyebrow raised.

"I think I trust you not to get all handsy, baby."

She huffs a soft laugh and walks to her side and slides under the covers. The bed is a godsend compared to the sofa. I roll over to face Ruby, and she does the same. I resist the urge to touch her face, to trace the soft outline of her lips and cheekbones in the dim room. Her shampoo and soap fill my senses.

And lying next to the most beautiful girl I have ever seen, with only a foot of mattress between me and her, I'm hard as stone. I close my eyes, willing my body to stop reacting to hers so close.

To stay friends.

To be what she needs from me.

To not screw this up.

So instead of pulling her close and smashing my mouth to hers, I say, "Tell me about your family."

At first, she doesn't respond, and a beat passes between us.

"What do you want to know?"

"What are your parents like?"

"Nothing like yours. They are career-driven, always have been."

"Ah, I know a girl like that," I tease.

"Well, they make me seem lazy."

"I highly doubt that. What about your sisters?"

"Tammy is a lawyer, works with Dad. And Sienna is in finance. And then there's me, in the planning and events sector. Nowhere near as prestigious as law or money. They love to remind me of that. But I guess for older sisters, they are normal. We love each other, in our own way."

"Sounds ominous."

She chuckles. "Maybe, but they are all I have known. Until your family, that is."

"Yeah." I roll onto my back and shove my hands under my head. "My family has a knack for thinking everyone should belong. Or at least, they are welcome to be, if they want."

"That's nice you have that. Addy was right, your family is incredible."

"Adds said that, hey?"

"Yup. I don't think you could get rid of her even if you wanted to now."

"Not sure Hudson will ever let her leave."

"She's lucky to have found Hudson."

I glance at her now. In the dark, I can see the sorrow in her face.

What's that about? Who the hell hurt this sweet, amazing woman?

"You want to talk about it, Rubes?"

She huffs a laugh and runs her hand over the mattress between us. "I don't do relationships, Reed. My rules. But sometimes I wonder if all this effort I put in, all the sacrifices I make, professionally and personally, will be worth it in the end."

"What's the end?"

"To run my own planning and events firm; one day,

that is. And I have been working and saving for over a decade. I'm so close, I can't let up now."

I roll over and push up on one elbow, looking down at her. "You'll make it, baby. I see how hard you work. The attention to detail. Everything you do comes off amazing."

"Thanks. Some days it doesn't seem like I'm getting anywhere. More like I'm spinning my wheels on someone else's hamster wheel."

"One day, you'll be the hamster wheel master."

She laughs, tossing her head back into the pillow, and I can't help it when my knuckles brush her cheek and tangle in a strand of her hair before dropping beside her. Her laughter dies out, but her eyes burn into mine through the dark between us.

I pull my hand back.

My chest heaves.

Keeping time with hers.

"Ruby," I say, but it's raw and too soft. She makes a job of straightening out the duvet and pulling it over her shoulder as she rolls over to face me. Her lips are pursed together before she closes her eyes with a little shiver. "Night, Reed."

I sit up and tuck her blankets into her sides, two hands at a time, down her sides. "Snug as a bug in a rug."

She giggles, and it sends the heat in my core surging around my body. "Night, baby."

A smile blooms over her face, but she flattens it as quick as it appeared.

"Night, Reedsy."

I lie on my back and stare at the ceiling, hands by my sides. It takes a solid hour to calm down enough to fall asleep.

When I'm dozing off, she touches my forearm with one of her arms, now out of her snug cocoon. "Reed?"

"Yeah, baby?"

"I want you to be happy."

A stone forms in my throat as I drag in a ragged breath. "I want that for you, too, Rubes."

When I wake up early the next morning, Ruby's sweet ass is pushed up against my rock-hard cock, her hair plastered over her face, arms hugging her pillow. I lie on the edge of the bed, on my side. And it takes everything I have not to wrap my arm around her belly and pull her into me.

Because right now, that's all I want to do.

What I wouldn't do to wake up with her, like this, every day, for the rest of my days.

Somehow, nothing else would matter.

And I could take on the rest of the world, and whatever it threw my way.

I sit on the end of the hotel bed, dressed up in a suit and bow tie. If my buddies saw me now, I'd be the laugh of the town, or at least the bar. I can just see the look on Mack's face if he knew where I was and what I was doing. I spin the wedding band on my finger, staring at the carpet.

The bathroom door opens, and Ruby steps out.

The air in my lungs disappears as I stand. Electricity flings through my veins, sending my heart into a gallop as I run my gaze over her in those red heels she loves. The black dress she wears molds to her shape, the sweetheart neckline highlighting her breasts, small cap sleeves, and the skirt finishing above her knee. She's all class.

Her hair is curled and swept around her neck to one side. Her brown eyes, smoking with a little eye shadow, render my voice useless.

And when she smiles at me and spins for me to see the low-scooped back that shows off the small of her back, a keening noise slips from my throat. She laughs and comes back around with an elegant wave of her hands. "Think it will earn the Mary-Sue stamp of approval?"

I take a step toward her. "Baby, you look . . ."

She closes the distance between us and fixes the bow tie I didn't realize needed fixin'. The ring on her finger shines. Another one with a small cluster of diamonds sits beside it. That's new. And more legit, I guess, and I kick myself for missing the chance to fix that little issue myself.

"Thanks," I rasp.

"You're welcome, sweet man."

Something low in my gut flips. This isn't supposed to be real. It isn't supposed to feel like this.

"Oh, shoot. I forgot my perfume." She ducks back inside the bathroom and sprays something that trails to the bedroom. When she pops back out, the scent surrounds us.

Strawberries.

This woman is stunning, head to toe. And the fact that she is incredibly smart and talented at the thing she loves most sends a warmth through my body.

We make our way down to the enormous ballroom. When the ushers at the door wave us in, she stops still, and I slide my hand into hers. "You did good, Rubes. This is magnificent. Breathe."

Her hand squeezes mine, and she glances up and nods.

A heartbeat later, Mary-Sue is by her side. They chat logistics for catering one last time before Ruby assures the older woman that everything has been checked and triple-checked, and I couldn't be prouder of her. I know she worries about every last detail and the clients being happy with each aspect of her planning.

The entrée comes around, and I take enough for me and Ruby, ensuring she has the chance to eat as the night goes on. When we are seated for the dinner course, she is making conversation with the owner Bill. His attention slides to where I sit, and he nods. "Hi there, you must be Mr. Robbins."

"Absolutely. Great to meet you, the name's Reed. Bill?"

I shake his hand, and he starts talking about business numbers and some other boring things I pretend to be interested in.

"What business you in, Robbins?"

Ruby and I haven't talked about our backstory or what I am supposed to tell people. So I wing it and hope it doesn't land us in trouble. "Few things, but real estate, mainly. Have a few clients over by Lewistown, so this trip was good for both of us."

Not a total lie. I do have a vested interest in land and

the ranch I now own. And Harry owns more again, so real estate fits.

"Keeping you busy then, hey?" Bill asks.

"Yup. Always busy. But it keeps me occupied while Rubes takes on the world."

Bill laughs and slaps my shoulder. "Until the day you make her a mother, buddy. Then you'll be the one bringing home the bacon. The way it should be."

I clench my jaw and glance over at Ruby. How the hell does she work with this complete douchebag?

I pick up my beer and take a swig. "Excuse me."

I stand and bend over Ruby's shoulder. "Heading outside for a minute, baby."

Her fingers brush over my knuckles as she nods, not breaking eye contact with the woman she is talking to. I wander outside. I can't stand another minute sitting next to the chauvinistic old shit. I wouldn't take away Ruby's —or any woman's—career so I can *bring home the bacon.*

What an asshole.

Outside is the pool area that meets the outdoor café area we sat at yesterday. Tonight, the shrubs and palms are lit up with fairy lights. The pool is lit up with rainbow lights. Soft music plays outside as it does inside. A few guests mill about, but most are too busy talking to notice me. I tug at my bow tie and suck in a breath.

Chlorine races into my senses as I lean over the pool fence and hang my head for a moment. Clacking heels behind me see me lift my head and turn back. Ruby closes the distance between us. "You okay, Reedsy?"

Looking back inside, I shove my hands in my pockets before meeting her gaze. "Yeah, I'm alright."

"Good. Another half hour or so, and we can go back upstairs. I know this must be getting old."

She gestures between us.

She means this fake marriage thing.

"Nah, it's fine. Just needed some air. Bill's kind of—"

"He's an ass. But Mary-Sue is nice. I'm focusing on that."

I chuckle. "I see your coping strategy, Ruby Robbins, and raise you one."

"Oh, yeah? What did you have in mind?"

"Dance with me?"

"Reed, I'm working."

"I know. It's only three minutes or thereabout. You are allowed breaks, aren't you?"

"I—"

I press a finger over her lips as Mary-Sue walks up behind her. "No buts, Mrs. Robbins. We're dancin'."

As we pass Mary-Sue, Ruby glances at me, lips parted in a covert *oh*.

I wink at her, and she takes my hand and bumps her shoulder into my side. The second we reach the dimly lit dance floor and the soft music plays, I pull her into my hold. How long have I waited to do that?

I hold her hand and spin her around. Mary-Sue and

Bill watch on, a lovestruck expression on the older woman's face. Bill simply shrugs with a smug smirk before walking back to the bar. A few other couples move onto the dance floor. We move around them all, trying not to bump into other people.

Ruby rises to her tiptoes, bringing her mouth to my ear. "Thank you."

I tighten my hold on her and dip my head. "Anything to see you smile, baby."

A grin lights up her face, and I twirl her out, holding her hand and pulling her back in. She rolls back and lands at my chest with a palm splayed over my heart. I step back and take her with me. We have a comfortable rhythm when I crash into a guy behind me. I turn back to apologize.

But a familiar face greets me.

Fuck.

"Rawlins, what are you doing here?"

Justin fucking Morley.

Of all the assholes to grace this place with their presence. If he doesn't keep his mouth shut, he's going to blow my cover. Our cover. Ruby's job.

"Same as you, Morley."

"You're invested in the inn, too? Or was it your father?" His gaze darts around, as if Harry could be somewhere in the room.

"Nope, only me."

Ruby's hand moves on my jacket. "Ruby, this is Addy's old boss, you remember?"

She doesn't move to acknowledge Morley. "Yes, I remember." Her voice is almost vicious, and I tamper the smile that wants to stretch my face.

"Ruby?" Mary-Sue calls from behind us.

"Later, Rawlins," Justin says, swinging his dance partner, who has been ignored this whole time, away from us.

We turn back to face Mary-Sue.

"Rawlins?" Confusion twists her face. "Ruby?"

"Yes?" Ruby pulls out of my hold, dazed. She looks like she's going to be sick.

Mary-Sue glances from me to Morley. The shithead has all but blown our story to the heavens. With a glance at our hands, I'm guessing she is scanning for the wedding bands. God, these people really have some nerve.

"If you'll excuse us, Mary-Sue. I'm going to take my wife and turn in early." The words are sand in my mouth. Like I would be able to look at myself in the mirror ordering any woman around like she had no choice in the matter, no say in what we do.

"I'm sorry, I have a splitting headache." Ruby rubs her temple and leans into me.

"Very well. I will catch you two tomorrow sometime. Good night." Mary-Sue's gaze is still alternating between us and Morley, face pinched.

Sweet Jesus.

"Night." I can't get Ruby out of that room fast enough. She's quiet all the way back to the elevator. And when we stop at the silver doors, I smash a finger into the Up button. She takes her hand from mine, putting a step between us.

Fuck.

I run a hand through my hair and turn to apologize. But I slam my mouth shut when Mary-Sue is walking toward us in a hurry.

Here goes . . .

"Ruby! Honey, you forgot your purse."

"Oh, thank you, Mary-Sue." Ruby takes her purse from her client and offers a smile.

Mary-Sue glances between us and frowns. "Do you know the Rawlinses from Lewistown?"

Sweet Jesus.

"Nope, don't think so." I push the button again.

She steps closer. "My cousin went to high school over there. There was a Harry Rawlins in her grade. Nice enough guy, bit rough around the edges for most people. But she always spoke highly of him. I think she was sweet on him in senior."

"Still not registering. Sorry, not sure how it's related to Robbins?" I say, desperate to throw her off the trail.

"Oh well, must be getting my wires crossed. Night, you two."

When the woman is out of earshot, Ruby curses. "She's on to us, Reed."

Worry floods her gaze. I have to fix this. Mary-Sue is milling about in the lobby as if waiting to catch us in a lie.

"Rubes."

She turns back to me, and I take her hands as the elevator bings. "Don't let her doubt you, not for a minute."

She looks up at me. "How do I make sure she doesn't?"

Mary-Sue is straightening the business cards at the front desk, obviously watching us. Waiting for a sign our story isn't right.

"You trust me, baby?" I say softly.

When her brown eyes find mine, she breathes, "Yes."

I take her face in my hands and cover her mouth with mine. Her soft lips are like silk. My body automatically presses into hers. She tastes divine. Sweet, fruity like the wine she was drinking and something very Ruby. Her fingers tangle in the opening of my shirt, and heat coils in my core, sending my cock hard in a heartbeat.

When Ruby breaks away from the kiss, I stay frozen, still holding her face. Still pressed against her. She's breathing heavy. So am I.

A small smile pops over her stunned face. "That ought to do it, Reedsy."

"Yeah, that did it," I rasp.

The elevator doors swing open again for the third time since it binged. She pulls me inside. But the second the doors meet, she drops my hand, and a blush covers her neck and face. "Sorry about that."

"It's okay. I kind of thought that might come up eventually."

She huffs a strained laugh.

"If I made you uncomfortable, I'm sorry. It was the only thing I could think of to solidify our story."

"No, it was a good strategy. Thank you." Her words are breathy.

When we reach our level and step into the hallway, she walks to the door and opens it with the card. When I step through after her and shut the door behind me, I lean on it. She kicks off her heels and reaches under her shoulder as she tries to undo the zip. It doesn't budge.

I close the space between us and put my hand over hers. "Let me."

Her hand lowers, and she sweeps her hair around her neck, away from the zipper, lifting her arm. I tug at the zip. It's tough, but it comes away a heartbeat later. I pull it down a few inches to start and drop my hand. She catches my hand and lifts her brown eyes. "Thank you."

Her breathing is ragged as we stare at each other for the longest heartbeat.

I step away and slide the jacket from my shoulder and rip the bow tie from my neck before undoing the first three buttons of the shirt.

"I think I need a shower," Ruby mutters and disappears into the bathroom.

What I need is a cold shower.
A long, cold, sobering shower.

The bed is cold and empty when I wake up, despite the heat that was coursing through this room mere hours ago when we returned from the gala. Reed in his suit was the hottest thing I have ever had the pleasure of laying eyes on. And when he kissed me by the elevator, I thought my heart would explode.

It took everything I had not to climb him like a tree the second the doors closed. And again when he helped with my zipper. And now, the man in question is nowhere to be seen. I push out of bed and wander to the bathroom.

No Reed.

His boots are gone. But his bag is here. He went out for something?

I track to the toilet and make a quick stop before brushing my teeth and hair. Still tired from last night, I pad back to bed and climb under the duvet. But not wanting to go back to sleep and miss Reed, I flick the TV on.

The door to our room rattles open a moment later, and Reed strides in. Two takeaway coffee cups in a tray rest in one hand, while a brown paper bag swings underneath. I sit up and he smiles at me with that gorgeous megawatt grin I adore.

Oh shit.

I snap my gaze to the duvet.

No, Ruby.

What the hell was that?

I like being around Reed. He's an amazing guy. Funny and thoughtful. Hot as hell. But adore? Yeah, that must have been some sort of brain conniption. How long has it been since the last guy I was with? Apparently, far too long. I so need to get laid, so my monkey brain can settle the fuck down.

When the bed dips and coffee appears under my nose, I wrap my hands around it, brushing his fingers.

He sips his coffee and passes me a chocolate Danish wrapped in a napkin.

I whimper a little at the smell of the chocolate pastry and coffee. A girl could get used to this. Breakfast in bed delivered by a handsome man.

"Thank you, Reed."

"You're welcome, beautiful."

He sinks his teeth into his pastry, and his throat works as he swallows. "Get dressed, baby."

I finish off the food and hop out of bed, grabbing my laptop. His large, warm hand folds over mine. "Nope. Not today, Rubes."

"But I need to check for feedback and emails. Manage any social posts from last night."

He shakes his head.

"Reed, come on."

He pulls the laptop from my grip and places it on the table by my tote. "The only thing you are doing today is a full day of R & R."

"Really, R & R? What does that even entail?"

He tilts his head, giving me an incredulous look. "Exactly my point. Now, jeans and boots and a polo or something."

"I don't have boots, Reed."

He feigns shock. "Thought you might say that." He pads to where his duffel bag sits by the wall and digs into it. When he returns to where I sit on the edge of the bed, he hands me a large brown box.

"What is this?"

"Well, you can't visit me at the ranch without these."

I open the lid. White tissue paper is folded neatly around whatever is inside. The smell of new leather starts my heart racing. I rip the paper from the box. Inside sits a pair of western riding boots, tan on the bottom covering the toes and ankle, but from there up, it's all pink. Intricate stitching in the shape of swirls and flowers covers the pink top part of the boots.

My mouth gapes.

They are so stinking pretty.

And like nothing I would ever own.

"I'm hoping you have socks," he says, rubbing a hand behind his neck. "Kind of forgot that part."

"I have socks," I whisper. Emotion chokes me up, and I press my lips together. No one has ever given me a gift this thoughtful—or useful, for that matter. "Thank you. Guess this means I have to come visit you whenever I can."

"They're a gift, Rubes. Visit or don't, they're all yours."

I slide across on the bed and hug him tight. He chuckles and folds me into his chest.

"I see how hard you work, baby. You deserve nice things."

"I usually buy my own nice things," I say, pulling away to take in his face.

"I know you do. But it's not the same. And I . . . I like taking care of you."

I can't breathe.

I can't respond.

Tears burn behind my eyes.

"Come on, outta those PJs. R & R awaits." He packs his bag. I hadn't had time to think about what happens after the opening night for the inn. What happens with Reed and me. And when we go our separate ways for the months between events for the inn.

I hunt through my bag for the clothes I need and slip into the bathroom and change. When I walk back to the bedroom, Reed is waiting on the bed, my new boots in his hands. He pats his knee. "Foot, baby."

I hesitate before lifting my foot onto his knee. He slides the first boot on. It's so comfortable. The leather is like butter. Oh my lord, they're divine. Who knew cowgirls had such stellar boots?

I offer the other foot and he works the boot on, gripping my ankle a little longer than necessary before he lowers my foot to the floor.

I spin around and show him the complete outfit. But he only frowns. He stands and plucks his Yankees cap from the table and pops it on my head before sliding his aviators on.

"Better." His voice is gravel.

"Where are we going?" I ask.

"Home, baby."

And the smile that blooms over my face is the most genuine one I've felt in a long time.

We make it to the reception desk to ask for his truck to be valeted. Not having said a word since we left the room, something electric hangs between us. And when Reed's truck rolls into the driveway, he scoops me up in his arms and heads for the doors. I giggle and hang my head back. And when I glance back, Mary-Sue is watching from just inside the restaurant entrance. Reed must have seen her there.

"Reed," I huff through a laugh.

"Yeah, beautiful?" We reach the passenger door of his truck.

"You can put me down now."

"Yeah, I know."

But when he doesn't loosen his hold on me, I lift my gaze. His green eyes burn into mine, and for a second I think I see something like I saw last night, right after he kissed me. And I can't help myself when my hand traces his jaw. He stills for a moment, then clears his throat and lets me down.

A second later, he opens the door, and I climb into the truck. I slide onto the seat, heart beating so fast it would put a hummingbird to shame.

When Reed is behind the wheel and we roll out of the inn's driveway, I take in the inside of his truck. It's a premium interior finish. As upmarket as the Audi my dad drives. Napa leather surrounds me, the seat hugging my frame. It's so soft . . . it's delicious. The dash is matte black, with the latest high-tech screen. I'm impressed. So much for a simple country boy.

When the warmth of his stare blooms on my face, I turn to face him. The cutest smile twists his gorgeous face. I dip my eyes. "Thanks for that back there. With Mary-Sue, I mean."

"Not everything I do is for Mary-Sue's benefit, Rubes."

"Well, thanks anyway. The last thing I want to do is

cause Olive a headache, or worst case, lose my job over their ridiculous, outdated ideas."

"Yeah, that would be such a shame."

I roll my eyes at him, and he chuckles, dragging his eyes back to the road. He hits the power button on the stereo, and Nickelback floods the black cab. Fitting. We chat about work things and Reed's family as we drive the hour and a half.

"You never told me what our R & R entails?" I say. I like to know what I'm in for.

He turns to me with a grin. "Reed & Ruby time, of course."

I laugh at him, and he winks at me. I feign a groan, and he returns his gaze to the road.

When we turn into the driveway of Reed's new ranch through long, open wooden gates, I can't help but sit up like a golden retriever, rolling the window down and looking around.

Reed pulls in by the house and shuts off the engine. When he appears at my door, I lean back and can't wipe the smile from my face. Opening the door, he holds out a hand like I'm stepping out of a carriage, and I laugh.

The man makes me happy.

When my new boots meet dirt for the first time, Reed crooks his arm, and I slide mine through. It's almost habit now. He tilts his head, bending to my ear. "Welcome home, Rubes."

"Your home, Reed. My place is a fifty-square-foot apartment on the east side."

He smiles at me and says, "I would love to see your city one day."

"You've never been to New York?"

"Nope. Not even a little."

"But Lawson lives there."

"I'm aware. Just never had the chance to go. Harry insists idle hands are the devil or some nonsense."

"Idle hands are the devil's work. My father says that, too. But he's right. And I would rather be busy, building a career and a life, than not."

"I've seen your version of busy, Robbins. It's a lot."

I chuckle and bump my shoulder into his. "You're probably right. Would you rather I be barefoot in the kitchen, spending my days chasing after a bunch of rowdy kids?"

He stops on the spot and looks down at me. Heat rises to my cheeks. I didn't mean it the way it sounded. Like I would be in *his* kitchen with *his* children. But by the pure cheek scrawled over his face right now, I'm going to wrangle a guess that's how he took it. "Reed."

"I think you'd look magnificent in my kitchen, Rubes. But that's not your plan, is it?"

He is close; we're only inches apart. And no, it's not what I want. I want an event planning business of my own one day and working as hard and as long as I can in high-end agencies is how to garner the best experience.

But I don't want to waste my day of R & R thinking about work, so I slide my hand into his and drag him toward his new house. "Tour, Reedsy. Show me your new adventure."

He crowds me from behind, my hand still in his, as I stall to a stop shy of the front porch of the house. Someone's inside.

"It's only Mack, baby."

"Oh, I didn't know he was here."

"Yeah, doing my chores while I'm living it up in Great Falls for the weekend."

"What? You didn't tell me you needed to be here—"

"I don't. Mack's here."

As the words leave his mouth, his older brother steps out onto the porch. "Ruby." He nods, hat already on his head. "How was your party?"

He's dressed in jeans and a button-down checkered work shirt, rolled up at the sleeves like his brother. He sips at a mug of coffee.

God, what I wouldn't do for a coffee.

"You want a cup, Robbins? Or do you always give mugs that longing stare?" Mack says.

Reed strides inside.

"I would love one. Busy morning?"

"Nah. Waters and a few fencin' jobs Harry wants taken care of."

"Do you ever take a day off?"

He raises an eyebrow as if I ought to talk. "Not usually; ranching is a year-round, three-sixty-five gig. At least it is in Harry's world. In which we are involuntary participants."

He takes another sip.

"Oh, that must be hard."

"It's a lifestyle, that's for sure. You comin' in?"

"Oh, sure. Can't let Reed sugar my coffee."

"Sweet enough, hey?" He smiles and shifts on his feet as I walk past with a chuckle.

"Something like that, Mack."

He dips his hat, resting his mug on the small table at the front door and walking down the step and off the porch. "See ya round, Ruby. Have a *relaxing* day!"

I wave, smiling as confusion tweaks my face. Do these men share everything?

"Coffee, baby?" Reed says from behind me.

I spin back, and he deposits a mug in my hands, nodding his head toward inside. "Come on, house tour first."

I follow him inside. The home is small but cozy, and it's exactly what I imagined a farmhouse would be like. The kitchen is to my left and a living room with a hearth is to the right. You could settle in and lose hours here.

Reed walks up the stairs, and I wander behind. When we reach the top, he waves a hand to the right. "Spare bedroom." Then to the door in front of him. "Smallest room in the house; and this"—he walks to the open door on the left and leans on the doorjamb—"this is my new master."

I walk past him and into the room. It's rustic. Large. The polished wood gives it such a warm feel. Nothing like the concrete and glass of my place. The long window has an inviting bench seat underneath it, and I sit, taking in the view of the surrounding mountains. It's magnificent.

"It's gorgeous, Reedsy."

I sip the coffee; it's hot and earthy. Amazing.

"Looks better from the back of a horse. Come on, let's see the rest."

Reluctant to leave my spot by the window, I sigh and rise. We finish our coffees and Reed rinses the mugs, leaving them in the sink.

"So, what do we have planned for the day?"

"I told you, baby. We're riding. You want your own horse, or do I need to get comfortable with you getting all handsy with a double?"

I slap his arm. "I will have my own, thank you very much."

The barn is huge, as big as the ones at Harry and Hudson's place. Inside sits a giant red tractor.

"Morning, Red," Reed says as he walks past the behemoth machine, tapping the hood with a hand. He named his tractor. I stifle a chuckle. Gosh, this man loves his trucks and machines.

"Tack is in here." Reed leads me inside a small room. The walls are covered in hooks and metal brackets holding up bridles, saddles, and saddle pads. "You alright to carry your own?"

"Sure, load me up." I hold my hands out, and he does.

He grabs his own gear, and we head to the stables behind the house. I recognize Reed's horse, Magnet, right away. Two others are in the long building. The smell of hay and horse closes in around me. It's been years since I have been on a horse.

My heart picks up the pace as I tentatively hold up a hand to Magnet. He nickers and sniffs the extended offering.

"He likes you, baby."

I huff a nervous laugh. "Maybe."

"This here is Mira. She will be your ride today."

I raise my eyebrows.

"Mind out of the gutter, Rubes."

My mouth snaps open. "Hey! I said nothing!"

He taps the brim of the cap on my head as he leads Magnet past to a small concrete area at the end of the stables by the door. "You didn't have to. Your face is the same color as your name, baby."

Ugh, shit.

"Do I unbuckle this colored one and cover her face?"

Reed turns back, dropping Magnet's lead on the ground and closing the space between us. "Been a while?"

He takes the colored bridle thing from my hands and walks into Mira's stall. He unbuckles the side of it and slips it up her nose and over her ears before doing up the buckle. When he throws the lead over her neck and runs a hand over her leg, she shifts on her foot, plucking it off the ground instantly.

"Damn," he says, taking her hoof in his hand. "She's got a stone bruise."

He lets her foot down and unbuckles the colored bridle from her face.

"She's not coming?"

"Nope, sorry, Rubes. Looks like you ride with me. I'll have to get Addy out to make sure a stone bruise is all it is."

"Will she be alright?"

"Should be, but we can't take her. And the young'un over there isn't for beginners."

"Oh, we can't walk or take the truck?"

He smiles at me, and I know that was a dumb thing to say. "Nah, baby. Too far and too rough. My truck doesn't venture into the wild. She's too precious. Too pretty. You ride with me. Plus, Magnet has been asking to spend time with you for god knows how long. Honestly, I'm sick to death of him naggin' me over it."

I roll my eyes at him, glancing at the grey gelding who patiently waits where Reed left him.

"Okay, your call."

"Give me five. I'll have a thousand pounds of power between those long legs."

"Reed!" I pull the cap from my head, intending to toss it at him.

He doubles over laughing. His hat falls off and hits the

ground. He runs a hand through his hair and swipes the hat up. When he dumps it on my head and walks back to the horse, he glances back at me. "Hold that for me, baby."

I watch, mesmerized, as he saddles up Magnet. Arms flexing under the weight of the saddle. The quiet, kind words he says. His ass as he bends over, making sure the gelding's feet are clean and clear.

Lost in something like a dream, I don't notice when he disappears to the other side of the horse and slips on the bridle. Before I know what I'm doing, I'm at Magnet's shoulder. Reed ducks under his neck, almost bumping into me as he swaps sides again.

"Hey, you alright?" he asks, green eyes dropping to study my face.

"Yeah, I just—"

I push up onto my tiptoes and kiss his cheek. "Thank you for this."

"Beautiful, the pleasure is all mine."

It takes every fucking thing I have to stand still as Ruby kisses my cheek. A friendly thank-you kiss. A platonic gesture of kindness. Like you would give your grandma at the Christmas holidays. And my cock is stretching in my jeans with her this close.

But I will be damned if I'm going to make her uncomfortable. Besides, she's all New York and ambitious and wants a career and shit. And then there's me—the wanderer, the least driven person on the planet. Hell, I can't even decide on a direction, let alone head that way.

So, I tussle her hair again as I reclaim my hat, some kind of big-brotherly, friendly gesture. And I will the fire in my core to peter out before it burns me alive. But man, she smells fine. That sweet smile of hers is enough to suffocate a man with his own desire.

"Hop up, baby."

I pat the saddle and reaffirm my grip on Magnet's reins.

"Okay," she says, pushing the cap back on her head as she ducks to the other side of the horse to mount. Her boots bounce on the ground before she launches herself into the saddle. She adjusts her seat and grips the pommel. Leading Magnet outside, I round his head and flip the reins over his neck and hand them to Ruby, slipping her foot from the stirrup and sliding my own in.

I swing up behind the saddle and put my arms around her waist, taking the reins from her hands. She leans back a little and returns her foot to the stirrup. "This alright?" she asks, the two words breathy.

"Perfect, Rubes," I whisper against her ear.

She glances over her shoulder with a gaze that would bring the toughest of men to their knees. Her fire fades to sweetness as I nudge Magnet into a walk.

"Mountains, fields, or stream?" I ask.

She's quiet for a moment.

"Mountains, please."

"Yes, ma'am."

I squeeze Magnet forward, and he breaks into a lope. Ruby squeals and holds on to the pommel. I close my body around hers as we ride past the barns and toward the northern fields, heading for the mountains.

Thirty minutes and two hard-ons at being this close to the most beautiful girl I've ever had the privilege to know later, we make it to the base of the mountains.

"Oh, wow. They are much more intimidating up close." Ruby tilts her face up.

"Mother Nature's finest. Want to go up?"

"Maybe a little way? I don't want Magnet to be exhausted."

"He's tough."

We walk up the incline until we make it halfway up to a plateau. I rein in the gelding to a halt and swing down. Ruby kicks her feet from the stirrups and holds her arms out. She must have seen Addy do the same. I smile up at her, and she swings her right leg over the pommel. I catch her as she slides from the saddle.

Holding her up against my chest, she's the only thing I can focus on. Heart hammering like thunder, I let her down to the ground. But she doesn't let go of my arms. And I don't want to let go, either.

Sweet Jesus, Reed.

My gut ties into knots as I force air in and out of my lungs.

"Thanks," she rasps, pulling away with a ragged inhale, and walks away.

All I can do is watch her as she takes in the mountains and fields that will be my home for the rest of my life. And I'm grateful for what my parents have given me; I am. But it wasn't my choice. My decision.

And that smarts.

And I all of a sudden have an acute understanding of what it's like to be a caged animal. I come to stand at

Ruby's side. She studies everything in sight from our high vantage point. "This place is going to be wonderful, Reed."

I shove my hands in my back pockets as the wind plays with my shirt, and stare down at the ranch that Harry gave me.

When I don't respond, she turns back. "You don't think so?"

"I don't know, Rubes."

"Which part?"

"All of it. The part where I own it. The responsibility is solely my own. The part where I have to live up to Harry's expectations."

"You'll be fine. You're smart and you work hard. I've seen it."

"Maybe, but I—"

She holds my gaze, waiting.

"What if I can't do this on my own? What if . . ." My shoulders are concrete, and the air in my lungs burns. "What if I fail and let everyone down?"

"You won't, okay? You can do this, Reedsy."

My hands tingle and I walk back to Magnet, grappling for each breath. Trembling fingers find the saddle fenders and grip tight. Struggling to pull in air, I'm fucking drowning.

A small, warm hand rests on my back. "Reed?"

I drop to my knees when dizziness floods in. Bile rises, and I pull at my loose collar. My hat hits the ground. I choke in noisy breaths.

"Shit, Reed." Ruby is in front of me, hands cupping my jaw. "Breathe. Just breathe."

Each inhale I take is too tight, and a strangled moan slips out on every exhale.

Worry and fear tighten Ruby's eyes.

Goddamn it.

Shit, I'm scaring her.

No.

I close my eyes, desperate to take back control. My heart flings against my ribs, and I shake my almost numb hands out, forcing air in and air out.

"Reed, look at me." Her words are wobbly, her voice cracking at the last one.

I open my eyes and try to apologize for scaring her. She pulls me close, her head dropping against my neck. "You scared me."

Tears burn behind my eyes, and I fold her into my hold. Letting her warmth, her body pressed to mine, extinguish the raging torrent that stole the air from my lungs. Her smell swallows me whole, and her beating heart against my chest calms my own.

"I'm sorry, Rubes," I rasp.

Now she pushes out of my hold, holding me at arm's length, and I miss her already. "Don't you dare apologize. You hear me?" She's shaking her head. "Don't you ever be sorry for being who you are."

"Harry may disagree with you there."

"Harry can bite my ass. You are more important than his bottom line. Or any grand plan he has."

I stare at her. The fire she carries, the way she knows who she is. I run my hands through her hair. What I wouldn't do to kiss that beautiful mouth. To have her want me the way I have wanted her since the second I saw her that night in Great Falls.

"What caused this?" she asks tenderly.

"I can't do it. I can't be tied to the land for the rest of my life. I'm not Hudson or Harry. It's not who I am."

"You don't have to be either of them. You're *you*. You have no idea how incredible you are. You're kind, extremely thoughtful, hilarious most of the time and . . ." Her gaze drops to my mouth before returning to my eyes, laced with fire. "And if this was another time and I led a different life, I would—"

I run my thumb over her bottom lip, trailing it over her jaw. "I wish you could stay."

The words tumble out on their own accord.

"I can't—"

She closes her eyes as if she is thinking about what's right in front of us. Like she feels every single thing that I do and has been for months, too.

"I know. Sorry, baby. It slipped out."

She huffs a small laugh before wiping her eyes dry. "Why do you call me that?"

"Baby?"

"Yeah."

"Feels right, ya know. I know we will only ever be friends. But my brain doesn't have another name for you, Ruby."

I have to be honest. I know she's leaving. She doesn't owe me a thing. And I want her to have the life she dreams about. Just wish it didn't mean I had to lose the only thing I have ever been sure of in my entire life.

Fully recovered and in command of my own respiratory system, I bundle her back onto Magnet, and we head down the mountain. She's quiet on the way down, leaning back into me. Her hands are around mine on the reins, as if anchoring me in case I spiral again. My life preserver.

"There are other ways to make an income on a ranch that don't include being tied to the land and Harry's way of life, Reed."

"Yeah?"

"Absolutely." She twists in the saddle, our eyes meeting. "You have options. You want to check out some other business models?"

"Sure, baby, whatever you want."

"No. No, Reed. It's what you want. Stop people-pleasing, or you are going to end up miserable."

I hug her tighter and sink my face into her hair, never wanting to leave this spot. "If you say so, beautiful," I say, muffled against her neck.

"Maybe that's what happened to Harry?" she quips.

I laugh so hard my gut hurts. Apparently, I'm not the only funny one on this horse.

The ride home is too short, even with Magnet's over-loaded, lazy walk. And when I unfold myself from Ruby and swing down off the gelding, my world feels colder.

And I'll be fucked if I want that.

Ruby Robbins may have found a way to turn things around for me. But I'm the mug standing in front of Harry Rawlins right now, nerves sending me higher by the minute, as I try to articulate the idea we came up with that I can live with.

My palms are sweaty and my pulse bounds through my head, drowning out the words I struggle so hard to make come out of my mouth.

A ranch resort.

A holiday place for city folk to escape to and live like a cowboy, or cowgirl, for three to seven days. Experiencing everything Montana mountain country has to offer.

Ruby stands beside me, and Ma sits at her spot at the kitchen table with Harry at the head.

Always.

Ruby's shoulders are back, her work face is on.

Kind of feel sorry for the old man.

Nah, nope. Not a bit.

Ruby nudges me, and I slide the tablet with her

presentation down the table to Harry. He doesn't break eye contact as it moves toward him.

"With your perm—"

Ruby elbows me hard to remind me we talked about this. Time to make decisions.

"I have come up with a way to move forward with my ranch that will be a better, more profitable model. And I want to run it past you, since you have experience with business."

Harry's focus drops to the tablet.

"This model helps turn a profit even in the dry time and when cattle prices are low. Spreading the income generation to more than one basket, so to speak."

A small smile pulls over Ma's face. I glance at Ruby as she sits in the seat next to her. I take the one at the end of the table as my old man swipes through the slides. Which, after hours of research and calculations, Rubes and I put together. A working holiday ranch model with three tiers of involvement, from those folks who want a vacation and a bit of fun to people who want to dirty their hands and do the real cowboy work.

When Harry reaches the last slide, he pushes the tablet to Ma, who carefully goes through each feature of the presentation. It's the first time I have ever done something like this. But I'm sure Ruby has pulled this sort of thing off many times.

Harry steeples his hands and leans back in his

captain's chair. I have always found that ironic; that chair should be Ma's.

"You're not happy with the operation we already have?" Harry says. His gaze flickers between Ruby and me. As if this upheaval is somehow her fault. I sit forward in the chair, heat trickling through my veins.

"The current model is reliant on one income stream. This gives us two, possibly more. It's smart. And means I can enjoy my days, instead of being saddled with the entire workload and isolated from the rest of the world."

Ma snaps her head up. "You're not happy?"

I stare at her for the longest time, a stone growing in my throat. Her face falls as the seconds tick by.

"Ma . . ."

But she pats my forearm and says, "If this is what you want, you have my support."

"Now, hold on!" Pa shoots forward, pointer finger pressing into the table. "We have to triple-check the demand for what you wanna supply. These numbers need to be compared and accounted for by our accountant. And son, changing the way things are simply because you don't like them isn't a valid reason for change."

And there it is.

The sucker punch to my gut that only Harry Rawlins can provide. His subtle way of saying I don't stack up to his expectations.

"Harry," Ma warns.

He turns to her. "No, Louisa, he hasn't even worked a

full season on that ranch, and he wants to change it up. The way things are done around here are done for a reason. Some fad that city folk wanna come out here and blend in is just that—a fad. And when it dries up, we are back to ranching, pure and simple. But we will have debt and overhead that this resort takes to start up. Not happening."

Pa slams a hand on the table and stalks from the kitchen, snatching his hat on the way out.

"Harry!" Ruby stands, calling after him. Ma holds a hand up, rising from her seat. "Louisa . . ." Ruby's face goes from businesslike to pained.

I sink my head into my hands and tangle my fingers in my hair with a sigh. *Fuck.* I knew it was going to be a hard sell. But I thought we at least had a shot.

Fine fingers wrap around my wrist. "Reed, let me talk to him. I know more about this kind of thing."

"It's fine. Thanks anyway, Rubes."

Groaning, I slide my hands down my face, letting them drop to the hardwood surface. I'm doomed to be a rancher. Same shit every day. Maybe I'll get lucky and die of boredom. I rise from the table, but she doesn't follow.

Pushing through the back screen door, I pad to the table under the willow. Ma's favorite spot. The place where we have Sunday lunches. Our family tradition. But instead of sitting at one of the long bench seats, I slump against the trunk of the tree, partially hidden by the weeping, swaying green branches.

Dropping to my ass on the ground, I close my eyes.

Well, no one can say I didn't give it a shot.

Footsteps crunch on the grass, closing in slowly.

"You alright, gunny?"

Mack.

"I'll live." I don't bother looking at him, but when my brother sighs and the seat creaks, I force them open.

"What's got Harry's goat, saddlin' up poor Chancy like the ground's on fire?" Mack chuckles, but it's strained.

"Told him his whole way of life isn't up to par."

He releases a low whistle. "Geez, bet that went down well. The old man doesn't like being the dumbest guy in the room."

Always cut and dry, our Mackinlay.

"Yeah, well. That's probably because he's the smartest guy we know."

"Reed, the ranch is yours. You don't need his permission to do a damn thing. If you want to start a llama circus and grow cannabis for Canadians, he can't stop you. He signed it over to you."

With that, I snap my gaze to the house. Ma leans by the back door, studying us. When she sees me staring, she smiles and rolls off the doorjamb, crossing the grass to where I sit.

"You still think our plan is okay?" I ask.

I stand as she weaves her way into the weeping willow. "I do. I think it's a wonderful idea. But I do have one addition, speaking of adding income streams to the mix."

"Yeah?"

"Events, Reed. You should make it an event location as well. It's pretty as a picture over there and with a few strategically placed larger buildings, you could have weddings, birthdays, family reunions, etc. It would be good business for you and for the town."

My mouth gapes. It's as if Ruby and my mother are one person in this moment. Mack's attention snags on something behind the veil of willow tendrils, but I don't take my eyes off Ma.

"Events? Ma, I don't have the first clue on how to set up or run events. Or how much to charge . . ."

The curtain of green moves, and Ruby appears.

"But I do."

"But you already have a job, and in the city." Reed's face turns from surprise to concern.

"Yes, but I work remotely for most of the events I run. And I can do that for you, also. It won't be a problem." His wide eyes are stuck on me. A combination of desperation and excitement wrestle in their green tones. And my stomach is a bundle of knots.

"Harry isn't goin' to be happy with this," Reed says to his ma.

"You let me handle your father. And you adjust your plans and projections to include events. Aim for two to four each month. They will give you the extra cash you need to develop the property, add cabins for guests, convert that largest barn to be your big celebration or wedding reception space, and all that without the residual debt after twelve months." She rests a palm on Reed's cheek.

God, I love this woman.

Fire and love all rolled into one amazing soul who would do anything for her children. The flame she continuously stokes for her family.

The pang of grief over my own distant parents and a sliver of jealousy hit me. Forcing air into my lungs, I purse my lips and will the burn behind my eyes to take a hike.

My phone pings.

Addy.

Ready for our girls night?

So ready! I'm out at the ranch, but I can be in town in forty with change. Can't wait.

Rosewood or Reed's?

Rosewood, talking to Harry and Lou with Reedsy.

Huh, okay I want to hear all about that tonight!

When I click the screen off, Reed, Mack, and Louisa are staring at me, eyebrows raised. What, did I pull a face or something?

"Sorry, just Adds organising girls night tonight," I offer.

"What time do you need to be in town?" Mack asks.

"Back by dark, I was hoping."

"I can give you a lift, if you like," Mack says, glance swinging between Reed and me.

"Sure, that sounds awesome. I'll grab my things."

"No rush, we can leave in like"—he glances at the bulky black watch on his wrist—"say, thirty?"

"Okay, thanks."

When Reed meets his brother's gaze, Mack dips his hat toward me and walks back across the yard.

"Well, that's my cue, too," Louisa says, wrapping me in a one-armed hug before wandering after her son.

"Subtle, your lot."

Reed pulls me into his arms, his hand running over my hair. "You don't have to do this. You have too much on your plate already."

I slide a hand onto his shirt and look up at him. I like his arms around me. It feels good. Right. Like someplace warm and sturdy.

"I want to. Besides, what are friends for, Reedsy? If I didn't help, when I am the best event planner you know, that would be unforgivable."

He chuckles, bending down so his mouth brushes my hair by my ear. "You're the only event planner I know, baby."

"That too," I whisper.

Air rushes in and out of my lungs like it's pulled by hurricane winds. I want to run my hand up his chest, let it wander over his throat and his Adam's apple that bobs as he swallows. His eyes drop to my mouth.

When he moves, still only inches from me, it takes everything I have to not cup his face and draw his mouth down to mine.

Friends.

We should stay friends.

Rule number one.

Rule num—

Reed smashes his mouth to my lips, and his hands are in my hair a heartbeat later. The air in my lungs disappears entirely. My body floods with electricity, the zing palpable where his fingertips meet my skin as they run down my neck and back up to hold my face.

I open for him, and his tongue sweeps in, claiming every part I offer up. Desperate to be closer, I press against his taut frame.

He breaks away.

"Shit, fuck. I'm sorry, Rubes."

His hands are in his hair, running through it as he walks a tight circle by the trunk of the tree. The willow shrouds us in its dangling, enclosed green canopy still. I stand rooted to the spot, arms by my sides, air churning in my lungs.

And I am definitely not sorry. I don't really know what I am, to be honest. But it's not sorry.

For some reason, whenever I'm around Reed, I feel things I don't usually. I haven't.

God, no one has ever wanted me that much.

Ever.

"Reed," I breathe.

"I know. I shouldn't have done that." He waves a hand toward me.

And when he leans against the tree, dark, fire-laced eyes burn into mine. After a heartbeat, he drags his hands down his face, the way he always does when he's frustrated and doesn't think anyone is watching.

I close the space between us. "It's fine. It can be whatever you want it to be. But I'm not sorry you kissed me. That we kissed."

"Yeah?"

"Uh-huh."

Now, his shoulders move in even deeper cycles, and his mouth parts. "Can I do it again?"

The smile that stretches my face is possibly the biggest one I've ever had. "Do you *want* to?"

This time when I rest my palm on his shirt, his heart slams against my skin. It mirrors my own, and I huff out a faint laugh. The heat that was racing through my veins just sank deep in my belly.

And Reed Rawlins doesn't feel like my friend. Not anymore.

He moves past me and sits on the bench seat by the

table, dropping his head onto the wood with a thud. I sit quietly beside him. "What are you thinking?"

"Hold up. I'm goin' to have to wait for the blood to return to my brain to do any kinda thinkin'," he drawls.

I laugh, throwing my head back. The sound rattles up through me as warmth floods in. God, I will miss this man.

He has earned a solid place in my frosty, somewhat vacant heart. And it's almost like I feel it stretch. Fine hairline cracks split their way through the concrete that makes up my heart. The one full of rules and habits protecting me from the things I fear most. Being redundant. Being dependent. Being a burden. Being distracted and failing.

So many things to fear when you're missing an essential tier on the Maslow hierarchy of needs. Specifically number three, belonging and love. My family is successful. They are driven. They are also completely emotionally unavailable.

There is no warmth in the Robbins household. Only trophies, achievements, designer clothes, luxury cars, impressive bank accounts, and a whole lot of meaningless small talk.

Reed clears his throat, pulling me back to the here and now. He studies my face, and I try to put the words together. To tell him that we can't do this. That there's no point because one, I don't date, and two, I'm leaving.

But I can't.

For the first time in my life, I'm resenting my rules.

Maybe it's the place. Or maybe it's the man in front of me. But my rules seem utterly insignificant.

"I can see the cogs spinning, baby." Reed tilts his head.

"What?" I laugh.

"You're thinkin'. Now *I'm* worried."

My smile fades, and I sigh. "I should go."

Reed nods, swallowing as he rises to his feet. He extends his hand, and when I take it and push to my feet, he crooks his arm. Because he's Reed and I'm me. It's our thing.

I tangle my arm through his and lean into his side. "I'm going to miss you, you know."

But he doesn't respond. His Adam's apple works as he homes his gaze ahead to where Mack's truck waits by the white gate at the homestead yard. The passenger door is open, and Mack sits in the driver's seat, looking at something on his phone.

Reed crowds me by the tray of the truck and brushes my hair behind my ear. "Goodbye, or see you later?"

"See you later," I breathe.

He plants a kiss on my forehead and bundles me into the truck. My bag and things are already on the seat between us. And when Reed shuts the door and steps back, my chest constricts, sending an ache through me.

"Ready?" Mack asks.

I almost forgot he was here. "Yeah."

He shifts the stick into drive and waves to Reed as we pull away from the homestead.

"Thanks for helping Reed; he'd appreciate the effort." Mack meets my gaze as he turns onto the dirt road.

"It's a smart plan. I can't wait to see it eventuate."

Mack smiles with a nod and turns on the radio. Some twangy country song plays over slight static.

"When do you have to go back?" I ask.

His hands reaffirm around the wheel. "Few months."

My gut sinks. I know Mack leaving for tour is hard for Reed. "How long this time?"

"Should be around six weeks. Be back for the county New Year's Rodeo, hopefully."

"That's still a thing?"

"Of course, you should come . . ." But his words fade out as he realizes that I won't be here.

"You live in another world entirely out here. I wish I could stay."

"If you don't like the city, you don't have to be there. At least, from what Ma tells me about your type of work, you can move around."

"Leaving New York isn't part of my plan."

"Never is."

He's quiet the rest of the way. I know he's talking about Addy and Hudson. It worked out for them. Really well.

But I'm not a vet or an animal person. My options would be limited around here, even if I was an honorary member of Louisa's clan. I focus my attention out the window. Not wanting Mack to see the grief I carry for my lousy family. And the jealousy that flares every time I'm at Rosewood, knowing I will never have what the Rawlins boys have.

Love and belonging.

Real, loving, raw, emotional—and sometimes messy—family.

"Ah, shit!"

The curling iron burns my finger as I tuck it under the last thick strand of blonde.

"You okay?" Addy calls from the her bedroom. It didn't make sense to go all the way back to Great Falls when the event is over and they don't need me back until the opening night.

It's been so long since we went out together. And I am beyond excited for tonight. I've never been around the small-town pub scene. My expectations are pretty low, but still, it's been an age since I let my hair down.

Makeup—check.

Gucci heels—check.

My favorite sheer black Chanel top and ebony Tommy Hilfiger dress pants—check.

I flip the power switch off and twirl for the mirror. I know it's kind of silly, but because I never had the chance to show off my outfits for anyone as a little girl, I like to do it for myself.

"Rubes!" Addy calls from downstairs. "Let's go, cowgirl!"

I chuckle, double-checking my makeup and blotting my lipstick one last time. I glide down the stairs in my favorite red stilettos. The color is a stark contrast to the black pants and sheer top with the shadow of my black Victoria's secret lingerie underneath. I do love fancy clothes. Always have.

Lewistown is small, and it doesn't take us long to walk the few blocks to one of the only bars open on a week-night. My last hoorah before I am expected back in the city. No bouncers or doormen here. Addy pushes through, leading me into a quaint bar.

The inside is well-kept, and the decor screams country town. I kind of like it.

"Booth, table, or bar?" I ask Addy.

She scans the room. I'm sure her idiot old boss sits at the bar with two guys around his age. I steer her to a table toward the back. The last thing we need is company. Both of us have been too busy for each other the past few weeks—hell, the past few months. And I want to talk to her.

"How's Huddo?" I say, sitting at one side of the table, placing my clutch purse on the polished wood.

She beams at me.

I lean in. "That good, hey?"

"He's brilliant, as usual. Busy. What have you and Reed been scheming this week? There appears to be a fundamental shift in the Rawlinses' universe. I take it you have something to do with that?"

She brushes her curly brown hair around one side of her neck. Her yellow blouse brings out her dark eyes. Those eyes have always grounded me. Even when my family was being a pack of insensitive asshats, Addy always had my back. And I hers.

"Well, it may not have occurred to the rest of the Rawlins bunch, but ranching is not something that Reed wants to slave at for his entire life."

"You make it sound like a bad thing, the life Harry and Louisa have built."

"It's not. It's also not a one-size-fits-all deal. Not everyone is Hudson, Adds."

"Thank god, imagine the women of the world if there was more than one of him."

We burst into hysterics. "Hudson Rawlins, limited edition, only ten in the world." I wave a hand in the air like I'm gesturing to a billboard. "Yes, I can see the chaos that would unfold should that happen, babes."

Addy recovers and glances to the bar. Her face falls. I take it, she's seen Cowboy Ken, a.k.a., her old boss and semi-sexual-harassment offender, Justin Morley.

"I got it, Adds. Your usual?"

"Yeah, thanks."

I weave my way back to the bar, leaning on it with a hip, my back to Morley. Before the next heartbeat, his oily gaze burns into the back of my head. The bartender waltzes over and nods. "What can I fetch you?"

He's a built guy, sleeves rolled up to showcase his arms. Brown hair gelled, with blue eyes that I'm sure have seen enough of the bad side of humanity in this place.

"Gin and tonic. Lime twist. And your best Merlot, please."

"Coming up." He turns his back to me, and a throat clears behind me. I put my clutch on the bar and turn back to find the roving eyes of Justin. They don't even bother rising to my face as he says, "You're new. Sweet spikes, baby."

Hearing the nickname out of his mouth is like swallowing sewage. "Is that so?"

"Yeah, haven't seen you round here before. In town for long?"

He obviously doesn't remember me from the inn's gala. Figures. "Long enough."

He smiles and anger rises in my core.

"Can I buy you a drink or something?"

It's now that I notice his words carry the slightest slur. "Oh, sorry, we city girls only fuck the Rawlins brothers."

His face blanks, and he recoils a little as recognition fades in. His features pinch when he finds Addy sitting at the table, and I close in on my prey. When he turns back,

I narrow my eyes and point a finger into his chest, hard. "Stay the fuck away from her. Or I will drive these sweet spikes into your eye socket. Got it?"

"Yup," he rasps, recoiling into his bar stool.

My drink appears at my side. "Thanks." I pull my card out of my wallet. The bartender raises a hand. "On the house." He winks before glaring at Justin.

Is there anyone in Lewistown he hasn't gotten on the wrong side of?

Drinks in hand, I wander back to the table and place Addy's glass in front of her.

"Morley wasn't annoying you, too, was he?"

"Not a bit." I smile at her, but she gives me the 'what did you do' face.

I raise my glass, and she taps hers to mine. "To Adds and Rubes," she says.

"To Huddo and Reedsy. Our *favorite* Rawlins brothers."

"To our favorites."

Addy takes a long sip. "Okay, spill, Rubes. How the hell have you ruffled Harry Rawlins's feathers and lived to tell the tale?"

I chuckle at her and turn the glass on the table, rolling the stem between my fingers. The fresh pale pink nail polish I spent a solid twenty minutes on last night reflects the light.

"I gave Reed options. Helped him find one he loved, and we did up a business plan, projections, staggered progress development, and all that. Harry wasn't impressed he wanted to veer from the traditional ranching route. But Lou loved the idea. I think we'll have a win. She's the captain, after all."

"That she is. Harry always wants what's best for his family. He probably got caught off guard after handing his son millions in property and putting in months of prep. Then some city girl waltzes in and shows him up. Babes, that will get you shot in these parts."

She's joking, I know. But I also know that ranching, this way of life, is cemented in traditions and generational family lines. But it shouldn't mean Reed has to live a long life doing something to make Harry happy if it makes him miserable.

"I can handle Harry. I grew up with Richard, after all. Plus, it's a smart option. The best of both worlds. Two, maybe three, income streams instead of one. It's not personal against Harry. But it's all I can do to help Reed."

Addy is quiet, stirring her drink with the short, black straw through the clear liquid, the lime already used and discarded on her napkin. "You sure you and Reed aren't more than friends?"

My heart beats, loud and heavy. And I can't take my eyes from hers.

"I mean, I tried leaving, Rubes. It almost killed me."

"But you and Huddo were . . ."

"And you and Reed aren't?"

I drop my gaze to my Merlot. We're not. Well, one *real* kiss doesn't say we are. I have rules. I have a plan. A timed trajectory to my own success. Robbinses don't do distractions.

"We're not anything, Adds. I can't."

"Alright, if that's what you want. The career. Not that man."

"You make it sound like I have to choose between one or the other."

"Don't you?"

"I—"

I slam my mouth shut.

Rule number fucking one. I don't date.

Addy slides her hands across the table and plucks the wine from my grip. She encloses my hands with hers. "Babes, I know you work hard. You always have. But please don't be afraid to be happy. To let someone in. Let someone love you, Ruby Robbins. You deserve that. And so, so much more."

Tears burn the bridge of my nose, filling the bottom of my eyes. Reed's words come flooding back in.

I like taking care of you.

The door to the bar swings open, hitting the wall. Two scantily clad women walk in, Americana hanging off every inch of them with boots shining with the flag, daisy dukes, white tops, and red sparkling cowgirl hats. Never in my life have I ever seen anything so ridiculous.

They make a ruckus strutting up to the bar. Oh great, some friends for Justin. I'm sure they're his type. One chews gum, a brunette. The other flips her red hair, popping a hip and pushing her chest out as she leans on the bar, eyes hunting for the bartender.

"From out of town?" the big guy asks as he polishes a glass before placing in the rack with a dozen others.

"Great Falls. I'm Starr and this is Skye. Mother Nature's gifts. We're here to conquer the *Great* Reed Rawlins," the brunette says.

I hear Addy swear under her breath behind me. I'm fully turned in my seat, watching this car crash of anti-feministic whore-mongering in action.

"Yeah, he kind of left us hanging the other night. We're here to collect," the redhead coos, twirling her hair through her fingers like a fucking child.

I rise from my seat and stride to the bar. The bartender offers me an exasperated smile. "Another?"

"Actually, two glasses of your most expensive red."

The two women turn toward me, eyes running up and down my clothes. When they reach my heels, Skye's mouth gapes, eyes contorting with something between disbelief and disgust. "Well, aren't you fancy."

I pay her no heed, as the bartender uncorks a new bottle of something deep maroon. The liquid glugs into the glasses, one after the other. When he turns back and sets them down, I grab my purse.

"Fifty-eight," he says, keeping eye contact.

I tap the card on the machine as he holds it out.

"Fifty-eight for two glasses. That's some serious gaso-line, girl." Starr snickers.

Now, I turn to them and close the space between me and the two dolled-up patriotic Barbies. "You're *hunting* Reed Rawlins?"

"You seen him out tonight?" Skye says, her eyes narrowing as if I'm the fucking competition.

"Answer the question, please."

"Yeah, we're hunting him, and whatever else we wanna do with him. He's more than willing with any girl that shows interest. All's fair in lovin' and whatever."

The anger that flooded my core earlier turns to lava in my veins. "Is that so?"

"You can have him after we do," Starr says with a wink.

I suck in a breath and briefly close my eyes. How fucking *dare* they.

I fling the glasses toward them. The wine hits their stupid faces a second later, running down their white tops and soaking into their skimpy threadbare short shorts, everything it douses staining red as I step forward. "You are disgusting."

"Urgh, you bitch!" Starr shrieks.

"Stop embarrassing yourselves and stay the hell away from Reed." I step closer, ensuring my heels are clear of the spilled wine as she wipes the red wine from her eyes, and snag her attention. "Understand?"

"Fuck you," Skye spits as she stands, arms out, wine dripping from her top, streaking its way down her bare legs.

"Little slow on the uptake, I see. That is the last thing you want to do. Have a good night, ladies."

I stride slowly back to Addy, who is now standing by the table, holding her bag. Yeah, we're leaving. But, holy fuck, there is no other way that could have gone down. Reed may drown his sorrows in female company. But it will always be *his* choice. Not some deranged team bully mission. Being hunted like fucking prey.

I push through the doors and suck in the cool night air. Addy bursts out laughing, doubling over as she does. I scoff a laugh at her. When she recovers and wraps an arm around me, she gives me a side look and head tilt.

"Oh, Rubes. You are so gone, girl."

"I am not!" I let my mouth gape. I can't stand people with loose morals, let alone straight up loose. If sex isn't practical, it should be meaningful. Not some conquest, or whatever those two bimbos called it. And the thought of those two anywhere near Reed makes my skin crawl and nausea roil in my belly.

Addy stands in front of me and puts both of her hands on my shoulders. "You know I love you like a sister, right?"

"Yes?"

"Ruby Jane Robbins, you have a thing for Reed Rawlins."

"No." I shake my head, but even the gesture is a lie. "I can't, Adds. I have to go back to the city."

"You can't, or you won't?"

I step backward until the building meets my back. I hang my head and close my eyes.

Breathe in.

I don't date.

We are just friends.

Rules . . .

Breathe out.

"Let me guess, you're running through your list of rules right now?" Addy says.

I groan and blow out a breath. "Stop knowing me so well. It's rude."

"There are worse things than finding the other half of your soul, babes."

"Shut up. Now I really do need that expensive wine."

"Let's go home and figure this out. We can grab the most extravagant bottle they have at the drive-through on the walk home."

"Fine."

Addy crooks her arm and waits by me as I peel myself away from the building. My belly coils with butterflies taking flight. I swear they are on fire, their little wings singeing to ash as they fling around my stomach at the sight of a crooked arm.

Another reminder of what is strung between Reed and me.

Saying goodbye to Ruby by Mack's truck was pure torture. I finally drummed up the courage to kiss the most stunning girl in the world, the day before she leaves. A real kiss, not the fake version at the inn. Fucking idiot.

And she has been gone almost a fortnight, and I'm like a lost sheep. Working the ranch Harry's way by day. Planning this working ranch resort by night. It's exhausting. Rubes has been helping as much as she can by calls and text. We are always pinging each other's phones. But I still miss her something fierce.

And I'm completely out of my depth.

But hell will freeze over before I mess up this holiday ranch concept. Something changed when Ruby believed in me. I changed. I started to dream about enjoying life. And I haven't done that since high school.

I have a purpose. And the thought of hosting people and putting smiles on their faces, seeing them experience things out here for the first time. It's so corny, but it lights me up.

Ugh, I hate myself in the best way possible right now.

Harry has mostly come around to the idea. I mean, what good businessman wouldn't? Multiple income streams with one property. It's a win-win.

Ma putters about the kitchen, getting the last of the food for our family Sunday lunch ready.

"Need a hand?" I offer. Mack is sitting at the bench, reading something on the tablet. Ma glances up from her work.

"Sure, my boy. If you can take the cutlery and plates out, please."

Mack studies me, chewing on a stick of carrot as if it's the most tasty fucking thing he's ever eaten. Okay . . .

Huddo and Addy file through the door, carrying a cooler bag which I'm guessing has Addy's now famous salad in it. It's become something of a staple for Sunday lunches and doesn't last long.

"Hey, Reed," Addy says, slinging an arm around me. I tussle her hair and slam a fist into Hudson's shoulder before picking up the cutlery and plates and heading outside. Hudson and Addy are hot on my heels. I wander over to the table under the willow and plonk the load onto the tablecloth. Charlie wanders by the tree. That mutt has it bad for Addy—it's hilarious.

When Harry rides in from the southern paddock, it's time to eat. Ten minutes later, we are seated at the table, waiting for the parentals to come out with the meat. Ma sits to my left, and I give her the side-eye. Not her usual spot. Hudson, Addy, and Mack sit across from us, and finally Harry drops into his seat at the head.

We say a quick grace, but before I can shovel food onto my plate, Ma grabs my hand.

"No, there's one more person to come."

I survey the table. Who's left?

Tires on the gravel driveway snap my head to the right of the homestead. Nobody at the table moves. I pick up my fork and trace patterns on the old, weathered wood. Killing time.

"Hey, sorry I'm late."

The air leaves my lungs as my head pops up. And all I can do is stare.

Ruby stands, bag in hand, at the end of the table. Addy beams at her. Mack gives her a small wave.

"You are not late! Not at all. Come sit," Ma says.

Ruby doesn't move; instead, she looks directly at Pa.

"Harry."

"Ruby."

Every gaze alternates between the two. And then Harry says, "Right here, darlin'. Louisa saved you a spot."

Ruby walks around the back of our bench seat and sinks onto the old wood between me and Harry.

"Thanks," she breathes in the old man's direction before turning to face me.

"I—What . . . what are you doing here, Rubes?"

"I took some leave. I'm here to help."

I can't say a damn word. A stone forms rapidly in my airway as she drops her bag by the chair. "This all smells wonderful; I'm starving."

"Well, dig in, sweetheart, there's plenty to go round." Ma picks up the salad servers, handing them to Addy, and passes the potatoes to me.

"Thanks, Lou," Ruby says.

My heart thunders a million miles a minute. Harry and Ruby must have buried the hatchet by the looks of things. And her being here is absolutely fucking everything.

I load food onto my plate and Hudson chuckles. "Share some with Ruby, brother. She came a long way for you."

Addy slaps his arm, and he winks at her.

God, this family. My family.

I smile at Rubes. Her brown eyes, rich and dark and lined with adoration, meet mine as she leans into me. "I missed you, baby." Her whisper is so soft I barely hear it.

A man has never eaten so fast in living history. I scarf down the plate of food and wait as the minutes tick past as Ruby finishes hers, chatting away to Ma. When Ruby finally wipes her mouth on the linen napkin and sets her cutlery on the center of her plate, I grab her hand and excuse us both.

Ma waves us off with a chuckle.

The car by the white gate is not Ruby's. Unease settles in my stomach.

"That's not your car, beautiful."

She shrugs, letting her bag swing in her hands in front of her. "It's a rental. I flew in this time; all that driving was getting old. I have to take it back before six tonight, to Great Falls. And . . ." She bites her bottom lip. "I need to meet Mary-Sue at the inn again. Can you drive me? After I drop off the car, that is?"

"Sure, whatever you need. But how are you going to get around if you don't have a car?"

"Well, your ma offered me a room here. But is that spare room of yours free? It will be easier to help you if I don't have to commute between the two ranches while I'm here."

She is giving me the cutest little cringy face. Something I've never seen from her before. She wants to come play house with me?

Abso-fuckin-lutely.

"Spare room is all yours. And I will happily drive you anywhere you want."

"Good. I was hoping you'd say that." She nudges my shoulder with hers.

"Olive gave you leave? Or should I rephrase that. You, Ruby Robbins, took time off?" I feign a stunned expression.

She chuckles. "Yeah, well, a few things in my life have

surprised me of late. It will be good to step back for a little bit and have room to think, you know."

"But not too much time, since you came here to work, unpaid?"

"Helping you is not work, Reed. I like taking care of you."

And there they are, my own words, outta her pretty mouth. Something in her bag buzzes, and we both startle. She plucks her phone out. "Shoot, I really should head over to Great Falls if I'm going to make it back before they charge me for another whole day of rental."

"Lead the way, baby."

Ruby pushes through the white gate, heading for her car, as I stay rooted to the spot in pure awe. Nobody has ever taken me seriously, apart from maybe Ma. But it's natural as breathing for Ruby Robbins. She doesn't seem to see me through the same lens as everyone else.

It's heart-wrenching, because the one person who actually sees me doesn't belong here. Sucking in a long breath, I follow her out. She is tossing her bag onto the passenger's seat as I lean on the side of the rental. "Did you want to grab something to eat after your meeting with Mary-Sue?"

She freezes as she stands back up. Pushing her shoulders back with a small smile that never reaches her eyes, she sighs. "Reed, I don't date, remember."

That sucker punch to my gut sends the wind from my lungs.

I know this. She told me.

But my hands slide into my back pockets as I try to hide my disappointment. "Yeah, sure, I remember. But you gotta eat, right? Friends eat, together, I mean."

"Yes, they do." She smiles now, her eyes lighting up as her hand lands on my shirt, a finger tapping over my heart.

Goddamn, Ruby Jane, we do not feel like just friends anymore. Not from where I'm standing.

But I don't tell her that. I nod and head for my truck, hoping the blood that rushed south to fill my now hard-as-fuck cock will disperse elsewhere.

The rental purrs to life behind me as I open the truck door and hop into the driver's seat. Ruby waves as she drives past. My forehead hits the steering wheel, and I release a groan. My rational brain knows we are only friends.

So, why is this thing between us so intense?

The rental place was quiet, as usual. And I sit in my truck outside the inn as Ruby strides inside, heels clacking on the paved driveway. I slump in my chair and scroll through my phone, letting Nickelback send my mind places with their grungy, soul-wrenching lyrics.

Ten minutes later, my phone vibrates, and a message from Ruby slides down the top of the screen.

> This is going to take a while. Come inside, husband. ;)

Husband.

Right, the fake marriage thing. I flip the glove box compartment open and snatch up the silver wedding band she gave me, sliding it onto my left ring finger. I roll the truck into the valet spot and kill the engine before hopping out and sliding my phone in my back pocket.

I turn back and grab the Yankees cap off the dash and dump it over my messy hair. Rubbing the three days of growth on my face, I walk through the front doors to find Ruby leaning by the front counter with Mary-Sue.

"Hi, Mary-Sue," I say, closing the distance.

"Hello, Mr. Robbins. Your wonderful wife here was sharing her ideas for our next event. You wouldn't mind if we had a longer meeting than planned, would ya, hon?"

"No, go ahead. I've got some work things to catch up on myself." I pull my phone from my pocket and wave it like that's where I conduct all my real estate business. Mary-Sue takes a call and Ruby glances over her shoulder and mouths *thank you.*

I crowd her against the counter, wrapping around her from behind. "You're welcome, baby."

My words are no more than a whisper, but when Ruby's hand rests on my arm and her brown eyes find mine, my heart stutters out. Her eyes lift to the cap a heartbeat later, and she traces a hand over my jaw, her fingertips floating over the scruff that's there. "I like this."

"Then it stays."

"Good."

"Well then." We both snap our gazes to a beaming Mary-Sue. Ruby goes to pull away, but I hold her close, not wanting Mary-Sue to read into that. Her scrutiny and outdated ideas are ridiculous, just as Ruby said. But I can't help feeling a small appreciation for the old-fashioned woman who made it possible for me to spend any amount of time with Rubes.

"I'll be a little while. Did you want to grab a coffee in the restaurant while we work?" Ruby says.

"Sure, you know where I am if you need me, beautiful." I dot a kiss to her cheek and head for the restaurant entrance to the right of reception.

The two women wander off to Mary-Sue's office as I sink into the small café chair. I open up my emails. I actually do have work email to respond to, despite it being Sunday and the fact that I've never run a business before.

I like having something important to do. Something that matters, that I want to bring to fruition. Like I'm building something from nothing, with my mind and my hands. Maybe that's what Harry was trying so hard for me to understand?

An email for a quote for holiday cabin construction sits in the inbox. I want at least three to be ready for the opening. And the kitchen will have to be expanded to accommodate all those people, not to mention the upgrade on the big barn. Hudson and Addy volunteered to help with that. Having a carpenter for an older brother sure helps.

Scanning the email for the figures in the quote, I decide it's whiskey I'm needing, not coffee. Holy hounds in hell. That option is not in my budget.

I place the phone down and lean back in the chair, hands knitted behind my neck, letting my eyes close.

"What can I get y'all?" a sugary voice drawls.

I open my eyes to a somewhat familiar face. A brunette waitress stands, pad and pen in hand, in a black top and short skirt, black apron tied too tight around her waist.

"Coffee, one sugar. Please."

"You don't remember me, do you?"

"Um . . . No?"

"The name's Starr, we met a few months back at the bar down the street."

Frowning, I sit forward and fold my arms over my chest. "Sorry, I meet a lot of people at the bar."

"Yeah, I know." She snaps a hand to her hip. "You can tell your vicious guard dog bitch to back off, by the way. This is a small town, and if you want to keep that reputation of yours, Rawlins, I suggest you tell her to take it down a notch."

"You've lost me. My what?"

The waitress saunters away. But she tosses a scowl over her shoulders as she says, "Oh, and she owes me a new top."

My eyes widen as I rack my brain for what on earth this girl is talking about.

When my coffee arrives, it's brought out by another waitress. She's much older and barely bothers with a smile. I scroll through more emails and reply to some that are in budget and seem okay to go ahead with. And an hour passes quickly as I tap out notes and random ideas for the holiday ranch.

"You look enthralled."

I glance up to find a smiling Ruby with her bag over her shoulder. "Ready? I'm starving."

"Yup, let's get out of here." I push out of the seat and drop my tip by the drained coffee mug. With my hand on the small of her back, I lead Ruby out to the valet space with harried steps.

"You must be really hungry," she says, shooting me a narrowed glance.

"Nope, tell you about it in the truck."

"Okay."

When I hear the sweet purr of my black beauty, she rolls into the driveway and the tension in my gut releases a smidge. I open Ruby's door, and she climbs on up. Running a hand through my hair, I reapply the cap before jumping into the truck and putting it into drive.

Clear of the inn, I turn to face Ruby. "I have to tell you something."

"Shoot."

"The waitress at the restaurant recognized me."

"Crap," she breathes.

"I'm sorry, Rubes. It's possible she won't put it together. And if she does, maybe she won't say anything?"

"Maybe. I hope so."

"But here's the deal. It was this girl, Starr, that I met at a bar one Friday, months ago. Nothing happened; I wasn't interested. But she apparently remembers me."

Now something like guilt sits in Ruby's eyes as she worries her bottom lip through her teeth.

"What?" I ask.

She cringes. "I may have spoken to her in Lewistown one night?"

I chuckle. "What did you do, Ruby Robbins?"

"I threw wine in her face. But"—she holds a hand up, her best lawyer face taking over—"in my defense, she was bad-mouthing someone *very* dear to me. And she so, *so* deserved it."

I am trying to stifle the hysterics bubbling up my insides. My grip turns white on the wheel. I pull over by a small barber shop and slide the truck into park. "You are telling me that Starr was smack-talking Reed Rawlins, and you took her out?"

"Well, not in the Mackinlay sense of taking someone out." She waves her hands in the air.

I should hope not.

But I slide a hand over my face as I fall apart with laughter. She huffs a small laugh and then her hand wanders over my jaw. "Reed, she was *hunting* you for—" Her eyes close as she shakes her head, so subtle. "For some kind of threesome, or something."

She swallows hard.

And the wind disappears from my lungs as her face turns to stone at the devastation lining her eyes. Her shoulders plummet with each breath.

"Rubes."

Her hand drops from my jaw. "I know it's none of my business, but god, she was so disgusting. I wanted to slam my fist into her face. She's lucky all she got was that top-shelf bottle of red."

I huff a laugh, and her eyes fly open. "Reed, it's not funny!"

Leaning over, I cup her face with my hands, and the wide-eyed devastation that was there moments ago returns. "You being jealous, baby? That's not funny at all. It's sweet."

Her breaths shallow out. Her fingers wrap around my wrists. "I—"

"Tell me, Rubes."

She pulls away and purses her lips, staring out the

window. I kill the engine and climb out of the truck. Outside her door, her brown eyes burn into mine through the tinted glass. I open the door, and she turns on the seat to climb out, but I wedge between her legs and put my arms on the top frame of the truck door rim. "You sure you're hungry?"

Now, every breath I take is not enough, and the stretch in my jeans from the solid hard-on she gave me with those eyes alone should be outlawed.

"Reed," she rasps.

Ruby saying my name will never get old.

"I'm right here, baby."

Her fingers wrap around my collar. The warmth of them brushing over my collarbones sends electricity straight to my heart. My left hand dangles from the rim of the doorframe, and she glances at the ring.

She swallows hard. "Maybe we should grab our food to go . . ."

Reed has my head all fucked up. My rules are fading from black-and-white to greyer by the minute. And holy hell, if Mary-Sue gets wind of his real name . . . I can't even think about that now.

The drive home is mostly quiet. The food, we eat on the way, not wanting it to go cold. And I take great pleasure in feeding him fries as he drives. He snaps one from my fingers before he returns the affection with cheeky smiles as we fly down the dirt road toward his ranch.

Reed rolls the truck into the barn as I yawn. It's been a busy day. And it's not over yet; I want to run some things past him and work on the website and booking system before bed.

But Lord, I could use a glass of wine.

Red.

Even better, Merlot.

My door opens, and I realize I've been staring into the abyss, thinking. I start and suck in a breath as I turn to Reed. His hands are held up like he's going to carry me from the truck.

"I got it, Reedsy." I grab up my bag and handbag, stepping out of the truck. The seats are so comfortable, I almost fell asleep. Luckily for this gorgeous man, his ravenous hunger kept me occupied. On tired legs, I teeter toward him, and he catches me in a warm hug.

When his face sinks into my hair and he tightens his grip, I stiffen, my rules heading for a full-out brawl with my heart. Never before have they been so much at war as they are now.

"Want me to carry you to bed, Rubes?" he breathes, face still buried in my hair.

I push out of his hold with a chuckle. "No thanks, I can walk."

His face falls a little, but he takes my bags and leads me to the house yard. The air is cool, the smell of hay and the mountain air mixing into a heady concoction. The stars out are magnificent. The blanket of shimmering silver points hangs low, like somehow, we are closer to heaven.

I follow close behind, not wanting to trip on the pavers as we head up to the dark house. No Mack here this time. And part of me is thrilled to be here with Reed. The rational part of me is screaming for my heart to let it go. To keep things cemented in the friend zone.

That thought makes me feel a loss like I've never felt before.

Not having the chance to have more of the only man that has ever wanted me for me, and not my bank account or status, is completely unfair. But the way things are, they're that way for a reason. For me. For my success. A success that has been the only thing I can ever remember wanting, my entire adult life.

The door creaks open and Reed flips the lights on with one hand, my bags dangling from the other. I step inside and take in the small farmhouse. I've been here before, but never at night and never to stay. And I can't fight the feeling of how right it feels. How cozy and grounding this place is.

"Let's get your bags squared away, and I can pour you some wine, baby." Reed walks up the stairs and to the right, and I follow a step behind. He drops my bags on the end of the bed and pads to the antique-looking wardrobe on the inside wall by the door. Pulling out two towels, he pops them on top of my bag. "That should keep you dry."

The towels are all of a sudden fascinating. As if thinking about the many meanings of what that sentence could mean for us. "Thanks."

"See you downstairs for a drink?"

"Sure," I say, turning to face him, hands in my back pockets. "Okay if I take a shower and slip into my PJs first?"

"Yup. Red or white?"

"Um . . ." I worry my bottom lip through my teeth. "Whatever you choose."

He nods and pats the doorframe as he walks out and back down the stairs. I wander about the room, taking in the simple farmhouse decor, cottage-style furniture, and soft furnishings. Something unwinds in my chest, and I sink onto the upholstered chair by the window. It's plush and way too good at coaxing my eyes shut. I snap up out of it and stand to tug the zip on my bag, before hunting for fresh lingerie and my shorts and singlet PJs. On second thought, it may get cool tonight.

I pluck out a t-shirt instead. A worn-out red one from an old cruise I went on years ago with faded *Captain's Choice* in white marine-type font set over an even more faded ship's wheel.

After a quick but hot shower, I pull on my PJs and head downstairs, drying my hair with a towel. The hardwood floor under my bare feet is cool but so good. Reed is in the kitchen, chopping something on a board. Two glasses sit out, a wine glass and a shorter tumbler. His glass has an inch of amber liquid. He lifts it to his mouth, drawing a sip before setting it down. I lean against the doorway, drying the ends of my hair, taking him in.

He looks good in a home of his own. His rolled-up work shirt and jeans have been exchanged for blue boxers and a navy shirt. His hair is wet. Wow, he's fast. I hang the towel on the end post of the stairs and clear my throat. He spins back, knife in hand. So much like his ma.

She always has a kitchen utensil of some kind in her hand.

"Hey," I breathe.

His cheeky grin that grows instantly when he sees me, fades to parted lips and a fixed stare on my chest. No, my shirt. He's reading it.

"Hey," he finally chokes out. He puts the knife down and heads to the cupboard. He grabs a bottle of red and pours me a glass. "Sofa, beautiful."

I do as instructed and flop onto the sofa. The fire is already on, despite it not being cold enough for one. But it warms my tired body, and I stretch out as he hands the wine glass to me.

"Ma sent over some of your Merlot from the party," he says softly, as my fingers curl around the stem.

"Oh wow. Tell her thanks. Actually, never mind, I'll text her in the morning."

He sinks onto the couch beside me. With a sip from his tumbler, he stares into the fire. "You two get along well."

The flames dance, their proximity tangling around one another. Like lovers in a never-ending waltz that mesmerizes. "I guess we do. She's different to my own mother. Much warmer."

"I know she loves having you here."

I push a small smile over my lips before tasting the red. It's floral and warm and delicious. I close my eyes and lay my head back on the sofa. I take a second to breathe through the warmth that lingers in my core, not a hundred percent sure it's the wine.

"I've never had a woman like Lou in my life. Not Olive, not my mother."

Reed moves closer and puts his tumbler down on the small coffee table between us and the fireplace. His palms are on my face, my eyes directed up to his. "That, Ruby Robbins, is a crying shame. You deserve that."

I huff a laugh, breaking the eye contact. "Thanks, but I'm used to it."

He is shaking his head, eyes pulled tight. "Nope, that's not acceptable. I officially give you Ma, for whatever you need."

Now I chuckle and wrap my hands around his and then slip them from my face. "Has anyone ever told you you're the most thoughtful, sweetest guy on this earth?"

"Not lately." He winks.

I roll my eyes at him and rub a thumb over his jaw. His gaze drops to my lips. The oxygen in the room is suddenly too thin. "Reed."

He stays where he is. His jaw feathers for a moment before he rises from the sofa and pads to the kitchen. Returning, he brings a tray of chopped vegetables and cheese. It's perfect.

"You think of everything."

He sits down, putting the food in between us. "I told you, Rubes. I like taking care of you."

"You're going to make an amazing holiday ranch host, Reed."

He forces a smile. I jump to my feet and dash upstairs, grabbing my laptop. Back downstairs, I sit on my spot on the sofa and flip it open. "So, I have made a website and embedded the booking system. It needs some finishing touches and your approval."

He moves the tray and slides over, our knees touching. Shoulders rubbing, I show him the site. "Of course, if you're not happy, with color scheme, theme, anything, I can change it. Here is where people come when they first click onto it."

His hand brushes my hair from my cheek, tucking it behind my ear. "Sorry, can't see," he rasps.

Hand frozen on the trackpad, I swallow down the stone that rose with his touch.

"What else do you want to show me, baby?"

"I—" I swallow. "The gallery and the accommodations page, which are still empty by the way. What did you decide about the cabins?"

He leans back on the couch. "Yeah, we'll be building those ourselves. I have to ask Huddo, but it shouldn't be a problem."

"Excellent, what time frame do you think? Will we make the fall opening as planned?"

"Listen to you, getting all event planner, business manager on me. Yes, Ruby, we will meet your deadline. Thanksgiving weekend."

"They're *your* deadlines, Rawlins."

He laughs, nodding. "Yes, they are."

When his gaze lands on me, it melts from humor to something deeper, something I've never seen in him. But when the air shrinks from my lungs and my gut flips, I have to rub a hand over my face to reset my heart back to something viable for life. Not the rapid flinging rhythm it's taken up.

"I should . . ." I drag my focus back to the screen. "I should finish this before bed."

He smiles and nods, plucking a carrot from the board, snapping it between his teeth. Carrot and whiskey. I huff a laugh at this amazing man and settle in to work.

When my eyelids become heavy and start their descent, I turn the brightness down a little. A yawn later, I close the machine and place it on the coffee table, taking to studying the flames, now smaller and a darker shade of amber.

Reed putters around the kitchen, clearing up. I take the last pull of the wine, emptying my glass. My head resting on my hand, and wrapped up warm with a blanket, I cover another yawn before the fire fades to black.

Chapter Fifteen

REED

Ruby is sound asleep on the sofa. And as much as I would love to watch her until dawn steals the last of the night's darkness, she is going to have one hell of a sore neck if I don't move her.

I peel the blanket from her and brush the hair from her face. She mumbles something I don't catch as I slide my arms under her legs and behind her shoulders. She's light. Soft. Her sweet strawberry scent winds into my senses as I take the steps up to her room.

The spare room.

That feels fucking wrong, if anything ever did.

My heart thunders, the blood rushing south with every breath I take with her in my arms. The curve of her gorgeous lips. The apples of her cheeks. The lines of her collarbones. Her long legs draped over my arm . . .

Fuck me.

Fire roars through my veins, burning my shallow breaths out, one puff at a time.

Sweet Jesus.

A moment later, I stand by the queen bed in the spare room. And I can't put her down.

Don't want to.

Asleep, so gentle, so fucking beautiful, my damn heart explodes. I clamp my jaw tight, the muscles feathering. But this isn't what she wants. To be tethered to a ranch, to a rancher. Even it's a whole lot of fun. And she's the best thing to ever have walked into my life.

Trying desperately to take back control over my now staggered breathing, I suck in a lungful. "Bedtime, baby," I whisper.

She moans, and it takes everything this man has to not crumble. Instead, I let her down onto the bed and step around to the other side and fold back the blankets. Wiped out, she doesn't wake, only sighing and rolling over.

I kneel on the bed behind her and lift her onto the side with the linen folded back, tucking her in. Two hands. Snug as a bug in a rug. Pressing a kiss to her cheek, I push from the bed and track to the door. Every step is hard.

I want to fold myself around her. Give her everything, every part of me she deserves. And selfishly, I want to keep her.

But that's not fair.

If I learned anything from Huddo and Addy, love isn't selfish. It just ain't.

I head downstairs and put her laptop on the kitchen counter away from the heat of the fireplace and tidy up a little before flicking off the lights and padding upstairs into my empty room.

I lie on the oversized bed and slide my hands behind my head, knitting them as I let my gaze rove over the stars above. They're stunning, yet they're dull compared to the brightness that thrums to life when Ruby is around. The full moon brightens my room with a soft grey.

Reed James Rawlins, playboy turned sap.

I chuckle, but the fact is, my life changed. My way of thinking, my bad habits, all shifted when I found Ruby. And I let my mind wander, playing out how things would go if she wanted me. If she felt for me the depth of whatever this is that I do for her.

With a hard-on that would take down a Greek god, I groan, rolling over onto my stomach, hoping it will extinguish the fire that started at the mere thought of Ruby and me.

Something creaks across the hall. A heartbeat later, she appears in the doorway, wrapped in a blanket. Her silhouette is an outline of every curve I adore. Her hair messy, her breathing steady.

"You okay, beautiful?"

"No."

I sit up. "What is it?"

She pads to the side of the bed and pulls back the covers, sliding in beside me. I lie back and weave my arm under her shoulders, pulling her into my chest. The emotion that clogs my throat squeezes in my lungs. "Were you cold?"

"No. I'm used to sleeping next to you when I'm out here. I want to be where you are."

I press a kiss to her hair and wrap her into me tighter.

"Reed?"

"Yeah?"

"Are we just friends?"

I swallow the stone that materializes with her words. "We are whatever you want us to be, Rubes."

She pushes onto her elbow, sliding her cold feet between my calves. "I can't tell anymore."

"I don't want to make your life complicated. I know you have plans. But . . ."

"But? Reed, what?"

"Dammit, Ruby." Nerves rattle to life, scratching through my veins, tightening my chest. *Say it, for fuck's sake, Rawlins.* I swallow hard and sink my face into her hair. "I have needed you from the first moment I saw you that Friday night in Great Falls."

She rolls over. Her eyes pinch, and realization spreads on her face as it gives way to surprise. "What?" The word is almost non-existent.

I fold my hand around hers. "It was the Friday before I

met you over at Harry's with Addy. I saw you pacing the street in those red heels, totally consumed by whatever was on your phone. You ran into me. You didn't look up to see me. But I saw you, Ruby."

Her mouth makes an *oh*. I drop my focus to the mattress between us, trying to find the words for what I want to say. I know she's not mine.

"It's okay, Rubes, I know—"

"I see you now." Her lips brush against my mouth.

My hands are on her face. Deepening the kiss, she pushes and pulls her way through my hair. I glide my thumbs over her soft features, over her jaw, down her neck. And when her lips part for me, my heart stumbles a beat before I sweep in, taking everything she wants to give.

Breathless, I break away. "You sure, baby?"

She studies my eyes, hands on my face, breathing hard. "I don't know where this leaves us, but I can't be around you and not touch you. Not anymore."

"Thank fuck for that."

She laughs and slaps my shoulder. "Now, I would like to know what all this talk is about."

"You've lost me."

"The *Great Reed Rawlins*. Bringing ladies to their knees since . . . Well, that part I didn't have the privilege of hearing."

Heat floods my face. And I choke on the air leaving my lungs. Ruby bites her bottom lip, trying to stifle a giggle.

"It's okay, sweet man, I'm not bothered. And I've had my share of gu—"

I cover her mouth with mine, winding my hands under her t-shirt. The shirt that held me captive earlier as my air stalled out in my lungs at seeing the word *Captain* sprawled over Ruby's chest. Harry's disbelief in coincidences has rubbed off on me. This woman literally running into me that night is no goddamn coincidence.

"Take it off, please," Ruby begs, almost breathless.

I slide her t-shirt off and let it fall to the floor beside the bed.

"These too." She rises to her knees, and I push her PJ shorts over her hips. But I can't pull my eyes from her, the shape of her, her perfect breasts bouncing as she moves, unfazed. Like we are already so comfortable with each other, and this too is natural for us. My body aches to hold her, touch her where she wants me to.

"God, you have no idea how long I have been thinking about this," Ruby whispers.

I swallow. My throat is now akin to the Sahara Desert in a dry spell. I trace the back of my hand over her cheek, letting it fall to the curved bone of her collar. Her gaze follows my touch, her brown eyes darkened, every breath choppy.

Fire lances through my core, ending in my rock-hard cock. I let my knuckles sweep past the underside of her breast, one then the other. She gasps, her lips parting.

Sitting on her heels, she wriggles the shorts off and flings them to the floor.

"Yours too, Reed."

Tugging the shirt from my back, I throw it onto the pile with hers. My hands grab my shorts, but she slips a finger behind the waistband and shakes her head. Wavy blonde hair, now lit up by the moonlight, sways across her bare shoulders.

"Mine. Lie back."

"You're the captain." The words fall from my mouth before I have the chance to reel them back in. I do as I'm told and lay on the bed. Ruby tugs the boxers down, letting them slide off my legs and over my feet. I think she's enjoying herself, by the cheeky expression on her face as she straddles my thighs.

"God, look at you, Reed."

I sit up and lift her onto my lap. "I'm looking, but my view is much, much better, baby." I flip us over, and she squeals, collapsing my chest in on itself with that one sound. So fucking happy. And if I could spend the rest of my days repeating this one . . . I would.

Ruby's laughter fades and her brown eyes hold mine as her breaths shallow out. "Maybe—" Her gaze snaps away, her cheeks blushing. Ruby Robbins, the toughest, most capable woman I've ever met, has turned shy.

"What is it, beautiful? No judgment here, only you and me."

"Slow. Can we go slow? It's been a while. And I don't

want to ruin this." She glides a hand up my neck and cups my jaw.

The thundering between my ribs has stolen every single word along with the air in my lungs. So I nod, tucking her hair behind her ear with a kiss to the forehead. She rises from the bed, hands around my face, pulling my mouth to hers as I shuffle closer, fitting between her legs.

Every move she makes has me consumed. Her lips part, and I can't help it when I tangle my tongue with hers, wanting to taste and be connected in any place she will let me. A little moan purrs from her lips, making me impossibly hard. Fire pools, turning to lava as she presses her pebbled nipples against me.

I break the kiss and hold her face with gentle palms. "Where do you want me, Rubes?"

Her chest is plummeting, desperation lining her stunning brown eyes. "Everywhere," she whispers.

"Aye aye, Captain." I wink at her, and she falls back onto the pillow with a giggle. The smile that breaks my face sends fresh warmth around my already fiery body. I crawl over her and nuzzle her neck. Her hands wander up the back of mine and into my hair.

"Ruby Jane Robbins, you are so fucking gorgeous."

Her breath hitches.

"Reed."

I push up, hovering over her. "I'm serious. The first

time I saw you. Well, let's just say you occupied more of my head than you should have."

"And now? Am I still in there?" She traces a finger over my temple, her gaze dropping to my mouth.

"Now, you're a permanent feature. A different showing every night. I have an excellent imagination."

She scoffs and slaps my shoulder.

"You never had wet Reed dreams, baby?"

She stills briefly, closing her eyes. Her hand slides over her right breast, pinching the nipple. Her mouth parts, and her hand descends until it slips over her center and down. "Oh Reed, baby. Please, don't stop."

Sweet Jesus, that's hot.

She snorts a laugh, tossing her head back on the pillow, her hands resting on her blonde hair now splayed over the pillow as she loses it to a fit of giggles.

"That was the hottest thing I have ever seen. And pretty soon, you're gonna be repeatin' yourself." I crawl backward, dotting kisses over her collarbones, to the tops of her breasts, skirting the nipple where I know she wants me.

Ruby wriggles on the bed and nudges my thighs with her knee. "You're missing all the good places. That is definitely *not* everywhere."

Now I chuckle at her. "This is your punishment. And I will make you suffer, beautiful. I'm not giving you what you want until you're writhing underneath me."

"Them's fighting words, Rawlins."

"Hah." I wink at her and travel my kisses back up to her neck. Reaching the shell of her ear, I nip it before whispering, "Come undone for me, Ruby."

I track back the way I came; this time I nip and kiss her as I go, making sure to cover every inch of her soft skin. Bracing myself on one hand, I cup her breast and nip the soft flesh, avoiding the hard peak. "Do you play with these when you touch yourself, imagining me, Rubes?"

Her eyes flicker. Like she knows it's a challenge.

"Okay, don't confess. I will have to resort to harsher methods to extract answers."

I nip the swollen bud.

Her back arches off the bed instantly.

Fuck me.

I nip the other one, and the soft moan that tumbles from her lips sends pre-cum leaking out of my tip. "Sweet Jesus, Rubes."

"Please, don't stop."

"There's those pretty words."

She wraps her legs around my waist, cheekiness claiming her face.

No fair.

My rock-hard cock lines up against her entrance, the slippery wetness coating me where we touch. I could so easily sink into her. God knows I want to, so fucking bad. But that's not what she wants. Slow, that's what Ruby wants.

That is exactly what she's goin' to get.

To keep my bloodless brain from doing something stupid, I crawl backward, tracking more kisses down her belly and eliciting more huffy laughter. With a dot to each hip bone, I nudge her thighs open with my head.

"Reed," she rasps.

"Yeah, baby?"

"You sure? No one's done that before . . ."

I have never been more sure of anything in my life than I am right now. So fucking sure. "If you want me to stop, say so, okay?"

She nods, hands gripping the blanket at her sides. I run my thumb over her clit, and she sucks in a breath. She is so wet. For me. That fact alone squeezes my heart tight, sending a pulse along my rigid cock. In a long sweep, I send my tongue through her wet center. Her back flies off the mattress as she whimpers.

"God, you taste so fucking good, Rubes."

She moans as I sweep my tongue over her clit, suckling it.

"Reed," she gasps, hands sinking into my hair.

"More, baby?"

"Yes, please." Her answer is more breath than words.

With a finger, I slide into her wet center. Her teeth bite into her bottom lip, her choppy breath turns manic. I work them in and out, curling them a little to find the spot I am right now one hundred percent sure no man has ever bothered to do for her.

Fucking losers.

How can someone this amazing not have had this before?

When I suck hard on her clit, working my fingers, she shoots off the bed, her grip in my hair so tight a sting starts. "Oh my g—Reed!"

She throws her head back, hips bucking as her walls clamp down. Every wave of her orgasm tightens around my fingers as she does exactly what I wanted and comes undone for me.

And it is the most magnificent thing I have ever seen.

Her grip loosens a moment later, and she cradles my head, leaning down, letting her hair tumble around my face. "Thank you."

I rise up to meet her, kissing her. She tastes my lips with little kisses, her thumbs running over my chin, taking her release from my skin.

"Told you, you taste incredible, baby."

She smiles at me, but it falls. "No one has done that for me before. I don't—"

"Rubes, that's fucking unbelievable."

But she shrugs. And when she shuffles backward off the bed a little, I move between her legs again, but this time, I sit on my heels and pull her up onto my lap. She sits straddling me as I pull her peak into my mouth. Her hands are behind my neck with the next breath.

"I want to return the favor. Your turn to fall apart, Reed."

"In a minute, baby," I say with her nipple still in my mouth.

She giggles and leans back, as if reveling in each stroke of my tongue around her sweet peaks.

"Careful, you'll make me come again doing that."

I release the hard bud with a pop. "I *really* want to see that."

"But it's yours I want to see."

Something bangs downstairs. We both still, staring at each other. When another bang and a crash ring out from outside, I pick Ruby up, depositing her on the bed. I push to my feet and head for the door.

"Be careful," she whispers harshly.

I walk down the stairs, stark naked, blood bounding in my veins. When I reach the bottom and turn on the kitchen light, I glance around. Nothing.

Something rustles outside.

I swing the front door open. Raccoons.

"Get outta here!" I lunge at them, arms flying up. They scurry off, and I close the door. They'll probably come back. Next time, I will be ignoring them. I pad back upstairs to find Ruby leaning on the doorjamb, still in the suit god gave her. The moonlight behind her illuminates her hair. She looks like a fucking goddess.

She *is* a goddess.

I move toward the door. She puts her hands on the frame either side. "Not a step further."

"Okay, baby."

"Stand and hold the frame, Reedsy."

She backs up a step, letting her hands fall to her sides. I do as I'm told. If it comes out of her mouth, I will always be listening. My grip firmly on the doorframe, she leans in and whispers, "Come undone for me, Reed."

Air is stuck tight, not budging, and no words form. But I manage a nod as she drops to her knees, holding my gaze the whole way down. Watching her sends my breaths choppy. Her fine hand wraps around my cock, and I roll my head back with a groan that could wake the dead.

"Tell me if you want me to stop. Otherwise, this only ends when you are completely and utterly undone."

"Alright, Rubes," I say, every syllable gravel. She pumps my cock with one hand before tangling her tongue around the tip. My grip on the door turns white.

"Don't think this is gonna take long, baby."

Her smile moves against my hard shaft. God, that is fucking *it*. It takes everything I have not to fuck her pretty mouth. To sink into her throat. "Ruby," I groan.

She releases me, her mouth disappearing. She's on her feet, kissing my neck a heartbeat later. Her teeth graze my thumping vein before she trails kisses downward.

"A man has to suffer a little."

If this is her idea of torture? Sign me the fuck up.

Reed's big and perfect and so hard. My insides curl up at the sight of him, desperate to be impaled on this man. This gorgeous, funny, kind, thoughtful, amazing man. But for now, I sink back to my knees after pretending to make him suffer. Who am I kidding—not straddling his lap and letting him stretch and fill me up is my own personal hell.

I take his hard, perfect cock in one hand and slide him into my mouth, as deep as I can go. One of his hands snaps from the doorframe and sinks into my hair. He likes this. I like this. I pull back up, increasing the suction.

"Baby, slow down." His voice is pure gravel.

The things that sound does to me. Heat pools low in my belly again. I'm so wet, I'm not sure there isn't a puddle between my knees. The fire in my core is killing me. Reed's eyes are closed. His face is twisted with something like beautiful agony. I sink down and pull up quick, pumping with my hand as I go, and his stance falters as he hisses a breath. I pop off the top.

I need to slow down.

"Look at me, Reed."

Slowly, he lowers his head, brilliant green eyes locking onto me. "Don't take your eyes off me, okay?"

He nods, jaw feathering as he slaps his hand back to the doorframe. I grip my breast with one hand and roll the nipple between my fingers. I can't help the soft moan that falls from my mouth.

"Sweet Jesus, Rubes. Baby, you're killing me."

"This hurts?"

I pluck the nipple and move to the other breast. This time, I whimper as the pressure on the nipple has my core twisting on itself.

"God, beautiful. I need that sweet pussy wrapped around my cock."

"Oh, this pussy?" I glide my hand down my belly until my hand cups my wetness.

"Yeah," he rasps.

I pump two fingers inside. "Like this?"

He doesn't respond. His gorgeous face is devastation in motion as his jaw works, his lips part, and he grabs his cock with one hand. I bat it away.

"Ah ah, that's my job."

I pump my fingers in and out a few more times, closing

my eyes. When I open them, Reed's strung out in the best way possible. I wrap a hand around his cock and take him deep into my mouth. This time, I tangle my tongue around the tip, teasing the small opening. Sucking my way back up, I repeat the action before sinking back down.

His legs begin to shake. "Bab—" The word turns to a heady groan.

Good man.

I suck and pull, sweeping my tongue over the tip with every stroke up. The taste of him, I catalogue away, along with every other part of this man who has been my friend for so many months. Every single thing I adore about him is stored securely away in my heart.

On the next stroke, his cock pulses. I keep up the motion, tightening my grip, increasing the suction even more as Reed Rawlins falls apart above me. And the look, the shape of his face when he lets go, *that* I stash away for later.

That's something I will never forget.

When the last wave peters out, I reluctantly release him from my mouth, wiping the last drop from my lips with a finger. I close my eyes, breathing in the moment. Something thuds in front of me, and when I open my eyes, Reed is on his knees in front of me. His hands move to cradle my face as his mouth covers mine.

I break the kiss a moment later. The wood, as lovely as it is, has my knees aching. I push to stand. When Reed doesn't follow, I tilt my head with a shy smile. "Coming to bed?"

"Yeah," he breathes.

But his gaze doesn't leave me as I crawl in between his covers, bare as the day I was born, and curl up.

The bed dips a minute later. His finger glides over my cheek, brushing strands of hair from my face. A kiss lands on my temple. "Night, baby."

"Night, Reedsy."

When he wraps his body around me, his breathing is steady. His hold is tight. His heart pushes into my back with every beat.

A girl could get used to this.

"We need to find at least five spots for camping and day trips. Mountains, the stream, open fields, etc. for guests." Reed is looking at me over his coffee cup, a slice of toast in the other hand. Disheveled and in his PJs still, he is damn cute. I try to keep things all business this morning, not sure whether last night was simply two people who got carried away and needed to blow off some steam, or something else entirely.

"Yup, can do. I have to sink some holes for Harry first, replace an old fence line. Then after we can do that."

"Sweet, the website should be up and running by the end of the week. Any word on the cabins?"

"Oh shit. I was goin' to call Huddo."

"Reed!"

"I was busy, baby."

"Ring him now. I'll wait." I give my sweetest smile. But he lowers his mug and tosses the toast to the plate. Rising from the chair, he comes to stand by my side. He crooks a finger. Brows furrowing, I do what he wants and stand. My red captain shirt rubs against his, the brush sending my nipples hard.

He grips my waist and hauls me up onto the table. "I will do nothing of the sort. Mornings are for eating; for slow, pleasureful things. Not Huddo's short temper."

"You're almost done with breakfast, though."

"Nope." He tugs at my shorts and pulls them and my panties over my hips. "Still starving, baby."

The cotton of his PJ shorts is tented. I huff a laugh at him. Looks like this is our thing now. Fooling around. Getting each other off.

"You need my mouth on this, Reed?" I rub the hard length through his shorts and his forehead drops to my own as he moans. I'm soaking wet for him already.

"Yeah, amongst other things."

All I can manage is a raspy laugh as he buries his head between my legs. Anticipation has my body trembling already. After last night . . . I'm not sure anyone else will ever come close. Pun intended. I groan internally at the lame joke and run my hands into his messy dark blond hair, leaning back and closing my eyes. He runs his tongue through my center, and I arch up involuntarily. He nips my clit and suckles lightly as I moan, my grip tightening on the table's edge.

A knock rattles the door.

"Fuck." Reed pushes to his feet fast, slipping my shorts up my legs. "I forgot Mack was coming over to pick up hay this morning. Jesus. Sorry, Rubes."

I catch my breath and slide my feet to the floor, hoisting my PJ shorts up as hysterical laughter swallows me whole. He is about to answer the door with a raging hard-on that's very visible through his worn, too-thin boxers. He starts for the door, and I wrap a hand around his arm. "Let me." I nod to his very obvious erection.

"Oh, yeah. Maybe you should."

He moves to stand behind the kitchen island. My panties are soaked through, but nobody is going to notice that.

With a glance at Reed, I pull the door open. Mack's beaming smile greets me. "Mornin', Ruby."

Oh god, he heard us.

Fuck.

I fight to tamper the heat that's flooding my cheeks and step aside, hoping he will stop looking at me and come in. *Ugh.*

"Good morning, Mack."

Reed sips his coffee. How did he get that from the table?

"Looks like it." Mack nods at Reed. "You need a bib, little bro?"

Reed's mouth and chin has my wetness all over it. Praying the floor will do me a solid and swallow me whole, I close my eyes and grip the doorknob like it's the only thing that can hold me up right now.

Reed grins and wipes his face with the tea towel that hangs on the oven door. Making a mental note to throw that piece of linen away, I shut the door and make my way to the table. Sitting, I take up my coffee with both hands, homing in on the brown liquid that will hopefully save me.

No luck.

"I can wait in the barn, if you two wanna finish what you started?" Mack says. His smile is genuine, albeit full of cheek. They are so similar, these two.

"Actually," I start, barely brave enough to make eye contact, "I should go change. Lots of work to be done before we start out."

"Going for a ride, Rubes?" Mack winks.

"No, you idiot." Reed tosses the tea towel at him, and I cringe, holding my breath. Mack catches it with one hand as Reed drains his coffee cup. "We're going out to find some spots for the guests to ride to, camp out, etc. Me and Rubes."

"Just you and Rubes?"

"Mack"—Reed grips his shoulder—"follow us and I will back the tractor over you."

"Taking the new wheels for a spin, hey?"

"Yeah, Harry wants post holes dug for a new fence line. Two birds, one stone, and all that."

"Sweet Jesus, Harry and his fencing. I swear, it's his favorite fucking sport." Mack tosses the tea towel at Reed's head. "See you at the barn, lover boy."

"Fuck off, Mackie."

Mack chuckles, walking through the door. When it closes behind him, heat is still blazing its way across my cheeks. I'm not embarrassed about being with Reed, but being caught doing that at all is mortifying. Like it should only be something the person you adore the most in the whole world is privy to.

My brain short circuits with the realization that the man standing in front of me is that.

And like that, The Rule, number one—no dating, no distractions—that I have lived by for so, so long, goes up in a brilliant ball of fire.

Fuck, fucketty, flaming fuck.

The big red tractor purrs next to me. And to say I'm dwarfed by its enormous size and power would be an utter understatement. Reed putters around the barn, plucking up a toolbox and a bundle of rags. Okay . . .

When he climbs up the step of the tractor and opens the cab door, he dumps the items behind the seat. Back down, he walks to the back of the machine, muttering to himself, something like a checklist. A few clangs, and he reappears.

"Right, ready for a ride in my big shiny tractor, baby?"

I chuckle. "I think so."

He climbs up and opens the door. The seat sinks on coiled springs when he drops into it. Tilting his head, coaxing me in, he holds out a hand. I put a foot onto the grilled foothold and push up into the tractor. In his Wranglers, a faded blue work shirt, and brown cowboy hat, he is so damn fine. Even in his worn-out, old clothes, this man is god's gift to women.

When I'm securely inside, he closes the door behind me and pats his thigh. "Have a seat."

In my new cowgirl boots, I spin and drop onto his lap. A huffy laugh rattles through his chest. The white sundress I wore seems silly now. But with no underwear on, I plan on making the most of our time alone in the middle of the gorgeous Montana countryside.

Reed's arms wrap around my waist, resting one hand on a lever and the other on the wheel. He slides the lever forward and the already loud tractor roars. I swear a moan rumbles from Reed behind me. This man really loves his machines. The giant wheels behind us turn slow as we roll out of the barn and into the morning sunshine.

"Hold the wheel for me, babes. I got to check the PTO."

"Oh, okay."

The tractor all but stops as he flicks a toggle switch, and the long shaft swinging behind the tractor rumbles to life, turning on its axis. He lets it run a minute and then flicks it off. When the metal spiral stills, his hand covers mine, and he pushes the lever forward again. We chug along to the first gate.

"This is the part where you earn your ride. Grab the gate, baby."

So a dress was not the right thing to wear, at all. I climb down and open the wide gate, and he drives through. The red tractor passes, still way too huge, still making me feel like the smallest thing on the planet. When it stops at an idle, I shut the gate and climb back up, returning to his lap.

"You're a natural gate maid, Rubes."

"For that, I'm going to grind on you until you can't see straight, Reed Rawlins."

He tosses his head back with a hearty laugh. "Go on, give me what you got. If you're lucky, I can find a bumpy road for you while you sit on my lap."

I turn and kiss his mouth. "Don't tempt me."

He nips my ear, and we roll forward again. Ten minutes later, we come to a fence line that looks like it has seen better days. Guess Harry was right about this one.

"We have to sink a hole for every post along this old line. Should take about an hour, and then we can go for a wander." Reed points to the ragged length of weathered posts and sagging wires.

The gorgeous face I have become so used to looking at, to seeing lit up with mirth, is currently frozen with stony concentration. The spiral digger sinks into the ground like a toothpick into marshmallow.

Reed watches every second of its descent into the brown earth as dirt is flung out all around it. When it slows with a shudder that reverberates through the entire machine, he curses under his breath, easing back on the lever that controls the spinning digger's speed and ferocity.

Fascinated, I stare at the heavy implement as it groans through another slow turn until it reaches the hilt of its shaft. A moment later, Reed snaps the lever back and the digger comes up, every spiral skirting covered in dirt and rock. He reverses the motion, snapping it to one side, and the dirt falls to the ground like rain, leaving the spiral as clean as it was before we started.

I huff an amazed laugh and he pecks a kiss to my cheek. "You want a go, beautiful?"

"Um, I have no clue how to work that thing. And we still need to get around to find those spots."

"Aye, aye."

With a half salute, he turns and steers the tractor to the next withering fence post in desperate need of retirement. It takes another hour and a half to dig out the rest of Harry's post holes. And as much as I love sitting on Reed's lap, I'm one hundred percent I'm in the way, so I take up a spot on something I'm sure he called a rumble seat. It's captivating, watching him work. In his element.

The way he operates the enormous machine like it's an extension of himself is impressive. He really has a way with the machines. Trucks, tractors, and the like. My phone, in the lone pocket of my dress, vibrates. A text from Mary-Sue.

Howdy, Ruby, I had a thought about our next event. When is a good time to call?

Shit. I can't call her with the tractor humming in the background. Not exactly a New York City sound.

"Reed, I need out."

He spins and glances at me from the PTO controls. "Yeah sure, let me turn this off first."

When the tractor fades to a gentle purr, he pushes the cab door open and lets me out. I jump onto the grass and step away from the machine. Putting distance between the farm noises and me, I tap the screen, dialing Mary-Sue back.

"Ruby! Thanks for callin' me back, hon. Can we video chat? I want to run through some options for decor I found for the event."

"Oh, I don't think that will work, I'm in traffic at the moment."

A cow bellows in the field over.

Shit.

"What was that?" Mary-Sue says.

"Oh nothing, some random making animal noises on the subway. You know how it is." I feign a laugh, but my insides are twisting like the old wire hanging from Reed's decrepit fence line.

"I thought you were driving?"

"Ah, foot traffic, sorry, you know how it is in the rush."

Ugh. My lies don't even add up.

I am so out of my depth.

Ruby on my lap on this rough dirt road is a special type of torture. She's quiet. And I don't know if it's the string of hard-ons I've had since we left the fence line or something else. But I would do just about anything to see happiness light up her face, so I wheel the Case into the paddock by one of the streams on the ranch.

It's almost as good as the one at Harry's. But at this one, it's only us.

So it's fucking perfect.

I park by a bunch of trees and let the tractor idle for a minute before shutting her down and pushing the door open. I love my machines, but after hours on end of being cooped up in the cab, even I want out. Ruby jumps down, heading for the stream. She pulls out her phone, taking photos then sliding it into her dress somehow.

I walk up beside her and wrap an arm around her shoulders. "What about this spot?"

She glances up at me, resting her head on my shoulder with a sigh. "It's beautiful."

"You wanna go for a swim?" I ask.

She straightens up and wanders away into the trees without a word. Pacing through the trees, she runs her hands through her hair. Something's not right. She's strung out.

Shit.

I follow her, leaning on rough bark a few feet from where she is walking a tight circle.

"Rubes, baby. What is it?"

A lump the size of a boulder forms in my throat when her worried brown eyes finally land on me.

"I can't do this . . ."

I push off the hardwood, air straight-up sucked from my lungs before the next heartbeat can flop. "What are you talking about?"

"This fake marriage, lying to people. It's not who I am. I can't do it. God." She moans through a strangled laugh. "I can't even manage one decent lie. I'm going to lose my job, Reed."

Her face is twisted with a fear so desperate it cracks my heart. As if her career is the only thing she has in life worth holding on to. Fucking unacceptable.

I close the distance and wrap her into a hug. "You're not losing your job, Rubes. You are brilliant at it. And those fuckers are lucky to have you. You can do this. We can do this. Even if it means we have to . . ."

"Means what?" Her eyes search my face for the meaning of the stupidest, most right thing I have ever thought.

"Even if we really gotta get married, baby."

She steps out of my hold. "Reed."

"Sorry, that was—"

"No, it was generous and kind, and so *you*. But I can't let you do that purely so I get what I want. Besides, it's a permanent solution for a temporary problem."

I can't speak.

Not a single word is able to edge its way out as Ruby wanders back toward the stream. I follow, but I sink to the ground by the nearest tree, leaning back. She pulls off her shoes and tiptoes through the waterline, skirt bunched up in her hands. Her wavy hair dances over her shoulders. She kicks up the water and it sprays my face.

"Hey!" I spring to my feet, tossing my hat off, tugging my boots off one by one. It takes all of three strides before I sweep her off her feet and into my arms. Launching us from the muddy edge, I cannonball into the water. She squeals as we hit the deep stream with a *thwack*.

And my heart all but stops.

We sink into the blue-grey depth, her dress billowing around her, my shirt making the perfect blue button-lined balloon before the air escapes, and we slow under the surface. Ruby's hands trace the line of my jaw. Her brown eyes locked on mine, her lips part, bubbles racing to the surface. I stay still as her fingers explore my face here beneath the water, where the world can't find us.

When she dots a kiss to my cheek and pushes upward, swimming her way up, I stare at the blank watery space where she was until my lungs burn. Water churns above me as she makes for the water's edge. The fire that lances through my tight lungs is nothing compared to the weight crushing my chest right now.

The homestead comes into view as the tractor bounces along the narrow dirt road. Ruby is on my lap. But this time, her shoulders rise and fall with a depth I've not seen from her before. And it may be the blood thundering through my veins right now, or the fact that I've been hard since we left the stream, but this cab is alive with electricity.

When I let Red roll into the barn and reduce the throttle to an idle, Ruby's palm presses over my knuckles. The sensation sends heat through my core. I pull the hat from my head and toss it to the small side seat. Her breath hitches. And I drop my forehead to her back.

"You would do that for me?" she whispers.

Ah, the stupid marriage idea. The real version, that is, not the fake one we are currently sporting.

"In a heartbeat, beautiful."

She stands and turns. I reach for the ignition. But she catches my hand, lacing our fingers. "Leave it on."

When I meet her gaze, it's pure fire. Her breaths are so ragged, her face is flushed, her hair disheveling as she runs a hand through it,

"Rubes . . ."

"No one has ever wanted to do things for me, Reed. Not even the smallest thing. And then you came along. You have changed the entire way I think about family. Lou and your brothers helped, too. Even Harry."

"Ma sure likes havin' you around."

She straddles my lap, lifting her dress, as the hat on her head is plucked off and dropped to the floor. "We really don't have to talk about your ma right now."

"No, we don't. But, Ruby—"

Her mouth is on mine and her hands crawl through my hair. The raging fire in my core that has been steady for the last half an hour flares to life, sending me impossibly harder.

Ruby moans but pulls back. "So we are clear, I am *not* marrying you, Reed Rawlins. I would never do that to you, you deserve so much better than some arrangement of convenience."

"Sure thing, baby," I rasp.

The sucker punch that my gut took with her words

rolls away, and I tuck the disappointment and grief away somewhere small and inaccessible, forcing my mind to focus on her movements.

The rational part of my mind knows she is talking about a fake marriage for her job's sake. But the part of me that adores her with every inch of my soul may never recover.

"God, I am so wet. How do you do that to me?" she utters, leaning her head back with a grind of her hips. My hands snap to her waist, tight.

"Goddamn, baby. Don't do that."

She circles her hips despite my hold. "What? This?"

I growl at her, and she giggles. But I nip at her dress, over her nipple that is now a hard peak. I would rip that pretty thing off her body and eat her alive if she gave me half a chance.

"Please, Reed." She stops moving, hands cupping my face.

I reach under her dress, fingers trailing down the inside of her thighs. Kissing me, she parts her lips. I sweep inside, desperate for her, always. But the kiss is brief. When she breaks away, her legs widen as my fingers trace up her soft skin and into her pant—nope, no panties. *Sweet Jesus, Ruby Jane.*

"So fucking wet, beautiful."

"You do that to me." Her hand slides downward, over my stomach, before finding the hard ridge in my Wranglers. The cab windows are completely fogged up, and we can't see a thing outside. Too bad if Harry's waitin' around. I chuckle at the thought.

"What's funny?"

"Just thinking of Harry having to wait for us." A cheeky smile pulls up on her lips and she tugs her dress down over her bare breasts. No bra. How the hell did I miss that, too?

"Making Harry wait make you hotter, baby?" I ask.

"A little."

I swirl my tongue around her nipple before pulling it into my mouth, sucking hard. She arches into me with a whimper. I slide two fingers through her wet heat. Sweet Jesus, she feels so good. What I wouldn't give to be buried deep in this woman right now.

Ruby Robbins, the only girl I've ever wanted with my heart and soul. And the one I can't fucking have.

That almost wrenches my heart from my chest.

She is doing so much for me and I—

What if I can't make this resort ranch thing work?

Hell . . .

I move my hands to her hips as the inkling of prickling heat crawls through my veins and my breaths shallow out. I tense up on the seat, my grip on her hips too tight. She gasps.

I try to breathe past the stone in my throat with each burning, shallow breath. My fingers tingle.

No, fuck.

Heartbreak cracks me right in two, stealing the last of the air in my lungs.

I gasp for breath.

"No, no, no, no . . ." Ruby whispers frantically, hands on my face. Her face blurs, right in front of me. "Reed, breathe."

The door to the cab swings open, her foot propping it wider. Cool air floods in. Ruby's thumbs run over my cheeks, palms pressed into my jaw. "You're okay. You're okay, please. Breathe, you have to—" Her head hangs. "Please be okay."

Sobs tumble into my now shallowly rising shoulders as she moves a little, hands gripping my shirt. The sound of her in tears is a slap to the face. I straighten, angry at myself for making her upset. For causing her anything but happiness.

"Ruby," I rasp. "Baby, I'm alright." I fight with the tightened muscles in my torso, forcing air into my lungs. She chugs a sob, and the last of my reserve splinters. Tears burning the back of my eyes, I hunt for her face through her hair with both hands, desperate to find her brown eyes.

"Beautiful, look at me, please." When she finally pushes up, and I snag her gaze, her face is broken. "I'm sorry, Rubes."

She shakes her head. "No." Her hands tremble as she wipes away moisture from my cheeks. Shit, I didn't realize it was there. I swallow hard, and she kisses my lips, tender and loving like the beginning of something else entirely.

"How can I ever leave you here? What kind of friend does that?" she sobs.

"You have to, baby. You have a life to lead."

She stares at me, flattening the wobble that threatens to steal her composure, before standing and picking up her hat. When she's safely down the tractor and out of the barn, I scrub my hands down my face.

Life is utter bullshit.

Ruby dances around the kitchen, prepping a tray of food for us to eat by the fire in the backyard. It's something else, the way she fits here. Her music is loud and fast, white headphones sitting over her head as she munches on a celery stick.

I am so not eatin' that.

I draw the line at carrots.

I take the plate of meats to cook on the grill out back and pad through the back door. The backyard is small, but intimate. A fire pit sits in the center with four white Adirondack chairs bordering it. Ruby found some old-fashioned lanterns in town and has them lit up and dotted about the garden along with copious amounts of fairy lights. It's amazing. And so Ruby.

An hour later, the meat hisses on the heat and the smoke billows into the cool night air. Addy and Huddo are coming over. It's been an age since we saw them. And things have been so busy with the ranch and planning the holiday experience aspects, time got away from us.

The back door snaps open, and I find Ruby leaning on the doorframe, tray in one hand, a glass of wine in the other. She's dressed up a little now. Tight, dark jeans and a boatneck top that looks like it was made for wearin' on a fancy yacht in international waters, not middle-of-nowhere Montana. Her face is done up with a touch of makeup. Her hair ironed, I think that's what they call it. It's dead straight, anyhow.

"Hungry?" She shoves the food under my nose as chatter comes from inside the house.

"Can I eat you instead?" I ask, looking from the tray up to her.

"Save it 'til we're gone, Reed," Huddo quips, striding through the open door, a bottle of whiskey in one hand, rolled up papers in the other.

Fuck.

Ruby strangles a smile, scoffing back a laugh. I snatch the roll from Huddo's hand. "What you got, bro?"

"Your cabin designs."

"Oh wow!" Ruby pushes off the door and comes to stand beside me. I put the tongs down and roll the papers out, holding them up. The blueprints for the one-bedroom accommodations are lit up by the fairy lights.

"Geez, Huddo. This is great," I utter as Ruby takes the plans and moves closer to the firelight.

"Should be straightforward to build. And with the four of us, we can have two or three up in a month."

"Four?"

"Yeah, Harry's pitchin' in."

Addy walks through the door, her happy smile landing on my puzzled expression. "He told you, then. Hey, Reed."

"Hey, Adds." I lean over to give her a tight hug.

"You better be taking care of my girl well, Reedsy," Adds whispers.

"Who, Mira?" I quip. She slaps my shoulder, glancing at Ruby, who is now standing by Hudson, running a finger over the plans.

When I track Addy's gaze, she's looking at my big brother like he's the last man on earth. What I wouldn't give to have Ruby stare at me that way. I wrap an arm around her. "He gets more Harry every time I look at him."

She laughs and pecks my cheek. "You'll keep. But I'm serious, Reed, about Ruby."

Now, I let my arm fall and turn to face her. "Me too."

She smiles before messing up my hair with her hand. Always the little brother to this lot. Guess it could be worse . . . I could have Ruby's trash bag family.

"Reed?"

I snap my attention to the pretty brown eyes I know so well, now topped with furrowed brows.

"Yeah?"

"Hudson wants to know what you think." Ruby beckons me over with a finger. I'm by her side a heartbeat later.

"Do you want them all identical or different? Floor plan wise, that is."

"Whatever you think is the most cost effective. I want to make more changes, so sticking to the budget is a must."

"Who the hell invited Harry to this party?" Addy snorts, almost losing the white wine she just sipped.

"Ha, ha. I don't wanna screw this up, Adds." I let my eyes slide to Ruby. ". . . It's too important."

"Yeah, well. I'm proud of you, little bro, taking the helm, so to speak. Going against Harry is never easy, but you two seem to have pulled it off, and unscathed, too. You'll have to tell me your secret," Huddo says with a half smile.

"You do just fine with Pa, Hudson Rawlins, now sit down and have a drink before this night goes from fun to all business." Addy ushers him into his seat the same way Ma would to the old man.

Uncanny, really. But it's sweet, and I'm happy for them. They both deserve something amazing and all-encompassing.

Ruby is still poring over the blueprints as she sips her red wine, sunk into a chair by the fire. And for the first time in my miserable existence, I wish time would slow down. Because her leavin' when this holiday ranch is a roaring success and her events are all lined up and she can phone it in, that's gonna leave a gaping hole.

Not even Harry's approval or Ma's cooking could fill that.

Chapter Eighteen

The ground sways. I grip the pommel tight. Reed's grin lights up his face. If it wasn't for the man on the horse beside me, I would have slid out of the saddle and hiked my way back to the house.

"You wanna pick it up to a lope?" Reed asks.

I stare at the grassy field between Mira's ears, sucking in a deep and steady breath. I'm not scared of horses, per se, more like of falling off them. After seeing everything Addy went through.

"Ah, okay?"

Reed shortens his reins, and I do the same, only half remembering how to do this horse-riding thing. He clucks his tongue, and Magnet bursts into a lope. His shirt billows at his back as he gets farther from Mira and me.

Shit.

I give her a squeeze with my legs, and she takes off after Magnet. I hold on to the pommel with one hand, the reins with the other. And soon her rocking gait has my tensed muscles melting into the saddle. Wind whips through my hair and the hat flies off my head and into the grass. Ah, I'll grab it on the way back.

Reed slows Magnet a little and we catch up. "You're doin' amazin', baby."

I roll my eyes at him, and he tosses his head back with a laugh. The hat on his head teeters, and he shoves it back down with a hand. We lope toward the field we are hoping we will be a guest camping spot.

With two riding trails mapped out, we need one more private area, and we have our locations pinned down. All that's left is the cabins, to convert the larger barn to a usable space for events, and to get the marketing up and running. A three-month pre-launch period for that should be enough.

Fingers crossed.

No, no hoping and praying.

All hard work and planning.

Rule number three.

We have been working our asses off to pull this off on time and under budget. But I must admit, this is the most fun I have ever had on a planning project.

"Rubes?" Reed lopes beside me, eyes studying my face.

"Sorry, was thinking about the to-do list."

"Nope, no work stuff this afternoon. Only two friends, riding and feeling the wind in their hair."

"We're scouting out locations, Reed. This *is* work." But I can't help the grin that splits my face. And the adoration and happiness that fill his face as he watches me ride sends a hurricane of butterflies up from my stomach.

"Come on, baby. Let's take this up a notch." He leans forward, and Magnet flattens his ears, bolting forward.

Fuck.

I reaffirm my grip on the pommel and squeeze Mira into a gallop. Her hooves thunder under my seat. I can understand why this could be addictive. Why Addy missed it so much. The power underneath me, moving along as fast as the wind, tunnels through my body. I rasp out a laugh.

Reed disappears behind a group of trees before reappearing out the other side and up the flank of the mountain. I push Mira in that direction, and she forges ahead. When we slow and round the copse, her strides change, every muscle pulled tight as she puts her head down and lopes up the incline after the gelding. Like these two are playing the same game Reed and I are. Only she gets to stay.

Lucky girl.

Clearing the rise, we spill up and over an edge to a plateau where Magnet and Reed stand, looking out over the ranch. I ease the mare to a walk and close in on the boys. Chuckling at the thought of the horses in a long-term relationship, I dismount on legs of jelly and wobble my way to where Reed stands.

"Perfect spot," I say, breathless, running my fingers through my wind-knotted hair.

He turns back and tucks a strand behind my ear. "Yeah, sure is." The words are all gravel.

I drag my focus back to the view of the ranch. "What are you going to call it?"

"What?"

"You need a name for your holiday ranch. It will be a huge part of the brand."

"Oh yeah, I thought about that."

"You did?"

"R & R Ranch. Fits the purpose and the founders."

Heat rises through my neck and face as he turns back to me. If he's talking about me—

"Rawlins & Rawlins," he says with a smile that doesn't meet his eyes.

My mouth opens, and I huff a breath before biting my lip. For a second, I thought R & R stood for Reed and Ruby. But that's not it . . . and the pang of that stifling thought sends my gut into knots. Reminding me I'm a passerby. Transient help. No matter how much going back to the city feels like something that shouldn't be an option anymore.

"I love it. It's like you said, fits the purpose. Very on-brand."

But even I can hear the disappointment in every syllable. Reed doesn't meet my gaze. Instead, he walks the perimeter of the plateau, looking around and muttering to himself. He's good at this. Taking care of people. Thinking of all the details. This life is going to suit him. Much better than the one Harry had pegged for him.

Mira nickers and nudges my shoulder with her muzzle. I turn back and rub her cheek, dropping my forehead to her long face. "You have no idea how lucky you are, sweet girl."

As if on cue, Magnet sighs, shifting to rest one back foot, a hoof tipped up. Like an old married couple. I snort a laugh into Mira's soft fur and close my eyes. Letting myself imagine, for a handful of seconds, staying here with Reed. Making these rides a regular thing. Building my life here.

"You two need a room?"

Shit.

I snap my head from Mira's face and meet the green eyes lit up with cheek that are homed in on me. "I think Mira's already taken." I nod to Magnet.

"Oh, these two? Just good friends." Reed winks.

"With benefits?"

"No, that's you and me, Rubes." Laughing, he gathers the reins and swings up into the saddle. Magnet is on right away. Ears forward and all four hooves back square on the ground. I am up in the saddle a heartbeat later. This will make an incredible camping spot.

And for the first time in my life, I am envious of people I've never met.

I stare at my phone in disbelief. I have no idea how this woman got my number. But the photo of Reed and her and her friend in Great Falls is anything but innocent. And she's Mary-Sue's fucking waitress. More importantly, this is evidence to my lies.

Fear snakes through my body and sinks like a stone in my gut.

"Rubes? Where you at?" Reed's voice calls up the stairs. I can't get my grip around the phone to loosen. The only thing I can do is force air into my lungs, one shallow, useless breath at a time.

"Baby?"

He's standing in the doorway. Crossing the floor, he's on his knees in front of me, his eyes level with mine. "Rubes? What's wrong?"

What's wrong?

Right now, I can't decide if I'm upset about losing the inn's account or about the two women sitting on Reed's lap in this sordid, questionable photo. With nothing to say, I turn the phone around. His eyes drop to it straight away. His face falls.

"Beautiful, that was ages ago. Before I met you."

I know that.

"That's not the problem." I point to Starr, Mary-Sue's waitress. "*She* is the problem."

It takes him a moment, but his mouth gapes when he realizes who she is.

"Ah, fuck. I'm sorry, Rubes. I don't even remember them taking a photo. Someone else must have."

"I haven't replied yet. I'm not accustomed to being blackmailed. And I'm guessing that if I don't pay up, she is going to talk to Mary-Sue."

"What the fuck?" He pushes to his feet, running a hand through his hair.

I drop the phone on the bed and walk from the room. Padding down the stairs, I sigh, rubbing a hand over my face. How could I be so stupid? Lying never works. I'm not good at it. This was the stupidest thing I've ever done.

I wander to the porch and sink into the swing seat. The breeze is cool tonight, and I wrap the tartan blanket around my shoulders, tucking my feet under myself. I need to figure out a way to make this go away, or at least a reasonable explanation that doesn't end with my fake marriage being blown.

Being taken off the inn's account means no more trips to Montana. No more visits to R & R Ranch. No more Reed. And, worst-case scenario, I lose my job for unprofessional conduct. The job I have spent the last ten years working my tail off at to build up my career. My reputation.

This couldn't be any worse.

The floor creaks by the door, and I turn toward the front door. Reed stands in the doorway, hands gripping the frame above his head. The t-shirt he's wearing slides up a little. His green eyes are narrowed with worry. With a sigh, I close my eyes and dip my head. Everything is too much. I'm tired.

And for the first time in my life, the things I am supposed to want—the career, the status, and the money—are at war with the things I need. The seat sways and dips. I open my eyes, and Reed is sitting beside me. Arms open, inviting me into his space, he tilts his head with a sad smile. "Come here."

I slide closer and lean into his embrace. His arms wrap around me, his warmth cocooning me with something so grounding and absolutely necessary, I almost forget the last ten minutes. He rests his chin on my head. His heart-beat drums into my cheek.

"I could say we met in the city, and it was love at first sight and we went to the chapel the next day?" he offers, his voice raspy.

I huff a laugh. "Who falls in love with someone the first time they see them?"

"I have."

I push out of his hold and study his face. "Really?"

I don't know if I'm surprised that he has been in love before or gutted that it wasn't me.

"Yeah, really." His eyes are fixed on mine, his breaths leaving with every plummeting wave of his chest. She must have broken his heart by the way he is reacting while talking about this.

I hate her already.

I run my thumb over his jaw, and it flexes at my touch. "Her loss, baby."

A small, crooked smile hangs on the corner of his mouth. "Maybe."

"Reed, promise me something. When I go back—"

"Anything you want, Rubes."

"If—I mean, when you find someone again. Make sure they know who you *really* are. That they love you for you. Promise me that."

I think he's stopped breathing.

"Reed?"

He swallows and gives me a shallow nod.

"Good," I whisper, resting my palm over his heart. "You deserve the woman who makes you feel it's okay to be yourself. Don't hide this."

His mouth opens, his eyes crinkled with emotion, and he slams it shut again.

I dot a kiss to his cheek and rise from the seat. "I'll fix the Starr problem. You concentrate on building your ranch."

After all, the Robbins family has had their fair share of gold diggers before this. I know how to handle it. We have a lawyer on speed dial from the last time some ingrate tried to screw us over. Starr is about to take a plummet from the heavens and into the earth's scorching fucking atmosphere.

After sending through a rough explanation to the lawyer along with forwarding the text and photo to him, I step into the bathroom and peel off the day's clothes as if peeling away the scandal of the last hour. When steam fills the room, I slip into the hot water, letting it scald the stress and annoyance over this whole fake marriage debacle from my bones.

It would be a lot easier if I was married to Reed. Less chance of being sacked and losing my career. But I wouldn't do that to him. It's not fair. Plus, who knows, one day I might meet some Wall Street banker who sweeps me off my feet.

I still as horror creeps through my veins at the thought of someone other than Reed "sweeping me off my feet." And when the realization hits, I slide down the tiles and slump onto the shower floor.

Fuck.

I try it on for size again, to be sure.

I imagine getting home from a long day in the city office to find my corporate king husband chopping up veggies on the wooden board. His back is to me as I say hello, his hair disheveled as he runs a hand through it, the veins in his forearm popping.

I swallow.

Heat pools in my belly as the water swirls around my ass on the shower floor, sending my toes tingling with its delicious heat . . . Wait, maybe that's my husband having that effect on me? Maybe I can do this? Fall in love and be happy with some city guy.

I slap a hand over my mouth with a gasp.

Rule number one.

Obliterated.

I close my eyes, homing in on my fictional husband in our imaginary east side apartment. I dump my bag on the sofa table and pad to where he stands. And when I slide my arms around his waist and bury my face in his back, he smells so familiar. His body so well traced. I know every inch of this man who is mine.

He spins in my hold, dropping the knife to the counter. And when his rough hands cup my face and his mouth dips to my own, his green eyes and dark blond hair steal my breath.

Oh god.

I can't even come up with an imaginary future guy who isn't my current fake husband.

Ruby Robbins, you are so fucked.

And . . . so worked up.

I slide a hand over my breast, rolling the nipple. The other drops to my center, slick with need for the man who inserted himself into my made-up scenario. The same man who is downstairs, that my heart has latched on to like he's the fucking air I breathe. I run a circle over my clit and let my head fall back to the tile with a thud. I don't even care.

I moan, imagining Reed's hands on me, his mouth on every place I want him right now. Arching my back, I slide two fingers inside, and I can't help the cry that slips through my lips.

Oh, fuck.

"Rubes? Baby? You alright? I heard a thump." Reed's muffled voice calls from somewhere on the stairs.

Oh shit!

"Ah—I'm, I—"

The bathroom door opens, and a heartbeat later, his eyes dip to where I sit on the floor. Then drop lower again.

Heart thundering, my breath stops.

Zero to one hundred in less than a heartbeat.

That's what Ruby touching herself does to me. And it takes every last ounce of control I fucking have to stay rooted to the spot outside the shower door.

But when she doesn't move, slipping her fingers in further as she holds my gaze, I'm pretty sure I am as close to combustion as humanly possible. I want to taste her. I want to hold her. I want her wrapped around me, riding my now rock-hard cock until we both unravel.

"I can't do it, Reed," she rasps.

I swallow past the stone cutting off my air supply as she pulls her fingers out and pops them in her mouth.

Jesus fuckin' Christ.

"What can't you do, baby?"

I'm a thousand percent positive I've swallowed glass.

"I can't imagine anyone else," she utters.

"Baby, I told you, those girls were before. And it was—"

Her hands fall to the tile by her legs. She's shaking her head . . .

Why is she shaking her head?

"Come here." Ruby rests her head back on the tile. I drop to my knees and crawl into the steaming hot shower where she sits. The water soaks my t-shirt, then my jeans. Drenched and inches from her now vibrating body, I wait. Absolutely wound up. Painfully fucking desperate for her.

Her hands cup my jaw, and she pulls my mouth to hers. But I resist, stopping before our lips touch. "What do you want, Rubes?"

Her face turns pained, like she's holding back a sob. A heartbeat later, she forces a smile, running her hands through my wet hair, those brown eyes burning. "I want you."

Before my brain has a second to analyze the situation, I slam my mouth to hers, moving forward until I'm kneeling between her legs. She peels away from the wall and is wrapped around me a second later. I rest back on my heels, and she straddles my lap. Her kiss is hot, hungry, and blowing my goddamn mind.

We've gotten each other off, but this is different. Like there's something strong and permanent tugging between us, both ways. It was tentative before. Now, it's pulling my heart through the cage that keeps it, seeing her this way. Because after the heat and the desire wears off comes the fall. With anyone else, I wouldn't care.

With Ruby? There would be no coming back.

I must have stilled, because she is leaning back. Water runs over her face, neck, and over her peaked nipples. Drops run over those perfect breasts, cascading onto her stomach.

"Reed?"

Worry lines her eyes. Fuck.

"You don't want to?" she whispers.

She has no idea how much I need her. But that's just it. This is more than some spontaneous thing for me. Has been for a long time. I could almost deny it before, but now?

Having her here has been amazing, but every time I think about the grand opening and what that means for us, knots fill my gut. When R & R Ranch opens, Ruby goes home. And I keep thinkin', if Adds had never come off her horse, her life, Hudson's life . . . they all would have been different. And I never would have met Ruby.

Color me sentimental. Maybe I'm more like Harry than I wanna admit, but fate doesn't screw up, unlike me. And I can't—I won't—find anyone like Ruby again. Those odds don't exist.

Soft, light kisses brush over every angle of my face.

"Wherever you went just now, sweet man, please come back." She searches my face.

I suck in a ragged breath and meet her gaze.

"There you are. What happened?"

"I'm alright," I rasp.

"Caught up in your head again?"

"Kinda, but it's not the anxiety."

In fact, my head is clear. I guide her to her feet and stand. The water rushes over me, matting my hair and running down my shirt, plastering it to my toned torso as I dip my head. Wet hair falls forward, sticking to my forehead.

"You told me it was always okay to stand up for myself. To choose the things I want in my life."

She nods. "I did, and you should."

My jaw feathers. "I can't do this, Rubes."

Her lips part as she sucks in a breath, hurt flooding her eyes. I walk from the shower. The hardest fucking thing I have ever done in my life.

Back in my room, I pull the sodden clothes off my shaking limbs and walk into my own shower. Under my own warm stream of water, I lather soap over my body and let it soak, chest heaving around the ache that bloomed with those five little words.

I can't do this, Rubes.

Arms crossed, hands tucked under my armpits, I hang my head.

I did the right thing.

Ruby gets to keep her rules, her career, and her life.

I keep my heart intact.

Well, almost.

Water patters around my feet, lulling me as I close my eyes.

"What exactly is it that you can't do?"

I snap my head up and my eyes to her. She stands in the doorway, wrapped in a towel, wet hair hanging over her shoulders, hands on her hips. Face stone, her stare is hard. She's all business.

Atta girl.

I hang my hands by my side for a heartbeat. Both of us are naked. But the only fire is that of burning disappointment. For the loss of things I want and can never have.

"This," I finally mutter, waving a hand between her and me.

"Why not, Reed?"

Always direct, my Ruby.

"Because you have your life, and I have mine. And there ain't no way to make the two combine; so before either of us gets hurt, we just stop altogether."

"Do I have a say in this?" She folds her hands across her chest.

"Nope."

"Fine, then you don't get a say in this." She drops her towel and walks into the shower.

"Rubes. Stop."

She stands shy of the water. "I haven't done anything yet."

My traitorous cock is concrete and pointing to the sky.

Looking at her has me breathless. "It's not just foolin' around for me anymore."

"And you think that's what I'm doing? Leading you on, having a bit of fun?"

"Don't think you and fun have ever met, baby."

She scoffs a laugh, glancing outside the shower, but closes the space between us. "For the record, you broke every single one of my rules, Reed Rawlins. And I wouldn't have it any other way."

"So, you changed your mind about a few things, hey?"

"You could say that." Her gaze drops to my mouth, her hands landing on my jawline. "But mostly . . . about you. I don't want to be your friend anymore. It's not enough."

You don't need to tell this man twice.

I slam into her hard, my mouth on hers, gripping her hips and pressing her into the tile. The whimper that leaves her throat drives the last of the sanity from my heated veins.

"Reed, slow down. I don't want to miss anything."

Her mouth is open in a pant. Her back arches off the shower wall. I drop my head, kissing her neck. Her fingers crawl through my hair. When my lips find her hard nipple, her grip tightens. Letting my hands wander, I play with the softness of her other breast with one hand and trail a finger toward her clit with the other.

When I brush my knuckles over her slick center, she moans, sending me harder than ever before. The memory of her walking past me on the street of Great Falls as she bumped into me with her strawberry scent wrapping around me like a snare floods in . . . And now, driving me completely off the rails, she stands bare in my shower, begging me to touch her. That is not lost on me. The enormity of the gift she has given me by being here never will be.

Emotion steals my air like a baddie in an old-time ransom movie. I shake my head and focus. On Ruby. On making her feel all I can give her.

Ruby's eyes flutter shut as I slide two fingers inside her.

"God, baby, you are so damn hot and tight." The warm leak of pre-cum floods over my tip. I'm going to need to pace myself to not screw this up. There is no way in hell I'm not giving this woman everything she wants.

I pull back a little, and she gasps. When my fingers fall from her center, I raise them to my lips. But she grabs my wrist and feeds them to me with a cheeky smile. Fingers clean, I drop to my knees.

"Oh god, Reed, please."

"You don't have to beg, baby. Let me watch you come on my face."

Her legs widen a little as I grip her thighs with my hands. This beautiful woman is so fucking perfect it hurts. I glide my tongue through her wet center, and she writhes against the wall.

Good girl.

Slow, Reed, slow.

With a little nip to her clit, I look up at her and spread her wider. She drops her gaze to mine. "Why did you stop?"

"Making it last, baby."

Breasts moving with every heaving breath, her cheeks are flushed pink. My fucking heart explodes behind my ribs.

"We are going to go so, so slow. And then, when we're done, we are gonna start all over again, beautiful."

"I—" She swallows hard. "Reed, I—"

I thumb a circle over her clit and sweep my tongue through her center again before she has the chance to finish her sentence.

"Oh." Her palms slam to the wall by her sides. Her legs tremble. "Reed . . ."

I pull back, and she growls at me. She literally growls at me. I can't help the grin that splits my face. Sweet Jesus, this woman is something else. "We'll get there. Patience."

"I can barely breathe when you do that to me."

"Baby, I can barely breathe just looking at you." The words are out of my mouth before my brain can snag them back. But Rubes and I don't have secrets. And I guess right now is as good a time as any to wear my heart on my sleeve.

She bends down and takes my head in her hands, guiding my mouth up to hers. Her tongue is in my mouth a second later. I groan at the taste of her. She tastes like she smells, all strawberries and sweet things.

When she pulls back, I grip her hips and hold her to the wall, sinking my face into her center. This time, I'm the one who's desperate. And I lick and flick her clit, sinking my fingers inside her. Needing to feel her, taste her, and bring her to the edge.

My entire body is vibrating, watching her tremble against the tile. Every slight move I make has her writhing, gasps falling out of those delicious lips like candy from an upturned jar.

"Reed," she rasps. Her hips buck from the wall. She's close.

I suckle her clit and curl my fingers inside her, still working them in and out. Still tracing my tongue over every delicious part of her I can. When her hands fly into my hair and her grip turns savage, she bares down on my mouth, riding out her orgasm.

I have to grab the top of my cock to stop from coming with her. This is too much. Ruby coming all over my mouth is too fucking much.

And I need her wrapped around me, now.

Chapter Twenty

RUBY

Soul-splintering ecstasy spirals through my core, flooding my body. I ride each wave, with Reed coaxing every last tiny piece of pleasure through my veins. The man is a literal god.

A moment later, limp against the wall, I try to steady my breath as I stand on wobbly legs. Sex really is a thousand times more intense when you care about the person you're doing it with, and we have only just gotten started.

None of the guys I have been with have ever been a romantic interest. Purely around for the physical. Associates with benefits? Sounds so very clinical. And the thought of it makes my heart hurt. It never worried me back then. But now, it's sad to think I could've had more.

Rules . . .

My rules. The ones I thought I needed to thrive. They were keeping me from the best things in life. Reed clears his throat. Looks like he's not the only one getting caught up in his head tonight. When I drop my gaze, he pushes to his feet and spins around, turning off the water. "We're not doing this in here, baby."

"We're not?"

His arms are around my back and under my butt instantly. Sweeping me off my feet, he carries me to his bed. My heart picks up its pace. The giant rustic king bed that Louisa picked for him as a housewarming gift is comfy. And very Reed.

He sits me on the edge of the bed, and I wiggle back a little. His hands are around my face, his mouth against mine, tongue wanting in. I open for him. Gladly.

He sweeps in, and I taste him. Needing more.

But first . . .

I pull back and grab his wrists. I want that delicious cock of his in my mouth. Looking at it makes me ache. "Tap me if you want out, okay?"

He frowns a little, but his lips pop open with a gasp as I slide him into my mouth. Oh god, he tastes amazing. He's rock hard yet velvety soft. I take him in further.

"Rubes, baby," he growls.

Hell yes. I suck hard and pull my way back up.

"Fuck, Ruby."

But I ignore him and pick up the pace. I want him as close to undone as I can manage. I take him in again, even deeper this time. With a hum, I suck my way back up.

"I—" he rasps.

A little closer . . .

I plunge down until he hits my gag reflex and pull up quick, swirling my tongue over his tip. He shakes against the bed, knees hitting the mattress, fencing me in. "Rubes, enough."

I pull back and lean on the mattress, elbows propping me up, my breasts bounce with the movement. His eyes are the darkest green I have ever seen them. He is feral, and I fucking love it.

"Where do you want me, Reed?"

He groans, closing his eyes as if trying to think of something else and pace himself. He's right, we should make this last. My first time with this gorgeous man is going to be *everything*.

"Definitely not under me," he breathes. "That's not you, beautiful."

He sits at the head of the bed, holding out his arms. "I want to look up at you every time you fall apart." I spin and walk up the bed on my knees until I'm straddling his lap. The way he watches me, the awe and adoration . . . Fuck.

The air rattling up my throat burns.

Reed takes my hips, moving me forward. He leans to the bedside, reaching for the top drawer, but I grab his arm. The veins over his wrist run under my fingertips. "No, we don't need it. I don't want it."

"You sure?"

I nod, breathless.

"Okay, baby, you're drivin'."

I huff a soft chuckle. Always with the vehicle talk. My hair, almost dry again, falls over my shoulders and surrounds his face as I rise up on my knees. He moves his soft, wide tip against my entrance, and my breath hitches. His face is strained as his hands return to my hips, and I suck back a sob. Emotion is commandeering this ship, as it always does when he is around.

His chest plummets as I hover in place. And when I lower a little, he groans, his grip turning so tight on my hips it bites. A few inches lower and my entire world is going to change. Tell that to the heat searing a hole in my heart, the fire lancing through my veins, and the threads of my scattered soul that are weaving back together after decades of not feeling loved.

It takes a moment to rein in my thundering heart and process the feelings now flinging around my heart like rogue javelins. The ones that I have suppressed for years after growing up in a house where affection was considered unnecessary. And love, well, that was something my parents and family never discussed, let alone showed.

I sink onto him and watch as his face wrecks in front of me.

"Ru—"

I snatch his face between my hands and devour his mouth before he can say a word. And when I rise back up, feeling every long, hard inch of him, I whimper against his lips.

Fuck me.

All the way to Sunday, Reed Rawlins.

Oh. My. God.

His hands are in my hair. Lips and a little teeth close over my hard nipple, and I take up a steady rhythm. Back arched and moans cascading from my mouth, heaven will never compare to Reed inside me. "Gorgeous man, you are everything."

"Steady, beautiful. God, you're perfect. Too fast and this ain't gonna last long."

He clamps down on my hips, driving further inside me, and I buck, heat spiraling in my center as lava tracks up my spine, heading toward release.

Never before has anyone sent me over that cliff while inside me. And the feeling working up to it is so intense. Driving me to the brink of no return faster and faster with every long, controlled stroke. I cup his face with my hands and tilt his head up. When I take in those gorgeous green eyes, the words I want to say to him solidify, squashed down by the rock that wedges its way into my airways. But my face must be etched with a thousand phrases, because he says, "I know, Rubes."

I slap a hand over my mouth to hide the stupid fucking emotion that is bubbling up through my insides.

"Hey, you're okay. I will always take care of you, baby. It's my privilege."

I suck in a handful of breaths and recover, not wanting

to cry during our first time. "Where did you come from?" I whisper, running a hand through his hair.

"Sometimes God gets it right, beautiful."

I huff a strangled laugh and bend down. "You're not supposed to be thinking about God right now."

A laugh rumbles through him, and he sweeps his arms underneath me, flipping us over. But he pulls out and I'm on my stomach a heartbeat later. Rough hands pull my hips up, and he sinks into me again. So much deeper, the fit tighter. I slam my hands onto the rustic headboard.

"Damn, Ruby, I can barely control myself," he pants.

"Then don't."

"Jesus, baby."

I widen my knees and push back with every stroke. The stretch is incredible. And I plummet toward sweet agony faster than before. And when Reed grabs my hair and leans over, dotting kisses down my spine, gooseflesh ignites along my spine, sending me over the edge.

"Reed! Oh, don't stop. Plea—"

The words accelerate into a cry as I contract around him, wave after wave, and he meets me there, with long, fast strokes that make my mouth water and my heart fling against my breastbone, like a captured bird.

When I catch my breath and the last wave is wrung from my body, I grind back into him. Still, even after that soul-shattering orgasm, I am desperate for him. I push off the headboard, rising up on my knees until my sweaty back meets his chest.

"Baby, you're ruining this man for anyone else."

I slide my hand up and behind his neck and drag his mouth down, kissing his lips. "Good."

"Want some more, baby?"

"Yes," I rasp, resting my head back on his shoulder.

He thunders into me. Each harsh thrust comes with his thumb circling my clit.

Again, I explode around him.

This time, he groans. His body starts to shake, and his hand slips from my center. "We need to move, baby."

I don't argue, and he's off the bed and waiting with his arms outstretched for me when I walk on my knees to the edge. Scooping me onto his hips, he pads to the wall. My back meets the wood, and he adjusts his hold on me and thrusts inside. Oh, wow . . .

Holy shit.

"I like this." I grip his shoulders, nails biting into his skin. All I want to do is arch into him, but I don't want to hit the floor, so I tilt my hips, taking him deeper.

He smiles under hooded eyes and slams a hand onto the wall above my head, thrusting harder. Reed tenses, and his body starts to shake again. God, I want him to unravel. Just like he said. What I wouldn't give to have him do that while I'm wrapped around him.

"Reed." I take his face in my hands. "Look at you."

I kiss his mouth, his jaw, and trail nips down his neck. When he groans, I meet his gaze.

"You are my whole heart, Ruby Jane Robbins."

The words hit hard.

I've never been anyone's first priority, let alone someone's everything. The words tangle around my heart with a squeeze. And . . . like that, I can't breathe. I want Reed to take it all. All I have.

A growl rumbles from his lips as his movements turn erratic.

He's close.

So am I, again.

I close my eyes and let my head fall to one side. Warm lips tease my nipple, and I explode around Reed. Letting go of his shoulders, I open my eyes with a whimper. Hands through his hair, I tighten my grip as my heart and soul shatter for him.

"Beautiful, god," he rasps, slamming into me hard. He spills into me in hot waves. Giving me everything he has.

Trembling all over, I fold around him as he buries his head in my shoulder and peels me from the wall. He's moving, but I don't know where to. Wrung out and thoroughly satiated, I breathe him in, my forehead on his temple, our air mingling as he lowers us. When I open my eyes, we are on the bed, his back to the headboard like before.

I kiss his mouth, but it's not hungry—not anymore. It's more than that; it's adoration and contentment, swaddled into a feeling I can't really explain.

His arms are still tight around my waist as he hugs me close. "I don't want to let you go, Ruby."

The words are soft, too quiet, almost like a well-kept secret I'm not supposed to hear. I pull back a little and search his face. His green eyes are creased with emotion. He traces his fingers over my cheekbones and down to my jaw. Each breath as heavy as the last, he's still as worked up as he was moments ago.

"Please don't," I whisper.

Something painful flashes across his face, and he schools it back before he folds me into his embrace. Exhausted, I nuzzle into his neck, happy to stay put for a while and be held. Be wanted.

The slow pull of sleep creeps up on me, and my lids droop. When a small sigh slips from my lips, he moves. A heartbeat later, I'm lying on the bed on my side. His warmth has all but disappeared, and I glimpse over my shoulder. "Reed?"

"It's okay, beautiful. Not lettin' go, I promise."

He slides in behind me and pulls my weary body against his, arms folding me into him, his chin on my head. The thump of his heartbeat taps against my back. Like a comfort. I lace my fingers through his and let sleep drag me down.

Time, if you don't mind, you can stand still now.

Chapter Twenty-One

REED

Magnet trots along the newly cut dirt track at a steady pace as I rise and fall in the saddle. The sun is hanging halfway up the blue sky, cooler air rolling in. I push the gelding into a lope, wanting to be home already. Rubes went into town to grab some groceries and run errands while I mark out the last of the trail for guests.

Nobody drives my truck, not even my brothers, but Ruby? She gets everything she needs. Even my damn F-250. Because she fucking deserves it. Sacrifices are made. That sweet ride used to be my greatest love. Now?

I shake my head to dislodge the thought.

Trying my hardest to not let it sink in.

I just can't.

The cabins are coming along well. Huddo has done an awesome fucking job. Mack, too. Even Harry has been here from dawn 'til dusk, working on the builds. Ruby has ordered a bunch of furniture and soft furnishings for each one. They're going to be nice when they're finished. Which, if all goes to plan, will be the week after the roundup. So, in two weeks' time, this is going to be very real.

But there is still a ways to go. We have to complete the finishing touches on the cabins, the barn, and have the trails all marked out by next week. The last one I can safely say can be checked off the list.

Ruby has already started the marketing. With the grand opening being on Thanksgiving weekend, families can do dinner here or come and stay. I would be lying if I said I'm not nervous about this. Is anyone going to want to spend their holiday out here?

We have to pull off the roundup before the R & R's debut, and Huddo has us all on the roster for that, as we are every year. Addy is riding along again. But Ruby is going back to the city for the fortnight after she sees Magnet and me off to catch up in the office, since I will be stuck up the mountains somewhere.

Sweet Jesus, that'll be the longest two weeks of my entire fucking life, I swear. The truck is still gone when I lope up to the barn. I swing down from the saddle and walk the gelding to the wash down bay. When he's cooled off and clean, I let him out into his field and put the tack away.

Tires on gravel fade in, and I can't help the smile that tugs up on my lips.

Ruby's home.

Two words.

One big emotion that goes with them.

I pluck my hat from my head and run a hand through my hair as I walk from the tack room and out of the barn. She jumps out of the driver's side of my truck, all dressed in her designer jeans and her favorite boatneck top. Her heels are black and shiny. Her hair is curled and bouncing over her shoulders as she pulls bags from the back seat of the dual cab.

"You're home early, baby," I rasp into her ear as I wrap myself around her from behind. She drops the bags and spins in my hold.

"No point wasting time. There's so much to do before I leave."

"Ugh, Rubes. Way to spoil the moment with all this leavin' talk."

I sink my head onto her chest. The soft chuckle that slips through her lips sends me hard fucking instantly.

"Your brothers around today?"

"Nope, no way. Told them to stay away. Plus, I'll be stuck with Mack and Huddo for a week straight. Gotta pace myself, you know."

Now she laughs. "I like your brothers. They're sweet, even Hudson."

"Do not tell Huddo that. He likes being a chip off the old block, I swear."

"Promise. Anyway, help me bring this stuff in, will you? Then we can go over the remaining details for the opening night dinner, okay?"

"Sure thing, beautiful."

But the last thing I wanna do right now is stare at a screen. Not when I can be lovin' on the only woman in the world my heart has ever needed. I take the bags from her hands and follow her inside. The sway of her hips, her ass in those tight jeans, produces a groan. Which I promptly tamper down.

Ruby wants her jobs done before she leaves. I get that. I do. We have been nothing but hustling since this idea of the holiday ranch was set in motion. It's so incredible to finally have a direction that I am excited about.

An hour later, we are staring at the computer screen. My mouth hangs open, and Ruby is doing some sort of squealing dance around the kitchen table. The opening weekend over Thanksgiving is sold out. Every cabin is booked. All the tables for the evening dinner-slash-soiree event are full. And there is a *waitlist*!

This woman is a fucking genius. Ruby Robbins is too good at her job. The sinking feeling that this is very real tightens between my lungs. I force myself to look at Rubes, her happy face lit up with emotion and excitement. We can do this. I can do this.

I will not let her down.

Period.

Ruby lands in my lap, hands on my face, kissing me briefly. "Wanna celebrate?"

"I thought we were too busy?" I growl, feigning a stern face. She tips her head back, laughing.

"We are, but this is definitely worth losing a few minutes for."

"A few minutes? Ruby Robbins, it is going to take much, much longer than that."

She giggles as I push to my feet and lift her onto my waist. Her quick, elegant fingers make short work of the buttons on my old shirt, and it hits the floor. "Where do you want to celebrate, Reedsy?"

She hasn't called me that in a while. It has unrequited vibes tangled between the two syllables. "Outside in the sunshine. I want your cheeks flushed, baby."

"I'm pretty sure you do that to me anyway, gorgeous man."

Something warm and all-consuming floods my veins with her words.

"Why don't we try out that camping spot by the spring?" she whispers in my ear, sending gooseflesh down my spine.

"Abso-fucking-lutely."

When I reach the truck, I open the passenger door and release her to the soft leather seat. But her brows scrunch as she meets my gaze.

"You don't take your truck out into the fields?"

"What can I say? You broke all my rules, Ruby Robbins." I wink at her as the words she used for me take full circle and realization spreads across her beautiful face.

"Wait here a sec. I need to grab some things," I say.

She nods, sliding her phone from her back pocket and tapping the screen. Always workin'.

Ducking into the house, I pull a cooler bag from the pantry and load it up with anything that looks like it could contribute to lunch and a bottle of red for Rubes.

Booking out for the first event is a milestone, and I'm not letting her hard work go unrecognized. I shove baskets from the sofa under one arm and head to the truck.

Head down, most likely immersed in her emails, Ruby glances up when the truck jostles with the back door opening. I pop the items between us. She raises an eyebrow.

I slide into the driver's seat and fire her up. "We're celebrating, remember?"

She smiles back. That one small expression sends my heart through my throat.

Three gates, two boners, and twenty minutes later, I pull up beside the water's edge of the spring that is nestled into the side of the mountain. Complete with a modest waterfall from the overhanging rock formation, it's flanked by rocky slate ledges. The view here is spectacular, and even though I found this spot months ago, I can't bring myself to add it to the list of places guests can spoil.

"Oh wow," Ruby breathes.

She is out the door in a heartbeat, walking the shoreline of the small lake the spring creates.

"This is stunning! Why didn't you tell me about this before?"

"Was saving this for a special occasion." I smile at her, it's all warmth and heart, and the flush of crimson that spreads over her cheeks tells me she gets it.

This thing we have built together *is* special. So's the holiday ranch . . .

I pull the tailgate down and spread the blankets out, placing the cooler bag and the wine in the center. Arms slide around my waist and the weight of her head meets my back. Every steady breath she takes presses against my spine. But when she releases a wobbly sigh, I spin in her hold and take her face in my hands.

Brown eyes filled with silver look up at me.

I study her face. "Hey . . . what's wrong?"

"Sorry." She pushes from my arms, but I don't release her wrists. "I know we're supposed to be celebrating. But—"

"But what, beautiful?"

"Will you be okay, I mean *really* okay, when I leave?"

Her eyes search my face, breaths coming quicker now. She's worried about me. Fuck.

"I will be fine. You'll be busy with your career, and I

will be surrounded by people every day. I won't have time to freak out, I promise."

Her eyes flicker to the side and close. "That's not what I meant."

I cant my head, brows lowering.

If this isn't about my anxiety, then what is it about?

"Ruby?"

She sucks in a breath and forces a smile. "Never mind, let's celebrate, hey?" Her hands grab the hem of her shirt and it's on the grass a second later. She wriggles out of her shorts and turns, heading for the water, hips swaying. Naked.

The blood supply that was fueling my processing of whatever she was trying to say to me disappears south. Distraction successful. *I see you, Robbins, and raise you.* I rip the clothes from my body, tossing them with hers and run, buck naked, to where she stands toeing the water-line. She turns, too slow, when she hears me coming, and I scoop her up and jump into the water.

When the water settles and we are both huffing laughs and wiping hair from our faces, I tug her into my body. She wraps her legs around my waist, and I drop my head to her shoulder. With a quick inhale to breathe her in, I wade toward the waterfall.

Ruby dots kisses over my face, hands in my wet hair. The cool water does nothing to douse the raging hard-on I have. And her body is hot on mine, her breasts pushed against my chest. The waterfall cascades behind Ruby's back. I move closer so it hisses over her skin, and she moans.

Inching her further into the water, I watch the smile that grows on her face. "Into the water, baby."

She leans back, letting the water tangle through her long hair and rush over her shoulders. Back arched, her nipples are pointing up at me. I latch on to one with lips and teeth, sweeping my tongue over every place I can. The whimper that tumbles from her lips makes my cock twitch. *Fuck me, Ruby Robbins.*

I suckle and nip each breast as she writhes on my hips. I know what she needs now. The same thing I am desperate for. Her wrapped around my cock. Her tight, wet heat.

"Inside me now, Reed Rawlins," she growls.

I huff a chuckle and line up my tip with her center. Hungry, she kisses my mouth. I pry those pretty lips open with my tongue. She lets me in, eyes slammed shut, nails digging into my shoulders. Hungry and on the brink of losing control, I thrust up into her. She gasps, light and airy, into my mouth, and I swallow every sound she makes as I move harder, faster.

"Reed," she whimpers, eyes flying open.

"Yeah, baby," I rasp, barely able to catch my breath.

"I—" Her face cracks, her body rocking with each delicious wave as she milks my cock. With a groan, I pluck her nipple with my teeth, sending her higher. Every breath she takes is lined with a little desperate cry. And the overwhelming feeling that things have unwound into yet another level for Ruby and me sinks into my soul.

A sharp ache flashes through my chest, and I swallow past the rock in my throat. Willing it away with every erratic thrust I make. Her strawberry scent that weaves through my senses has me entranced.

I'm a dead man walking.

And the minute this is over and she leaves, you may as well bury me, because I will never be alive like this ever again. Without Ruby, my days are going to be one hellish stretch after another.

Her hands are on my face. And if I look anywhere near the way I feel right now, that look of worry on her face is warranted. Because *fuck*.

Closing my eyes, I slam into her as she whispers my name on repeat. Spilling hot and fast into her, I swear the sound of her soft plea will haunt me for the rest of my damn life. The moment I open my eyes and her hands lift my face to hers, a tear rolls down her cheek. Not water from the fall behind her. No, these drops I witness swell, bob, and then slide over her lashes, tracking a path down her cheek.

"I love you, Reed."

My heart cracks in two. I let my eyes fall shut as something tight snakes through my rib cage. "Don't say that, Rubes, please . . ."

Her breath hitches. "Look at me."

I can't.

"Reed." My name is breathy desperation, and my heart squeezes tighter still. Sucking in a long, burning breath, I raise my gaze to hers. Her chin wobbles. She tries to compose herself and fails. Tears burn the back of my eyes at seeing her this way.

"Hey," I say, running a thumb across the stream of tears that fall over her face. "Rubes, please don't cry."

She huffs a laugh, surprise claiming her face, and she kisses my forehead, my brows, nose, cheeks, jaw, and then finally my mouth.

How the hell am I supposed to live without this woman?

Chapter Twenty-Two

Louisa's arm is slung over my shoulder. But the nervous energy flinging around my body is making me dizzy. I'm trying to steady the breaths that leave my lungs and am failing miserably. The men and Addy are mounting up for the muster. And for the first time in my life, I wish I was as good on a horse as Adds. What I wouldn't do to ride along with Reed, the only person in this world to make me feel everything.

But I can't. And I'm leaving for two weeks.

Going home.

To the city. But the words don't fit like they used to. With everything for R & R Ranch's big debut organized and triple-checked, I have to go back and put in some office hours before my position at the firm is overrun by some rookie.

I wait on bated breath as Reed walks Magnet around

inside the barn, then readjusts the saddle's girth. When he swings up into the saddle in the doorway, I strangle a sob back, scrunching up my face to quell the tears that are filling up my eyes fast.

Louisa hugs my shoulders again, like she knows I'm falling apart. God, it's so stupid; he will only be gone a week. I will only be away for fourteen days. I'll be busy. He'll be with Mack, and he's done this a million times before. He will be fine.

But when I catch a glimpse of the rifle slung over his back . . .

My breath stutters out.

Fuck.

When did I become so attached to this man?

The envy I have for Adds riding along surges back to life. Magnet trots in my direction, and I wipe my face and plaster on the biggest smile I can muster.

"You two be alright without me?" Reed quips, a grin lighting up his cheeky face.

"We will be fine. You look after yourself, my boy." Louisa releases her hold on me, and I step forward. Reed leans down in the saddle and dots a kiss to my forehead. I catch the way Louisa's eyes light up and the way she purses her lips.

Not even subtle, Mama Rawlins.

"I will miss you, baby." The words are so soft against the shell of my ear. A tingle shoots up my spine.

But I grab his face and press a kiss to his cheek. "See you in two weeks, Reedsy."

He winks, sitting back up in the saddle. With a click of his tongue, Magnet is off at a trot toward the huddle of cowboys and horses. I wonder if guests would want this experience? Another tier? I can only imagine the insurance paperwork and waivers a trip like that would entail for a guest. But it would be an extraordinary adventure for them.

Making a mental note to ask Reed when he gets home, I shuffle closer to Lou and listen to Hudson giving out the orders. As he finishes, he beams at Adds with a smile that would melt a thousand suns. Envy has nothing on me today. Ugh.

"Alright, y'all. Let's go!" Hudson yells.

Yahoos split the air, followed by thundering hooves as the men send their horses toward the mountains. Reed trots in a circle and comes back to where we stand. When he reaches us, he looks to his mother before meeting my gaze. He raises two fingers to his forehead under his hat and salutes me.

Automatically, I salute him back. The movement is slow as my heart thunders. His face scrunches, and I swear he sucks back a lungful before pushing Magnet into a lope and heading off after the others.

"Nothing like a man on a horse to melt a girl's heart," Lou says quietly beside me. I almost forgot she was there. Too bad mine is already liquefied.

I huff a laugh and turn to face her. "You need a hand with anything, Lou?"

She has been packing for the men for days, cooking up an absolute storm.

"No, darlin', all under control. But we should sit and have some coffee before my legs give out. Every year, I wave them off. Every time is harder than the last, I swear."

"It's hard watching them ride off, knowing they won't be back for an entire week. Living in the snow and elements. I don't know if I could get used to that."

She stops inside the white gate and turns back. "You don't, hon, but this life asks things of us that most folks don't comprehend. And in return, we are blessed with all this." She waves her arms out, and I stare off at the mountains, the ranch, and all its parts. This family that I have come to love more than my own, oddly.

"I'm starting to understand that."

She smiles at me and touches my cheek. "Come now. Coffee will do the trick. This old woman needs sustenance."

I follow as she wanders inside and pours two cups of coffee. When she hands one to me and sinks into her seat at the kitchen table, I do the same, sitting in Reed's spot.

"How do you get used to this life?" I ask.

Louisa runs my question through her mind, the effects visible on her face as she takes a sip and swallows. "Well, it helps if you want it—this life, that is. It's not for everyone. The isolation. The long, hard days; long, hard seasons. But . . ."

I stare at her, holding my breath like the next words she will say may change everything I ever thought I knew.

She leans forward. "This isn't the life I had planned when I was young. Nowhere near it."

I'm stunned.

I can't imagine Louisa anywhere else.

"What—" I shake my head. "What do you mean?"

"Oh, I had big plans. I even left, determined to earn a life in the media—TV chef, that sort of thing—in LA." She waves a hand, as if California is over to the left of us. "I worked my tail off to earn a spot on a cooking television program. I thought I had made it. It was what I had wanted my entire life. And then, it wasn't."

"What happened?"

"I couldn't do it. I froze up on set. Every time. The pressure, it would . . ." She dips her attention to her cup, as if the words could be swirling inside the dark brown liquid, waiting to be fished out. "I panicked each time the guy behind the camera gave the signal to start. It was like I couldn't breathe, couldn't keep on my feet, or steady. The room felt like it was cavin' in, you know."

I stare at her, mouth agape. Anxiety. From everything I have read, it is usually hereditary. Louisa has it. Or had it. Reed *has* it.

"Well, that was it for my big TV cooking career. Guess

I'm no Martha Stewart." Her words are lined with a chuckle, but the ghost of regret covers her face.

"Martha Stewart has nothing on you, Lou. You are a real, living, breathing cooking legend. Everyone who has had your food would take that over some shiny celebrity food any day of the week." I slide my hand across the table and take hers. She smiles and tilts her head.

"Ruby." She turns her hand over so it folds around mine. "You are always part of this family. You know that, don't you?"

I still. The air in my lungs stalls out. I'm barely part of my own family, let alone one as tight-knit as this one. But she isn't going to take no for an answer, by the look on her face. So I nod, and she squeezes my hand.

"Good. Now, what time is your flight?"

"In four hours."

"How about you and I do some shopping, and then I will drop you at the airport?"

"That sounds wonderful, Lou."

She beams, looking so much like her youngest son. My heart almost grinds to a halt.

"Excellent, it's been an age since I hit the shops."

I recover and laugh as I rise, taking our mugs to the sink. A moment later, she is changed, and we head to the barn where the Chevy that Harry and Louisa take to town is parked. It's silver, and the inside is nearly as fancy as Reed's truck. I toss my bags onto the back seat, and she starts it up, buckling in.

The drive is fun. We chat about the boys and the ranch, and she quizzes me about New York City and my work. She asks questions that I'm excited to answer. My parents are not interested in my "silly little party-planning job." If it's not high-end, it doesn't count. Little do they know the companies and budgets we work with. But it's okay; it's better this way. I have my life. They have theirs. No need to mix the two.

The Great Falls shops are quaint, but Lou and I have fun regardless. I buy her a bottle of perfume that she swears Harry would skin her alive for buying, and she folds me into her hug. God, I am going to miss this woman. Almost as much as I'll miss her son.

We are back in the car when I have an idea.

"Lou?" I settle the bags between us, and she looks up. "Can I help with the base camp for the roundup?"

Her face lights up. "Sure, hon. Always needin' more hands on deck."

"Thanks." I run my bottom lip under my teeth. "Can we not tell Reed? I want it to be a surprise."

She winks at me. Now I know where her sons get it from. "Mum's the word, sweetheart."

I laugh as she shifts the truck into gear, and we head for the airport. I tap out an email to Olive, updating her on my travel plans for the week. Feeling more than a little excited about the prospect of seeing Reed sooner than planned, I all but skip out of the truck when we reach the airport parking lot.

Lou walks me inside, hugging me tight before gripping my shoulders. "I will see you in a week, then?"

"Yup." Reed's casual language rolls off my tongue these days. I can't wipe the smile from my face, and I don't want to. I readjust my bag strap over my shoulder and turn to go.

"Ruby?"

I spin back on my red heels. Only fitting I leave wearing the spikes I strolled into town on. "Yeah?"

"Thank you."

She doesn't elaborate. She doesn't need to. The silent exchange between her and me is like some unspoken truth that we two have always known. Incredibly, Louisa Rawlins and Ruby Robbins are unlikely, but very well suited friends.

And if I'm honest, really *deep down in the depths of my soul* honest, she is more like a mother to me than anyone I have ever had in my life before. And I have needed her for so, so long.

The office is cold. And not in the first-snowfall-of-the-season way.

Not today.

Olive's hard stare drills into me over her glass desk.

The same one I used to occupy. The top floor has been commandeered by Olive and her latest mentee. In other words, my replacement.

"I'm gone for a few months on assignment, and you hand over my entire portfolio to some random rookie?"

I can't keep the venom out of my voice.

She folds her hands over the file in front of her on the desk. My employee file.

"When I told you to find some perspective, Ruby, I didn't expect you to lose it altogether."

I grip the arms of the chair and set my shoulders back.

"I haven't dropped the ball on any of my accounts, Olive. In fact, being in Montana has only opened up more opportunities, more business."

"We do not need redneck clients with tiny budgets, Robbins. We are a prestigious firm with a high-class reputation."

The word redneck raises my hackles like it never would have before. But I hold my composure and focus on turning this sinking ship around.

"My work on my other events hasn't slowed down, Olive. I have been working remotely."

"This isn't a job you can phone in, Ruby."

Liar, it most definitely is.

We do it all the time. Something else is going on here.

She pushes to a stand and plucks up her tablet. "If I can't trust you, Ruby, then there is no future for you here."

"What the fuck, Olive?"

Her face turns to stone. She has never had a problem with my language, but today something is off, and I fear I've overstepped. What in hell's quarter happened here while I was gone?

Olive stalks through my door and slips past the PA who no longer takes direct orders from me, apparently.

The ship is going down, no matter how fast I bail out the water. It could well be the Titanic.

And I'm Jack fucking Dawson.

Chapter Twenty-Three

The snowdrift has well and truly set in. The only thing keeping me warm right now is the memory of Ruby wrapped around my waist and me buried deep inside her as I tail a small herd of furry cattle across the ridge. Mack is at the head, and I keep an eye out for mountain lions and wolves.

We came close to losing a run-in with a pack of wolves last night. Despite the rifle strapped to my back, I have no desire to fend off a pack attack with gunfire and then have to gallop after a stampeding herd.

When we finally reach the halfway point for the muster, and the rough, timbered forest opens up, I can breathe easy. Trotting around the cattle, I find Mack checking his mare over. The two men that ride with us have started the camp, and I lend a hand, thrilled to hand

Magnet over to my brother. As much as I love my horse, I am happy to be out of the saddle.

"Where's your hot little blonde, Rawlins? Not ridin' along like Addy?" Curly says. His dark hair pokes out from under his hat, his old, leathery hands stacking firewood to make our campfire.

"Back in the city" is all I give him.

He shakes his head. "Good luck trying to tie that one down. I hear she's somethin' of a spitfire."

"How the hell did you hear that?"

"At Louisa's party. Harry was talking about her."

I can't help the smile that stretches my cold, tight face. The dry air up here has my skin paper-thin, clinging to my bones. The chafing is so bad it keeps me from sleeping well most nights. I can't wait to get home.

"Ruby tells things like they are. Like everyone should," I finally respond.

"Yeah, *that's* why you like her. I've seen the body on that one," Stan pipes up as he walks over, carrying the rolled up tents.

I snatch one from his arms and throw him a dirty look. "Watch your mouth, old man, or I'll feed you to the wolves."

Curly laughs, and Mack slaps my shoulder. "That oughta keep them off our tail."

I grunt, sinking onto a fallen log by the campfire. The trees around us sport branches weighed down by snow, and the cold air slides its icy tendrils into every tiny gap between my clothes and skin it can find. I shiver, rubbing my hands over the now roaring flames.

We eat in silence until Mack yawns.

"Well, I'm gonna call it a night. Reed, you right to take first watch? We can't let those doggies spook the herd."

Always the sergeant.

"Sure, not like I'll be gettin' sleep anyway."

"Too many thoughts flying around your head about that blonde?" Stan has another crack at me.

"Fuck off, Stan," I growl.

Something about him talking about Ruby riles me up. Maybe it's the exhausting days, or the fact that I haven't seen her for so long. Or maybe it's the fact that I have finally found her and we have created something incredible, and her life—the one she wants with her whole heart and has worked a decade for—doesn't include me.

And being out here in the middle of nowhere reaffirms how magnificently different our two worlds are. How far apart they really span.

I wander to the pile of tack and lift the blanket that's draped over to protect the saddles from the elements and pluck the rifle from the stack. Settling back down by the fire, I let my gaze meander over the trees, searching in the dark spaces between the trunks for movement.

After nothing for an hour, my mind skips to Ruby. I stare up at the stars. The milky blanket hangs over the glistening, white-covered canopy, and I imagine she is looking up at the same sky as me.

"Any movement?" Mack's words jolt me back to the present. The cold, Ruby-less present.

"Nothin'."

He settles on the log beside me and leans back, lifting his blue eyes to the sky. "You know, the change I have seen in you since you and Ruby took on Harry is impressive, gunny."

I huff a laugh. "Maybe."

"You don't think so? I know Ruby does."

"Ruby is—"

"I know. She's really somethin', that girl. Pity she's headin' back to the city when it's all done and dusted. You'll have your holiday ranch; she'll have her big career. It's almost perfect, little brother."

His words are playful, a little taunting. But he's right, and I hate him for it. I hang my head, clasping my hands as they dangle between my legs. "Yeah, almost."

"Reed, tell the girl how you feel. You'll be kickin' yourself later if you don't."

"You know I can't do that."

"Why not?"

I groan and rub my hands down my face. "I was a first-class idiot about what I said to Hudson when he and Addy were in this situation. Should have kept my fuckin' mouth shut."

"Possibly. But you were fighting for him and Addy—he saw that. You're more Harry than you know what to do with, little brother."

"And now, I am acutely aware of why he wouldn't ask her to stay. How could I do that to Rubes, after all she has worked for? Everything she's done for me."

Mack slaps a hand on my back and rises to let me past the fire. "Go on, you head into the warm, I'll take this one. Can't sleep much these days, anyhow."

What's that supposed to mean?

We never ask Mack about his work. Ma can't, and we don't. Like some unspoken family code essential for survival.

"How 'bout I keep you company for a little longer?" I offer.

"Suit yourself, but one of us should sleep."

He plonks down on the log again, wrapping his coat tighter around his body. For all the horrible things my brother has seen and lived through, he is the most grounded of us all. At least, that's my take. He plucks a snow-covered stick from the ground and pokes at the fire. Embers rise and sparkle before burning out in the cold air.

The only sounds are those of the night birds and soft scurries of whatever is up and about between the trees at this hour.

Mack sighs, and I slide my focus from the flickering flames to his face. It's unreadable, as usual. "What's got your cogs turnin', Mackie?"

"Nothin'."

I raise a brow, and he smiles half-heartedly. "Tallied up the days I have left, is all."

I swallow at the sudden thickness that has closed my throat over. Mack leaving for a tour is always a bad day. Every time he leaves, it feels like a gamble. One I don't want anything to do with but can't escape.

"How many?" I ask, not ready to hear the answer, each syllable way too heavy.

"Eleven days left." He pokes at the fire, like it deserves his wrath, like it is responsible for his leavin'.

"Fuck."

"Yeah."

"When you gonna give that shit up?"

"I like my job, gunny. And I'm not seeing no city girl turnin' up to save me."

I still and meet his gaze. A shit-eatin' grin stretches over his face, and I punch his shoulder. He howls a laugh, tossing his head back.

Fuck you, Mack.

Just fuck you.

"Make sure you come back, you hear?" I utter on threadbare breath.

"Abso-fucking-lutely, Reedsy." He winks.

I roll my eyes at him, but the fire blurs in front of me and I swallow past the boulder that formed with his last words.

Huddo's precious herd at my back is bellowing up a storm as we roll down the side of the mountain and start out along the stretch toward base camp. The two large white tents that Ma puts up every year sit behind Harry's Chevy. Small figures wander around, stopping to watch as we push the herd closer. Ma must have wrangled one of her friends to help.

We're the first to arrive. Hudson and Harry's crews must be still coming down. Mack calls out behind me, his voice cracking after a week of hollering, the same as mine. Magnet ducks from side to side with the slightest leg pressure as I try my best to keep the cattle back. Last thing we need is a stampede barreling toward Ma. The stretch between us and the camp may as well be miles, at the slow pace we're going at.

Shouts split the air a moment later. Chancy plows down the side of the hill beside Harry's cattle. Who are, by the looks of it, flying blindly down the face of the mountain.

"Fuck! Mack?"

"Yeah, I see it!"

"Curly, hold the herd!" Mack and I gallop toward Harry and Chancy. The hat on my head flies from its tight hold and tumbles onto the short, snowy grass. The herd is frenzied, and I can hear the cuss words from the old man's mouth from here. His men are struggling to catch up in the rough terrain, and Harry is a one-man show trying to slow a runaway train.

I push Magnet forward, and his ears flatten. The thousand-odd pounds of gelding under my seat moves in quick powerful strides. A heartbeat later, Mack flies up beside me. We intercept the runaways, and Harry throws us a look mixed between relief and pure fire. The herd getting away from him has gotta burn.

"Whoa!" I spin Magnet around and duck him fast and sure, side to side, as the lead beasts slow. Adrenaline blazing through my veins, I draw in a breath and hold on to the pommel. Magnet lowers his head and turns on a dime again and again between bursts forward. Mack and his mare do the same on the other side at the head of the rushing cattle.

Something like a million dips and sways later, the herd is back to a walk. Harry trots over, Chancy frothing at the bit, her flanks covered in sweat and slushy mud up to her hocks.

"I got it, son," Harry says. The closest thing to a *thank you* I'm gonna get from the old man. I nod and move out of position, letting Harry take my spot. One of his crew relieves Mack, and we lope back to our herd, collecting my hat en route.

"Reckon it was wolves?" I ask.

"Most likely; guess Harry'll say when we're back."

With all the excitement, we have closed in on base quick. Ma stands with her arms crossed in front of the main tent. She saw the whole thing. Sometimes I wonder if she ever worries about Harry. They both exude confidence and partnership every day. But with the work we do, surely, she must worry about him. He's not gettin' any younger.

When the cattle are herded and a few of the crew take sentry, I trot over to the main tent and swing outta the saddle. The second my feet hit the ground, I release the collective breath I have been holding since the moment we left the homestead.

God, it's good to be almost done. Almost home.

Something strawberry drifts in the air.

My overactive, Ruby-obsessed imagination.

Or, more likely, Ma's cookin'. And I miss Rubes like nothin' else. It hits somewhere deep in my gut and sends an ache to my chest.

"Ma." I walk to where she stands and wrap her in a hug.

"Hello, my boy. Long week?"

"You could say that."

"It's about to be worth it." She winks, and confusion sets in on my face.

No idea what that's about.

"Harry having some fun?" She laughs, but the happiness doesn't meet her eyes, and her gaze falls away. Yeah, she worries about him. But when Harry pulls Chancy to a halt beside us, she simply looks up and smiles. "Hello, my love."

He tips his hat at her and swings down from the saddle, drops the reins, pulls her close without a word, and buries his head in her hair. I murmur an "excuse me" and wander around, hoping to find Mack.

"Oh, Reed?" Ma calls, and I turn back.

"Yeah?"

Excitement fills her pretty features. "You're in the tent first, bath's waitin'."

"Sure, thanks." I pull off my hat as I push through the oversized tent flap to where Ma will have the bath ready. Steaming hot. God, I can almost feel the heat of the water on my skin. And I'm first into the tub. First time for everything. The wooden bath sits in the center of the tent, rugs laid all around it, with a table laden with food off to the right. This has always been my favorite part of the yearly roundup.

But when I cast my eyes to the other side of the bath, I freeze.

My heart rockets from my chest, and the hat slips from my fingers to the ground. Her beautiful smile lights up the room as she runs for me.

Ruby.

I steady my stance as she closes the distance fast and jumps up onto my hips. I open my mouth to say something. Anything. But nothing comes as I rock under the weight of her crashing into me, wrapping herself around my waist. Her mouth is on mine. Hands in my hair.

God, Rubes.

My throat closes over.

"I missed you," she breathes, leaning back, her palms framing my jaw. "So. Damn. Much."

I huff out a strangled laugh and rest my forehead on her collarbone. "Me too, baby."

"But Reed?"

I lift my eyes to meet hers, and she shakes her head with a chuckle. "Heavens above, you stink."

I chuckle and pull her in tighter. She giggles and sinks her face into my neck. "If I pass out from the smell, you're going to have to take a bath by yourself, cowboy."

"Like hell, beautiful."

She wriggles, and I let her down. "Let's get you in the tub, then?"

"You're the captain."

"You got it, Sailor."

Now my heart all but stops. I suck in each ragged breath. And the familiar tingles that precede the inability to fill my lungs with air start creeping in.

Nope, not fucking happening. No way in hell's garter am I ruinin' this. I steady my breaths and mentally tally five things I can see.

Tent.

Tub.

Love of my fuckin' life.

Food.

Rugs on the floor.

Three things I can feel.

Ruby's fingers tugging at my Wranglers.

The stretch in my jeans, my cock swelling as she pulls the shirt from my shoulders.

Her skin, soft and silky under my rough hands.

Breathing easy again, I step into her and take her face in my hold. I could eat this woman up—the way she looks at me, the way she smells, sounds. The way she melts in my hold. Folds herself into me. Like we were fucking made for each other.

"Longest week of my life, baby."

"Mine too, Reed."

Something like sadness flashes across her face. I tilt my head, and she catches the gesture.

"Not now. We can talk about it later." She makes quick work of my buckle and jeans. And before I can count a handful of breaths, she has me naked as the day I was born, pushing me toward the bath. But when I reach the edge of the old-school bath, I turn on her.

"I'm not gettin' in this thing without you, Rubes."

She laughs and tugs her shirt over her head, letting it fall to her feet.

"Fine, but I'm washing you first." She screws up her face.

"Can't wait, beautiful."

I wasn't expecting to not be able to breathe when Reed pushed through that tent flap. But that is exactly what happened.

I am so screwed.

Or maybe I'm the luckiest woman on the planet. Time will tell, I guess.

I run the sponge over his shoulders as he studies my face, like it's been so long he needs to rememorize every part of it.

"Why are you here, baby?"

"I want to be here."

He tilts his head and raises his eyebrows, and for the first time since we met, confusion and concern twist his gorgeous face. "That so?"

"Yes."

I switch hands and wash his other shoulder. All I want

to do is settle over his lap and wreck that handsome face of his with each smooth stroke I make with my body wrapped around his. But this is a communal bath.

So I tamper the heat swelling in my belly and clear my throat.

"Olive wants me to sort out the mess with Mary-Sue at the inn. Also, she insists that we finish out the events. And—"

"She knows?" Reed's face scrunches further.

"No, not from what I can gather, but she is uptight about me being out here and I . . ."

"You need to go back."

"I will be here for your Thanksgiving opening, that I do know. But I'm not sure what will happen after the event for the inn."

He doesn't speak, simply taking my face in his hands and touching my forehead with his. "Whatever you need, Ruby Robbins, ask."

I swallow, tears prickling the bridge of my nose. For someone who gets shit done and doesn't do personal, I have been more emotional in these last six months than in my entire life. Can humans have emotional deficits? If so, I'm absolutely sure mine has finally caught up to me. Between Reed and his ma, Addy, and this town, I swear I'm a mixed bag of hot and cold. Sad and happy. Determined and at the same time desperate to spend my days slow with Reed. And I haven't cried this much since . . . well, ever.

Yup. Totally fucking screwed.

Rules, who?

We wash up and dry off. Reed smells divine once again as he pads his way to an oversized enamel bowl and jug. I sit by the small table as he shaves with a single-blade razor. Like something you would find in an old western. Minutes later, he is clean-shaven and dressed, and we head from the tent to find the others.

Mack strides over, grinning like the cat who got the cream. "Rubes! Nice surprise."

"Hey, Mack. How was your week?"

"Oh, you know, same as everyone else's. Slow, cold, and tiring."

"Aren't soldiers supposed to be tough?"

He chuckles. "Something like that, little lady. Be seein' ya." He slips through the tent flap, pulling off his hat. Louisa sure has drilled the manners into these four boys. Reed hugs me into his side as we approach Harry and Lou.

"Come to make sure your client is in one piece, darlin'?" Harry says with a wink.

"Actually, I was wanting to help, if I can."

Reed rubs his thumb over the back of my hand before letting me go and moving to help his mom.

"The easy part's done, but you can help Louisa. Catering to this bunch is the hardest task, especially after the last seven days we've had." Harry folds his arms, eyes tracking his wife.

"What happened? I mean, apart from that last bit."

"Had a few run-ins with some wolves. Same pack, too. They get more brazen every year."

"That's why you carry the rifles?"

"Sure is. Every beast counts. But I don't need to explain bottom lines to you."

"No, business is pretty standard, no matter what industry. And it's always hard to make ends meet."

"You got that right, darlin'."

"We will make this holiday ranch a success, Harry, I promise you."

He turns, locking his gaze with mine. His mouth tips up in a smile. "I know you will."

He walks off, heading toward Louisa. With orders to help her, I follow. His words replay in my mind. Was that a compliment from Harry Rawlins? Hope the devil's still got his snow boots, because he's gonna need them with hell freezing over and all.

The last of the soft furnishings for the cabins were delivered to the house yesterday. I stand in the living room by the fire, doing a last-minute inventory check before Reed is back to help me deck out all three of the new structures. Hudson and Mack are busy converting the largest barn into something we can use as a function room, with a dance floor, bar, and small catering kitchen included.

I'm beyond excited for this opening. I've shattered the Ruby Robbins Rule List, and so far, nothing dire has unfolded.

Give it time.

I keep telling myself this is a test, to discover how life works without the rules. Maybe I have been too rigid for too long. Have I missed opportunities and people that could have enriched my life if I hadn't been so stuck on six arbitrary rules?

I guess I'll never know.

The front door opens to a grinning Reed. The space between us collapses the instant his gaze finds mine, and he scoops me up, planting me on his waist.

I waste no time smashing my mouth to his. Every day we are closer to the opening for R & R Ranch.

Every day is a day closer to me going back to the city.

His hands wander through my hair as my fingers tangle in his shirt. I bite his lower lip and he groans, pushing my back against the wall by the stairs.

Each day that creeps closer to my final two events in Montana, the air thins a little more. I devour Reed at every chance I have, like he's my oxygen and I'm starving for it.

He's my last meal.

And now I can't breathe.

My eyes are already shut, so I scrunch up my face and rub a hand over my breastbone, trying to coax air into my ever-shrinking lungs. I can't do this. I can't be here with him, like this. Like he's my entire world.

But . . . I don't belong here.

"Put me down," I rasp.

"Rubes?"

"Please," I rasp, "let me down, Reed."

"Okay," he says, lowering me to the floor, worry and hurt creasing his face.

Fuck.

I'm certain that face didn't exist on this gorgeous man before I came along.

"I have work to do." My words are breathy and weak. As if my whole existence is warring against pulling away from him.

"You still want me to help?"

I turn back to find him standing lax, hands hanging by his sides, his eyes searching my face.

"No, I'm good." I walk for the door, swiping up a tape measure from the small side table I bought for the front entrance.

In the sunshine, I stride for the first of the cabins. I'll double-check the measurements and then come back for the items when I can pull a solid breath back into my lungs. Right now, I need a minute. Space between Reed and me, so my body can settle down, my heart can stop racing. To redirect my head to where it should be.

Why am I so hot and cold about this?

Guests will be arriving tomorrow. Thanksgiving. The debut for R & R Ranch has to be epic. First impressions count, and if I'm truly honest with myself, Harry is who I want to impress. He's the pinch point that needs to be overcome to make Reed's life, from this event onward, better.

Crossing the grassy spans between the house and the first cabin, I step up the three steps and onto the wooden porch. Painted white with red R & R brand colors accenting the trim and eaves, the cabins look magnificent. The men did an amazing job.

I push through the screen door and open the red door with a silver number one smack bang in the center. Inside, the bare bones have been dressed up with farmhouse-style trim on white walls with dark hardwood floors. The windows on either side of the front of the cabin and the central living area have cream-colored cotton drapes that touch the floor. The new house smell is rocking the space, along with the cathedral ceilings and stained crossbeams that run through the entire cabin.

I measure the front room and swipe out my phone to check the numbers I got first time around. Yep, same as last time. Next, I pore over the master that's accompanied by a generous en suite finished with white subway tiles and black hardware. The measurements are correct, as I knew they would be, and I lean against the cool tile, dragging in a rough lungful of air, trying desperately to separate myself from this place and the man it represents.

"I can do this. Get back on track. It's not like we will never see each other. Friends is a smart compromise." I rub my hand over my heart. I don't believe a word I'm saying. I doubt anyone else is going to. Especially not Reed.

The screen door swooshes open, snapping shut. Boots work their way into the empty cabin with a sullen echo. "Rubes?"

I wipe my hands over my face, set my shoulders back, and force a smile. "In here."

He is through the en suite door and leaning against the opposite wall a heartbeat later, one boot crossed over the other foot. Those green eyes burn into mine. "What ya thinkin', baby?"

I huff a laugh. "Don't go accusing me of thinking, Rawlins."

I drop my eyes to the floor between us. The tile pattern is subtle, understated but elegant greys and white. Huddo did an amazing job, as always.

Reed drops his head, looking up from under those lashes that are enough to make any woman melt. I roll my eyes at him in an attempt to keep this casual.

But I know it's not going to work.

Emotion is rising in my throat already.

Fuck.

"Tell me, or I will torture it outta ya," he says, pushing from the wall slightly, arms folding across his chest.

He would, too.

Reed's version of torture would have me on the brink of unraveling on his face.

"Fine. I was thinking about what I need to do when I go back to the city."

The half smile that had grown on his face in anticipation falls. "Yeah, right. I mean . . ." His voice is tires on gravel.

"We still have the dinner tonight and the inn's opening gala. But after—"

He bolts forward, closing the space between us, hands on either side of my head. "Until then, we make every second count, beautiful."

"I don't know anymore. It'll make leaving harder, Reed."

He trails kisses down my neck.

The air leaves my lungs and doesn't return. When he reaches my collarbone, I drag a shoddy breath inward and flatten against the wall. Cursing my body for responding to his so intensely, heat trickles through my core, lightning sparking up my spine.

"Reed."

"Stop thinkin', Rubes."

"Why?"

"Cos." He straightens up, green eyes drilling into me.

Now devastation lines them like I've never seen before. "Thinking about you leavin' *fucking hurts*."

I try to tamper the sob that claws upward, my face twisting with the effort. His hands are around my face, his lips brushing mine.

"Don't cry, baby." His jaw feathers fast, face strung out like a man on the edge of something incomprehensible.

Deny, Ruby.

Deny.

I shake my head too fast, dislodging tears.

Who am I trying to kid?

I'm so far gone, there's no coming back.

With Reed, I feel *everything*. Like he's turned on an emotional faucet that I can't wrench shut.

And I'm scared.

But I can't turn back.

Not now.

I grip his collar and pull him closer still. His hands are under my ass, lifting me up the wall. I wrap my legs around his waist, plucking at the buttons on his shirt. He nudges my chin with his nose and covers my mouth with his. I open and take him in.

Hungry doesn't even cut it.

We are starving.

Desperate.

I tug at the hem of my shirt, and he leans back as I pull it up and over and toss it to the tile floor. With a groan, he sinks his face between my breasts. Quick, rough hands release my bra, and it joins my shirt. Dark blond hair tickles my collarbone as Reed's mouth finds my peaks. I arch, still not close enough to him.

Never will be.

"Reed?" I rasp.

"Yeah, beautiful?" The words reverberate through me, sending me higher and the heat in my belly lower.

"Clothes. We need to lose the clothes."

"Agreed," he growls, setting me onto my feet. He makes short work of his shirt and jeans, and my breaths shallow out as I take him in. No matter how many times I see this man bare for me, hard for me, it hits hard, every single time.

I rest a hand over his heart, letting it slowly trail downward. He watches my hand slide lower and lower.

"I love this part of you," I whisper, running a finger over the abdominal muscles that are honed to cowboy perfection. I trace the V that sits central to his hip bones. "And this."

Every breath burns with each second my finger stays on his skin. When I finally reach the rigid length and velvety soft head of his hard cock, I close my eyes and hold the last inhale in my lungs.

I count to twenty, trying to tame my wild, shattered nerves that are sending me lightheaded.

"My turn, baby," Reed drawls, stepping a little closer.

His hands start on the top of my head. I huff a breath. Trust him to start there.

"This soft, gorgeous golden hair gets me every time."

His hands glide down my neck, and his fingers wrap around my neck. I meet his gaze. The heat that had me consumed before roars to a bonfire, eating up the last of my control.

"This here. Mine."

His hand continues, light and gentle, to my breasts. "Now these are fucking priceless, Ruby Robbins."

I roll my eyes at him, and he growls a little, shaking his head with lowered brows. His hand reduces to a finger as he curls his fist and tracks it toward the clasp of my Levi's.

"This is where I show you how much I fuckin' love you." His voice cracks and fades, and he sucks in a short, abrupt breath. He plucks the clasp open and pushes my jeans and panties to the floor. "And I will love you for as long as I damn live, Ruby Jane Robbins."

He drops to his knees and grips my hips. I slide my hands into his hair and lean my head on the wall, tilting it up so the tears that formed with his declaration don't spill.

When his hands push my thighs open further and the first strong sweep of his tongue runs through my soaked center, I scream his name.

Now, there is no turning back.

Completely resuscitated by the kindest, most genuinely loving man to ever exist. And, I have no idea how I will make this work.

But to lose Reed?

That would break me beyond return.

Chapter Twenty-Five

REED

Ruby stands beside me, wringing her hands in front of her. If I wasn't as strung out as her, I would be giving her shit about being worried about nothing. But I ain't, cos I am.

The driveway stretches out before us.

Ruby checks her watch again. The tablet she will use to check in the guests balances on the top of the fence.

Ten minutes until the arrival of the first official guest of R & R Ranch.

The knots that are turning my gut into a hurricane tug tighter. But seeing Ruby anxious over this has my protective streak lit up and blazing. "They will come, baby. I promise."

"You can't promise that, Reed. What if they don't? The dinner we all pitched in and made, the outlay for the cabins and catering, the rebuild of the barn will sink us before we even start!"

She starts pacing. "Harry is gonna kill me."

And I realize right here, this is not the usual calm-and-collected Ruby Robbins. This event is personal to her.

To us.

She has stakes in this one.

Anxiety etches its way onto her face. I turn to her and grab her hands, caressing her knuckles with my thumbs. "Breathe, beautiful."

And like that . . . the student becomes the master.

Or whatever the hell they say.

Anxiety can kiss my Wrangler-covered ass.

"This has to work, Reed."

I nod. "It will. But right now, I need you to take in some air and look at me. Name three things you see."

"Green eyes." Her voice is breathy. "Square jaw, and —" She closes her eyes. I squeeze her hands. When her eyes snap open, she opens her mouth to speak, but the sounds of tires on gravel sees both of us turn.

A light grey Suburban rolls up to where we stand. I give them a wave and lean into her, my lips brushing the shell of her ear. "Told you. You did good, baby."

She releases a huffy breath and forces a smile.

Good girl.

The driver, a middle-aged man with salt and pepper starting to show in his otherwise dark hair, steps out of the car and stretches his back, looking around as his partner climbs from the passenger's side.

"Oh, wow." Her blue eyes and straight brown hair whip about in tandem as she spins, looking every which way.

I step up to the man and extend my hand. "Reed. See y'all found us alright."

He shakes my hand, firmly. "Tim. Bloody great to meet you, mate. Some place you have here."

His accent is strong. Australian.

Ruby introduces herself to the woman, taps the tablet awake, and checks them in.

"You're welcome to park here, but if you wanna, there's parkin' by your cabin. Number one, first one on the right by the stream." I point out the first white cabin to Tim and he nods, climbing back into the car. When he rolls past, I wander over to the women, who are deep in conversation about Montana and all its wonder.

"Hi, I'm Reed." I extend a hand to the woman.

"Denise. Gosh, it's so pretty out here. I'm so excited we were able to nab a cabin! This place is going to be bloody popular; good for you."

"Well, thanks. What brings you to Montana?"

She leans a little, eyeing her husband as he pulls the bags from the trunk of their car. "You could call it a midlife crisis, I suppose. Not mine, though. But that can stay between us, hey?"

Ruby chuckles. "Mum's the word. Nothing like a trip

around the world to give you some time, space, and perspective."

"Oh, you nailed it, love. But I can't complain, beats the North Queensland summer, hands down."

"Wow, you will have to tell me about home. You are signed up for the dinner tonight, so I will see you there. But if there's anything you need, shoot me or Reed a text, okay? Our numbers are on the welcome info right inside the front door on the small table," Ruby says, excitement lining her gorgeous brown eyes.

"Righteo, thanks, you two. I better help unpack before I hear about it." She offers a smile and walks toward the accommodations, snapping pictures on her phone as she goes. Traveling around the world. That's been on my bucket list since I graduated high school. Maybe one day.

When Denise disappears through the screen door, Ruby squeals. She's doing a little dance, the tablet firmly clutched in one hand. I chuckle and crowd her against the yard fence. Her excitement peters to a grin.

"I like happy on you, Ruby baby."

"Me too," she whispers.

I take her face in my hands and kiss her mouth. And when she melts for me, I can't help but press my body into hers. She opens, and I sweep in, tasting her. The blood that was racing through my veins a moment ago with the arrival of our first guest sinks south fast.

The wind picks up, sending a hiss through the trees by the house as gravel crunches again. I break from Ruby reluctantly to find two vehicles creeping along the drive-way. I dot a kiss to her forehead. "Showtime, baby."

"Let's do this, Reed."

I wink at her as we push off the fence and walk toward the approaching guests.

The absurd amount of fairy lights currently twinkling all over the ranch and specifically arched over the double doors to the barn could be mistaken for a small city from space. But the absolute wonder that fills the face of every guest that pours out of their trucks was worth the effort.

They love it.

And it was the right choice. Fairy lights are always the right choice. Harry and Louisa's silver Chevy rolls in, parking over by the house. Soft country music plays on the speaker system that we installed in each corner of the barn. The long tables inside are filling up fast. And with the catering from Lewistown that we booked months ago, this night is turning out to be stellar.

Harry and Ma walk over, arm in arm. Harry's gaze runs over the building, inspecting our hours of last-minute prepping, and when those grey-blue eyes meet mine, he smiles. And it's a sight to behold.

"Harry," Ruby says as he folds her in a one-armed hug,

squeezing her tight. All cologne and clean-faced. He's handsome for an old man.

"Well, you have outdone yourself here, Ruby, darlin'. The place is looking damn fine."

Ma pulls me into a hug as I stand a little stunned. The fragrant smell of what must be her new perfume from the shopping trip in Great Falls Ruby and her made shrouds me in the embrace. "Y'all have done a wonderful job. We are so darn proud of you both."

When she releases me, she scrunches her face, as if trying to quell the silver now lining her eyes. She cups my cheek with her hand briefly and leads Harry inside. Their gasps are audible from where we stand. I fold Ruby into my chest a heartbeat later. "I think the old man is impressed, baby."

She huffs a laugh. "Seems that way. Everyone find a table okay?"

"Yep, got Tim and Denise squared away. They are practically begging for the dancing to start. But first, we need to stab a big, fat bird and make this thing official."

"You mean slice the turkey. Let the catering do it so people don't have to eat hacked-up white meat, Reedsy."

"I miss that."

"What?"

"Reedsy."

"Ah, but that was my friend zone name for you. Not entirely appropriate anymore."

"So, what do you want to call me—"

A hand slaps my shoulder. Hudson messes up my hair with one hand, leaning over to kiss Ruby's cheek as he does. "Nice work, Robbins. You sure have pulled off a stunning event."

"You haven't been inside yet," she says brightly.

"Oh, we are about to. This old man needs a whiskey."

Addy walks up behind him. "You ain't old, Huddy. Just tired. Let's find some gasoline and a chair."

"My lord, Adds really is one of us now." I shake my head with a laugh. "You seen Mack yet?"

"No, actually. You?" Huddo says.

"Nope. Guess he'll turn up."

I crook my arm like I have so many times and tilt my head. It took Ruby twenty minutes to pick my clothes, saying everything had to be perfect. I'm dressed in a crisp light blue shirt, sleeves rolled up as always, the top button left open, white t-shirt, and dark Wranglers that hug my ass. My caramel leather jacket, the only semi-city piece of clothing I own. Cowboy boots under the jeans like the ones Ruby wears right now that I bought her months ago. My once neat hair is now slightly mussed, and by the sparkle in Ruby's eyes, she loves it. She smells divine, sending the blood straight to my cock every time she moves closer. Her brown eyes bore into me. "Beautiful?"

She beams up at me. The crooked arm, the 'milady,' it's kind of our thing, and she slides her arm through and takes my hand with her free one. Rising on tip toes, lips brushing against my ear, she says, "To a magnificent first event."

My breaths shallow out.

Ruby has always taken my breath away. But this? This is a whole new level. Doing the thing I love with the person I adore—it feels too good to be true.

So, I smile and track my gaze to inside the double doors. Guests mingle, some by the rustic bar on the right that marks the front of the servers' kitchen, some by the tables, already settled in and waiting for the meal. Some wander around the big old barn, pointing and chatting. The drone of the music is an elegant background for the night.

And, of course, draped strings of fairy light twisted with long sheer panels of cloth, strung between the rafters. Countless candles blaze along each table. The wildflowers that Addy is so fond of that grow on the hills of Rosewood Ranch are dotted across them in jars, rattan chairs in front of each place setting.

The entrées are carried out to the crowd by a handful of servers as we enter. We head for the table closest to the dance floor, where Harry and Ma are already seated. Mack rolls in the door behind us and catches up. "Hey, sorry I'm late, got stuck in traffic," he says with a grin.

Red lipstick stains the corner of his mouth.

"What in the red-light district, bro?" I grin at him like a fool.

"Huh?" Mack says, wide-eyed.

Ruby steps closer and plucks a tissue from the pocket of her dress. "Here, you must have *hit* a red light."

I cackle beside her as I tap the corner of my lips to clue Mack in.

"Oh shit." He wipes the lipstick away and hands Ruby the tissue.

"That one's all yours, Mack. Keep it. Never know, you might need it later." She winks at him, and I swear our sergeant blushes.

We turn and make for the table as I lean down, arms winding around Ruby's waist. "What else you got in that pretty white dress, Ruby baby?"

"Wouldn't you like to know, Rawlins."

"Rawlins!" The familiar voice prickles the second it lands.

And when I turn back to find Justin Morley with the two women from the bar hanging off his arms, my gut plummets. Starr steps forward, still half swinging off Justin's arm. "Wow, who'd a thought you two would be a thing." She chews on her gum, running her stare up and down the both of us, and it snags on our wedding-band-less fingers.

How the hell did these three book seats for the dinner? Ruby's face falls, and I know she'll be scanning the last few months through her memory, fast. She grabs my arm hard, spinning me away from them. "I didn't vet the guest list. I always vet the list, for this very reason.

How could I be so damn stupid?" Her words are no more than a frantic hiss.

"Morley, sure you don't have somewhere else you'd rather be?" Mack says, stepping over to where I now stand rigid, palms sweaty and heart hammering. I move forward, putting myself between Morley and Rubes.

"So, you two *aren't* married?" Skye says with a taunting laugh.

Fuck off, bitch.

Rub salt into a man's wounds, why don't ya? I home in on her with a glare that could melt a glacier when Morley smirks.

"You oughta watch that mouth of yours—"

Ruby grabs my arm before I can make a scene in her honor. I absolutely fuckin' would, too. Mack is staring at us in confusion.

"Our personal life is not a topic up for discussion tonight. If you wouldn't mind returning to your vehicle," Ruby says in her best *I-mean-business* voice.

Starr glances at Mack, who sets his shoulders back. Hudson files in on the other side of me. Intimidation pouring from his posture, he says, "Guess y'all should head back to town, Morley."

"I paid good money to have Thanksgiving here, Rawlins."

"I ain't askin', Morley." Huddo sets his shoulders back, jaw clenched. The ultimate Harry move. An incredulous expression claims Starr's face as she checks out Hudson.

"Now, Justin," I growl.

"I will happily refund your money, Justin. Sorry for the inconvenience," Ruby says with absolute mockery. But we'll have to give him his money back—it is against the law to keep it if he's unable to attend. And with no refund policy to protect the ranch, we have no choice. That will be the first thing that is adjusted come Monday morning.

Justin scans the room, pausing on Harry, who is now sitting back in his chair, whiskey in one hand, his other arm wrapped around Ma. He tips his glass to Morley and winks at him. I tamper a laugh and flatten a smile as I gesture for the three to leave.

Luckily, this little scene went mostly unnoticed. And as Morley's truck roars away down the driveway, the first flakes of snow start to fall. They glisten under the twinkling fairy lights, setting the ground awash with a shimmering white glow. It's gorgeous.

Pretty as a picture—it's perfect.

When I turn back, Ruby stands between my brothers, their arms over their chests, smiles pushing their handsome faces. I grin at her.

"What?" she insists as I step back inside.

"Did you make a mistake, Ruby Rawlins?" Mack quips, turning to look at her.

Is he talking about Morley being here or Starr's fuckin' comment?

"I—"

"She did no such thing," I interject, alternating my focus from Ruby's stunned face to Mack's shit-eating grin. Realization hits me.

Rawlins.

He called her Ruby Rawlins.

I don't know whether to be annoyed or ecstatic. And when Adds wanders over, cuddling into Hudson's side to watch the snow falling behind me, I fix my gaze to Ruby's with a smile I couldn't tamper if I tried. But she simply steps into my arms and presses her back into my chest. "For your information, Mackinlay, I did make a mistake . . . Inviting you."

Mack slaps my shoulder with a chuckle as footsteps crunch in the snow outside.

"Well, I didn't expect a welcoming party, but I'll take it."

I turn back on a dime, still holding on to Ruby. Each of our gazes tracks to the man standing in the doorway in Levi's and a dress shirt with shiny loafers and a long, New York-style trench, the shoulders now dusted in snow. And the happiest fuckin' smile on his handsome face.

Lawson.

Chapter Twenty-Six

RUBY

Addy and I are on either side of Lawson, dragging him in from the cold a heartbeat later, under the adoring smiles of his three brothers.

"Laws," Hudson says, pulling him in for a one-armed hug.

"Huddo."

Mack fist bumps his older brother, and Reed slaps him on the back with a quick hug before casting his arms wide. "You like?"

"Reed, this is incredible. Didn't know you had a flair for decorating." A shit-eating grin splits his face as he turns to me. "You done good, Ruby. Awesome work."

"Thanks," I mutter as heat flushes my cheeks under the weight of all four Rawlins brothers grinning at me. But the excitement is marred by the fact that I messed up.

I forgot to check the guest list. It wasn't Reed's responsibility, it was mine. And it was missed. I missed it.

I was *distracted*.

A real-life, real-time consequence brought about by ditching the rules I have lived by for the last ten years. Excusing myself, I do a round to triple-check the run sheet on my phone that I practically have memorized at this point. The catering is rolling out on time. The music is setting the tone and atmosphere as planned, the barn is exquisite, and every guest has arrived, according to the tablet at the bar. Reed must have dropped it off here after seeing everyone inside.

I tap the screen and scroll through the list.

Morley and his two bottom-feeders have a red line through their names. I huff a small laugh. *Nice one, Reed.*

"Can I get you something?" a deep voice asks from behind the bar.

I glance up to find the bartender from the bar in town. Guess I have a face to the name we hired now.

Tanner Lewis.

"Sure, Merlot, top-shelf."

He grins at me and nods, walking back as he slides a wine glass from the rack over his head. Mack built that. Reed and Harry built the bar.

Hudson worked on the internal structures and the beams that flank the high ceiling that needed replacing and updated joinery.

It was a team effort. A family effort.

And it came out perfectly.

"You want it on the Rawlins tab?" Tanner says, handing me the glass.

I nod and smile, taking a sip. The heat winds its way down my insides, warming me up. "Lovely, thank you."

I turn back to find Harry.

"Another whiskey?" I ask.

"Actually, soda water; this old man is driving tonight."

I turn back to Tanner and order Harry's drink.

"Well, we oughta get this bird stuck, I reckon'," Harry says, taking the drink from the bar as it appears.

"We should."

We wander through the tables, stopping en route to chat with guests before finding our seats. Harry sits by Lou, and she whispers something in his ear. A half smile cracks over his face. Reed has a chair empty beside him at the head table. I slide into it, and he dots a kiss to my cheek and stands, whiskey glass in one hand, fork in the other. He taps the fork to the crystal with a *tink tink*, and the music softens. Every guest turns, all eyes on him.

He stills, swallowing hard.

His mouth opens, then closes. Shoulders lifting higher than before with each breath.

No. Not tonight . . .

I squeeze his arm and lift the glass from his hand, setting it on the table. He tracks his gaze down. Eyes wide and jaw set.

"Pretend you're talking to me," I whisper.

A few breaths later, he sets his focus back to the waiting guests and squares his shoulders back.

One Mississippi.

Two Mississippi.

Three—

"Welcome to R & R Ranch's first-ever event. To our grand opening, the beginning of something magnificent. It means a heck of a lot that y'all came out tonight in the cold and this season's first snow." He points toward the doors, where the light fall of fresh snow is still drifting down. "R & R stands for many things, but right now, it's all about the people we are here with tonight. Thank you for coming. Let's stab a bird!"

The tables chuckle with laughter, and Reed plonks back into his seat, hands gripping his thighs.

"That was terrifying," he rasps.

I lean over and nuzzle his neck, my mouth brushing his ear. "You were amazing. You're a natural host, Reed Rawlins."

He takes my hand under the table, rubbing his thumb over the back of it. "You always have my back, beautiful. How will I—"

Two servers push a silver service cart up to our table, lifting the turkey on the equally impressive tray into place in front of Reed. When one holds out a massive knife, Reed stands and glances at me before raising his glass. "A toast to the people we love and a new place to spend our days. Happy Thanksgiving, folks."

"To the people we love!" The crowd responds in muddled strains as glasses clink.

Reed stabs the succulent-looking turkey with the knife, and guests clink their glasses again, taking another drink. Removing the tray and the divine-smelling white meat, the servers return to the kitchen to plate up. Entrées on ornate round silver trays come forward on servers' upturned palms as they weave through the barn and set them down on the tables.

The warm bread rolls and churned herb butter are heavenly. Small skewers of grilled meats and tiny pies with marinated winter veggies make it to the top of my list for cowboy entrée options for future reference. Every part of this meal was designed to appeal to the cowboys and local folk of Lewistown. For the guests, this means they truly discover this part of the west through the sights of the ranch, the people they meet at the dinner, and the food that is locally grown and loved.

It's an authentic ranch experience, albeit a little more upmarket.

An elegant twist on the meat-and-three-vegetable diet these country folk are used to. And by their reactions to the entrées and the barn, it's a winner.

After dinner and a luxurious trio of desserts, the music kicks up a notch and guests head for the bar. Harry and Louisa are the first on the dance floor. Who knew?

Reed wraps an arm around my shoulders as his parents move across the parquetry dance floor Hudson installed. They're amazing, twisting and turning with the rhythm of the song. Harry has some serious moves!

"Bet you never would have guessed the old man can dance?" Reed whispers, his breath sinking into my hair.

"Wow, look at them go. That must be so much fu—"

Reed is out of his chair and pulling me from mine a second later. I stumble to catch up as we step onto the dance floor. "Reed, I can't dance."

"I got you, baby. Follow my lead."

He pulls me into his arms, and we are moving with the tune. His cologne is intoxicating. My heart races as I glance up to the cheekiest smile stretching that gorgeous face. The song fades out and "Lovin' on You" by Luke Combs starts up.

The air turns electric as people make their way to the dance floor. Reed takes my hands, spinning me around a full turn until I am back against him. But someone taps his shoulder, and he spins back. Harry winks at me.

When Reed steps away, he grins and salutes with two fingers on his forehead. I huff a laugh, and Harry has me in his hold a second later.

"You dance, Ruby?"

"Ah, a little." I grimace.

"Hold on, darlin', just follow my lead."

Like father, like son. Before I have the chance to catch my breath, he has me swinging out by one hand. When I roll back in, he grabs my hand and we are skating across the dance floor on quick feet, a sharp turn, and back the way we came. A ridiculous laugh bubbles up my throat. I snag a glance at Reed and Lou. They wave. But I'm whisked off balance, and I trip trying to keep up. Harry rights me in no time with strong hands and a direction change.

I feel left behind, and I hate it.

Listening for a few heartbeats, I make out the rhythm and match his pace. When he sends me spinning, I meet his intensity. The second my hands land in his, I give him a smile, but it's all cheek, and he grins back with a chuckle. "Let's see what you got, Robbins."

I match him, step for step.

Turn for turn, skip step and sharp turns, backward, holding his hands to my side as we walk forward. I spin before we reach the end, and he tosses his head back with a laugh, the way his sons do, and folds me back into his hold on my return.

"Checkmate, Harry."

"You got it, darlin'."

Something like adoration and pride mix through the light in his eyes. The song starts to wind down and Harry moves closer, two-stepping around in a tight circle. I do the same and study his face that has now faded to something more somber.

"Thank you for believing in him, Ruby."

The air leaves my lungs, and I press my lips together, hoping the emotion that clogs my airway doesn't show on my face.

Harry dips his head a little. "This version of the ranch, Reed's life, is better for it. Louisa and I want you to know that."

I open my mouth to respond, but the song ends, and I can't form the words I'm desperate to say.

Like, maybe it shouldn't have taken a complete stranger to figure out ranching wasn't something Reed wanted. Or maybe that's exactly what it needed. An outside perspective. Someone without stakes in this family's life and business.

"You're welcome," I choke out and break my hold as the last notes of the song echo out.

Reed meets me halfway to the table. I hold my hand up. "Give me a minute to catch my breath."

He nods, but his brows lower as I walk past and head for the door, plucking my coat from the hook inside the entrance.

Outside, the snowflakes settle on my hair and shoulders. I lean on the cold wall of the barn, the noise of happy people and upbeat country tunes spilling through the slightly open doors with the bright light. With a shiver, I pull my coat around my body tighter. The momentous scale of the situation I have woven my way into hits me.

I changed a life for the better.

I made him happy.

I made all these people happy. With one unforgettable night.

Nothing like the cold, impersonal corporate events I usually plan.

And suddenly, the thought of going back to that is incomprehensible.

But my place is not here.

It's back in the city.

If this hiatus from my career trajectory has taught me anything, it's that veering off the path might find you a little fun, but the things I have worked for pay the price for my inattention. Olive is pissed and has all but replaced me.

I'm making mistakes.

I push off the barn and wander to Louisa and Harry's truck. Climbing up onto the front bar, I sit with my knees up and shiver, tucking my head into my coat lining. Things may have worked out for Addy, but I'm not her. I'm not good at emotions and relationships and small-town living. They seem to swallow me whole and leave me drowning.

"Thought I might find you out here."

I look up to find Mack's handsome face, his worried dark blue eyes locked on me.

"I needed a breather after dancing with Harry."

He laughs and climbs up beside me. "Yeah, who knew the old man still had the moves?"

"He really does. He is a fantastic dancer."

"You didn't think Ma married him for his personality, did you?"

I grin and shake my head. "Knew there had to be more to Harry Rawlins; never expected fancy footwork."

"Thinkin' about trading up a generation to the old man, Robbins?"

I choke on a laugh. Mack nudges my shoulder with his. But the smile that rose falls, and I shiver, hunkering back inside my coat.

"Come inside, Rubes."

"Reed's okay? Getting around to the guests?"

"Come see for yourself." He jumps down off the truck and extends a hand. I slip my ice-cold one into his. It's warm and wraps around mine. There isn't one person in this family who doesn't seem to have my back. The feeling is so unfamiliar, it aches its way through my heart.

Safely on the ground, Mack wraps an arm around my shoulders and pulls me into his warmth. Glancing up at him, tears fill my stupid eyes.

Shit.

"Sorry," I whisper, wiping them away with the back of my hands.

"Hey, it's been a long few weeks. It's okay, Robbins."

"Yeah," I utter.

That's it, a long week. Filled with these amazing people, in this stunning place. And I am set to leave in a few days' time back to the lonely city. All by myself.

God, I'm a fucking Celine Dion song.

Good Lord.

I roll my eyes, hoping Mack doesn't catch it, as we walk back into the bright warmth of the barn.

"Hey, sweetheart. You alright?" Lou meets me within a few feet inside. I nod, and she winks at me before turning to study the room. When she looks to Reed, who is standing talking to guests, she says, "What an incredible night."

"It is, isn't it?"

"In more ways than one, darlin'." She squeezes my arm and walks away toward Harry.

"You should be over there. This is your accomplishment, too," Mack says, retracting his arm from my shoulders and waving at Reed. As if he senses I was looking at him, he turns and smiles at me. And that one look breaks my heart and patches it back together all at once.

"When do you leave?" I turn and ask Mack.

The happiness fades from his face. "Sunday morning."

Only tonight and tomorrow left. I wrap my arms around him, and he folds me into a hug. "Please be safe."

"Always am, Rubes."

When I break the hug, he messes up my hair like the little sister I feel like right now. The one who would do anything to keep him from going back on tour. To save Reed from having to say goodbye to his big brother again. To make sure Louisa's heart is safe.

But I set my shoulders back, tip up my chin, and dot a kiss to his cheek before striding through the tables and sidling up to Reed. His fingers automatically lace with my own. The couple he is talking to is our first guests from earlier this afternoon, Tim and Denise.

"Oh, love, I am parched. We should grab another drink," Denise says, meeting my gaze.

"Sure, let's hit the bar."

We leave the men to the farm talk and wander to Tanner and order drinks.

"You are one lucky woman, Ruby, he's gorgeous."

I chuckle a laugh, dipping my head. "Ah, thanks."

"No, I'm serious. Nail that down quick. You don't get that look twice in a lifetime, trust me." She's nodding.

I don't understand.

"What look?"

"The way he looks at you. Babe, that man is a goner. Sorry about my Aussie slang. How do I say this? You're *it* for him. That bloke is head over heels for you. *Deep.*"

She nods, her eyes widening even further on the word deep. I take a long, burning draw of the Merlot that Tanner set beside me. Swallowing, I glance at Reed. He's moving his hands in the air, describing something to Tim. My heart races, banging on my ribs faster with every beat. I down the rest of the wine and return the glass to the bar a little too hard.

"Don't tell me you didn't notice, love?" She's studying my face with lowered brows now.

I meet her gaze, sucking in a breath. "We were fooling around, and things got . . . but—" I choke on the next inhale.

I did tell him I love him. And I meant it. He is the best person I have ever met. I do love Reed, but loving someone isn't the same as giving up everything for them.

And this is the one thing I can't reconcile.

Struggling with how to fit both our lives together, I order another glass. Tanner raises an eyebrow.

"Tanner," I growl.

He holds his hands up, as in *okay don't shoot,* and I am sipping on Merlot a minute later, grappling for anything to change the subject, because Ruby Jane Robbins doesn't settle down, and she sure as hell doesn't abandon her ten-year plan because of a love hiccup.

But this is *Reed.*

I don't know what life will be like without him now.

But I can't give up on everything I have worked for, every dream I still want. I grew up believing that nothing good comes from choices made on emotion. Let alone love . . .

Logic over all else.

Achievement over life balance.

I can't bring Reed down with that way of living. He's not built like that. It wouldn't end well for us, for him.

And now, I have an impossible choice to make.

Chapter Twenty-Seven

REED

The low growl of thunder echoes through the air. The wind and snow flutter against the windows. The guests have all left, bar the three couples that are safe and warm and squared away in their cabins. Ruby pulled off the most incredible event I have ever attended. And I intend on showing her just how grateful I am for her. She took my breath away with those big brown eyes, that white dress, and those boots. She looked like she belonged.

The boots I bought her have scuffs and snow slush under them from wearing them all night and sit on the porch outside as I walk through the front door. The fireplace blazes, with Ruby curled up on the sofa, basking in its warmth. A blanket over her shoulders as she stares into the fire vacantly. What is going through that beautiful mind of hers?

I toe my boots off and toss them onto the patio and shut the door, keeping the frigid blizzard-like storm out. Sliding on my socks, I come to a halt by her feet. When she doesn't look up, my gut plummets. I sink beside her, tilting her head toward me with a hand under her chin. "Baby?"

She forces a smile.

Fuck.

"You tired? Or did something happen?"

She sucks in an abrupt breath and turns back to the fire. "I'm fine."

Sweet Jesus.

"You wanna take a shower?" I ask.

"I had one already," she says, opening the blanket to show her faded red captain's t-shirt and PJ shorts.

"Okay, sure. I'm goin' to have a quick one, and we can catch some sleep."

She nods, not looking at me. Hesitating for a heartbeat, I push off the sofa and pad up the stairs to the en suite in my room. I strip away my good clothes and dump them in the hamper before turning on the shower.

Ten minutes later, I'm head down, water running over me, and still at a loss as to what's happened. She looked like she was enjoying herself and the event was a huge hit, and we have five bookings for the start of next year and two Christmas parties booked in already. I make a mental note to secure booking deposits Monday.

Damn, listen to me, all business and shit.

Getting distracted by the other long list of items on my to-dos for the following week, most of them Harry's jobs, I jerk with a start when the water turns cold.

I turn the taps off and grab a towel, wrapping it around my waist and walking into my bedroom. The central heating is pumping, and the room is warm, despite the constant rumbles and howling winds outside. I pull on my t-shirt and boxers and run a hand through my damp hair. A soft voice clears in my doorway, and I spin back to find Ruby in nothing but her panties and those red heels that have caused me more wet dreams than I can count.

"Rubes?"

"I'm not tired," she whispers, running her hands up the sides of the doorjamb.

My cock swells to rock-hard inside a heartbeat, sending the air from my lungs as my feet track toward her. But something is up.

This moment and the last we shared don't add up.

"What's goin' on, Ruby?"

"Nothing, it's the post-event comedown. I'm fine. I told you that."

Her words are clear, but the feeling I had in my gut moments ago lingers. Her hand lands on my chest, reducing to one finger as she runs it over into the valley between my pecs and then down my stomach. I tamper a growl.

"Are you sure, because before you were—"

Her finger presses against my lips. "Shhhh."

Lightning lights up the sky outside.

And when the prettiest fuckin' smile blooms on her face, I forget my own goddamn name. Quick, rough hands have her around my hips in an instant. Cock pushing into her wet center as she wriggles. Knowing exactly how to drive the last brain cell from my head.

"Fuck, baby, those heels are doing all sorts of things to me."

"Good." She dips her head, cupping my face with her hands, the softest touch pressing into my jaw from her elegant fingers. "Because you have that effect on me, and then some."

I huff a chuckle, and she covers my mouth with hers, eating up the reverberation that rattles up. She's hungry. Starving.

I match her need with my own.

I'm steadily burning up with the ache to be inside her and have her wrapped around me until we fall apart. To watch her face shatter with release. So pretty it almost splits my chest in two every single time. I sweep my tongue over her lips, and opening, she lets me in. Coveting any part of her she offers up, I pad toward the bed.

Sinking onto the edge of the mattress, I run my hands through her hair and a thumb over her neck. The soft, satin-like skin washes with goosebumps, her nipples diamond hard and rubbing against my t-shirt. I break the kiss, and she rests her forehead on mine as a loud crack of thunder splits the air and rattles the windowpanes. "We playin' nice or givin' in to those damn heels, baby?"

"Giving in," she whispers.

Air rattles from my lungs as my chest plummets, my hands snapping to her breasts, cupping each one. She tilts her head back and parts her lips on a moan. *Sweet Jesus, Ruby.*

I could implode from seeing her like this.

I close my eyes, dragging slow, grounding breaths in through my nose and out my mouth. My last resort to keeping this from escalating so quick either one of two things will happen: I come before I have a chance to sink into her wet pussy and bring her to release, or things get rough.

And we haven't spoken about that.

When I haven't moved for a moment, she grinds on my lap again. Her breasts bounce with the slow, drawn-out movement, her lithe body illuminated by the constant flashing sky.

"Rubes, not the best idea with where my head is at right now."

A half smile plays over her lips as she takes her breasts in her hands, her gaze turning heated. "Where is your head at?"

"Flipping you over and pounding that sweet, wet pussy into the bed until you're screaming my name and have long forgotten yours."

Her face blanches with surprise for a heartbeat, and she swallows but raises an eyebrow and studies my face. "I want that, Reed."

"You sure?"

"Yes," she utters. Her breathing shallows out as she works on my t-shirt, tugging it up over my shoulders and tossing it to the ground. The wind picks up, howling against the house now.

"If I'm too rough, you tell me, alright?"

She nods.

"You promise, Rubes. I can't hurt you."

Now my air is wedged tight. I can't breathe.

"I promise." She follows the planes of my torso with her palm, as if mulling the idea over, and when she meets my gaze . . . "I trust you."

I inhale, running through the things I have wanted to do with her from the second I first saw her. Those fuckin' heels. Those ruby-red lips. I scoff at the phrase, opening my eyes. I lift her off my lap and steady her on her feet. Reaching for the top drawer of the bedside table, I grab an old tie. She glances at it, and a playful smile pulls up on her lips.

"Turn around, baby."

She does, without a word. I pull her hands behind her back and tie them with the long length of silky material. A breath wooshes from her as I spin her back.

"Reed," she moans, and I barely hear her over the storm.

"Let a man work his magic, beautiful."

I'm using every tactic I have to tame the part of me that wants to spread her open and plunder that wet center straight up. But I'm taking my time. Gonna make her come on my face, my cock.

"Spread your legs," I rasp.

Ruby moves, heels clacking on the wood floor as she follows the order. I run two fingers through her wet center, running circles around her clit with my thumb. A whimper claws its way through her lips.

I swallow hard, each breath burning. "Kneel."

When stunning brown eyes drift back up to me, I tangle a hand through her messy waves of blonde. Cock throbbing so hard it's on the brink of sending points of light in my vision, I take her hand and place it on the waistband of my shorts.

She tugs them to the floor. My cock springs free, right in front of her face. Her lips part, and her hand wraps around the base. "Suck."

Her warm, wet mouth covers the head of my cock a heartbeat later. Snow and sleet slam into the windows with a hiss.

Sweet fuckin' Jesus.

Every breath is a growl. I brace my legs, muscles strained tight, jaw set. Ruby takes me in up to the hilt, and I fist her hair, pulling her back. She doesn't wince, doesn't hesitate. Simply continues her shallow strokes down the shaft, twirling her fucking tongue over the tip like she was born to make me unravel.

Heat washes up my spine, my balls tightening.

I grab her head with both hands. "I'm driving, baby."

She lets me plunge deeper like she read my mind. Like she knows I'm too close. Her elegant lips wrap around my cock. The sight is too much. I keep the movement shallow, my thumbs rubbing over cheeks. Her eyes are homed on my face.

Her watching me shove my cock into her mouth riles me up like nothin' else.

Fuck me.

Groaning, I let my cock slide from her mouth and fist the base. Pre-cum mixes with her saliva, glistening under a white flash as lightning streaks across the sky and lights up the room. And when she licks her fucking lips, I slide a thumb into her mouth. She sucks on it, hard.

Lining the head of my cock up with her lips, I find purchase in her hair and drive into her mouth. I slam my eyes shut. Electricity flings through my veins, desperate to fill that sweet mouth with every last drop of my cum. But I shake my head.

Nope. Makin' it last . . .

I retract myself fast and lift her to her feet. She whimpers at the loss, and I spin her to face the bed and press my body to hers.

"On the bed, Ruby." The words are almost a growl, and when she crawls onto the mattress on her knees, those fuckin' heels spread wide, I take in every sweet part of her glistening pussy.

Desperate to eat her out until she is writhing on my face, I flip her over. Wrapping a rough hand around her ankle, I lift her leg up and rest it over my shoulder as I sink to my knees. I lift her other leg over my other shoulder, and the spikes of the heels scratch against my back. Thunder shakes the entire house.

The throbbing in my cock turns painful.

But I grip her hips and drag her closer to the edge, until her clit is inches from my mouth. My breath lands on her center, and she whimpers.

"This pussy is mine, Ruby Robbins. Mine to eat, mine to claim. Mine to fuck. You understand?"

She nods frantically. "Yes, I'm yours. I have been for a while, Reed."

My heart bottoms out.

Sending me more feral than the Great Reed Rawlins has ever felt in his entire damn life.

Chapter Twenty-Eight

RUBY

Reed's tongue sweeps through my aching center, and I arch off the bed like a rocket of fireworks bursting from its canister. The lightning outside has nothing on the man between my legs. I grip the duvet under my back like my life depends on it.

Oh. My. Lord.

Heat pools, and I'm drenched and still growing wetter by the second, if that's even possible. Every part of me is a live wire. Everywhere his fingers, his tongue land is electric.

I'm his.

His words.

My words.

I tremble uncontrollably, the storm shaking the house. Snowflakes slap against the glass windowpanes continuously. I can't grapple enough air. I don't want it. The only thing I need is Reed inside me.

I may be his.

But he is also mine.

Right now, I am loving him taking what he wants. It's so overwhelming to relinquish control and let him take the lead. It feels like love. Like being loved. The true sentiment of the word, in action. A real-time experience of something so deep and all-consuming that my body swells with emotion.

Heat tracks over my skin as he flicks his tongue over my clit. I whimper, wanting more. So much more.

"Fuck beautiful, you taste so good." He sweeps through my center and suckles on my clit. My hands are stuck, aching to run through his hair. To anchor myself to him with touch. My fingers would tangle through his hair, gripping tight when he sucked my clit.

"You alright?" Reed rasps.

"Uh-huh."

The syllables are raw, almost incomprehensible.

"You're gonna ride my face now, baby. Up you come."

He withdraws his hands and lifts me to sitting up on the bed. "Flip over and crawl over a little."

I push to my knees and crawl to the edge of the bed. Rough hands grab my ankles and drag me back a few inches. A moment later, Reed slides through my legs on his back, his mouth lining up with my throbbing center.

God, yes.

What I wouldn't do to have use of my hands right now.

"This is the last nice part, baby. Then we're turnin' up th . . ." Thunder drowns his words with its raw growl.

His mouth meets my wet center, teeth grazing my clit. My legs tremble. It's too much and not enough. I need him inside me.

I'm dizzy with it. He suckles, kisses, lets his teeth skate over the bundle of nerves sending me higher and higher with every small move he makes.

"Reed, more."

He slides two fingers inside me, excruciatingly slow. Mouth opening and head falling back, I force air into my lungs to tamper the orgasm that's teetering on the edge. His works in and out, eyes watching me by the heat that's flooding my chest, neck and face. His free hand tracks up my stomach, so light it leaves a wake of goosebumps.

He moans as I start to move on his mouth. I couldn't stop, even if I wanted to.

Adding another finger, he slaps my ass, hard. The fire of the slap melts to tingles as I pick up the pace on his face. "Reed!"

I want my hands free.

I want to kiss my taste from his lips, his chin, and his jaw. I want those green eyes locked on me when I come. I snap my gaze down. My face is wrecked with desperation, every part of it tugged tight. Each choppy breath is lined with a whimper.

He curls his fingers forward, sucking hard on my clit.

"Fuck, fu— Reed."

He slaps my ass and bites down on my clit, only hard enough to limit my movement. I spiral upward, into the heady bliss of release. He growls around my clit, and I explode, milking his fingers. A rough hand grabs my hip, and he smooths out my erratic rhythm, drawing out the orgasm.

I slump backward as the most intense orgasm of my life fades out, sitting on his stomach. The biggest grin spreads over his face, my release covering that megawatt smile.

And when it fades and his eyes darken, I move onto the bed and wait for my next order.

"On your stomach, Captain."

I rest my head on a pillow and slide my knees apart, canting my ass up for him, hands still tied behind my back.

"Sweet Jesus, Rubes."

"Yours, remember."

"Yes, it fuckin' is."

The head of his cock swipes through my soaked pussy. I wriggle backward, desperate for him. A hand slaps my ass, hard.

"So fuckin needy, beautiful."

Heat fills my cheeks, but my pounding heart loves it.

"Again, Reed."

His hand lands on the other cheek, drawing out a

whimper when his hands grip my hips tight and tug me backward. I turn my head to find his eyes closed, breaths plummeting.

"Fuck me hard, please."

"Beg again, Ruby baby. If you want it, you have to say it again."

"Please, Reed, fuck me so hard."

He lines up the head of his cock, slamming into me a heartbeat later. I cry out. The fill, the stretch. My mouth waters. The sky lights up, all oranges and yellows. Reed is backlit by Mother Nature, and he is stunning. I moan at the sight. But he stills, as if he has to pace himself.

"Oh, Reed. Fuck. Fuck."

"Thinkin' about anything else right now. Not gonna blow this, baby."

I huff a laugh and grind back into him. He snaps his eyes open with a growl.

"Like that, is it, hey?"

He pulls out, slow. So, so slow. I whimper when the tip falls from my entrance.

"Please," I whisper, face contorted with need.

He grips my hips so hard it smarts and slams back into me with a groan. And again, I cry out. Not even caring that our very first set of guests are probably hearing every syllable. Even over the storm.

He slides out again, making me whimper with the heartbreakingly slow deliciousness. Slamming in, he leans over and runs kisses down my spine. And when his hand leaves my hip and slides underneath me, tweaking my impossibly hard nipple. I strangle a moan, tightening around him.

He slams into me for another few strokes before lifting me from the bed with one arm, my back against his sweaty chest. He picks up the rhythm again, his choppy breath rasping into my ear. His heated, sticky skin pushes against mine.

"What's your name, baby?"

A bent smile grows over my slack face. "Ruby."

"Wrong answer," he growls and thrusts harder.

Cries slip through my parted lips, his hand pushing the soft flesh of one breast, the other hand rolling the opposite nipple.

Like a fucking god.

How he can concentrate on three things at once and keep his own body in check is awe-inspiring. But something is missing. As if he read my mind, his hand slides up to my throat. I lay my head back on his shoulder in answer. His face is all light, shadow, and gorgeous angles.

The Great Reed Rawlins.

A lazy smile pulls over my face, strung out by ecstasy.

His fingers squeeze around my airway, and I huff a heady moan against his palm.

"Name," he snaps, raw and gravelly.

Stars creep into the sides of my vision, my center coiling tighter as my breaths shorten even more. Each thundering thrust sends me higher and higher. Lightning cracks, loud and close.

"No fucking idea," I rasp.

On a huffy breath, he says, "Good girl."

Every stroke is strong. The bed creaks, shuddering with every rough movement that becomes more and more sloppy.

He's close.

Pushing my back to his chest, tilting into him with my hips, I want more. "I need . . ."

The hand that was cupping my breast has reduced to two fingers, and he finds my overstimulated bud and swirls them erratically. I spiral and explode with a breathy whimper that sends tears prickling behind my eyes. Reed follows with a raw rumble as he spills inside me with each hard stroke.

"Fuck, Rubes . . . Mine . . . baby."

"Yours."

Folding me back against his chest, he nips along my neck. "And I'm yours, beautiful. Have been since day one."

I rest my head back on his shoulder, and he dots kisses to my cheek and down my neck and shoulder, as he tugs the binds from my wrists.

"You're gonna need another shower," he breathes.

"I'll run the rivers dry if it means we can keep doing that."

His soft chuckle buffets the curve where my neck

meets my shoulder. "Keep wearing those heels and you'll be in for a lot more showers."

"Promise?"

Thunder rumbles, softer now, and his smile stretches against my neck. "Ten-four, Captain."

The devastation on Reed's face—he's trying his best to flatten—is breaking my heart. Mack holds him in a tight hug. "Later, gunny."

The Great Falls airport isn't much, but the few people who mill around offer sympathetic expressions directed at the army uniform Mack is wearing and the hollow faces of his family who are trying their best to see him off with smiles.

Louisa sets her face in a tangle of grief and forced happiness as Mack pulls her in for a hug, and I swallow back the sob that has sent tears stinging behind my eyes.

Harry stands, hands clasped in front of his waist, by his wife's side. His Adam's apple bobs as Mack whispers something to Louisa. She nods as he releases her.

I all but fly into his arms as he turns to me. It's stupid, I know. But a sensation akin to someone pulling my insides out through my teeth is unfolding at seeing Mack leave his brothers, his parents. They have a bond and love that I have never experienced, and it has me all messed up.

I clear my throat, not letting the emotion show through. That's what we're supposed to do, isn't it? Be brave. Pray he comes home safe. I catch a glimpse of Reed, his face twitching as he struggles to hold his jaw slammed shut, his eyes shiny.

This is eating him up.

I push from Mack's hold and plant a kiss on his cheek. "Make sure you come back."

He salutes with two fingers to his forehead, but he's not looking at me. His gaze is set on Reed.

I turn and wander back to Reed's side, sliding my hand into his before Mack has the chance to notice the silver that's flooded my eyes. Lacing my fingers with Reed's, I lean into him as Addy and Huddo crowd Mack. Hudson slaps him on the back, and Addy pulls Mack's head into a one-armed embrace as he leans down to her. Everything is so intimate.

So raw.

The air is so damn thin.

A woman's voice announces boarding over the PA system.

I blow out a breath. As one, the Rawlins family take a step back, like old habit. A routine they have been through many times. Mack shakes Harry's hand and lands one last kiss on Louisa's cheek before plucking up his army-issued duffel from the floor and walking toward gate number one.

Harry tucks Lou under his arm, saying something to her softly. When she nods and they turn and walk from the building, Addy and Hudson do the same. But Reed stands staring at his brother's receding form. Like some unspoken rule, Mack turns back at the gate's entrance and waves with a bright smile.

Reed's nostrils flare, his entire body tensing, but he returns the wave.

"Hey," I whisper, standing in his field of vision, hands on his face. "You will see him again. Okay?"

He doesn't respond.

He's barely breathing.

Taking his hand, I lead him into the weak sunshine of the late-fall mid-morning sun. We have the inn's opening gala tonight. And, despite the overwhelming want to run back to the ranch and hide under the covers and hold Reed for hours, I have work to do.

I can't mess up this event. And it has to go perfectly. Because if our fake marriage, with this relationship that doesn't feel so fake anymore, gets back to Mary-Sue I will have a catastrophe on my hands. And no amount of pleading will land me back in Olive's good books.

My phone buzzes in the back pocket of my jeans. I slip it out and tap the screen. Two messages. Three missed calls from the lawyer.

I open the message from Olive.

Make sure tonight goes off without issue.
I will see you back in the office first thing
Monday morning.

I tap out a reply and check the next message.

The lawyer. I tap his name and read the text twice. And on the third pass, my gut sinks.

A notification pings on the ranch's socials. I tap it open. I don't believe my eyes. My mouth gapes.

Two reviews for R & R Ranch, the grand opening flagged, both one-star reviews. The sentiments are beyond harsh. They are flat-out trolling the business. The names that sign them off hit harder than it should.

Skye S

Starr M

I glance at Reed. I can't show him this. Not now.

Chapter Twenty-Nine

REED

The only silver lining attached to this day is being with Ruby for the gala. Getting to be with her in her element. The tight evening dress that sweeps over her hips and dusts the floor in a stunning red silk is helping.

But Mack leavin' always has me down for days. It's hard saying goodbye, not knowing if this is the last time I will see him. And this is the first time I have ever had someone around after he waves off at the airport. That counts. More than she knows.

Ruby is everything.

And there is no way in hell I'm letting her down tonight. Not a fucking chance. I hold the passenger door open in the airport parking lot as she smiles at me with sad eyes and climbs on up.

My heart is heavy, but it's also full.

Some fucking contradiction that is.

I slide into the driver's seat and fire her up. The rumble makes me feel a little better. Stupid as it is, this truck has always been my safe space. Somewhere I can be myself and free. Nothin' like the purr of idling V8 engine and soft leather to lull you back to comfort.

I lay back, closing my eyes for a heartbeat, letting my heart rate steady. And I count my blessings. The biggest one sits next to me, whose stare is warm on my face. I smile, eyes still closed.

"Rude to stare, beautiful."

"I know." Her voice is strained.

I snap my eyes open and find hers. Her jaw is clenched, hands tight around her phone, breaths shallow.

I cant my head, narrowing my gaze. "What is it?"

"No, today is about Mack."

"I can handle it. Please, baby, tell me."

She breaks eye contact and stares through the windshield vacantly. "Your groupies are suing for harassment."

I ignore the phrase *my groupies*, even though it eats at me. Dropping my focus to the seat between us, I run my hands through my hair. "Fuck, please say it's the both of us?"

"Just me."

"Sweet Jesus, Rubes," I utter. "Don't give them a thing. Harry will know someone."

She gives me an incredulous face. "My lawyer is already on it. But technically, I did. So, there's that."

"But *I* threw them out of the Thanksgiving party."

"Yeah, well, apparently it's me they hate, not the Great Reed Rawlins."

Her face slackens as the last words leave her lips, like she didn't mean to say it. Like it's not what she wanted to say.

I drift my focus to the steering wheel. "We will fix this, we make it through tonight, and then get busy figuring out a solution for this mess."

She doesn't respond, eyes glued to her phone in her hands, not really seeing.

"Ruby? We will sort this out."

I move closer and turn her face with one hand. Her eyes are lined with silver. Fuck me. An iron grip closes around my heart, a stone forming in my airways.

"Hey, it will be alright, baby." I pull her into me, and she sobs. Her fingers tangle in the opening of my polo shirt. Rubes is the toughest woman I have ever met; this stress is eating her up. It's fucking unacceptable.

The event.

The fake marriage.

The harassment bullshit.

The past few months of nonstop planning and work.

The thought of her having to go back to the city by herself rips me apart. Life is utter garbage some days.

Some people sail through it, some have the weight of a thousand boulders to carry all by themselves. And I feel like the former used to be me. The latter, Ruby. What I wouldn't give to haul her burden for her. But knowing Ruby Robbins, the most she is going to let me haul around is less than half.

I push back and tilt her head up with my hands cupping her face.

"Now, you listen to me, darlin'," I say in my best Harry voice, "you work your magic and get that fancy party done. Leave the rest to me, you hear?"

She bursts out with a sobby laugh, picking up on the Harry talk. Her mouth wanders over my own a second later. God above, I love this girl.

I sink into the kiss and don't let her go until she wriggles free, her hands sliding up my shirt and over my neck to my jaw. "What would I do without you, Reed James Rawlins?" Her finger brushes over my bottom lip, and she watches as I entwine my fingers through hers and plant a kiss to her palm. To her wrist.

"Reed," she whispers.

"Yeah?" I rasp, all the blood from my clear-thinkin' head already disappeared south.

"We should go," she utters. But her eyes are hooded, her breaths short.

"We have a room at the inn?"

"Yes, same one as last time."

"Hold tight." I move back into my seat and tug the seat-belt over, clicking it in. She does the same, and we're flying down Main Street a moment later, heading for the inn.

When the valet leaves with my truck and I haul the bags through the door, Ruby's arm is linked through mine. It takes everything I have to focus on checking in.

Mary-Sue is at the desk, chatting to Ruby as the girl in front of the computer taps away, double-checking details. Every word she says is hazy, and when she pushes the cards over the counter at me, I all but snatch them up and tug Ruby away from Mary-Sue awkwardly.

But she only chuckles and waves to Mary-Sue. "I'll be down an hour before the event to do final prep."

"Y'all enjoy your last stay here." The older woman beams Ruby's way.

So, I am guessing by that expression, the waitress hasn't let on about our fake marriage yet. Maybe we will make it out of this unscathed, after all.

A long, excruciating minute later, the elevator door bings, and we are on our floor. Ruby walks beside me, all quiet. She taps the card on the door, and when she pushes it open, she doesn't move, staring at the space, the bed, looking around the room. As if remembering the way things were when we were here last.

I slide my hand into hers. "We can just go home if you wanna, baby."

Slowly, she turns to me, and a sweet smile blooms

over her face. "No, anywhere with you is my favorite place to be."

I scrunch up my face to tamper back the emotion threatening to send my nostrils flaring and my airways thick. "In that case, Mrs. Robbins, we should definitely do it on every surface."

She walks inside, stopping at the counter with the small fridge at the opposite end of the sofa. "Well, how about right here on the counter for starters?" Her hand sweeps over the shiny surface. I toss the bags onto the bed from where I stand, slamming the door behind me.

One hand plucking my jean button open, the other tugging my polo off, I stride toward her like a man on a fucking mission. She laughs and rests her hands on my bare shoulders when I stop, our bodies almost touching. "Gonna keep me up all night, baby?"

"Abso-fucking-lutely, Reedsy."

I groan and drop my forehead to her chest. Her smell is intoxicating, and my cock is rock-hard a heartbeat later. Gripping her hips, I kiss my way up her skin, over her collarbones, her neck, her jaw. She releases a breathy moan as my mouth works her over, and finally I cover hers with mine.

I slide my hands around her waist, pushing her shirt up.

"Off. Take it all off, Reed."

I pull the soft, light blue t-shirt over her head. Perfect fucking breasts are pushed up and spilling from her lacy red bra. Her fingers tug at her jeans, and she steps out of them a few seconds later. I step back and fist my cock, wanting to take her in for a moment.

So beautiful.

So mine.

In her underwear, she moves a little closer, playing with herself, running a thumb over one nipple. Her other hand slips past the waistband of her panties, and I can't fuckin breathe.

With a growl, I snap my hands around her waist, picking her up and depositing her on the counter. She smiles playfully at me. But she has me so goddamn wound up, I can't respond. With a rough hold, I pull her panties off and run two fingers through her wet center.

Fuck, she's soaked. "Rubes."

"Fuck me, Mr. Robbins."

"Yes, ma'am."

But not before she rides my face. Then she can come all over my cock. Not a second before. She giggles, tossing her head back. I spread her legs and drop to my knees. With the first run of my tongue through her delicious folds, I'm on the edge of coming all over the marble tiles. I sink two fingers into her and suckle her clit like a man dying of thirst, and she rides my face like I've wanted her to since I woke up this morning.

"Fuck, Reed."

She whimpers as I coax out the last of her release. I push to my feet and rub my palm over the swollen head of my cock. Looking at her, wet and ready, is sending my head too high. She wriggles forward, her hands on my hips pulling me closer. I line up the head with her soaked center.

"Give me everything, please," Ruby breathes.

I slide the tip in. She huffs out a small cry, and her face falls apart a little. When I don't move, she opens her eyes, desperation lining them. I edge forward a half inch, tampering the smile that's trying to pop up on my face.

"Reed," she growls.

How this woman has my heart. Good Lord.

I give her another inch. Now she sits up off the counter and takes my face in her hands. "That's just mean, Reed Rawlins."

"Making it last, baby."

Her eyes narrow. "Fine, your call. Tell me what you want."

"I want you. Being inside you. Going excruciatingly slow. Seeing you fall apart. Seeing you desperate for me, Ruby."

"I want that, too," she whispers.

Emotion swells, warm and raw.

I smash my mouth to hers, and I'll be damned if I have an inch of self-control after that little confession. I slam into her, up to the hilt. She cries out, and I swallow every last sweet sound she makes, thrusting into her hard. Pulling out so slow, it makes my head spin.

It only takes a few minutes before Ruby is trembling,

legs wrapped around my waist. I pick up the pace, rubbing a thumb over her clit. When her stunning brown eyes lock on mine and she unravels beneath me, I make myself a promise.

To always love this woman. To always make her happy.

Whatever that means for me.

Chapter Thirty

RUBY

I t's magic.

Pure, glittering, wondrous magic.

The entire conference room has been transformed from drab beige and paneled walls with pastel carpet to a transcendent space. You could say the inn has had a glow up. It's my best work yet.

Half of the room is under round dining tables. Tall centerpieces stud the centers, tea lights, crystal, and fine bone China adorning each place setting. The theme of white-on-white has washed out the outdated tones, creating something heavenly. Stunningly whimsical.

Servers with silver trays weave through the black-tie crowd. Reed slips his hand around mine, lacing his fingers through. "This is magnificent, beautiful."

I cast my gaze about the room, doing a visual check of every element that was planned. String quartet, check.

Abundance of flowers from the local florist, check. Bar flowing and hors d'oeuvres circulating, check. Guests spill in through the open double doors where Mary-Sue is greeting each one.

"I need to do the rounds and help Mary-Sue. Save me a seat?" I ask Reed.

He leans in, all clean-shaven, cologne, green eyes, and square jaw. "You bet, beautiful."

I twist the wedding band on my finger. I'm not usually nervous at events, but today has been too much already. And despite the event prep coming off without a hitch, something's off. Reed's focus drops to my hands.

He closes his fingers around my left hand and raises it to his lips. Pressing a soft kiss to my knuckles, he winks. "Go impress the panties off them, Mrs. Robbins."

With a wry smile I peck his cheek and wander through the growing crowd to where Mary-Sue stands. She greets me with open arms. "Ruby, you have outdone yourself, darlin'."

"I'm so happy you like it. Elegance was the element I was going for, I thought it suited the inn *and* its owner." I lean into her, and the older woman squeezes an arm around my shoulders.

"Where is that gorgeous husband of yours?"

"He's finding our table." I glance Reed's way. He is mid-conversation with Bill.

"Well, I imagine you two will want to settle down and

have yourselves some beautiful babies very soon." Mary-Sue grins at me.

"Ah, actually we—"

"Ruby Robbins, or is it Rawlins? I'm getting it all mixed up between New York, Great Falls, or is it Lewistown. Tell me, which is it, Ruby?" The light voice should sound friendly, but its familiarity sends a chill down my spine. I hesitate before turning to find Starr, dressed in an apron with a silver tray propped on one hand. Her smirk is almost sickening, and when she tracks her attention to Mary-Sue, my breath stops.

Fuck me.

"Rawlins?" Mary-Sue says, confusion lowering her brows. "I thought Reed didn't know the Rawlinses, are they relations on your side?"

"Ah, they are, um . . ."

"So, which is it, Robbins or Rawlins?" Starr says too sweetly.

"Robbins," I choke out.

Mary-Sue's staring at my wedding band, her focus shifting to Reed as he laughs at something Bill says. Heat rushes my neck and face. A waiter floats past, and I snatch a tall glass of champagne from the tray, throwing it down in three gulps.

"It's Robbins, hon," Mary-Sue says to Starr. "You know that. You should keep moving, we can't have the guests going hungry or thirsty. That's not in the event plan."

"Sure, wouldn't want to ruin anyone's evening." She swaggers off, tray held high as if that's her *fuck-you-Ruby* trophy.

"That girl is so daft, I swear, she'll forget her own head one of these days." Mary-Sue turns from the receding waitress's form to me.

Fuck. That was too close. I thank my lucky stars she didn't bring up the lawsuit. I have no idea how I would explain that away to Mary-Sue.

My last event in Montana must go smoothly. Stalking my way to the hostess at the other side of the big doors with the tablet to check in guests, I give her a warm smile. "Everyone here?" I ask.

"Every last one. Your party is goin' to be stellar, Ruby."

"Mary-Sue's party, and yes, it's all going to plan. Thanks. Keep me posted if you have any worries with guests or anything else, okay?"

"Sure, enjoy your night."

I weave through the mingling of perfumes, tuxes, and shimmering floor-length dresses toward Reed. The seat beside him is empty, his arm draped over it, as if he's saving it. He's chatting, laughing, and when he takes a sip of his beer and I scan the table, the next man I find runs heat up my spine.

Morley.

Fuck me.

And he's sitting right next to Mary-Sue.

I lean over Reed and let my hair fall around his face as I level my lips to his ear with my softest whisper. "Morley is here *again*? How the hell does that happen twice?"

He turns, glancing up at me with a cheeky wink. One that tells me he's got everything under control. I hope he does.

Since when does Ruby Robbins hope?

Hard work, all the way. No glitches. And Morley here is definitely a glitch. How the hell did he make the guest list without me realizing? Again!

But if Reed isn't worried, that's good enough for me. And then I see it, the chair by Morley is empty. Who is he waiting for? A vacancy that could end in disaster. I sink onto the seat by Reed and adjust my dress. His hand, warm and strong, finds my thigh before his fingers tangle through mine.

When the music fades, Bill stands, glass in hand.

"Welcome! First off, thanks for coming out tonight. And a big thank you to the investors who were here for the last event and this one. The revamp and opening would not have happened without you. To my lovely wife for helping with the plans for this, my new venture. Have a great night, y'all."

His new venture? Mary-Sue does all the grunt work and the long hours. What an ass.

A few men wander over, congratulating Bill on the inn. Mary-Sue sinks further into her chair with every dismissive comment that leaves his fucking mouth. The hurt on her face drives me wild. How can she sit there and let that jerk of a husband claim her success and hard work? It's inconceivable.

Food appears at my place, and Reed orders another beer.

"So Ruby, Reed was telling me you two have other business. Something about a holiday ranch."

I stiffen and Reed gives me a nod, a manic smile filling his face.

"Yes, actually, we were working on a ranch in the area. The opening was almost as good as this one." I force a too-bright smile.

"And how exactly did you get that job, Ruby?" Morley asks, malice glinting in his eyes.

Tampering down the overwhelming need to stab a fork through his eyeballs, I clear my throat and smile. "I worked a party for Louisa Rawlins over by Lewistown. So, word of mouth, I guess."

I shrug, hoping . . . No, *praying* Morley will drop it.

"The Rawlinses, what did you think of them?" Morley leans forward, eyes darting between Reed and me.

"Lovely. Are you from around here?" I ask, innocence plastered over my face.

"Oh, Justin here is our nephew. And one of our newest investors," Bill says, slapping Morley on the shoulder.

"How wonderful."

I guess Morley and I are both faking who we are and what we know now.

"Yeah, we like to keep it in the family round here," Morley says, sipping his beer, eyes narrowed.

I catch my eye roll before anyone can notice and dig into my food. When nobody else has anything else to say, I glance up. Morley's smirk is set on me before it tracks to Reed. Who is happily ignoring him. Like they really just met, and they have nothing to talk about. I relax a little, enjoying the flavors of the meal, sipping on the champagne.

"Oh, my lord! I'm so sorry I'm late, babe," a woman says, rushing past, bumping my chair as she rounds our table and flops onto the chair by Morley.

Skye.

My gut sinks.

And when she scans the table and her focus slams to a halt on my face, I push my shoulders back and suck in a breath. I can almost see my career swirling the drain with the next lungful of air I drag in. Reed shifts on his seat.

Fuck.

"What the hell?" Skye says to Morley before turning to Mary-Sue. "This is the woman that threw the wine in my face at the bar!"

Fuck. Please, please don't mention the lawsuit!

Mary-Sue's face goes from happy with Skye's arrival to confusion to outright disgust. I'm guessing Morley is a *close* nephew. And Skye has been automatically made part of the family.

"Ruby, is that true?" Mary-Sue says quietly. I can see the disappointment bloom over her face.

"It was a—" I look to Reed. I can't lie. Not anymore. "You know what? Yeah, that was me. Skye and her friend were harassing Reed. It was . . . unwholesome, to say the least."

I know exactly how much weight 'unwholesome' carries for Mary-Sue. And I weaponised it. Heat flushes my body.

"He was good for it, until you came along," Skye says, screwing up her face.

Mary-Sue glances between us, horror and confusion tangling across her face. "But why would your husband be at the Great Falls bar looking for—" She shakes her head. "Never mind, gossip is nobody's friend, and definitely has no place in this room tonight. Why don't you tell me how you two met? How long have you been married, Ruby?"

Thankful for the redirect, I focus on Mary-Sue, not Skye, who right now is burning a hole through my head with her glare. "We met in the city, one of those fundraiser events, you know."

"I was working a development job on the east side, got a last-minute invite, you know how it is. And Ruby was there," Reed adds.

I stare at him, but he simply smiles and squeezes my hand. The air leaves my lungs, and I swear my heart swells.

Morley chokes on his beer, and only then does he shift

his gaze to the rings on our hands. He huffs an incredulous laugh. "Oh, for fuck's sake! Aunt Mary, they're not married. That's Reed Rawlins. Harry's son. She's from New York." His focus swings back to me. "Are you two even together?"

And there it is.

I freeze as fear snakes up my spine.

Desperation twisting my face, I glance at Reed.

His face is stone, eyes homed in on Morley. His hands curl to fists. And when he closes his eyes and shakes his head real slow, I know it's time to go. I stand and excuse myself, grabbing up my purse. I pull Reed from his chair. He stands beside me, close, and wraps an arm around my waist.

"Ruby? I don't understand?" Mary-Sue's face is devastated.

"I'm sorry, Mary-Sue." I suck in a breath and swallow past the stone lodged in my throat. "I hope you enjoy your event. *You* deserve it." I glimpse at Bill as I turn and head for the double doors, Reed beside me.

"Well, that was unexpected, baby."

"It's fine. It's—it will be okay." I fight the sob crawling up my airway as we pass through the doors, and they thud closed behind us.

Reed turns me to face him and takes my face with both hands. "Hey, you did so good. Mary-Sue got the event she wanted. Her inn is going to be a huge success, and you were part of that."

I wrap my fingers around his wrists, wrangling air into my lungs. I've never felt like more of a failure. Not even with my overachieving family. I really wanted this to work out. I thought I could do this.

"Let's go home," I whisper. Everything deflates in this moment. My hopes, the tunnel vision that I have held for my career for so long. Tears swell, lining my eyes.

"Ruby?" Mary-Sue says from by the door.

We both turn toward her. Reed drops his hands from my face and pulls me into his side, as if that can protect me from her wrath.

And I meet the older woman's gaze, running my bottom lip through my teeth.

"So let me get this straight." She steps closer. "You are a Rawlins"—she waves at Reed, then turns back to me—"and you are Ruby Robbins?"

"Yes, ma'am." Reed nods.

"Why did you lie to me, Ruby?"

"You wanted a married woman working on your event. And I—"

"You're not." She shakes her head.

"No. I'm sorry I lied, Mary-Sue. But I saw how much you wanted this to work out. And, it sounds pretentious, but I knew I could make your events so much more than any other planner you'd find out here. It's literally my life's work. And—"

The older woman holds a hand up. "I'm not happy you lied and even less happy you and Skye had an . . . incident. But what hurts me most is that you thought it was okay to rope this young man into your schemes."

Suddenly, the air in the inn's enormous foyer evaporates. I force air through my nose and into my lungs, each too short and burning, pressing the back of my hand to my mouth.

"I will be emailing your boss, Olive, in the morning. Good night, Ruby Robbins. Reed." She turns back, disappearing through the doors.

"Rub—" Reed reaches for me. I back away, stalking for the front doors.

I need air.

Like, now.

Crisp, cold air rushes my face and fills my lungs as the sliding doors snap closed behind me.

"Vehicle, Mrs. Robbins?" the valet asks.

"Yes, please." I steel myself against the will to let every last horrible thought and emotion out. And when the rumble of Reed's truck rolls around the corner and stops in front of me, I thank the young guy and slide into the driver's seat. Hands gripping the wheel with white knuckles, I drop my forehead onto it.

The passenger door opens, and Reed climbs in. "Where we off to, baby?"

"I don't know. Anywhere but here."

"You wanna go home? I can go and grab our bags."

I shove the stick in drive and roll into the street. Reed was right, the rumble is comforting.

"I can drive, Rubes," Reed offers.

"No," I breathe.

I let the truck idle at the last set of lights of Great Falls, and when that round glass goes green, I sink my foot onto the accelerator. Tears roll down my face as we pick up speed, busting through the small-town limits until we're flanked by snow-covered fields.

Northbound and no clue where this leads, I choke through each sob. Reed grips the door handle with one hand, the other a fist on the seat beside him. I have ruined everything with stupid, stupid lies. The holiday ranch could be affected by my thoughtlessness. A fucking fake marriage? Who is idiotic enough to think that would have panned out?

This is *all* my fault.

"Beautiful, slow down." Reed's face is stone, eyes on me.

Reed reaches over, turning the headlights on.

Fuck, I can't even remember the basics.

"Rubes, it will blow over, baby. Please slow down."

"No, it won't Reed. I've screwed everything up. I—"

"Deer!"

"Fuck!"

I slam a foot on the brake as the deer ambles onto the road, dazed by the headlights bouncing off the snowy road. My heel slips from my foot with the pressure. The deer stops in the path of the truck. I wrench the wheel to the right.

"No! Don't swer—" Reed lunges for the wheel.

The animal slams into the front corner of the truck, the headlight burying into its side. Its limp body disappears underneath the truck as the vehicle spins to the right, clipping the culvert railing. The snowy road too slick, the truck leaves the ground, careening into the air, rolling.

Weightlessness grips me as we are tossed in our seats.

I can't breathe.

Reed's eyes burn, frozen, panicked. He reaches for me. The tips of our fingers brush.

White bursts from the dash, engulfing the cab of the truck.

Airbags.

I cover my face with my arms as the hiss of white power fills the space between Reed and me.

"RUBY!" Terror floods his voice.

The ringing in my ears drowns out the thunderous crash when the truck hits the ground and rolls. Glass shatters, raining inward through the gaps between the airbags like chaotic wind chimes. We jerk to a stop. Instantly, the steering wheel flies up and cracks into my head.

Hissing.

Then the nothingness of quiet.

Darkness creeps in from every angle.

Chapter Thirty-One

REED

Every inch of me is so heavy. My head pounds. The droning in my ears, so loud. I shake my head to dislodge it. It doesn't budge. Glass falls. Warmth trickles down my forehead. Sharpness cuts into my hands. The inside of my truck is blurred and wrong. The roof lining of the truck is beneath me.

Upside down.

We're upside down. The seatbelt bites into my hips and one shoulder.

Ruby . . .

God, no. Please no!

I push the airbags aside, reaching to find her.

Hanging from the driver's seat, her hair is littered with glass. The side of her head by her ear is soaked with a streak of bright-red blood. She's out cold.

"No, baby," I rasp.

She's still.

Her chest is barely moving. I tug at the belt, raging against its hold with a scream. The scaly fingers of heated anxiety claw through my center, stealing the last of my shaky breath. The seat belt tightens, and my lungs cave in.

I shake my head until stars burst into the sides of my vision.

Snap out of it, Rawlins! Ruby needs you.

I grind through a groan and push the button on the seat belt with one hand, bracing myself with the other on the roof. The second the belt releases, I crash into the roof lining and the truck sways. Ruby swings with the movement. Tiny pieces of glass dig into my neck and shoulders. The sting barely registers.

Pushing myself upright, I shuffle on my seat cautiously toward Ruby over the glass. "Rubes, baby, wake up."

She doesn't move. But the truck does. Fuck.

I can't see well enough past the airbags to tell where we are. But by the way the truck rolls and shakes with my slightest movement, it's not somewhere stable.

I wedge myself under her and support her shoulders. "Beautiful, you gotta wake up." My voice cracks, my body screaming with the pain of impact and hundreds of tiny bits of glass weaving their way under my skin. "Ruby Jane Rawlins, *wake up!*"

I sob into her shoulder.

Sweet Jesus.

God, how could I let this happen to her? I should have insisted I drive. Made her pull over.

A sweet, coppery tang winds through my senses.

Blood and strawberries.

I sweep my thumbs over her cheeks. "Baby, wake up, please. We gotta get outta here," I whisper.

The warmth I felt earlier reaches my shoulder. My white dress shirt is now red on my left side. Bile rises in my throat, burning. I run my hand over her neck, hunting for a pounding pulse, only to find a thready one.

We need help.

I scan the truck for one of our phones. Mine is wedged between the seats above me. I grab for it. My hands shake too badly to tap the screen.

"Siri, call 911, on speaker."

"Calling 911." The ringtone starts.

"911. What's your emergency?"

Eyes closed, I swallow down a ragged breath.

"Help, please. Highway 87 northbound from Great Falls. The truck has rolled. She's out cold. Please, hurry."

"Stay on the line, sir, an emergency unit will be . . ."

Hushed voices float around. The pounding in my head is gone. But something holds me in place. Body heavy with fatigue, I open my eyes. Florescent lights burn my eyes, and a light-green curtain sways, surrounding the hard bed I'm on.

An IV is sunk into a vein in my hand. The cotton stretched over me is not my shirt. I push to sit up. My head spins, but the sensation fades with a few deep breaths.

Ruby.

I swing my feet from the bed and rip the needle from my hand, tossing it onto the covers. The curtain moves, and Ma has me in her hold a heartbeat later.

"Oh, my boy. You should be resting, sweetheart."

"Where's Ruby?" I choke out.

Ma pushes back, holding me at arm's length. "She's down the hall. I tried to call her family, but her father's receptionist said he wasn't to be disturbed."

"Did the hospital try?"

"They did. Same response."

"Fucking hell. Pack of lousy, good-for-noth—"

Ma's hand lands on my arm, and she gives me a sad smile. "She has you."

I push past Ma and make for the curtain. Cool air swirls up my legs and over my ass. Fuck me.

"Here," Ma says, handing me clean jeans and a t-shirt with a sad smile that sends my gut plummeting. She slips out, and I pull the clothes on as quick as my aching body will let me. Every single cut on my skin burns. The glass is gone, but the sting remains. On bare feet, I rip the curtain back and stagger toward Ma, who is standing outside a bay marked Emergency 1.

Closest to the nurse's station. That's not good.

When I reach the curtain, Ma grabs my hand and nods, scrunching up her face. I know that look. She is trying to prepare me. Air leaves my lungs like a fucking vacuum. Harry appears by the corner of the hall and walks over, wrapping himself around Ma.

I turn back to the curtain and will my lungs to expand, to fill with air so I can move forward. With a shaking hand, I slide the fabric back. Ruby lies on the bed in the same gown I had on a moment ago. Her hair is still caked with blood, her face is cut up from the glass. A bruise the size of my palm is over her forehead and temple. Her chest rises and falls in a steady rhythm, her hands by her side. One finger is covered by a gadget, the other hand has an IV drip in it. The machines nearby monitor her vitals.

I fiddle with the bed rail, getting it to go down, and sit on the side of the bed. I trace my fingers over her cheeks and tuck a stray piece of hair behind her ear. The curtain hisses, and a doctor walks in.

"Mr. Robbins?" His glance drops to my hand, where the wedding band still sits on my ring finger.

"Yes." I offer up my hand. "Reed."

He shakes my hand, confusion filtering over his features. "You were in curtain six. Isn't it Rawlins?"

"Long story. Can we focus on Ruby?"

"Fine. I take it you're discharging yourself?"

"Yep." I return my focus to Ruby.

He stares at me for a heartbeat before tracking to the bed. "Your wife has had a hard knock, but her scans came back clean. We sedated her a little earlier. Nothing major, only a Valium. She woke up agitated, she was panicking, calling for you."

Ruby needed me. And I wasn't fucking here.

"How long 'til she wakes up from the sedative?"

"A few hours and she will be up. I suggest you be here when she wakes up this time."

He nods and writes something brief in her chart before walking out and replacing the curtain. Ruby scared is one thing I can't accept.

I lean over and dot a kiss to her cheek. "Hey, baby. I'm here, beautiful. Whenever you're ready."

She doesn't move.

Just lies there, breathing slow and steady. I can only imagine the dreams she is having right now. I hope to hell she's not reliving the truck careening off the road. I don't want her to be scared. That tears me up. Standing, I drag the only chair in the cubicle to her bedside and sink into it. Dropping my head on the side of the bed, I fold her hand between my own.

My body is sore and tired. My head more so, from the

months hustling, trying to reconcile with the fact that Rubes is leaving soon. I close my eyes and the room spins. I press her hand to my lips again and let sleep take me wherever the fuck it wants.

"Reed . . ." Ruby's voice is weak and raspy. I snap my head up and jolt onto the bed. She leans forward, and I help her sit up. When she is steady and sitting comfortably, I lean back to study her face, needing to see in her eyes that she is okay.

"Baby, you scared me," I choke.

Her eyes widen, pulling with fear.

I take her face in my hands and move closer. "Hey, hey, you're okay. You're safe. I'm right here."

She shakes her head. "Olive . . . my work . . . your—" She tilts her head with a whimper. "Your *truck.*"

Sobs spill from her lips, her fingers sliding into her hair.

Fuck my goddamn truck.

"Ruby, I don't care about the truck. It's just a vehicle." I don't know what to say on the other two points. I don't know Olive or how Big Corporate deals with this sort of misconduct.

"You loved that thing." Tears track down her reddened cheeks. Her face crumples, and she winces.

"Ruby Jane Rawlins, I love you so, so much more."

She loses it, sobbing hard as I pull her into a hug. I rub her back, dotting kisses to her hair as she lets out every ounce of fear, stress, worry, and hurt. The last few days have been too much. What I wouldn't give to make all the hard things in her life disappear.

As her sobs fade, she leans back and wipes her face with her hands. Her brown eyes land on mine. "I need to go home, Reed."

"Sure, baby, I'll take you home. I'll grab Harry's truck."

"No." Her voice is barely a whisper. "I need to go to *my* home. I've ruined everything. It's a disaster. I need to try and fix it."

The stone in my throat sinks, transforming into a full-on fucking anvil in my gut. And it must show on my face, because hers breaks again. She schools it back and sucks in a breath.

"I need to figure out what I want. And where I go from here. I need to talk to Olive. Maybe my parents?"

Forcing air into my lungs, then back out, I stare at our hands, tangled together.

"Sure, Rubes, whatever you need. I could drive you. We could talk."

"No, Reed. I have to do this by myself. I'll fly home. Take a week or two. Maybe a little longer."

The tear in my heart grows with every beat it takes. If Ruby needs time, I'll give it to her. I'd give her anything, no matter the cost.

"I'll book your flight and pack your stuff, beautiful." I stand and release her hands.

"Reed." Tears stream down her cheeks.

"It's okay, Rubes. You don't owe me a thing. You take care of yourself this time."

I wander into the hall and toward the exit. A hand rests on my shoulders, and I turn back, dazed. Harry stands with my boots and cap in his hands. "I'll take you home, son."

I don't respond, simply following him through the doors and into the midday warmth. Ma waits by the truck. I slide into the front passenger's seat, and she shuts the door and hops into the back. As we pull away from the Great Falls hospital, I replay Ruby's words over and over in my head.

The hour and a half that it takes to drive to R & R Ranch flies past, me lost in my head and all. I spill from the truck and wander inside.

"Let me pack her things, sweetheart," Ma says.

"No, I'll do it."

I pad upstairs and into the room that has been Ruby's for months. Not that she slept in this bed even one night. Her clothes are neatly stored in the cupboard and dresser, and it doesn't take me long to have the woman I would give up everything for packed up. The only item left is her

Coach Love perfume. The one that had me addicted to her from the moment I met her.

Strawberries.

I can't bring myself to pack it, so I don't.

Ma clears her throat from the doorway. "So, you two really married?"

I still, hand holding the zipper halfway. "No."

"Would that be such a bad idea?"

I turn to face her. "Ma," I say incredulously.

She shrugs and waves her palms up. "You're amazing together, just sayin'."

"Ruby has plans."

"So do you. Look at everything the two of you have created. I see the way you are with her, hon. That matters —it's so important. It is what makes this life worth it."

Maybe, but it's irrelevant.

Sickening sensation winds through my core, spreading to my arms. The tingle in my hands starts, and I sink onto the bed.

Fuck.

I try to pull in air, but it's too thin.

I strain to hear the sounds around me, but she's not here. I hear nothing.

I grope to feel my surroundings, and don't find her soft skin, her soft, velvet lips.

I can't . . .

I can't without Ruby.

I grapple to pull in a breath, and stars creep into my

vision. My hands cramp up as my shoulders heave, my lungs screaming for air. Choking sobs tumble out.

Ma is in front of me, her palms on my face. Her face blurs as I slide from the bed, knees hitting the wood floor. I lean forward, trying to shake the pain from my arms.

Nothing gives.

". . . Reed," Ma coaxes.

I rock back and forth. Images of Ruby, her cut-up face, her hanging from the seatbelt upside down. Her happy laugh and smile, all faded as she lay still in the hospital bed.

Ruby distraught over those fucking hussies that ruined her event and her plans. The lawsuit. The months she lost on her own work because she was here, helping me.

Sweet Jesus.

I groan, pushing to my feet.

"Reed? Are you alright?" Ma's face sharpens, her brows lowered, her eyes devastated.

"I can handle it."

She grabs my hands. "No, you— You got this from me. The anxiety. I'm so sorry." Worry lines her face.

"I'm fine, Ma. I can handle it. Ruby taught me."

Yet another thing that beautiful woman gave me. How can I ever repay her for that? For giving me my freedom back. All she did was give and give. She helped me, and what did she receive in return?

A fucking nightmare.

I'm not going to take away the things Ruby wants so I

can have the one thing I want. God, I'm an utter idiot for telling Hudson what to do when this was where him and Addy were at. It's not as simple as being in love. It ain't.

"Can I borrow your truck?" I ask Ma as I push past with Ruby's bags and head down the stairs.

"Of course." She doesn't follow.

Harry is waiting by the door, arms crossed. Hat pulled down, brows lowered. God above, what now?

"Your truck was towed to the wreckers."

"Sounds about right."

"Insurance will cover the cost of a new one."

"Thanks."

I couldn't care less. I grab my coat from the back of the door and make my way to Harry's truck. "I'll be back in a few hours."

"Take your time, son."

I toss the bags in the back seat of the silver Chevy and climb up into the driver's side. When the engine fires up, the first sob lodges in my throat, cutting off my air supply. After everything that has happened, never in a million years would I have thought this is how Ruby and I would end.

My forehead hits the steering wheel, hands gripping it until my knuckles turn white.

My heart cracks right in two.

Chapter Thirty-Two

The second the door of my east side Manhattan apartment closes behind me, I know I don't belong here anymore. Everything is cold. Foreign. Clinical.

Lifeless.

After a week recovering in Lewistown and a red-eye back to the city, I have two days to recover before I go in to meet with Olive. To find out if I still have a job. With all that's happened, do I even want it anymore?

One thing I do know, losing my rules, spending time with the Rawlinses . . . I don't see life the way I used to. I dump my bags by the door and pad to the kitchen. The space is so clean, so void of living, it's like a hotel, not my home.

My phone pings.

Addy.

Hey Rubes, make it back to NY alright?

And Lou.

Let me know when you make it
back, hon.

New York, back. Not *home*. Even Addy's siding with Montana.

I huff out a laugh—of course she is. Who wouldn't? We think living happens here in the city. But it's more like the skeleton of survival, not the flesh and blood of life that sees your heart pumping and pulls laughter through your lips. That lets love bloom from somewhere deep you didn't even realize existed in your soul.

Fuck me, I'm a Hallmark card now.

Sweet Jesus.

My breath catches at the automaticity and ease of the saying the Rawlins men use.

I wander aimlessly around the small apartment for an hour, touching the things I thought I valued. Picking up frames without photos, still the happy stock photo families from the factory nestled behind the glass. The one plant I own is sporting a generous amount of dust on its plastic green leaves. And when I reach my bedroom, I flop onto the bed. The crystal chandelier that hangs over the bed glitters.

I tap a message back to Addy so she doesn't worry. But I find myself scrolling through the back-and-forth texts between Reed and me. I come across a photo of him and I, beaming as we sit by the fire, me on his lap, huddled against him. Addy took this one and sent it to Reed. He sent it to me later that night, with a text: "R & R—the only thing I will ever need, baby."

God, he looks so happy.

We look so happy.

I chug sobs, letting the phone fall onto the bed. Every breathy cry that tumbles from my lips takes a little of the worry and sadness that I have been carrying around my entire life. I roll over and scream the last of the tension and anger into my pillow.

Five minutes.

You have five minutes, Ruby Robbins, to let it out, suck it up, and start fixing this clusterfuck.

Now is the time for the soul-searching sliver that lies dormant in me to bubble to the surface. Because there are a few things in this life that are more important than best-laid plans.

Olive is livid. I mean, who can blame her? Not me. I screwed up, and I'm at peace with that now. I may or may not have a job at the end of this meeting. And for the first time in my life, I'm okay with that.

"How did this happen, Ruby?" she snaps, leaning over her desk, finger pointing at the tablet in front of her. The screen has a photo of the inn, Mary-Sue standing out front with none other than Justin fucking Morley. "I have multiple emails from the Heritage Inn owners claiming the events were amazing, but they will not be working with us because of your deceit."

"She assumed I was married. And you told me to fix it, so I did."

She leans back in her chair and taps her pale pink manicured nails on the desk. "I did not tell you to lie to an entire town, to use your position to have some sordid affair with a stranger."

The heat of shame turns to a fire of anger. What the actual fuck?

"There is nothing *sordid* about Reed Rawlins and me. And yes, I asked him to attend the events as my husband. But that was all to appease a pedantic client with values so outdated they should have left with the Ark!" I throw my hands up.

"So you thought it appropriate to lie to the very people who were building your career, allowing you to spend their budget and influence their peers and friends."

My mouth gapes. She is blowing this way out of proportion.

"What the hell, Olive? You told me to fix the problem. I did, at least until the last minute, when everything turned to shit."

"I'm sorry, Ruby, we can't have dishonest staff in this company. Our integrity is our major strength, and I will not weaken it with your scandals. No matter how far removed from our upmarket clientele."

So, she's firing me.

Fucking perfect.

I stand and straighten my tan pencil skirt. The red heels that I wear like a second skin dig into her plush carpet. "You know what, Olive? I quit."

"You won't receive severance pay, Robbins."

She rarely calls me by my last name. I can remember the one occasion she did. She was irate with me, but back then I was a junior. So much has changed since then.

I have changed.

"Not bothered, darlin'." I give her my best Harry voice and stride for the door.

"Ruby!?"

I turn back with one hand resting on the silver door handle. "Hand in your access cards before you leave, please."

I flash her a smile that would freeze lava. She jerks in her chair. The girl at the assistant's desk sinks into hers as I walk toward it.

"She reamed you out, too?" she asks quietly, glancing at the door that just closed behind me.

"I quit, actually."

"Lucky you. She has been horrid ever since her

husband was caught cheating on her. I know I should feel bad for her, but she is so mean."

Oh, that explains some things.

For a moment, my heart bleeds for Olive. But with bridges burned, I know better than to try and backpedal over ashes.

"Give her some space; she'll come around." I smile, sweetly this time, and salute her with two fingers. By the time I reach the elevator, my brain has caught up with my actions, and I slam my eyes shut, slumping against the wall.

Captain.

Mack had told me what that salute meant between Reed and me.

And the way he reacted the first time I wore the faded red Captain's Choice t-shirt with my PJ shorts . . .

But I have some things to work out before I can consider where Reed and I stand. If we stand together at all.

Back in the apartment, I pull out boxes from the spare room closet. Dust drifts down as I flip the lid off the last box. I can't remember why I started hunting through the rubble of my childhood and the past ten years, but I'm on the last box, so . . . Why stop now?

Books and a journal sit in the box. I blow the remnants of a decade from the surface of the journal and open the cover.

Ruby Jane Robbins

Age: 10

I slip the pages across with a finger, reading the ramblings of a ten-year-old prone to daydreaming. The spine is cracked on the sparkling hardcover book, and when I place it on the floor, it spills open to the center spread.

My ultimate dream: To have a home where I feel I belong and people who love me, lots and lots and always, no matter what!

I stare at the page as the words I wrote eighteen years ago deliver a sucker punch with acute precision. I never felt loved in my childhood home. And I never really let myself think about it.

Until recently.

Until the Rawlinses.

Until Reed.

Until Louisa and Harry.

I've always had Addy; she's my sister in so many ways my biological siblings never will be. But the Rawlinses, that was the first time I felt cherished and loved. Spending my days with Louisa was like finally having that unconditional love only a mother can give.

My days with Reed.

Nothing else compares.

I doubt anything ever will. And not one of the days in Montana had a single thing to do with my rules. I lay on the floor and stare up at the ceiling. It's time to rewrite the rules. Course correction is required.

A new heading for this captain.

I smile, stupidly happy, as tears flood the floor under my neck. This captain needs her first mate. Our ship and whatever comes with that will be enough.

The old Ruby would be fighting this way of thinking. The old Ruby would insist on sticking to progress and achievements, to drive forward and carve a place for herself in the big world with a plethora of plans and checklists. The old Ruby was a miserable bitch. No way in hell am I going to end up like Olive.

I peel myself from the floor and rush to the bags I left by the front door. Snatching up the laptop bag, I rip my MacBook out and flip open the screen as I slump into the sofa.

Reinvention.

A new plan . . . new rules.

That is what I want. Ones that revolve around the heart of my ten-year-old mindset, a happy home with people who love me unconditionally. I open a fresh tab and type "google" into the URL bar. The blank search engine glares back, its endless potential and infinite possibilities cracked wide.

I click the Notes icon, fingers hovering over the keyboard.

Six rules are too many.

Too much restraint, and that's what landed me in this position to begin with.

Three. Three is a good number of rules for any girl to

have. Nobody likes a control freak. Just enough for some direction, so I don't end up lost.

I let my eyes fall shut and my mind wander.

What do I want?

What do I really want . . .

First, to *belong*.

What do I need?

That feeling I had in Louisa's kitchen. In Reed's home.

Unconditional love, so I am free to live and grow without fear of failing the people I cherish.

What can't I live without?

That one's easy.

Reed James Rawlins.

Everything else—the career, the plans, and the status —is superfluous now. But I do need some way to spend my days and fill my soul. To fuel my independence.

Louisa's party flashes through my mind. The happy faces. The way Lou's face lit up when Harry led her outside to her family and friends. The close-knit community of people who know each other so well and have been through thick and thin.

I want that. I need that.

To be able to create those moments for other families, that would be priceless.

Bingo.

With a little research and a new focus, I can start working on big family parties, reunions, and maybe even weddings?

A party planner who's like part of the family.

God save me, that's corny. And exactly what I'm going to do.

I tap away, pulling up inspiration from Pinterest, making mock run sheets and checklists for all three of my new ideas. And when I begin the business plan, my fingers still over the laptop as the screen shows the most recent tab. R & R Ranch, holiday ranch business plan.

I smile at the screen like it's an old friend as the memories of working through the proposal with Reed scroll through my mind. And that unfamiliar feeling of something I know down to my bones I need but have never been able to grasp . . .

Warmth swells as I fly through the times I shared with Reed's family at home at Rosewood Ranch. Belonging blooms in my core, steady and bright. And when it steals my breath, I slam the MacBook shut.

Good Lord, how could I have been so daft?

Ma keeps calling my phone. I let it ring out, and then I let it go flat. I'm in no mood for chit chat and even less in the mood for her suggestions. Especially since each one of them ends with me in New York.

Ruby wants space.

She asked for it, straight up. And I am goin' to give her as much as she needs. Even if it means she never comes home to R & R Ranch. It's the one thing—scratch that, the only thing I have left to give her. Huddo's truck rolls into the driveway. And he parks by Harry's Chevy, which is still my loaner for the next few months while I sort out the insurance garbage. Fucking red tape paperwork shit. Who would have thought that because I wasn't drivin' it could make so much of a difference in claimant matters?

When Addy jumps out of the driver's seat, I lean the rake against the doorframe of the stables.

"Hey, Reed." She waves as she walks over to the stables. Charlie flies out of the truck and winds through her legs, sniffing the ground. Those two have been inseparable since Addy started her lessons with Huddo. *Good for you, devil boy.* Her brown eyes find mine, and I freeze. I know they're not Ruby's, but since every single damn thing insists on reminding me of the woman I've lost, it hits hard.

"Hi Adds, you needin' something?"

She stops short of where I stand, and Charlie stalks into the stables, nose to the ground.

Her hands land on my shoulders as a grin blooms over her face. "Yup," she says, tilting her face, "you."

"I'm tied up here. Can't Huddo or Harry help?"

She huffs a laugh and shakes her head. "No, Reed, they can't."

I sigh and lift the Yankees cap from my head and run a hand through my hair. "What can I do for you, then?"

Her eyes narrow. "You forget what day it is?"

"Friday?"

"Yeah, no. It's Sunday. Your ma has been trying to call you for hours."

And the sun is high in the sky, so I'm late as well as moody. "Fuck. Shit, sorry. I'm not really in a Sunday lunch mood, Adds."

"That is *exactly* why you should be surrounded by people who love you, Reed."

She grabs my hand and drags me toward the truck. Charlie flies out past us, giving me the stink eye, no doubt for being in close proximity to his favorite human. I toss a narrowed look back at him, every bit as ridiculous and petty as I feel right now. I slow against Addy's grip, and she turns back. "Adds, I have guests, I can't up and leave."

"They're grown men and women. You can let them be for an hour or two. Besides, your ma wants to see you."

I've never been able to say no to Ma. Even as a little kid, she could always pry the truth outta me, make me feel better with one hug. Louisa Rawlins has always been my kryptonite. That was, until Ruby Robbins showed up. Or maybe I have two types of kryptonite now?

Urgh.

"Fine, let me grab my phone and change my shirt to somethin' more respectable."

"Sure, don't take long."

I jog into the house and pluck up my phone from the kitchen counter. I plug it into the power and take the stairs two at a time before swinging around the top of the banister knob and into my room. A minute later, I have a light blue checkered shirt and a fresh white t-shirt. Rolling up the sleeves, I lope down the stairs.

Swiping up the phone, I turn it on. Three more missed calls from Ma. Sliding it into the back pocket of my Wranglers, I readjust my cap and grab my coat from behind the door, walk through, and pull it shut. Charlie is sniffing around the front porch as Addy wanders the yard. She is taking in the fairy lights Ruby hung, staring into the canopy of the trees.

"Right, let's go," I utter, reaching the front gate.

Addy shoots me a smile and whistles for Charlie. He's in her arms a heartbeat later. We pile into Huddo's truck, and Addy fires her up. She doesn't force small talk as we drive down the dirt road for Rosewood Ranch. Love her for that.

And when we pull up in front of Ma's white gate, Addy kills the engine. But she doesn't make a move to leave the truck.

"Ruby loves you, Reed. I know that for sure. The last few weeks haven't been easy, I realize. But she does. So much."

I can't respond. The stone that has grown over my Adam's apple is stuck tight. I nod and push the door open and climb out of the truck. Inside, Ma is fixing something in the kitchen, bent over a large steaming pot on the stove. She drops the wooden spoon to the counter when she sees me, rounding the counter to fold me into her arms.

"I was worried," she whispers.

"Sorry, Ma."

She hugs me tighter. Harry waltzes through the front

door and I hear the words before they leave Ma's mouth. "Boots."

He waves her off and slips his boots off, dropping them onto the rack inside the door. The pair beside his dusty ones catches my eye. Tan bottoms, pink tops.

I push from Ma's hold and scan the house, as if Ruby would be hiding in here somewhere. Did she leave them here last time we came over? My head is so full of running the last few weeks on repeat, I can't even find the memory of what happened the last time Ruby and I were here.

Dumping his hat on the hook by the front table, Harry pads past. "Guests doin' okay over there this week?"

"Fine. All three cabins booked for the entire week, trail rides and the likes scheduled for Monday and Wednesday."

"Sounds like a well-oiled machine to me." He winks and wanders to where Ma is now checking her whatever-it-is on the stove. Wrapping his arms around her waist, he sinks his face into her hair with a groan.

Right, I officially need to be anywhere else but here. I grab up the basket of cutlery and linen, my permanent assignment for Sunday lunches, and push through the back door.

Huddo and Addy are outside already, Addy on his lap. Hudson's hands are in her hair as he pulls her down to him and her forehead rests against his.

Sweet Jesus, all this lovin' could kill a heartbroken man without tryin'.

I dump the basket on the table harder than I need to. Addy jumps but chuckles as she stands to help me with the linen.

"You alright, bud?" Huddo asks.

Fuckin' hell, not only do I feel like the world's most heartbroken loser, now I'm back to the useless little brother.

Fuck my life.

"Fine," I grind out, placing the cutlery around the table while Addy straightens the cloth.

"Smile, Reedsy," Addy says. "Life is not *that* bad."

"Says you, Adds."

"Shoot, can you grab the beers for me?" Huddo says, bending down to inspect the underside of the table. What is it like broken, or something?

"Whatever. Adds, you want one?"

"Nah, just you two."

I wander back inside, hoping to steer clear of the happy couples. The back door slams behind me as I pad down the hallway.

"Here, taste this?" Ma says from the kitchen. Someone is getting a sneak peek of whatever is bubbling in that enormous pot, I guess.

"Mmmm." The soft sound sends electricity through my veins. I jerk to a halt in the hallway, out of sight.

"You like it? It's a new recipe I've been working on."

"It's incredible," the soft and all too familiar voice says.

Her words have me out of breath. My heart sinks into my gut. Leaning against the wall, I close my eyes and listen.

"I'm glad you like it. Maybe we can use it for the catering half our new venture."

"It's got my vote, Lou," Ruby says.

My hands crawl through my hair.

"Brilliant! It's so wonderful to have you home, hon. Gosh, we did miss you, sweetheart."

I swallow, lungs burning.

Ruby came back, and nobody told me?

"Thanks for letting me come home, being here with you and Harry was the only place I felt I could sort all this out. You are—" Her voice cracks. Ma must have folded her into one of her famous hugs, because Ruby's next words are muffled. The sniff that follows tells me Ma has let go.

"Tell me what to do, Lou. Will he ever forgive me?"

"Oh hon, you would have to ask Reed that."

I push from the wall and wander back through the screen and out into the yard, dazed. She came back. She came to Ma to sort her life out. To have the support she needed to move forward. Part of me is so proud our family could be that for her. And part of me is devastated she didn't come home first.

"Reed?"

I turn back.

Harry holds a bundle of cold beers and a bottle of whiskey, glass upturned on top. I close the distance and take the beers. "You wanna talk about it, son?"

I open my mouth to respond and close it again as the back door opens and slams.

Ma.

When she reaches me, she cups my face with her hands. "Someone is waitin' for you inside." Her smile is pure joy.

I can't move.

I will move.

Ruby is waiting.

She needed space. And if she needed Louisa Rawlins to help her plan and execute the next stage of her life, then I am happy she has Ma. Sucking in a breath, I push through the screen and walk into the house. The kitchen is empty.

Dining table, also empty.

"Reed?"

I turn toward the soft sound of her voice. She stands by the crackling fireplace. Her wavy hair is around her beautiful face, dark jeans and a dark red checkered shirt, the sleeves rolled up. Her bottom lip slides through her teeth.

"Hey, beautiful," I rasp over my thundering heart.

Her face breaks, and she presses the back of her hand to her mouth. I jump the sofa and close the distance, and she's on my hips a moment later. Her hands are on my face, her lips smashed to mine. The scent of strawberries is everywhere. She opens her mouth for me, and I claim her with my tongue. Fingers crawling through my hair, her grip tightens, and she moves my head backward. "Sweet Jesus, I missed you, baby."

I chuckle, heart so tight it could burst. But I take to studying her face before I say, "You sure this is what you want, Rubes?"

She nods. Her thumbs wander over my jaw. "I went back to the city, and it all felt so foreign. Every single rule I'd made and lived by doesn't even fit anymore. And then I found something, well, a reminder of it, that is, and I realized I already had the one thing I want."

"And what was that?"

"When I was ten, my dream was to have a home that I felt like I belonged in, and people who love me unconditionally. I know it soun—"

"Nope, it sounds perfect."

Her face lights up and she bites down hard on her bottom lip. The last of the blood supplying my brain floods south, my cock stretching my jeans.

"What are we doin' here, baby?" I rasp.

"Well, I was making lunch for the love of my life." She smiles, and it's the most beautiful thing I have ever seen.

I claw back the sob that is fighting its way up.

"I'm so sorry I left you," Ruby whispers.

"Don't apologize for taking care of yourself, Rubes. Ever."

"As long as you do the same, okay?"

"Deal. You hungry?"

"A little, but . . ."

"But what, baby?"

"Reed, I don't wanna fake it anymore."

Stunned, I stare up at her, wide-eyed. I search her gorgeous brown eyes for any hint of mirth, for some sign that she is playing. But her face is dead serious.

And I find none.

Chapter 34

RUBY

I wait outside the Heritage Inn, pacing the sidewalk like a woman possessed. The family lawyer told me to leave it alone. But I can't do that. Too much is at stake to let this play out and go whichever way a judge decides on any given day. And having enemies in a small town doesn't sit well with me.

The fact that they are two women tugs at my soul. We may come from very different backgrounds, but we should have each other's backs, not be fighting like street cats over stupid shit—and especially not over the opposite sex. So I am going to fix this. The Ruby way. I guess you could say I'm getting into the Christmas spirit a little early this year.

The door swings open, and two women spill out into the midday sunshine. By the way they are chatting and shouldering their bags, I'm guessing it's their lunch break. I stride up to where they stop, checking their phones. My heart hammers, nerves lit up like lightning through a rod.

"Ladies?" I say, pulling my best smile and wringing my own phone through my hands.

Starr glances up from her screen. "Say what? Where's your fake husband, Robbins? Or is it really Rawlins?"

"No, it's not. But I'm not here to cause trouble. I want to apologize."

Skye slides her phone into her bag and folds her arms, raising an eyebrow. "I'm listenin'."

"No way, she only wants out of the lawsuit, don't give her an inch, babes."

"This isn't about the suit, I promise. It's about Reed."

Now Starr snaps her hands to her hips and harrumphs. "Fine, what is it?"

"I have a proposition for you."

Starr's eyes go wide. "We are not hookers, bitch."

Good Lord.

Okay, let's try a rephrase. "I have a deal for you. I want to help you."

"In exchange for what?" Skye tilts her head.

"So, here's the stats, I can help you to make headway in your careers, or help you find something better than this waitressing gig. Something that pays better, something you love. Name it, I'll help you get there."

"Why would we want that, and what does that have to do with Rawlins?"

"You want to be waitressing the rest of your lives?"

I study their faces. I've seen enough of small towns and low socioeconomic families to know how this will play out for them both. Work as a waitress, get married, get knocked up. Back to waitressing, a tiring job with shit pay. Having to pick up a second job to make ends meet.

Nope, it doesn't have to be this way.

"So like, any job we want?" Starr says.

"Probably nothing with NASA, but you never know. My connections are pretty vast."

Their faces don't change. *Okay, no more jokes, Ruby.*

"What about nursing? I always wanted to be a nurse. Mama wouldn't pay for the studies."

"Sure, we can do that."

Starr's face lights up. "Are you for real?"

"I am." I beam at her, arms wide. She pulls out her phone and taps on the screen for a moment before turning it to show me a site from her favorites tab. A nursing college one town over sits on the screen. "That looks amazing, we can do that."

Skye chews her bottom lip between her teeth. "And what do you want in return?"

"I need you to leave Reed be—his business, his family. He has worked so hard to bring the holiday ranch to where it is, he can't lose it. Please, anything to help the ranch prosper and grow would be amazing."

"So, you will give us tuition and stuff and we just have to not troll his business?" Skye's brows lower.

"That sums it up, yes."

"Why are you doing that for him? Your fake marriage was busted and shit." Skye tilts her head, as if trying to comprehend.

"Look, all I know is that sometimes it's hard to do the right thing. And sometimes instead of fighting, we should all make the best of what we have."

"Sounds alright to me. I can take down the review. And the lawsuit, I'll ring the lawyer and drop it," Starr says. A smile peaks over her face.

"Wonderful. Skye?"

Her gaze drops to the sidewalk, and it takes a moment before she returns it to me. "I want to leave this place. I wanna write, you know. Not like a journalist or anything. Stories or whatever."

"How about a literary degree?" I prompt.

"Really?" Her face turns stunned.

"Sure." I grin, and her mouth gapes. "I know a fantastic online degree. You can keep working while you study, and when you're done, you can submit some work to publishers."

"Oh shit! You're serious, aren't you. I don't know what to say."

"Nothing to say. You're welcome."

"Maybe I could do a blog or something for the ranch? And of course, I will take down the shitty review and drop the suit also. Was Morley's idea, anyway."

"Figures. And we'll see." I chuckle. "What about a town gazette or the likes?"

"Can I grab your number?" Starr asks.

"Sure, give me your phones and I'll pop my number in. Text anytime you want."

"Can we attend R & R events?"

"Sure thing. But please, leave Morley at home."

Starr nudges her friend.

"I dumped him last night, such a creep."

"Yeah, I can see that."

I hand their phones back to them and they glance at each other. "You want lunch?" Skye asks.

"Oh, I don't want to impose."

Skye readjusts her bag over her shoulder. "Can you tell me some more about this degree?"

"I can. Actually one of my friends back east just graduated. She loved it."

"Come on, then. The pub has the best steaks in town."

I walk with the two women toward our reconciliation lunch. They chat about their dreams and plans that don't include Great Falls, Montana. And a little spark of warmth blooms to fill my chest, knowing I have taken something sour and turned it sweet, filling me with happiness.

Lou's red sauce should be outlawed. It's that damn good. The earthy flavors hit so right. So good. We stand shoulder to shoulder in her huge kitchen, making Christmas dinner for the family. My family. The one I have waited twenty-eight years for.

The Robbins household doesn't do Christmas, and I have spent half of my childhood holidays with Addy and her family. This year, Addy's parents are in Greece. So we are here, at Rosewood Ranch, and it feels like home.

The men are outside grilling. Addy wanders in, arms loaded with more wood for the hearth, Charlie at her heels. Light snowfall drifts outside, and the trees covered in glittering white are lit up with the fairy lights.

Reed insisted the lights be on, and the entire homestead yard looks like a nativity scene, lights glowing from under the snowy branches and up the massive trunks. A mix of carols sung by country artists plays over the stereo that Reed is once again designated DJ for. Mistletoe hangs in the front door, in the arch of the hallway, and over every bedroom door.

Harry's idea.

Apparently, the only day Harry Rawlins softens is Christmas with his family. Figures. The man is a walking human barometer, and the holidays bring out the kindness in most people. I think he is secretly trying to give Louisa the grandbabies she so desperately wants.

It's sweet.

The pot on the stove in front of me bubbles over.

"Shit!"

I turn the heat down and slip the lid off. The pasta I was assigned to cook has risen to the top. The white frothy cloud simmers down, and I stir it.

"I think it's done, hon." Lou nudges my shoulder with hers, smiling.

"If you say so, Lou. I'm not the best with food. Maybe you should have Addy help next year."

She hugs my shoulders with one arm. "But I love cooking with you, Rubes. Luckily, since we are going into business, sweetheart."

"True, but when we created this event and catering partnership, I was imagining me doing the planning part, not the cooking part."

She laughs and whips her tea towel at me. "You do just fine. Anyway, I think both sides are a two-woman job. I'll teach you food, you teach me events."

"Sounds amazing." I can't wipe the smile that has spread over my face and Lou rests her hand on my cheek. "I'm so glad you're here." Silver lines her eyes.

Tears burn. "Wouldn't be anywhere else."

Strong arms slide around my waist, and the smell of Reed tangles through my senses, shrouding out the Italian fragrances we have been working on for over an hour. His face buries into my neck. "Don't go gettin' all emotional on me, baby. The day is only just started. Long lunch, lazy supper, and then wine by the fire. I don't see us fallin' into bed any time before midnight."

I lay my head back on his and close my eyes. Louisa chuckles, clicking the stove off. I cover Reed's hands with my own. He pushes upright and spins me round to face him before pushing me into the counter beside the stove. He kisses me with equal parts hunger and playfulness. Fingers crawling through his hair a second later, I forget we are smack bang in the middle of his ma's kitchen.

"Alright, you two. Save it for later." A familiar chuckle.

Breaking apart, we turn to find Hudson carrying in the tray of cooked meats. The door stays open behind him as Lawson files in with Harry.

I release Reed and skirt the counter as Lawson pulls me in for a hug. "Hey, Ruby."

"Lawson, you made it. Merry Christmas."

"We did," he whispers with a wink. When he loosens his hold, I step back, and Reed grabs his hand, and they pull in close for a one-arm man hug. At least, I think that's what it is.

"Can you give me a hand, Ruby?" Addy pipes up. I wander to the hearth where she sits stacking logs. The Christmas tree that almost touches the ceiling stands over a pile of presents. Another thing the Robbins family never does—gifts.

Reed and Hudson talk to Lawson, cracking beers as they sink into the sofa. But my smile fades as I realize not every Rawlins made it.

"You okay, Rubes?" Addy says softly.

I glance at Reed. "Yeah, I wish Mack was home."

I force a happy face. I know how much Reed loves his brother and worries when he is on tour. The stress eats at him. He tries to hide it, but I notice it slip through some days. What I wouldn't do to make that go away.

The wind picks up outside, a low whistle funneling past the snow-coated windows as the white fall gets heavier.

"Dinner, y'all." Lou stands by the counter. The men file into their seats like they have since they were small, and Addy and I take our places by Hudson and Reed. Lawson sits by his mother, Harry at the head. One seat remains empty beside Reed. Mack's.

Harry holds out his hands on either side of his plate. Lou slides her hand into one. Hudson places his hand in the other. We link hands until everyone is joined.

The soft twang of the country Christmas songs fills the quiet moment as we hang our heads and Harry starts. "With these and all his merc—"

The door swings open. Snow swirls inside around a camo silhouette. The tall figure of dulled green and greys moves. "You not startin' without me, are you?"

Mack.

Emotion bubbles up my throat as I look to Reed. His face is wrecked in an instant. He is up and across the floor before the next heartbeat. Mack drops his duffle bag and hugs his brother tight. Louisa stands, hand over her mouth as she sucks back small sobs.

"Hey, Ma. Merry Christmas." Mack folds her into the hug.

"They let you off early, Mackie?" Lawson says, pulling Mack's seat out.

"We got pulled out."

Louisa fusses over him, and Reed comes back to my side, dropping into his seat with a kiss to my cheek. His hands tighten to fists on his thighs. I slide my hand under his and lace my fingers with his. "Breathe, gorgeous."

He huffs a strangled laugh.

We eat, chatting and laughing, wine and whiskey flowing. Mack entertains us with his funny barracks prank stories. Reed hangs on every word. And when my gaze tracks back to Louisa, she beams at me. She raises her glass, and the table goes quiet. "To *all* my beautiful children." She gives Addy and me pointed looks, and the men chuckle.

"Welcome to the family, darlins'." Harry's blue eyes sparkle and Louisa stares at her husband with something so ethereal it sends butterflies soaring in my stomach.

Lawson slaps the table. "Must be time for presents!"

"God, yes." Reed shuffles out of his chair and drags me along with him. I stumble behind with a giggle. I've never seen him so eager to sit on the floor before. He sinks onto the rug by the fire and pulls me into his lap. A moment later, he's hard underneath me. I lean back and whisper in his ear, "Don't think we're going to make it to midnight, baby."

"Don't need a bed to make you come, beautiful." His lips brush my temple, his words so soft they send goosebumps over my entire body.

When every last Rawlins is settled in by the fire and whiskey and wine is repoured, Louisa kneels by the tree and hands out presents. Harry unwraps a new watch. The navy-blue velvet box looks something like a TAG Heuer piece. *Fancy, Lou, nice work.* Our shopping trips are brushing off on her.

She flashes me a smile.

Addy hands an envelope to Lawson, and he opens it. Tickets to a Yankees game. Four of them. One for each brother. Reed gets to go to New York, after all.

When only one more present sits under the tree, Reed bends forward and plucks up the silver-wrapped box and hands it to me. An envelope rests on the top, larger than the box and red ribbon. I shoot him a curious glance and slip the card out. The room is silent except for the crackling fire.

Opening the card, I take in the handwriting. Reed's.

Hey beautiful,

I know I'm probably sittin' right by you. But since I want this to last, I thought I better write it down.

That way there's no faking it . . .

I stare at Reed. Every single face is homed in on me. Addy is almost jumping out of her skin on Hudson's lap. Hudson has a hand over his mouth, head tilted down, eyes drilling into my face. My heart picks up the pace.

Faking it . . .

The fake husband thing.

"Reed," I breathe.

"Keep readin', baby," he rasps.

Harry and Louisa beam at me. I drop my eyes back to the handwriting.

> *I literally can't breathe without you. I want to take care of you, Rubes. No, strike that, I love taking care of you. I want you as much as I need you. I adore you. Dammit woman, I love you so damn much.*
>
> ~~*Will you*~~
> *Just open the box, baby.*
> *Reed xxx*

I let the card fall from my fingers and tug the red ribbon from the silver paper. But I hesitate and move off his lap, settling on the floor to face him. I want to watch his face. You only get one chance in this life to see what I think is coming when I open this small box.

The paper falls away, revealing black velvet. I glance

up at Reed. The most gorgeous smile stretches his face, his green eyes lit up.

I open the box. A solitaire diamond sits nestled in a white velvet cushion.

"Holy shit . . ." The air leaves my lungs as my mouth gapes.

Harry tosses his head back with a hearty laugh. Louisa leans into him, tears rolling down her cheeks as she smiles at me. I look up at Reed. He's stilled, that gorgeous grin has slipped, and his hands are in his lap. His breaths are shallow. All three brothers' concerned gazes are locked on his face, and something like surprise and worry tangle on each of their handsome faces. They haven't seen him like this before.

I crawl back into his lap and take his face in my hands. "Breathe, baby. Then put that pretty rock on my finger."

He smiles through a ragged breath. Pressing my forehead to his, I run my thumbs over his jaw. His eyes close, hands on my waist as he pulls me closer. His body is trembling. I hold him tight, whispering, "I will always be yours, sweet man."

When he relaxes and releases me, I lean back and hand him the box. He takes the ring out and finds my hand. Green eyes lit up, he slides the engagement ring onto my finger. Now tears burn their way past my eyes and roll down my cheek.

God, I love this man.

Every single part of him.

But there is one more surprise for the day, thanks to Lawson's help. And this moment feels like the right one.

"You alright?" I ask.

"Am now, Rubes."

I smile and push up from the floor, pulling him up with a hand. His family watches as I lead him to the door. Slipping on my boots with the pink tops I love so much, I hand him his coat and nudge his shoes toward him with my foot. He dons both as I pull my coat over my shoulders.

Outside, the snow swirls around us as we head for the barn. It's freezing out here, but I don't plan on being in the cold long.

"Where are we going, Rubes?"

"Close your eyes. This is your Christmas gift, but I couldn't wrap it."

"Don't tell me Huddo palmed another horse off on us."

I turn back. His face is lit up with mirth.

"Close your eyes, Reed Rawlins."

"Yes, ma'am."

The snowfall is frigid. But it's forgotten the second Ruby's elegant hand slips into mine. I peek through one cracked eyelid as we cross the barn threshold. It's slightly warmer in here than outside.

"Hey! Your eyes are supposed to be closed!"

Shit.

I snap my eyes shut and let Ruby lead me over the hay-littered floor. She stops me, hands on my shoulders. "Stay."

Her strawberry scent fades. Something crackles, hissing as it falls to the ground, I'm guessing.

"Hand out," Ruby says excitedly.

I put a hand out and warm fingers turn my palm up, as something that clinks drops into it.

Ruby's smell closes in on me and her soft lips brush

against my own. A heartbeat later, she breaks away. "Open your eyes, baby."

I crack an eye, and she jumps up and down, grinning, her hands wrapped around my free one.

Both eyes wide, I stare at it.

Mouth gaping.

Heart frozen on the last beat.

Ruby is grinning from ear to ear, but her excitement fades a little when I don't move. "You like it?" She chews her bottom lip and glances between me and a brand-new Black Widow Limited Edition F-250. The exact same one I had, but next generation.

Sweet Jesus, Rubes.

I step toward her. "I—"

She drags me to the driver's side door. "Sorry I totaled your old one. I know how much your truck meant to you."

She opens the driver's door and maneuvers me closer to the inside.

The new car smell hits me in the face. I scrunch my nose up as the bridge of my nose burns. This woman. She is more than I fucking deserve.

"Rubes . . . I can't." I swallow past the stone wedged behind my Adam's apple. I am *not* fuckin' cryin'.

"*Yes,* you can." She pushes me closer. "Unless you want me to drive?" Her eyebrow hitches, and she gives me that *don't argue with me, Reed* face she does so damn well.

"Nope." I chuckle and slide into the seat. The soft, buttery Napa leather is heaven. I grip the wheel with both hands, running an eye over the dash. It's similar to my old one, with a few upgrades.

"Does it feel as good as the old one?"

I turn back to her. "Hop in, baby, let's find out."

She closes the driver's door and walks around the front. Her blonde hair bounces over her shoulders as she runs an elegant finger across the hood, holding my attention. My blood sinks fast, and my cock stretches my jeans. I start the truck up and get the warm air pumping.

When she slides into the passenger's seat, I reach for her. She crooks a finger. I slide on over to her seat and she rises up and spins, coming back down on my lap, one leg on either side. Dainty kisses pepper my lips and jaw. Her hands under my shirt are freezing now, sending goosebumps over my back and shoulders. "Sweet Jesus, Rubes. Let me warm you up."

"I like it when we steam up the windows."

"Same, baby."

She wriggles on my lap and heat rushes my body as I take in the most amazing woman on the planet, right in front of me. I will never deserve her. But I will do everything I can, every day, to try to. My wife.

Ruby Jane Rawlins.

Sounds fucking perfect.

Hungry hands shove the coat from my shoulders, crawling back under my shirt. I sit, watching her. The way her eyes catch me. The way she comes alive at my touch. The hitch in her breath when I cup her face with my hands and pull her in for a kiss. She opens for me, and all of a sudden, I can't breathe . . . but in the best way possible.

Hands dropping to her striped boat neck navy shirt, I tug at the hem. "This all comes off, Rubes."

"We're gonna have to fog up these new windows good to keep warm," she utters.

"Listen to that Montana talk slipping past those pretty fucking lips."

"They'd look better wrapped around your cock."

She slides from my lap and makes short work of my jeans. I rise off the seat as she pulls them down. My rock-hard cock springs free, and she grips the base with one fine hand and pumps it. Gaze burning into mine, she takes the tip into her mouth. Closing her eyes, she takes it all.

My head falls back on the headrest, my hands sinking into her hair. She pulls back up, suction tight. I groan, fisting her hair. I want her wrapped around me, those gorgeous breasts in my face while she rides my cock. "Rubes, up here, now."

Hands under arms, I tug her up. She licks her lips and I slide her jeans off, leaving the lacy red panties behind. Sending the seat backward, I remove the rest of her clothes. The windows are well and truly foggy now. Our breathing heavy, every touch is so desperate. I run a hand down her belly, finding her apex.

"Reed."

"Tell me what you want, Rubes."

"You, everywhere."

"You have me, beautiful."

I slip two fingers inside her. She's fucking soaked. She wriggles forward, straddling my lap. I retract my fingers and line up the head of my cock with her wet center. When she leans forward, those gorgeous breasts in my face and her blonde hair surrounding me, I slam up into her.

The sweetest whimper tumbles from her lips. Seated up to the hilt, I kiss my way from her neck to her hard peak. Tangling my tongue around the left nipple, I grip her hips and lift her up. This time, Ruby drives down, taking up the rhythm between us.

The windows are a white out.

The truck rocks on its wheels as we meet each other, stride for stride. And the beautiful wreck claiming her face tells me all I will ever need to know.

Ruby is mine.

And I'm hers.

The diamond on her finger is the first of the many ways I'm going to show this gorgeous girl how much I love her, for as long as she will let me. Rubes sits back up, her hair falling behind her back, her breasts bouncing as she pushes her palms to the ceiling of the truck.

Unshed tears burn the bridge of my nose.

This moment, right here, is one I will never forget.

She slows, opening her eyes, as she drops her gaze to mine. "Reed . . ."

The rasp in her voice sends me spiraling as her lips skate over my jaw. I take her face in my hands, stilling her, and she breaks away. "What is it?"

"Your turn on the soft leather, baby."

I flip us over, holding her against me to keep from being apart from her for even a second. When she is settled on the seat, her head on the reclined headrest, I grab up her boots and slide them on her feet. The smile that blooms over her face takes the last of my fucking breath. I tug her forward and drop to one knee.

I lean down and run my tongue around her clit. She arches off the Napa leather. The smell of new truck mixed with Ruby Robbins wet for me might be my new favorite thing. Lifting her leg, I rest it over my shoulder and straighten 'til she is spread wide for me.

"Fuck, baby. Best damn Christmas ever."

"This was on your list?" She smiles at me, cheekiness shining through her eyes as she plays with her breasts. It takes everything I have not to come all over her belly.

I grip my cock and nudge her entrance. "This was not on my Christmas list. But you're in my mind every single minute of every single fucking day. And this"—I nod to her lying on my front seat—"is going to keep my mind spinning 'til the day I die."

"Well, how about you fuck my name right out of my head?"

"Yes, ma'am."

"You make an incredible first mate, Reed Rawlins."

I close my eyes as my breath peters out with her words. Captain's Choice, that's what her t-shirt said the first night we spent together at the ranch. I knew it then. Hell, I knew it the second I saw Ruby Robbins clacking her way down that sidewalk in Great Falls.

But I never for one minute thought I would be worthy of this girl. I slam into her, and she lifts her hips from the seat. I rub a thumb over her clit, and she hums my name like a fucking prayer.

"Right here, Rubes . . ." She tightens around me. I hold her ankle and pick up the pace. Her fingers roll her nipples, and her face breaks. Every long, languid stroke sends me higher. Warmth coils at the base of my spine. My rhythm shatters as she explodes.

"Reed! Baby, fuck."

"Good girl, Rubes." I slam into her with erratic, hard strokes.

Fuck me, nothing on this earth compares to Ruby. Never will.

Her fire.

Her faith in me.

Her loyalty.

Her unconditional and all-consuming love for a man who shouldn't have been worthy.

I burst, hot and fast, into her. She tightens again and follows me over the edge. Exhausted and ecstatic, I peel her from the leather seat and pull her close. When my face sinks into her hair, it takes every last ounce of energy to not fall apart.

The overwhelming happiness she gives me is so precious.

"God knows how much I love you, Rubes."

"He's not the only one who knows." She pushes back, hands on my face, her big brown eyes studying my face. "Rule number one . . . Reed Rawlins is my reason for breathing."

I choke through a laugh that turns to a sob.

Sweet Jesus.

So much for not fucking cryin'.

Epilogue
RUBY

Two Years Later . . .

Reed's hands hold mine. All warmth. Addy stands by my side on the hillside that Reed first took me to on R & R Ranch. The day that my perfectly constructed life cracked, the day I wanted something so badly for someone else that it broke my heart clean in two. How could a man this thoughtful and kind, this bright and full of life, suffer and not be seen.

Harry and Louisa stand behind their sons, who are shoulder to shoulder with Reed. Mack smiles wider than I have ever seen.

My parents didn't come. No surprise there. But Addy's did, and that's something.

The breeze winds around my hair, jostling it over my shoulders. The preacher opens his book. Reed rubs his thumbs over the back of my hands. The diamond ring sits on my finger, and a new bracelet hangs from my right wrist. Sterling silver, a captain's wheel charm hangs from it with Reed's name engraved on the back.

Family tradition. At least that's what Louisa said when she and Addy gave it to me. Now all three of us have one. It's sweet. And it's the first time I have felt part of a family dynamic. Felt treasured. Like I belong. Am wanted.

And it's more amazing than I ever imagined.

Grounding, fulfilling.

Like being wrapped in the warmest blanket, mesmerized as stars burst out overhead.

Harry gave a speech about a man being complete with the right woman at lazy supper on my first Rawlins Christmas. But I think it goes both ways. Reed makes me a better, kinder, and more thoughtful person. He shows me every day the things that make the difference. He makes me so damn happy. For the first time in my life, I actually *feel* alive. Not just ticking boxes on the way to some huge goal that's always years off.

And I wanted him to be happy, to be free. Back here when he first fell to his knees, gasping for breath. The first time I saw what he hid so well from everyone else. He was so desperate for more to his life than being stuck in a small town, doing the same thing each day for the rest of his life.

I had felt so helpless. Here was a man, my *friend*, who couldn't see a path forward that he could live with. How could I leave and let that happen? It put everything I had thought I knew until that day into perspective. That was the day my rules first stood on shaky ground.

I watched them fall in the months that followed. And I savored every minute of it. And we did it, together. We created a business and a life that we both love. One where we have the ranch, the lifestyle, but we can travel when we want. We can choose what path we take next.

And the next adventure for Reed and me is marriage. A real one, not the fake charade we started out with. Although I wouldn't change our first few months for anything.

"We are gathered here today . . ."

Reed slides the wedding band on my finger, the one he first gave me. It's like an old friend. It fits just right. The way it did the first time, back in Great Falls at the inn. Only now, I won't be taking it off. I slide his ring onto his finger, and he scrunches up his face. I know he's trying not to cry. His jaw grinds together.

Mack slaps a hand on his shoulder.

A tear dislodges and tracks down his cheek. I wipe it away as my own tears fall freely.

"You may kiss your bride," the preacher says with a smile.

A grin cracks over Reed's face and his eyes light up with mirth. He steps forward and scoops me up, skirts dragging across the grassy ground. His mouth is on mine as he leans to the side, and I dip backward.

Hudson's hearty laugh is followed by the family's cheers.

I melt into Reed's kiss, fingers brushing over his jaw.

When he sets me onto my feet and spins me around to face everyone, I look up at him. He hugs me to his side, pressing a kiss to my forehead. "Shall we, Mrs. Rawlins?"

"Abso-fucking-lutely, Mr. Rawlins."

His hands slide from my waist, lacing through my fingers. We walk through the small crowd of family and a few guests. Addy greets me first. "Hey, we are officially sisters!"

"Oh Adds, we are, too!"

"This changes everything." She grins.

Of course it doesn't. Adds will always be my sister. I will always be hers. Louisa has the both of us in a squishy hug next. And when she releases us, Harry steps forward and shakes Reed's hand. "Well done, son."

"Thanks, Pa."

Wonder stretches my face. That is the first time I have ever heard Reed call Harry Pa.

Harry has me in a tight hug a heartbeat later. "We love you, darlin'."

Emotion bubbles up, sending more tears to my eyes. "I love you guys, too," I rasp.

He hugs me tighter. "We will always have your back, Ruby. We take care of family, you hear. And you're a Rawlins. It's my guess you've been one since the day you two met." Last, he plants a kiss on my cheek.

I chug through a strangled laugh.

"Just don't call him dad, or you'll hear about it," Mack chimes in, wrapping an arm around my shoulders.

"Hey, Mackie."

"Hey, Rubes. Or is it little sis?"

"Whatever makes you happy, Mackinlay." I dot a kiss to his cheek, and he messes up my hair the way a big brother should.

Reed closes in and presses his forehead to mine. "Did I ever tell you about the time I saw this girl in ridiculous red heels stalkin' her way down the sidewalk in Great Falls?"

"Tell me again . . ."

His hungry kiss claims me.

The Italian sunshine is bringing out a whole new level of happiness for Reed. He's so damn fine, lying on a picnic blanket on the side of the Tuscan hill of our Airbnb. The guests back home are happily being taken care of by Harry and Lou. Hudson and Addy have Rosewood under control. And we are catching up on well-earned R & R.

Reed rolls over, a strawberry between his lips as he wriggles his eyebrows. The morning sun kisses its warmth to my bare arms. I slide my fingers through his messy dark blond hair and swing over his hips, plucking the strawberry from his teeth with mine.

"The outdoors looks good on you, Mrs. Rawlins."

"Yes, they do. You know what looks better?"

"What, beautiful, tell me?"

"Nothing on me."

"I can't picture it, you're gonna have to show me." Cheekiness fills those gorgeous green eyes.

I slide my tank top off, letting my bare chest soak up the warmth of the Italian countryside. There is nobody around for miles. Just the way we like it. This New York City girl never would have dreamed in a million years this would be something she'd like. But I do.

And happiness makes Reed more alive, if that's possible. He spreads my legs, lifting the knee-length skirt up, fingers finding the spot I need him straight away. When he wriggles down, disappearing under my skirt, I moan.

His warm tongue finds my clit and my hands shoot into his hair. My knees are digging into the blanket and legs trembling a heartbeat later. The Great Reed Rawlins has my body well-tuned to his moves. My hardened heart now mush and wrapped around his little finger.

He sends his fingers through my wet folds, and I grip his hair tight. He groans, slipping them inside me. I buck against his mouth as release explodes through me and he laps up every wave he creates.

When the orgasm fades, I shuffle back, kissing the wetness from his lips, his chin, his jawline. Aching for him, I pull his shorts down, exposing the hard length that always sets my mouth watering. Tugging him upward until he's sitting up and looking at me with hooded eyes, I sink onto his lap.

"God, Rubes . . . the things you do to me, beautiful."

I rise on my knees as every inch of him moves through me. He leans back, palms flat on the blanket, toned chest soaking up the sun's rays, muscled arms flexing with each movement. He is stunning. And he is all mine.

This woman has new rules.

Rule one, Reed Rawlins is my reason for breathing.

Rule two, build the life *we* want.

Rule three, always stick to rules one and two, no matter what.

Remember, Ruby . . .

No matter what.

Need more Ruby & Reed?
Grab the BONUS SCENE now!
https://BookHip.com/MVDHVVD

Continue the Rosewood Ranch series with
Mack & Grace's story,
Saving Grace!

Sign up to the newsletter to make sure you never miss an Alexandra Banks book!!

ALEXANDRA
Banks
CONTEMPORARY ROMANCE
AVAILABLE NOW!!

HEART & HOPE

playlist

CONFIDENT — Demi Lovato ... 326

FOOL — Thomas Rhett ... 301

LIFE AIN'T ALWAYS BEAUTIFUL — Gary Allan ... 345

WHAT ARE YOU WAITING FOR? — Nickelback ... 339

SHE THINKS MY TRACTOR'S SEXY — Kenny Chesney ... 408

I JUST WANT YOU — Cole Swindell ... 356

WHAT COULD GO RIGHT — Thomas Rhett ... 332

LOVIN' ON YOU — Luke Combs ... 315

THUNDER IN THE RAIN — Kane Brown ... 7??

WITHOUT YOU IN IT — Kelsey Hart ... 318

TROUBLE — Josh Ross ... 335

KEEP IT TO MYSELF — Cooper Alan ... 3?

ROSEWOOD RANCH SERIES
SAVING GRACE

Acknowledgments

A love story like this one is all consuming to write and it is my hope that readers find themselves immersed.

As always, thanks to my editors, Lindsey and Zainab. Your input and guidance is always wanted and appreciated.

To every ARC reader who volunteered to read this book, thank you!!

And lastly, but most certainly not least, my family for putting up with the endless country music playlist that I made them endure during the writing process to get into the zone. Sorry... ;)

Alex xx